Demon's Bane

DAVID DOUGLAS

One Five One Press

Munich · Palmyra

Demon's Bane
First Edition

Cover design and map by David Douglas
Front cover illustration by J. W. Parente
Artistic consulting by Dylan Masells
Author photo by Udo Hartmann
Edited by Elizabeth Douglas

ISBN 978-0-9842547-0-5

Published by One Five One Press
Munich, Germany · Palmyra, Virginia

I have many people to thank for
their help with this entirely self-
created book: photo subjects, test
readers, online reviewers, artists,
photographers, and many more.

At the top of the list is my mother,
without whom this novel would
still be a pile of unedited pages.

Thank you, Mom!

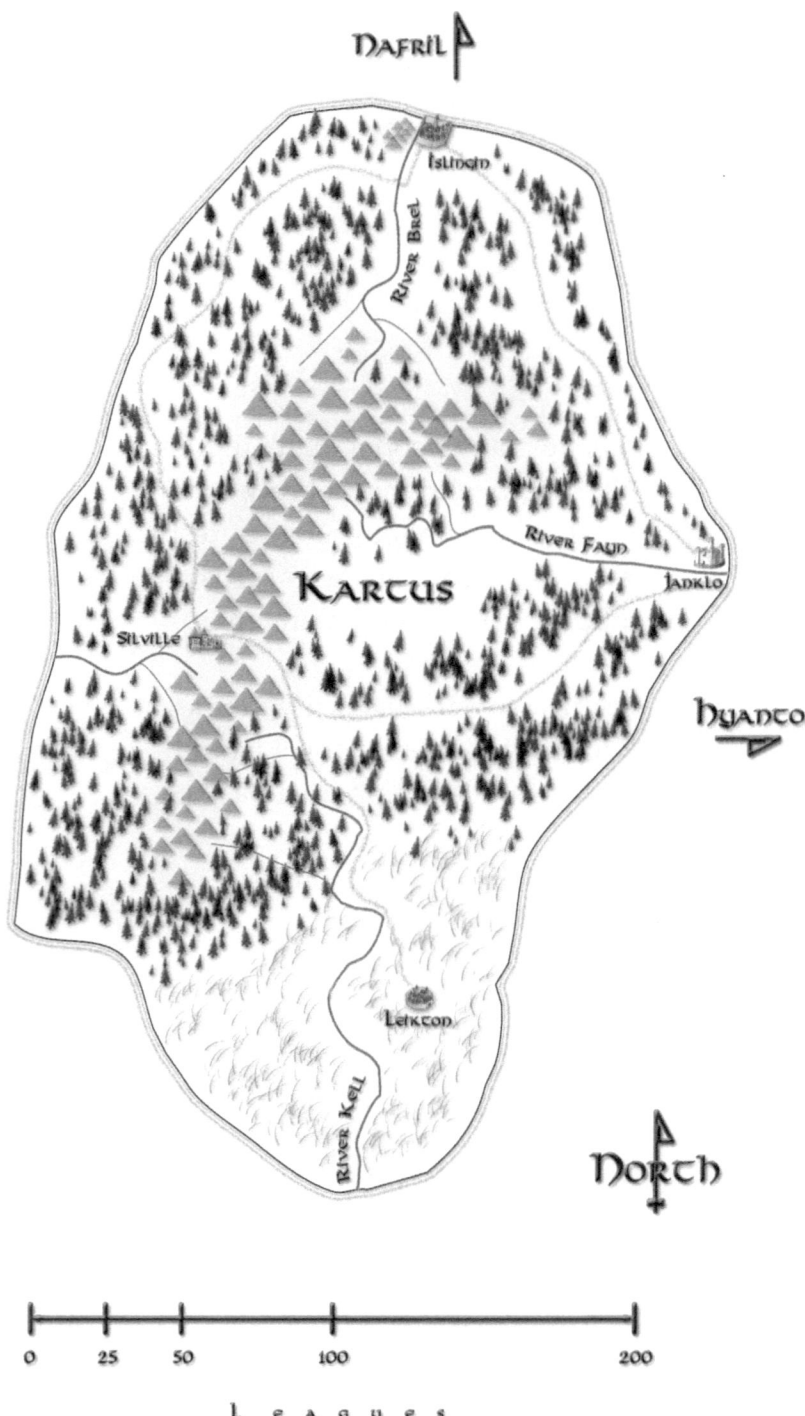

NAFRIL

ISLINGIN

RIVER BREL

RIVER FAUN

JADKLO

KARTUS

SILVILLE

HUANTO

LEIKTON

RIVER KELL

NORTH

0   25   50   100   200

LEAGUES

Demon's Bane

Prologue

The spring morning was a foggy one, and Senn Morel was not enjoying it. Mist wreathed the trees of the forest as if hanging from their branches alongside the dangling moss. He could hardly see far enough to find any firewood, much less find his way back to the camp. As if it weren't enough to be left behind while his friends grew into their magic, he was stuck at the age of twelve scavenging for firewood and food with the much younger children.

Squish . . . what was that? Senn looked down to find he had stepped in a pile of dung. Great, just what he needed on a morning like this: cleaning his only shoes of some wild animal's excrement. At least that task would only last a few minutes, unlike the firewood treks. Those would only end when the clan had exhausted the fallen wood supply, which unfortunately was plentiful around its new camp. They'd been here a moon already, and probably it would take another moon to pick clean the surrounding forest, before the older kids would have to start felling live trees for wood. But, looking on the bright side, maybe traipsing around in the damp forest would scour most of the dung off his shoes by the time he got home.

Off to his left there was a shout. "Aah! Help, I'm stuck!" Senn raced toward the sound, sliding to a stop on slippery leaves at the lip of a small ravine. A creek had apparently run there once, but had found a new route when a cave-in blocked its flow. Little Sephora had slid in, and she could not climb out. The muddy walls were several times his own height; probably Senn couldn't even get out if he fell in himself.

"Hold on, Sephora. I'll think of something!" He looked at the surroundings: wet, slippery vines and sodden branches that Sephora's small, muddy hands could never grip. There was no one else in sight to help him. But there was one possibility—a pine tree by the ravine whose top third had been split off by lightning. The split piece hung point-down among the pine's remaining branches above the ravine. "Move back, I don't want you to get hit!" Senn uprooted a small, flexible sapling and climbed up the tree until he was level with its broken top. Using the sapling, he pushed and prodded until the broken piece came free from the boughs holding it up. The spring in the flexed sapling pushed the length of pine outward as it fell, and it crashed into the ravine at an angle. Sephora clapped her hands and then climbed up the sticky pine branches, emerging from the ravine sap-covered but unhurt.

"Thank you Senn! You saved me!" She gave him a big hug, pressing her tear-streaked face into his chest. He hadn't exactly saved her—he certainly could have run back and brought an Adept to hoist her out—but it was satisfying to have managed it by himself.

Just then, he heard the horn. It called loud and long, then sounded long again. The signal for an attack! What bad luck: it had only been a bit over a moon since the last one, and the consequent move of their camp. At least that last time only a single demon had attacked, and no one had been killed. Maybe they would be lucky again. Senn took Sephora's hand and they ran back to camp, trying to keep quiet to avoid being noticed by a demon. The horn sounded again, three short calls, which meant they'd received a magical warning—three demons were coming. That was bad . . . the most he'd seen at once was two, and that was no lucky day.

The fledgling camp was just starting to look like home: a cluster of cozy huts in a large clearing surrounded by tall, ancient trees. As Senn approached, a momentary burst of flame lit up the space between the trees, burning off the mist. His mother's spell, most likely; she was Magus-level and the only one strong enough for that. The warmth continued as she reduced the heat to a mist-cutting bake. He could see all the way across the camp now, and more importantly, so could those who would be fighting off the demons. He ran toward the small hut he shared with his mother.

Lieh Morel stood outside to direct the clansmen. She was a tall, imposing woman, and her strong voice echoed loudly across the clearing. "Drop your packs and valuables in my hut. Then pair up as drilled, spellcasters with your strongmen. I want at least four pairs by each trail coming in. We have three demons coming, no telling from where. At least I got the warning in advance this time." She saw Senn run up. "Thank the stars you made it. I hope all the youngsters will return before the demons arrive. Get on the platform up in that tree and take two or three of these little ones with you." Right . . . another drawback of being a kid was that you couldn't get near the action! At least up on the platform, Senn and a lucky few would have a good view of the fighting down below. He grabbed Sephora and a couple of the other wood scavengers who had filtered in from the forest, and hurried them up the ladder to the narrow platform in the crook of the tree.

Below, the adults had begun to organize quickly, guarding the four trails coming into camp. Among them were most of the clan's strongest spellcasters, Minor Adepts. Unfortunately, there were no Major Adepts in the camp—and only Senn's mother was at the Magus level, the most powerful among spellcasters. Alongside the Adepts, weapons in hand, were the camp's fighters, men and women with little magical ability but strong physical skills. As for the rest, some herded children into tents or up into the trees. Several other clansmen found trees to hide behind and checked their weapons, making ready in case some of the attackers fought through to the center of camp. Most of these were Medi, with so little magic as to be almost useless in a battle.

Two of the archers climbed into tree stands and readied their bows. They looked like Beagan and Elam, who were only a few years older than Senn. His mother stood next to their hut at the base of the tree in which he was hiding. She would protect the valuables of the whole camp: some imbued items, books, and other irreplaceable treasures from the time before the demons. Wildon Herst, the old magic tutor, headed over to join her. As a Sabi his magic wasn't fighting strength anymore, but he'd been a Major Adept once upon a time and could put up a decent shield in a pinch.

Up on the platform, Senn hid and waited. After some time his knees ached from crouching behind the tree trunk. Then a globe of light appeared between the north and west trails that led into the camp. The glowing ball flew in toward one of the outlying huts and blasted the side of it, causing the whole structure to burst immediately into flame. The green branches comprising the hut gave off a dingy smoke as they burned, creating a low cloud over that corner of the clearing. Several fighters from the nearby trailheads shouted and ran toward the source of the energy ball. As they closed in, a strange woman stepped forward out of the haze of fog and smoke, hands raised. That wasn't good, as the possessed woman could obviously wield some powerful magic, unlike demon-possessed animals that had only claws and teeth at their disposal. As soon as the fighters saw her, they readied their swords and their partners raised walls of solid energy in curving shields around them.

As the battle was joined with the possessed woman, the remaining demon combatants entered the fray. Two massive black wolves bounded out of the misty distance on different tangents toward the nearby trailheads, moving with a speed Senn had never seen in a normal animal. They closed the gap in a few massive bounds, jaws snapping. One wolf barreled into the few clansmen at each trailhead and scattered them like sticks, having moved too fast for them even to set up their solid energy shields.

After that it was difficult for Senn to follow all the action at once. At the center where the demon woman stood, it seemed as if one or two of the shimmering shields held, although several others fell as their creators were distracted or overwhelmed. Arrows streaked toward the woman, but the wolves were too close to clansmen for safe shots. A couple of arrows burned up in midair. Damn, that woman must have had some strong magic! An energy ball flew into one of the charging clansmen and he lit up in flames, sword still swinging and nicking the woman's leg. She was letting loose energy balls as if it were child's play. One exploded a nearby tree and sent trunk and limbs flying, along with a haze of shrapnel.

At least one woman from the clan was down on the west trailhead with a wolf tearing at her. The beast had a few burned patches from small energy balls, but none of the Minor Adepts could cast a spell powerful enough to do real damage. Artie Tenko pummeled the wolf with blows from a huge hammer, and Senn recognized Rikk Janus, from a neighboring tent, coming up with a sword to finish it off. Even after he slashed it to the guts, the wolf managed to tear a chunk out of Rikk's leg. "Aaaahh!" He let out a pained battle cry as his sword came down point-first and speared the wolf in the head, its body finally going limp.

Senn shook his head in despair: in the north there were at least two men down. Jarel Linker's hounds snapped at the second wolf, although one of the dogs was already crawling away, badly mauled. Jarel's axe cut into the wolf's back, blade biting deeply. The demon wolf kept snapping though, until with an axe, a hammer, and one long sword closing in, it turned and started off into the woods, limping badly. Jarel whistled his dogs back, probably not wanting to lose them in a fight he couldn't see. Several archers loosed arrows which stuck in the wolf's hide before it disappeared from view.

When Senn looked back to the fight with the woman, it appeared to be almost over. She had two arrows sticking from her chest and one in her remaining arm. A swordsman had chopped the other arm off, at the expense of all the hair on his head, which must have been blown off by the edge of an energy ball. He staggered back behind one of the remaining energy shields as a huge cracking noise split the air. A massive tree split about five strides up, and the top half of it fell toward the demon woman. One of the branches impaled her through the chest and pinned her to the ground. Finally she was still, as the ground beneath her grew red with blood.

"Alright, pack it up and let's go!" His mother was sweating with exertion: first the spell to burn off the mist, which was a massive one; then, splitting that tree. She was the only spellcaster left standing who could have done it. Yet she still had the energy to give orders, always thinking about the safety of the clan. That always came first, sometimes even ahead of keeping her own son safe. Why did she have to ignore him half the time? Well, Senn had learned to look out for himself, anyway.

Climbing down from the tree was difficult, since every muscle was twitching nervously after the last few tense minutes. Back on the ground, Senn looked toward the hut where his pack was prepared and ready to go, as it was every morning. They would be gone within the hour. Two possessed had been killed, and their demon spirits were probably reassociating already. It was quite a shock for them to be ripped from a dying possessed body, but eventually the spirits would recover and would have to find other hosts quickly. No one in the clan wanted to be around when that happened. Plus there was the other wolf. Who knew if it would die, or tear out the arrows and come back for more? Probably it would take some days for the wolf to heal even if it lived, which would provide enough time for the clan to escape and cover their tracks with magic.

Another fine camp made useless. Senn faced more moons of scavenging for wood in a new place while he waited for his magic. From the looks of it, several of their clan were dead, gone to the spirit world. What was the point, to live a life like this? Something had to change. Maybe the next time, in the next attack, it would be different. Maybe Senn would have his *own* magic by then.

The kids he'd taken to the tree platform finally clambered down and looked up at him. One cried, "My Daddy's on the ground over there!" Another piped up, "What's that smell Senn, did you have an accident?" He looked down at his dung-caked shoes and frowned. Had that really just happened this morning? The incident with Sephora already felt like part of the distant past.

CHAPTER ONE

Lessons

I n the small clearing, today's lesson was just starting. Senn sat on a stool across from Wildon Herst, both facing a large stone that acted as a worktable. Finally he had his magic! Senn had waited most of the way through age fourteen to get it. Now to find out if it was as powerful as his mother had always promised. He concentrated on a sliver of wood, built the matrix of the fire-lighting spell in his mind, and fed energy into it. His excitement at being able to test his newly developing powers crackled in the air, burning as he wanted the wood to be. As he directed the energy toward the sliver, it vaporized in a puff of smoke, leaving only a few sparks to settle down on the blackened stone where it had been laying. Argh . . . it was supposed to burn, not explode!

"Excellent, you're almost there. But, my boy, you've got to control yourself and thus your magic." Wildon Herst smiled warmly, his short, neat white beard contrasting with his unkempt hair and bushy eyebrows. He was a spindly old man, a Sabi whose magic had weakened with age, but he was an excellent teacher of the arts he had once practiced as a Major Adept. "I know it's exciting to reach this point at last, but you must relax your mind and remember to calculate the factors properly. At least you got all the other parts right! The lines of energy, the closed matrix . . . and so forth."

Senn twitched in annoyance. Of course he had gotten everything right except the factors for how much energy to use. "I should be able to do this. I've thought about it ever since the last lesson, and my mother . . . well, she can light a fire while doing two or three other things at once."

"All in time, lad, I'm sure one day you will be every bit as powerful as your mother. It seems you are a Magus. From what I've seen of your first try at this spell, you only need a bit more practice. Relax for a moment, and tell me what you remember from our last lesson about the types of magic."

"Sure. There is energy in the form of heat and cold. Then there is solid energy that can hit like a hammer or provide a shield. Air energy works like an artificial wind. With earth energy you can make plants grow and heal wounds."

"Right. Now, think how lucky you are to be a Magus amid the sea of powerless Medi, with a river of energy at your command. Let's see that river flow! Try the fire lighting spell again, and remember the factors."

This time, Senn moved more slowly through the mental motions of casting the spell. First, he visualized the target: a new sliver of wood that Wildon had placed on the stone. Next, he must channel the magic energy —that was essential, because aiming non-directed power at the wood would be like trying to blow a leaf off a table with one's breath from a hundred feet away. He formed a picture in his mind, drawing lines where the energy would flow out of his body, making a channel toward the target. Then, in his mental image, he created a matrix around the wood sliver. If there were any gaps or leaks in this imaginary model, the nicely channeled energy would leak out, heating up the stone or diffusing the whole spell. Senn's model would hold the energy in the right place for the duration of the spell. He calculated enough heat magic to light the splinter of wood, based on his estimate of its mass, density, and composition. But this time, he didn't use so much power that it would disintegrate into sparks. He drew in heat energy and felt it run through him, like a tool responding to an artisan's hand. As he released the magic, he slowly metered it out down the channel and it filled the matrix around the wood. The sliver started to smoke and finally burst into bright, orange flames.

"Bravo, Senn! Now, try it again." His eyelids drooped from the effort, as Wildon pulled a handful of sticks of various sizes from his robe. "The only way to perfect a spell is through practice. Just imagine: you go to light a torch, taking some lovely girl out for a nighttime walk in the woods, and you miscalculate how much energy to add. You'll either end up with a smoking mess of hot but not burning pitch, or you'll explode the torch and ruin your tunic in the process. Now, once you've lit these dozen pieces as well as you did the last one, your lesson will be over for the day." Wildon smiled, and Senn felt a hint of irritation flicker across his face at the assignment. But life wasn't meant to be easy. He turned reluctantly to the pile of sticks, and arranged them one by one on the stone.

The afternoon was warming up nicely. But Senn wasn't paying any attention. As he walked back home, all he could think about was putting one foot in front of the other. And of course, lighting fires with his mind. From watching the adults around the camp, one would never guess that magic was such hard work. But it was fun, too . . . what else would he be able to do? Where would his talent lie—fire and ice spells, cutting and forming with solid energy, working the air—hopefully not the slow-growing earth magic?

He walked through the clan's makeshift village and flicked his eyes wearily over the houses. Some were simple shelters, boughs lashed together with wood and vines and covered with evergreen branches. Others were made with earth magic, the saplings or vines persuaded to grow and leaf in such a way that they provided weather-proof walls with less physical work. How each clan member constructed his dwelling depended on his skills. Apart from the varied construction, some of the buildings were showing traces of age. That was a good sign; it had been almost two years since the last demon attack, the longest he had ever lived in one place. A life of moving every few moons was no fun, and no way to grow up.

That last attack—two demon wolves and a possessed woman—had been brutal. The demons had worked together, instead of fighting amongst themselves as usual. The casualties had been grave: four warriors and magicians hurt by the wolves or by energy balls, with another four dead, one of those almost torn in half. In addition to the loss of life, the clan had lost half its supplies to fires as several huts had been hit by energy fireballs from the demon woman.

The following weeks had been a frightening time: packing their remaining belongings, loading up the animals, walking long hours and many leagues, and sleeping badly with furtive looks into the dark woods. Those with enough magic worked in shifts, using spells to smooth out their path, to cover their tracks, and to leave no scents for the demons to find after they reassociated or healed. Finally, they had built this new camp some fifty leagues away.

There were ways to avoid this painful move. But to keep the demons from finding their way back to the camp, one had to capture them alive and contain them. Normally, once the borrowed body died, the possessing spirit would be ripped out unnaturally. Then it had to reassociate and quickly find another human or animal to possess, or it would fade back to the spirit world, like water evaporating from a wet cloth. Wildon Herst had once recounted a story of a magical box that could force demons back to the other side. Senn wondered if someday his own magic might be strong enough to capture demons and send them back.

Senn's thoughts were wandering as randomly as his feet when he stumbled in the door of the home he shared with his mother near the center of the camp. It was a small two-room construction of tree limbs thatched with evergreen; Lieh Morel had little patience for the time-consuming spells required to bend plants to her will. One room contained the packs and sleeping rolls, always readied each morning to depart at a moment's notice in case of danger. The other contained a small table and chairs lashed together with simple rope, set next to a fire pit in the center of the room. Senn's mother was just arranging firewood to cook the midday meal. She was never one to waste time with small talk, so when he walked in, she stood up to her full, towering height and pursed her lips.

"Back already? I don't know if that's good or bad. So. Tell me about your lessons today."

Senn sighed. She had taken much more of an interest in him since he had gotten his magic, which was a bit annoying after years of being ignored and going his own way. "Wildon let me try out the fire lighting spell, I got it on the second try, then I had to light a bunch more sticks one by one. I could do it, and I didn't explode any more of them after that first one. I don't see why we can't just have the spells explained to us, and start working magic on our own."

Lieh frowned. "I bet without Wildon's guidance you would have exploded a tree and burned down the forest by now. Someone has to teach you to understand how magic works, and to use it in the proper way. Remember what happened with the earliest spells you learned? I seem to remember pebbles flying through the air with no direction. Even at your age you could hurt someone with your magic. I should say especially at your age, when the magic is new and your understanding of it is limited."

"Yes, well, I have to make up time, since I got it later than all the other kids!"

"Senn . . ." she shook her head and fixed him with her eyes. "With the power that your father had and I have, you are almost guaranteed to be a powerful Magus. Just learn how to use it carefully and wisely, to avoid your father's fate. Don't experiment too much with what you don't understand."

He frowned. "You always bring that up about Father, but you never tell me exactly what happened. There is just some warning about experiments. When will you finally tell me?"

Lieh glanced away, then turned back to him. "Senn, I've been waiting to tell you that story until after you started using magic. It's most important that you know the truth, but I needed you to be mature enough to understand and handle it. Let's talk about it over the meal. Will you light the fire? Keep your concentration and show me I'm right about your strength."

Finally Senn was about to hear the story he'd been waiting his whole life to know. He wanted to learn about his father, whom he'd never met—but wait. First he had to focus, and light the fire. The firewood was arranged neatly, just waiting for his magic to do its work. Did he even have enough energy left to make a single spark fly? Senn closed all the excitement and exhaustion out of his mind and concentrated on the spell. Channels, matrix, factors, energy . . . go. The fire flared quickly to life and within seconds was blazing warmly, fast on its way to becoming coals to cook their dinner.

All the young men and women in the clan knew the story of Islingin. The city had become a major hub of trade, culture, and ideas. The Magus Conclave ruled Kartus from Islingin Keep in the center of the city, with Magi representing different areas. But deep in the bowels of the Keep, a tear between the physical and spirit worlds opened. Rumors abounded about how this had happened, but if anyone had solid evidence they weren't sharing it. What *was* known was the result: a once-bright culture was reduced to small clans of frightened demon fighters.

When the tear opened to the spirit world, corrupt spirit creatures squeezed through into the physical realm and began wreaking havoc. As demon spirits alone they had little influence in the physical world. But their power multiplied once they possessed a hapless creature and took over its added strength, magic energy draw, and weapons (whether man made tools or natural claws and teeth). The first to die or be possessed had been the members of the Magus Conclave in the Keep, and the Major Adepts around them. With the most powerful spellcasters out of their way or in their control, the demons ran amok through the city, destroying everything not made of solid stone. Only those who fled had survived.

These remaining stragglers had tried to regroup. But each time, they drew the attention of scores of the demon creatures at once and lost even more lives in the process. Some demons had possessed forest animals and grown to become huge, bloodthirsty, powerful beasts. Others would possess a Magus or Adept whenever they could break down one's mental barriers, with the victim ending up as a powerful spell casting demon. Additional cities had been razed by the spirit invaders: the mining town of Silville, the mercenary center of Janklo, and the southern city of Leikton. Even the smaller towns and farmsteads were destroyed in the end. Everywhere that people tried to settle down, the possessed demons found them in numbers that couldn't be turned back.

Finally the survivors split into small, mobile clans to avoid attracting so many demons at once. As the demon creatures all seemed to fight amongst themselves, they were unable to organize the kind of offensive that would be required to track down the many clans. Besides, the magic of a few dozen clan members combined with the swords of a few dozen more was usually enough to take out the occasional lone demon, even if it often meant relocating to escape being found again.

Senn's father had died in this attack on Islingin, but so had many others. How was his father involved? Senn's family name was from his mother, so she must have had the more powerful magic of the couple. But she had incredible power, so that didn't say much about his father's ability, which was also Magus level. The possibilities were turning over in his mind in time with the chicken roasting on the spit. By the time his mother served the bird, he was perched on the edge of his seat in anticipation.

"Here. Chicken, carrots, some potatoes." Lieh poured fresh water from the jug. Their camp was lucky to have a stream running from the mountains to the north.

"And? What about the story?"

"Senn. You must learn the patience that your father lacked." Slowly she started to slice her food, and took a bite of chicken. Senn followed, realizing with the first mouthful that he was famished. He dug into the tender chicken.

Finally Lieh paused between bites and began. "Marek Seltin, my husband and your father. He was a powerful Magus, and a member of the Conclave that governed Islingin. My father, Talen Morel, was also a Magus in the Conclave. That's how I first met Marek, through your grandfather. Marek was several years older than I, but in fact my magic was even more powerful than his. Hence you bear my family name instead of Marek's. We both shared an understanding of magic that was deeper than that of any others we had met, and we quickly fell in love. I'll spare you those details."

Senn snickered. "Yeah, I didn't realize this was the story of how you fell for each other."

Lieh frowned and gestured at him with her fork. "This is serious, boy. And what I tell you now is not to be repeated to another soul, until we find a way to reverse it. Some might not understand, might take it the wrong way."

Senn missed the last part entirely. "Reverse ... whah?" He leaned forward, elbows on the table, knife and fork poised, a bite of chicken still half-chewed in his mouth.

"The rift that Marek and his Magi opened up to the spirit world."

CHAPTER TWO

The Orb

"**D**o you mean that . . . my father caused all of this?" It couldn't be true! Senn looked around the sparsely furnished shelter and imagined living in a stone keep, his father still alive beside him.

"Yes, Marek is responsible. But . . . it's not as simple as it sounds." Lieh sighed. "Let's start at the beginning. The warring tribes of the olden days of Kartus had been united for many years under the common banner of the Magus Conclave, ruling from Islingin. Each region had a Magus to represent its people in the Conclave's decision process. The other cities were prospering as well, trading with Nafril and Hyanto by ship—"

Senn rolled his eyes. "Yes, Mother . . . we all heard about how towns and trade used to work, and a pile of stories about Islingin."

"Yes. But what's behind it is most important, and that's what you never hear about. The Conclave invested a lot of time and energy keeping all this going. Then, once their new society stabilized, Magi in the Conclave began to get restless and push their own agendas. By the time the rift was opened, the factions among the Magi were almost at war in private, even though in public they appeared to be the closest of friends.

"The different generations pushed opposite agendas. Your grandfather Talen Morel advocated careful magical research, to be concentrated more in the areas of health, farming, and handcraft. But your father Marek wanted to push the limits of what was possible, and to find the boundaries of our world. We all knew there must be something more than what we can see with our eyes, and he wanted to find out what it was. The energy on which we draw for our magic must come from somewhere, after all."

"You must have tried to tell him, right? Something bad could happen?" Senn had been anxious to find out the heroic truth about his father, but now it seemed the ending might not turn out as expected.

Lieh looked down to her plate, drawing lines in the grease with her fork. As she looked up, she closed her eyes for a moment and gestured with the fork. The grease rose into the air in tiny droplets, illuminating from within to make a brilliantly glowing winged serpent. Its eyes turned to Senn and he almost cried out. After a few seconds the brightness increased, and the grease monster disappeared in a brief burst of yellow flame. Lieh sighed. "I was caught up in Marek's ideas too. It's just too amazing, isn't it? All the things we can do with magic! I had to know where it comes from and why it works, not just how to use it. And you see where those ideas led us.

"I wasn't a Magus of the Conclave, but heard all about both sides of the disagreement. Early on, your grandfather still discussed matters with me from time to time, and I kept his confidence. After all, we had been sharing talks about magic since I was first able to channel energy. Talen worried about the new theories and spells developed in the last few years by Marek's faction, thinking they toyed with dangerous, uncontrollable forces. Nonetheless, Marek plunged ahead with his ideas to follow the magic energy back to its source. After finding the spirit world, he decided to try to go there, even though physical matter has no meaning in that realm. At the end, he and his followers created a tear, a hole between the two worlds. Unfortunately the spirits figured out how to push through it before Marek did." Senn gasped in amazement. It really *was* all his father's fault!

Lieh continued, "Your grandfather, well, you know he was one of the most powerful Magi of the time. He created the Orb." She stood up and walked to the shelf in the sleeping room, and took down the wooden box where she kept everything of value. Senn had never been allowed to look inside, always being told when he asked that the contents were too valuable and fragile for the little paws of children. She opened it and took out the ebony Orb, bringing it over to the table where she set it in the center of the tablecloth.

Senn had seen it a few times before; his mother had taken it from his grandfather's study during her flight from Islingin. The Orb was his mother's most prized (and most protected) possession. Its dark ebony surface seemed to absorb light, except around the center ring where it was embossed with a silver pattern. "It has spells sealed in the wood, right? Like the imbued objects?" He tried to remember what he knew about these artifacts. A powerful spellcaster could 'burn' a spell into an organic object so that others could cast that spell as well. Wood was the best material for creating such magic objects.

Lieh touched the Orb lightly, caressing it with her fingers. "Yes, your grandfather imbued the Orb with a lot of powerful spells. The one that warns us about demons nearby, for example. I feed energy into that spell on the Orb every day, and I feel the alarm immediately if I'm within a stone's throw of it. But the spell is so complex, and goes so deep into the Orb, that even I can't figure out how it works."

"Not even you? But how could that be!"

"Talen spent years working on this magic Orb, and told me if anything ever happened to protect it at all costs. Unfortunately he didn't tell me anything about the spells it contains, or how to use it. When the first demons and possessed Magi began killing everyone they could find in Islingin Keep, I ran to the study to check on Talen and the Orb. I found your grandfather there at his desk, dead. His eyes were fixed on the Orb as if it were his last hope. It wasn't enough to save him, though I've no idea exactly what killed him. I took the Orb, along with a few of Talen's most important items, and ran. As far as I know, that was the last any free human saw of Islingin. I was the last to leave the Keep alive. Well . . ." She bit her lip and looked away. "We were the last. I was pregnant with you."

Senn's eyes opened wide in understanding. He had never seen his mother shed a tear in his entire life, and now he realized why. After what she had gone through—her husband setting the wheels in motion that destroyed the city, her father dying as a result, and she herself barely escaping with Senn inside her belly—nothing much could affect her now. He reached out to touch her hand, which was resting on the table next to the Orb. "Mother, I . . . you . . ." What could he say?

Lieh locked her eyes on his. "This knowledge is just for you. No one else can know! It would be too dangerous, for both of us. Listen to me!" She took his hand and gripped it tightly. "Don't trust anyone but me, do you hear? We'll never know what they might do! If someone were to blame our family . . ." She closed her eyes for a moment, then looked up and let out a deep, slow breath, steadying herself.

"Now that you're old enough for magic, you'll soon have to care for the Orb and learn what it can do. Let's wait another moon of your lessons before we start. When you can do a few of the more complex spells that Wildon teaches, we'll start to study the Orb, just the two of us. Don't tell anyone about this, not even Wildon—it will be safer that way. Once you know more about magic items, when you can levitate yourself and cast energy balls . . . then we'll proceed."

"Energy balls and levitation? Most of the people in the clan can't even do that! You think I'll be able to cast those spells by next moon? Today I can barely light a fire!"

Lieh concentrated and held still. Her chair slid backward out from beneath her. She quickly folded her legs underneath herself, holding position a few feet off the ground. Senn blinked as she smiled warmly at him, she who never smiled. "Senn, most young men and women need weeks to learn the fire lighting spell, and trying it twice is exhausting for them. You've learned it in one day. And if I know Herst, you've done it at least a dozen times already." It sounded as if she were proud of him, instead of half-ignoring him as usual. Could that be true?

Another morning peeked into the windows of the Morels' small dwelling, casting a few rays of sunshine where the sun found gaps in the towering canopy of trees. The days had been getting warmer, and it was already hot under the thick sleeping roll. Senn woke to the smell of sizzling wild bacon. His mother spent a few hours a week hunting, so their pantry was always well stocked. Wild boars weren't much of a match for magic weapons wielded by someone of his mother's strength.

Anxious to get started, Senn wolfed down several slices of bread with bacon and headed out for the day's lesson with Wildon Herst. His progress had been remarkable, as his mother had promised. In two weeks he had mastered spells that the clan's dozen or so teenagers had taken several moons to learn, or never managed to cast at all. As Senn walked, he passed some of his friends who already had several years of magic use under their belts. They stared at him, their eyes reflecting a mixture of jealousy and awe.

Besides Senn's speed at learning, his spell-casting stamina was a curiosity to everyone, including Wildon. Senn could practice complex and energy-hungry spells for hours, whereas the next best youngsters could only handle a few tries per day.

This gave Senn a new standing among the clansmen, who realized what an asset he would be in case of future demon attacks. It was fantastic to leave behind that scrawny kid who had to stay with the younger children—to now be an aspiring Magus and future protector of the camp. Combining his new skills with his mother's power, the clan would have a front-line defense that could take out several demons, maybe even without any casualties. Because of that, he was given far more time than the others with the clan's tutor for one-on-one lessons.

On the way to the clearing that served as his classroom, Senn ran through the most recent lessons in his mind. He had learned to throw small energy balls, to lift objects as heavy as several stone, to cut firewood, and to perform a dozen other similar spells. But today was to be different, as Wildon would start explaining magic objects: how a spellcaster imbued them, and (more useful for the average user) how to cast the spells imbued by others. This was the foundation of the learning that would lead to the secret lessons with his mother about the Orb.

Wildon Herst was already waiting by the stone table. He stroked his neat beard with his fingers, while his hair was an explosion of disarray as usual. "Good morning, Senn, I hope you're feeling rested."

He smiled. "Absolutely, Master Herst, ready for whatever you might throw at me today."

"Excellent. Let's start with a review before we move on to a new lesson. Explain the spell for splitting a tree limb into firewood."

"First you cut the limb into pieces by building an energy channel and narrowing it to a knife edge as it gets close to the wood. Next you create a matrix around the area where you want to cut, to hold the piece in place. You set the factors for a solid energy force, with enough power to cut through the wood. Most of the energy must be pushed into the channel like a ram, so that the knife edge cuts through cleanly, while holding the limb still with the surrounding matrix. Then, you split the resulting log, using a knife edge of solid energy as a maul."

"Very good, you remember the principles. Now, let's try it. Last time you did it with a log on the ground. I want to see you cut and split that limb there . . ." Wildon pointed to the lowest limb on a tree a dozen strides away, which was at least three strides from the ground. Senn stood up to walk closer. "No, boy, from here."

Senn's eyes widened: this was more of a test than a review. He looked, measured the distances and the size of the limb, and started creating the channel and matrix.

"Aah, Senn, one more detail. We don't want that massive limb crashing down and disturbing our peace, do we? Make sure it comes down gently."

Alright, if that's the way it had to be . . . two spells at once. Senn created a second channel leading to a wide, flat matrix below the branch, supported from underneath by channels connecting to the ground. First he fed energy to this support structure, making it strong enough to hold the weight of the branch. Then he pushed the power into his knife edge. There was a splintering sound of shearing wood fibers, and the branch fell gently onto the platform. Then it rolled halfway over to one side, fell off the platform, and crashed to the earth with a loud thump and a shower of small spring leaves. "Oops . . ."

"I guess you should have made some sides on your platform so the limb couldn't roll out. Continue."

That was embarrassing, but Senn continued nonetheless. First he sheared off the small branches and the end of the limb with a moving knife edge. This was going to be a lot of cutting and splitting spells. Why not streamline the process? He created a channel with a splitting knife edge on the end, and a matrix to hold the far end of the log. As Senn fed in the power, he caught Wildon smiling in satisfaction. The log split through the middle all the way down its length. Then he created a long channel with multiple cutting edges, spaced half a stride apart, and sliced the big limb into short sections all in one go.

Wildon laughed and clapped his hands. "Well done. That makes up for disturbing my morning when the limb crashed down. One more step ... I want to see you light up a pile of that firewood. And not with a fire-lighting spell."

"What ... ?" Senn was confused, then it hit him. "You want me to light the firewood with an energy ball."

"Right on, my boy. You aren't getting all this extra training for fun, you know. I need to show you how to defend us! I don't have the stamina for all this anymore; an old Sabi like me would be exhausted by cutting firewood the way you did just now. But you and your bottomless well of energy—you need to know how to use it!" Wildon closed his eyes and concentrated. He lifted a half dozen pieces of wood and guided them onto the stone table. Sweat beaded his forehead by the time he was finished. "I used to be able to work spells for half the day ... aah. Now my skill is mostly academic. But let's see what you can do. And remember, I want burning logs! Not exploding logs, hot air, or a shower of warm splinters."

What did that mean? Aah ... Wildon was subtly pointing him in the right direction. Senn had to throw a ball of energy at the pile of wood, and the ball was just a hollow globe of solid energy filled with heat energy. Too much heat and there would be a fireball of sparks. Not enough solid energy and the ball would not hold together as it flew through the air. Too much solid energy and it would hit like a sledgehammer, pulverizing the wood.

The two walked away from the table, Wildon leading them a few strides distant. The tutor raised his hands and prepared a spell to shield them in case anything flew their way. Senn closed his eyes and worked the energy ball spell. The main channel went to a short rail from which to fire the ball. The matrix was a thin wall of solid energy, filled with enough heat energy to start the logs on fire. Finally Senn pushed the ball from behind with solid energy, firing it toward the target. He tweaked its flight gently with guide channels. When it hit the logs they jumbled a bit, and burst into bright, crackling flames. He was grinning like a madman. Now *that* was a lot better than collecting sticks from the forest floor!

"Magic objects. They are among the most prized, and most complex spells that we know." Wildon Herst lifted a small polished branch of oak. "The power needed to imbue this wand with its levitation spell was more than you've expended in the several weeks you've had your magic. And that's accounting for the vast power you possess! So, you can imagine that average folks don't have enough energy in a lifetime to create something like this."

The small branch didn't look very special. It had no special carvings or symbols, only a surface smoothed by time and use. "This wand can lift objects up to a stone's weight. Using it is child's play for anyone with a whit of magic left. In fact, I got it from my father, who was infirm and used it to do tasks around his house back in Islingin. You only need to sense the inputs and outputs, then feed in minimal power, and the rod creates all the energy channels, guide channels, matrices, and so forth. Think of all the shapes of various objects you might want to move—eggs, cups, plates, a head of lettuce. The rod takes care of creating energy matrices to move all those. It calculates the factors for the user, based on his inherent knowledge of weights and sizes. Furthermore, it makes the most efficient use of magic energy, to minimize how much it tires the user. Here, take it. What do you sense?"

Wildon offered him the wand. Senn took it, turned it over in his hands, and felt for its magic. "I feel a lifeless spell in the fibers of the wood."

"Feed it a bit of energy and feel what happens."

He extended his own energy into the wand.

—*Concentrate on item*—

"Hey, I think it's talking to me!"

"Yes, in a way, it gives you a mental feedback asking for your inputs."

Senn looked to a wooden cup of water on the table and focused his mind on it.

—*Apply energy*—

There was a sense from the wand of how much energy flow it needed, though it was hardly even enough to notice. Senn opened an energy path to the wand.

—*Follow trajectory, relax to release*—

Senn continued focusing on the cup, and flicked his gaze to his free hand. The cup flew through the air and smacked painfully into his fingers. "Ow!" As the pain distracted him, he lost focus and the cup fell to the table, spilling water in his lap.

"The wand does exactly as you tell it. Your point of concentration moved too fast and was about as subtle as this morning's falling branch. Try again, and make sure you have your fingers closed around the cup before relaxing focus." Wildon placed the cup back upright and refilled it with water from a skin.

This time when Senn focused on the cup he moved it slowly toward his hand. As he closed his fingers around it he relaxed focus. "Alright, I see how it works, but how does someone make a stick of wood do all this?"

"Think of it as a blueprint for the spell, etched into the wood by the craftsman. He uses magic to imbue the spell inside the stick, like carving the inside of it with a hot knife. But the spell is far more complicated than what you've done 'til now. The magic object has to talk to the user, as you noticed, by an unspoken mental communication spell that uses earth magic. Then, it has to interpret what the user is focusing on: 'he's thinking of a cup, so big and with so much water in it, about that far away.' It relies on formulas in the imbued spell to tell the user how much energy is needed. Finally, it must work the actual spell: channels, a matrix of the right shape to hold the object, and so on. You can imagine: if the spell is not perfectly imbued, after days of hard work the craftsman ends up with a wand that breaks eggs and drops plates on the floor!"

All this sounded very complicated. Senn pointed to the magic rod, "Well, how can you imbue something like that? I don't know anything about those other spells you mentioned: talking to the user and so on."

"All in good time, boy. Let's start by making a simple wand: one that casts small energy balls of a preset size, usable even by a Medi. That should keep us busy the rest of the week, or at least you, after I explain it to you." What, a week to make the simplest kind of wand? This was turning out to be much more complex than expected!

After several more weeks of training, it was nearly time for Senn's mother to begin her lessons teaching him about the Orb. He had made his first wand, casting energy balls just about big enough to light a twig on fire. It wasn't much, but was more than anyone else in the clan could manage aside from his mother, and she didn't have the time for crafting that kind of item.

Then he'd learned about levitating himself, which was a lot harder than moving an object in the way Wildon's wand had done. Creating a moving matrix to carry a person was a lot of effort. On top of that, once you started levitating and moving around, the point of view from which you propagated the spell was also moving—making it complicated to readjust the support locations of the solid matrix that held you up. It was like creating and riding a giant wave of oatmeal while standing on a pair of floating logs. Screw it up, and you hit the ground hard, as Senn's several scrapes and purple bruises could testify.

He arrived home to an angry glare from Lieh. "Isn't it a bit late for dinner? You're usually home much earlier from the lessons with Herst. In fact I've already eaten."

"Yes, I know, but he had me perfecting the levitation spell. I kept falling off, but now I think I've got it." Senn winced as he sat down in a chair by the table. Why did he have to land so hard on his arse in that last fall?

"Alright. Well, as Wildon told me you are progressing fast, and you know a bit about magic objects, let's start experimenting with the Orb after dinner. While you eat I can tell you what little I know about it." Finally! The waiting had started to drive him crazy. But . . . what little she knew? That didn't sound too reassuring. His mother usually knew everything there was worth knowing.

Lieh served a cold dinner of sliced meat, cheese, and some root vegetables. "Here, eat, while I tell you what I know about the Orb. It was your grandfather's life's work, as I mentioned before. It's made of ebony, and as you should have learned from Herst, such a dense hardwood is perfect for a magic item. You can fit more into a small space that way. There are sixteen sectors that have spells worked deep into the wood, like half-wedges of an orange. Around the center there is a ring with another spell, but I can't for the life of me work out what it is. Of the sixteen spells, there are several I use, but the primary one that I need is for detecting nearby demons. Some of the spells don't seem to work, or were perhaps not complete when your grandfather died."

Senn finished his meal, and his mother got out the Orb, setting it on the tablecloth. "Here. Now, feel it for yourself, try this sector here."

—*Apply energy*— He opened a channel to the Orb and fed it energy.

—*You will be warned if spirits come near. Refresh this spell each day*—

"Great, so it will warn me in case something is coming!" Senn was beaming.

"Tell me about the other sectors, what do you find?"

He tried another. —*Inactive*— Then another, —*Inactive*— and another, —*Inactive*—

"They all say 'Inactive,' I don't understand!"

Lieh frowned and her eyebrows drew tight. "You must not be applying the right energy. Try the ring around the edge, where the pattern in the wood is. I could never get a response from that section. Maybe your fresh view on it will reveal something."

This was strange. She was asking him to figure it out? He tried the ring. Nothing at all; even trying to push in some energy gave no result. "It's not working, Mother." How frustrating! Now that he got to use this fantastic talisman that he'd been eying his whole childhood, there was nothing to it but a spirit warning. "What about the other spells you use?"

She did not look happy. "Well. Let's see what happens tomorrow, maybe we can try again when you're not so tired from a day of walking on air. Once you have your energy back, we might have a better chance for you to unlock some of the other spells."

"But I'm not tired."

"No debating this time. We'll try again tomorrow. Now we have to get to the rest of the chores: I'll need to restock some of our supplies, and you split and dry a tree so we have a ready stock of firewood for the next week."

She didn't even want to tell him what else there was to know about the Orb? Something didn't feel right. But there was no arguing with Lieh. All it would get Senn was another angry glare, and double chores.

—*Wake up*— Senn heard the whisper in the middle of the night, and his eyes popped open. —*No spirit is near, do not alert any others*— It must be the Orb. Why was it notifying him if everything was fine? —*Please bring this item outdoors—* Maybe there was something else. He silently slid out of his sleeping covers and padded over to the shelf, opened the wooden box, and took the Orb out, hoping that the hinges on the box wouldn't squeak. They didn't. He took his shoes and jacket and carefully made his way out into the cold. After a few steps he stopped and put on his shoes, trying carefully to avoid crunching any leaves or twigs underfoot. *—Farther, away from others—* He kept going until he was outside the camp.

—Hold fingers around ring, apply energy— Well, it couldn't hurt, could it? He created a channel and fed energy into the ring, waiting to see what the Orb would say next. As he fed in the power, a warm feeling came over him and there was a loud *—POP—* in his mind. Could anyone else have heard that? It sounded so loud . . .

—Alright my boy, that was an unfortunate burst of energy I caused at the end there, but we'll deal with it later if need be. You have no idea how good it feels to speak to someone after fifteen years cooped up in here alone— The voice sounded a little different, more like a person than the previous magical communications.

"What are you saying, who's talking?"

—Not out loud. Talk with your mind, like this. Otherwise you'll wake the others. I haven't heard a spoken word or shared a thought with anyone in a long time. Until you broke the seal, I could only get a sense of the people in contact with the Orb. You can call me Talen . . . what's your name?—

Senn didn't know what to say. Someone named Talen was stuck inside the Orb? It seemed that way, and he only knew one person by that name. *—Uhh, sure . . . Talen. My name is Senn. Can you explain a bit of what's going on? Do you know . . . my grandfather Talen Morel?—*

—Yes, Senn, that's me. Nice to meet you at last!— Senn's eyes widened as his world changed yet again, something which had become all too commonplace lately. *—Let's make this short and sweet, since we may have visitors soon. I think when you broke through my protective seal, it released all the spirit energy that has been building up in here for fifteen years. So if there are any spirits or Magi within twenty leagues of here, they probably felt it and know exactly where we are. Usually the magic we use is so little as to be undetectable, but that much at once might be noticed. I was worried about that, but there's nothing I could do. Anyway . . . to the crux of it. I made this*

Orb, a talisman of ebony with some bloodwood hidden in the core, as a last resort—

—Bloodwood? Isn't that what the old Magi used to magically store memories?—

—Yes, but no one in recent times has made much use of it, and it's very hard to find. Those spells weren't deemed interesting by your father's generation, who were far more interested in contacting the spirit world, the other side of our physical reality. Eventually they succeeded, and opened a small hole that let demon spirits through. I didn't want to give the spirits access to what I knew just yet, so I used my escape route, transferring my mind and soul into the Orb. All my physical magic was lost, and I've gained spirit magic. A pocket of spirit energy built up over time in here, as it had no way out of this imbued bloodwood.

—I've been living here, if you can call it that, for fifteen years just waiting for you to come of age. I knew you'd have strong magic, boy, and when Lieh handed you the Orb, I could feel it. I could tell you're a better type than she is, too . . . that's why I haven't allowed her access to any of the other spells. She's just as power-hungry, self-serving, and heartless as your father Marek, but she was the only one I could trust to get the Orb out of there in case something went wrong. Since she was pregnant, I knew there was some hope I could eventually communicate with her child, and it seems that I have. Now, tell me about what's going on here. All I knew until you broke the seal was the vague input I can receive through the spirit sensing spell, because the other spells are all locked down—

Senn told Talen about the recent tumultuous years. *—Well, people scattered when the demons ravaged the cities and towns, so we're pretty mobile now. Every once in a while we hear from another clan—* He told the story of the fall, their current loose society of wanderers, his own clan led by Lieh, and the way the demon attacks came at random.

There was an interruption, another sound in his head. The magical voice was back. *—Alert, spirits near. The number is seven—* It repeated.

Senn stopped in the middle of telling Talen about his recent magical endeavors. *—What? Is that the real warning, should I alert the rest of the camp?—*

—Damn. Yes. I feared this would happen when I felt that seal break the way it did. It seems that every nearby spirit must have felt it. It might be too

many for your clan to deal with, given what you said about your mother being the only powerful one. I could open some more spells up to you, but there isn't time to explain them, and your own magic use isn't very skilled yet. If the fight gets rough, grab a good friend or two and run! You hear? Don't let us get caught. I cannot fall into the hands of any spirits—

—But . . . what should I tell my mother about all this?—

—Don't tell her anything. Sneak back in there, and pretend you just woke up when you heard the Orb's spirit warning. Say only that there are seven demons coming, nothing more. That's all the Orb's spell would have told her, and since you refreshed it last, she'll be expecting you to get the warning. But, we both know what happened with that energy burst: demons could be coming from several directions, all uncoordinated. Keep me close. Now that the seal is broken, I am aware of what goes on nearby. Maybe I can help you if we get into a tight spot. Whatever you do, don't trust Lieh!—

CHAPTER THREE

The Seventh Demon

L ieh flew high over the world, skimming the mountaintops in her search, looking for her love, her Marek. She burst up above the clouds, looking down on a sea of white, knowing Marek was floating somewhere down there. She would lift his tall, strong body up from the foamy waves and be with him again. Together they would learn about the source of magic and find a way to contain the demons. Men would rebuild Islingin, and with new magics make it more than it had ever been under the old, argument-wracked Conclave. They would show those old men whose way was best in the end. But Marek was nowhere to be found, heard, felt, held, caressed. He did not seem to be in this world.

Lightning flashed up ahead. A wave of clouds grew taller, forming a dark thunderhead, roiling up in front of her too quickly to avoid. In another instant the clouds had built around her, and many old feelings flooded back, just for a moment. Her flight continued as raindrops stung her cheeks, and though Marek wasn't there in the storm clouds, her father was. Talen Morel flew up next to her in mid-air, shouting that she'd done everything wrong, that Marek was wrong. He insisted that she give up her search to find the roots of their magic.

She hadn't thought too deeply about her father in years, aside from cursing his near-useless Orb. If it had any power at all, she could have driven the demons back, and found out what really happened to the missing Conclave members who had been deep in the cellars of the Keep. But instead, all that work Talen had put into the Orb was unfinished, 'inactive', and worthless. She began to speak, ready to curse him for his uselessness—

"Mother, wake up! I just got a warning!" Lieh woke and sat up with a start, drenched in sweat. Senn was hovering over her as white as a sheet, with the Orb clutched tightly in his hands. "Seven demons, it said! We have to get everyone ready, right?" What? She must still be dreaming. But looking around, it was her shelter, her son, and the Orb which she'd had him activate the evening before.

"Senn ... slow down. You got a warning from the Orb? Seven? You must be mistaken, it's never been more than two or three before."

"Yes, but something ... must be different this time. I don't know. It just said 'Spirits near, the number is seven.' There was no mistaking it!"

"Oh hells. Seven demons?"

"Yes, mother."

"Then we'd better assume the worst." The clan might not survive the assault, but they had to try and fight. "We'll lose this camp for sure. But maybe some of us will make it out alive to rebuild." Lieh slipped out of her bedroll and started packing it up, already preparing to run at the end of the confrontation. "Can you stand and fight? It will require every ounce of strength in the two of us, and I'm not sure even that's enough." She looked at him and frowned. He was still scrawny, for a fourteen year old.

"Sure. I can do it, let's try. What other choice do we have, anyway?" There was fear in her son's cracking adolescent voice.

"Listen to me, Senn. If it gets rough, you get out of here, and hide yourself until it's over. Give me the Orb," she hesitated a moment. Should she come clean about how little she could do with the talisman? No. "I can use its power to aid in the fight."

Senn furrowed his brows at her. "No, I'll keep it safe!"

What was he doing? The boy was not in the habit of disagreeing with her. What was he hiding? No matter, there wasn't time for arguments or punishments. The demons could be here any minute.

"Fine, just don't make yourself a target. I want Herst with you, along with Jarel Linker and his hunting dogs. Jarel and his Adept Lani will keep you safe. I'll let you wake the others, then I'll be out in a moment to organize them." Senn looked a little surprised that she was letting him off so lightly. Later she would have to make sure he didn't start a habit of questioning her. That was, if they came out of this alive. How in all the hells had *seven* demons banded together? Normally any two of them would rip each other to shreds for the fun of it. Well, there would be time enough to answer questions later. Now it was time to fight.

Lieh threw on her clothes as Senn called out the alarm to the camp. Soon the horn would sound the clan's alert signal for all to hear. By the time she walked out of the crude shelter into the pre-dawn gloom, a few of the adults and older children had started to arrive. She gathered her thoughts. There were about sixty of them left in the clan, but only a quarter of them were fighters and a quarter spellcasters. That meant around four defenders for every demon ... not good odds when only two were Magus-level. The others besides herself and Senn would be tired out after the initial charge, and she guessed his green spells were just as likely to hurt their own people as the enemy. Add to that the fact they couldn't see in the near-darkness ... at least some of their teenage trainees should be able to help with that. It looked as if nearly everyone had gathered, forming a semicircle in front of Lieh's shelter. It was time to get started.

"Alright! We have a big fight coming, there are seven demons on the way. Let there be no illusions. We are fighting for the continuance of our entire clan tonight. Drop off your packs here by my hut. Namee, Kettin: split up, north and south, and find a good place to hide. I want you each to make a spell to light up the camp as well as you can, but remember you have to keep it going for quite some time." The young Adepts nodded, and started off in opposite directions. Nervous glances and whispers made their way around the remaining clan members. She had to keep the situation in control, to prevent panic.

"Herst, you and Lani and Jarel, stay with Senn, here in the center facing north. Remember, we have two Magi now!" There were a few nods of assent among the crowd. Hopefully that had reassured them, although Lieh wasn't too confident herself. "The rest of you, split up to cover the two southern entrances and the path to the north. Keep low and stay hidden until you see them. Let's get going!" Yes, that's probably what they should be doing—going. As in running, fleeing. But then it would be just as likely they'd encounter this band of demons as they fled.

Lieh walked to the south, where two beaten paths wandered toward the center of the camp. So far it seemed to be quiet. She looked around, watching her clan spring into action. They responded just like the well-oiled mechanism she had trained them to be. Strongmen and spellcasters were looking for spots to hide, and the less-capable were herding the children into the more centrally placed huts where they would be safest. Archers were climbing the trees to their prepared lookout and shooting points. She could see Beagan and Elam, two archers who had hit their marks well in the attack two years before. Slowly it got lighter as Kettin and Namee began working their spells, with two globes of light appearing, one north and one south. Lieh let out a long, slow breath, and sat down on a log to wait.

It was over an hour before Beagan called out a warning from the archers' perch: incoming demons! Within seconds, the largest grizzly bear Lieh had ever seen crashed through the woods on all fours from the west, making little effort to disguise its approach. Lieh stood up and edged around toward it, wary that it might be a distraction. An arrow or two dug into its hide, not slowing it at all—definitely a demon. She began by casting an energy ball spell: calculating where the bear would be, weaving the guide channel in and out between the trees, and finally launching her projectile. The ball smashed into the bear, burning off half its fur and a good deal of flesh, but it kept moving through a haze of smoke and flying sparks toward the center of the camp.

A loud crash from behind jolted Lieh—it sounded like a new threat, and much closer to her. Quickly, she called out, "Senn! Do what you can with that bear ..." Turning to the southeast, she saw a giant ... what was that ... ? A moose? Some of these demons were really desperate lately, judging by the animals they chose to possess. As it thundered up the trail, Rikk Janus slunk out from behind a tree and slashed the moose down its side with his sword. Rikk was a lot slower since his injury from that wolf two years before, but that made him all the more cunning. The gargantuan moose stopped and swung around, splintering a small sapling as it turned. Its huge antlers, twice as wide as she was tall, lashed out in response to Rikk's sword cut. Someone was pitched through the semi-darkness with a scream. It looked like one of the spellcasters, who would probably spend his last moments regretting the very existence of antlers. Suddenly being a moose didn't seem like such a bad idea.

How to help ... Lieh summoned up a black ball of cold energy, and routed it on a channel toward the moose. The energy smashed into one of its front legs just as it regained its footing. The cold froze the leg nearly solid and frosted the ground white around it. Rikk dove forward with his sword outstretched as the moose lost balance, almost hacking the leg off at the knee. The moose fell forward on him and thrashed around, kicking him hard with its rear legs. Artie Tenko entered the fray with his battle hammer, raised it two-handed, and swung at the demon's head. A shimmer of solid energy shield glimmered next to him as the shield deflected a few solid kicks of the moose's flailing legs. At least one Adept over there was still able to maintain a shield.

A wolf howl echoed from the north, and Lieh heard a grunting noise coming from the southwest path. It was strange that the demons were approaching from so many directions, several minutes apart. This kind of disorganization was no way to win a fight, but Lieh wasn't about to complain. She turned her attention to the new threat from the southwest, confident the demon moose was now in good hands. A wild boar was coming up the southwest path at a dead run. At that speed, it would be tough for the archers to hit. She started to create a wall of solid energy across the path. As she built the matrix of the wall, she heard a noise overhead, and looked up just in time to see a huge lynx leaping out of a tree to her left. The muscled cat slammed into Lieh's side as if the tree itself had fallen on her. She felt a crunch as the impact crushed a few of her ribs, then her head hit the ground hard, and the rest was blackness.

A flaming grizzly bear crashed through the woods in the distance off to Senn's left, leaving a trail of smoke and embers in the air behind it. By his side, Lani, Jarel, and Wildon watched the charging bear with apprehension. How best to intercept this demon with what he knew so far ... what about the wood cutting lesson? Judging the distance, Senn built a cutting channel by the trunk of a big tree between himself and the bear.

"Hurry up kid, make that bastard ugly." Jarel sneered at the half-burnt bear. He turned his double-bladed axe, inspecting its sharpness one final time. "I'll whistle my dogs on it once it looks near finished. No point in sending them to die right off." Senn fed in the energy, added a bit more of a kick at the end, and smiled as the back side of the tree exploded a few strides up. This blew the top of the tree down directly in the path of the charging bear, striking a solid blow on its left shoulder with a snapping sound audible throughout the camp. But the bear kept coming, hardly slowing at all. For Senn's first fight as a combatant, this was certainly a challenge. Maybe too much of one for his tastes.

From the path to the north, Senn heard a chilling wolf howl. Some of these demons didn't understand the concept of stealth, and to be honest, usually they didn't need to. Could the group on the north path handle the wolf alone? He had his own concerns much closer at hand.

Jarel was doing his part to slow down the bear. "Lani! Gimme a shield over there to the left! And Senn, don't toast any of my pups in the heat of the moment, or I'll put ya next on my list!" Jarel winked and took up a position several steps forward of the spellcasters, massive axe hefted over his right shoulder. He whistled and the four hounds bounded along behind him.

How could they stop that bear? It would be upon them in seconds now. Senn built a cone-shaped matrix just forward of the area where Lani's shield had shimmered to life. The cone dangled point-down from a nearby tree bough by a thin solid channel, and he filled the cone itself with cold energy. Wildon stepped up beside him. "I'm going to do what I can, Senn, but my best is about a minute of meager shielding for the three of us. We might have to get out of here fast, if it turns any uglier." What, abandon his friends and mother here? Senn glowered at him, then looked back to the bear approaching Jarel and his dogs behind the shield.

Senn released the icy cone, and it crashed down onto the bear's left shoulder, piercing deeply and freezing the limb solid. The bear took a header and rolled, going down in a massive ball of smoking fur, but came out of the roll just a few strides from Jarel. It stood up straight on its rear legs. By the stars . . . the bear was twice Jarel's height, and the warrior was a big man in his own right. Jarel leaped out from behind Lani's magic shield, axe swinging. It bit into the demon bear's good arm and lodged in the bone. The beast bellowed and swung its arm around, ripping the axe from Jarel's hands as the warrior stumbled backward, stunned. Senn had to distract that bear! He took aim at its midsection with an energy ball.

As the bright ball flew through the air, the beast turned toward it, shaking its body like a dog drying itself. The axe was jarred loose, its haft knocking Jarel in the side of the head as he tried to regain the safety of the shield. He slumped on the ground, dazed. But Senn's tactic had worked, and the bear took the ball of flame full in its chest. Its remaining fur ignited, at least the part which wasn't attached to the small chunks of airborne bear meat that now flew through the air.

Still it seemed the beast wasn't finished. Its head unharmed, it roared and started running on all fours toward Senn and the others, its frozen forelimb thumping awkwardly on the ground. "What more have you got, boy," whispered Wildon urgently as his shield shimmered to life in front of them. Lani huddled in behind it as the bear came on. She had dropped her shield and was setting up a new one at an angle to Wildon's, to prevent the bear from coming around one side. Senn froze for a moment as the beast slammed into Wildon's wall just a few hands' breadth from his face. He could smell the smoking fur and see blood dripping down the wavering surface of the transparent shield as the demon slavered at him.

A whistle from Jarel releasing his hounds brought Senn out of his panic. The strongman must have recovered from the axe blow. Senn had to keep this demon hemmed in! He created a third shield, cutting off another angle for the bear. The dogs came up behind it, going for the legs. As they distracted it, the beast slammed back and forth into his and Lani's shields, sending two of the hounds rolling across the ground. Finally, Jarel caught up to the dogs, breathing heavily and dragging his recovered axe behind him. Senn was relieved that the bear had stayed on all fours, trying to bite the hounds and swat them with its thawing arm. Jarel lifted his axe high for a two-handed stroke, and brought it down with all his remaining strength on the demon bear's head, which split halfway through. Finally the beast went limp and crashed in a smoldering mess on the ground with a muffled thump that shook the earth beneath them.

All three spellcasters dropped their shields. Lani and Wildon lay exhausted on the ground, and Jarel leaned heavily on his axe. Blood dripped down the strongman's neck from the wide cut on his head where the axe haft had hit. "Holy hells. The bigger they are, the harder to fell 'em."

Lani looked over, "Honey, you mean the harder they fall?" The warrior was always trying out some half-remembered saying from his youth in Islingin. But his wits apparently weren't as sharp as his weapons.

"Err, yeah. Something like that."

Senn himself was shaking like a leaf, a heady mixture of magic and fear coursing through him. Wildon raised his head, "What's that noise?" From the north there was a steady crackling.

Jarel turned and peered through the trees. "The forest's on fire. None of our people up there could have done that. There must be a possessed Adept over there, and from the sounds of it, a wolf as strong as the ones that came after us two years ago." He looked back to the three of them. "I think we'd best be going before the going gets gone. We can take our packs from Senn's hut here, and get the hell out."

Senn had to object. "We're still standing. I'm sure we can take down the rest of the demons with some help from my mother!"

But Wildon was on Jarel's side. "Senn, of the four of us, you're the only one with any fight left. You'll be on your own."

Senn glanced around, reviewing the grim situation in the camp. But he couldn't give up on the remaining clansmen, could he? "You wait in my hut, get the packs ready, but I think I should help my mother." Wildon, Jarel, and Lani looked at each other and started moving, shaking the weariness from their bones.

—*Senn. You handled that well, without my help. But now there is no time*— Talen's projected thoughts had an urgency Senn hadn't heard when they had talked earlier in the night. —*Listen: there is nothing but the sound of bones breaking and men screaming. Lieh may already be out of action. The others speak from an experience you've never had, as they only survived the fall of Islingin by abandoning it*— As Talen spoke, the light to the north abruptly cut off. Was Namee gone as well? That made up Senn's mind. He turned and followed the others to the hut.

Inside, Senn lifted his pack. Thinking once more, he grabbed the wooden box of magic items off the shelf. He wasn't supposed to touch it, but that hardly mattered now. His mother might not make it back, and someone should ensure their few heirlooms from Islingin made it out safely. Besides, according to Talen she wasn't to be trusted. Lieh had always seemed distant from Senn throughout his childhood. It was fitting that now he put more trust in a soul trapped in a wooden ball than in his own mother.

Senn hefted the box, and guessed it weighed about a quarter stone— no problem. He wedged it into his pack.

Jarel clapped him on the shoulder. "Glad ya came to your senses, kid. Sometimes ya just have to know when it's not your fight. We'd better not tempt fate again today . . . leave 'er those she's already chosen." The warrior's ever-present grin seemed to have faded for the moment, perhaps knocked out of him by the axe handle. "Let's go while we still can." Those already chosen . . . was it really true there was nothing they could do? Jarel squeezed hard, and Senn had to agree.

The four of them crept out of the hut to total darkness, Jarel talking quietly to the four hounds to keep them calm. At least all of the dogs were alive, though they had bruises and cuts from the final mêlée with the demon bear. Sounds of tearing flesh and occasional screams, both animal and human, filtered in from three sides. Wildon whispered, "We have to go east. It's the only direction that seems clear of demons. Boy, you have to use your magic to cover our tracks. There's no one else left to do it. Once we get a few strides away I'll explain the spell." They ducked down and started moving east.

Talen's voice spoke privately again. —*That won't be necessary, Senn. Activate this sector on the Orb, one to the right of the spirit alert. It's a powerful concealing spell that will drain a lot of your energy, so deactivate it when you sleep. Lieh never had a need for it, because she could always get by with her own magic on that count. So I never felt the need to unlock the spell for her. Might as well tell the others you've got a little toy, eh? Just don't say too much—*

He kept his voice low. "I can do it already, Wildon. I have a . . . a gift from my mother, and I can cast a few spells with it. They shouldn't be able to follow us." Wildon looked at him quizzically. Senn felt in his pocket for the Orb and activated the spell, opening a channel to feed it energy. He immediately felt the magical drain, tiring him as if he were walking double-time. From the north a wolf howl pierced the silence. Jarel grunted and picked up the pace.

Lieh woke slowly, her midsection a ball of pain, her head throbbing like a drum. Why did she feel like a prisoner? She opened her eyes, and slowly it all came into focus ... wait a minute. She *was* a prisoner. In her own hut no less: she sat at her own kitchen table tied to a chair she'd built with her own hands. A ruddy dawn had broken outside, tinged with wood smoke and the smell of death. Across the table, a middle-aged man with dark eyes and a pointy beard sat in the other chair, staring at her. His body appeared normal, with the soft musculature of a spellcaster, but his face was an unreadable mask of stone. She came back to the eyes and looked closer, shivering—they were black as the pits of hell. This was definitely not a normal, living being. She counted: flaming bear, frozen moose, wolf howling to the north, wild boar, tree-climbing lynx ... he made six.

A thin old woman with similar black eyes sat on the ground next to the table, a fiendish grin on her face. The seventh demon. The most noteworthy distinction about her was the blood ... ugh. Her hands were coated sticky red; her clothes and face were splattered with flecks and droplets of it. When the old woman saw that their prisoner (or prey?) was awake, she looked Lieh straight in the eyes and turned up one corner of her mouth in a devilish sneer. Perhaps guessing Lieh's disgust, her tongue flicked out and tasted a drop of the blood on her lips.

Why was Lieh still alive if the rest of the clan was dead at the hands of these demons? And how could she escape? She tried to focus her mind and then her magic, but the pain in her head was too great. After a moment of concentration she slumped back in the chair. The man spoke, with still no hint of expression on his face, and with a cold evenness to his voice. "Sorry that we hurt your head like that. I instructed our lynx Shyama to be careful. But now it seems quite an advantage, since we don't have to contend with your magic just yet."

Lieh moved her jaw; at least that part of her still seemed to work. Her tongue felt as if it were coated with coarse flour, and she could taste blood in her mouth. "What do you want? And why have you kept me alive?"

"Ah, humans, always asking so many questions. It's much easier to work with an animal. We speak to them with our spirit magic, tell their simple mind they will never be hungry, cold, or sick again, and they let us in without a struggle. But with humans ... it's always such an ordeal. The truly unwilling can take hours to break, and then we need time to heal from the wounds we inflict on them during the persuasion."

What, give up to one of them and be possessed? By the same demons that killed Marek, took her life and family, destroyed Islingin ... she spat in his direction, unfortunately not hard enough, and the bloody saliva speckled the table. "If you had any idea who I am, you'd know I'll die before I let one of you in."

"But we do know who you are." As if on cue, he lifted his lips in a cold, emotionless smile. "Your presence was announced by your father, Talen Morel, whom we had thought dead. Although, you see, his spirit never showed up on the other side with all the rest. Maybe he's still here somewhere, and just woke up from his slumber. A woman of your strength, so close to the source where we felt his presence ... you can only be Lieh Morel. Now that we've found you, perhaps we will find him as well."

Her father, still alive? How could it be possible ... and how could these demons have felt his presence? Then she put it all together: the Orb, that useless, broken, 'inactive' chunk of wood with only one working spell, and Talen's unexplainable death in Islingin. Perhaps he'd hidden his spirit inside it. Senn must have activated it one way or another, and all the demons in the area had converged! She cursed herself for keeping the Orb where the boy could get to it. But it was too late for self-recrimination now.

Still, she didn't want any part in aiding these demons after all their kind had done to her family and clansmen. "Even if I could help you, why in all hells would I ever do that? You must think I'm a fool."

"Lieh Morel. You were never a fool, even in love you chose the right man. Please allow me to introduce myself. I am Xipil, and this is Tamesis. You've already met Shyama, or at least your ribs have ... she's out hunting for stragglers right now. We were all once alive, and were as powerful then as those you call Magi now. For a longer time than you could conceive, we have been dead and locked away in the spirit world.

"After all this time in darkness fighting to remain sane, a ray of light appeared, thanks to one that you and I both hold dear. When he first met our kind, he thought he had made a mistake and he fought back, rather pointlessly. After some years in the spirit world, he saw the truth and changed his mind. He and I worked together on how to *properly* come back to the world of the living.

"As a man who hadn't yet been ravaged by centuries spent on the other side, he wanted to make sure you were compliant and in safe hands. Marek sent us from beyond to find you and take care of you."

Lieh's eyes glazed for a moment. If there were ever a statement that was hard to believe, it might be 'Your dead husband sent demons from beyond death to protect you.' Before the events in Islingin she would have laughed at the very thought, but now she had seen and fought demon spirits that had come across. This demon Xipil could be telling the truth! She looked up, "Compliant?" What did they—

"Of course, it means to keep you and your immense magic from doing harm to our cause—Marek's cause. The best way to do that is to let one of us be in control for a while. It's also quite convenient, because so far the best vessel we've found for Tamesis is this weak, old Medi. It's much safer for all of us if she shares your body with you for a time. Then she can use your powerful magic to protect us all, instead of worrying that you might use it against us."

Tamesis looked at Lieh with those black eyes, framed in deep wrinkles and straggly white hair. "Marek prefers we not have to hurt. But if you leave no choice ..." She held up one bloody hand. "You see Tamesis not squeamish. What about Lieh?"

No choice? There are always choices. "Give me a minute."

Xipil stood. "Generous as we are, we shall give you five. Tamesis, keep an eye on her while I survey the surroundings." He walked off to the south at a brisk pace. Tamesis rose slowly from the ground, and lowered herself into the other chair—a bloody, smirking guardswoman.

Lieh tried to organize the thoughts flooding her mind. Had Senn gotten away, as she had admonished him to do if the situation turned bad? She glanced around the hut. There was a pile of packs here from the clansmen, but in the bedroom, Senn's was missing. She didn't see the wooden box on the shelf, either—that was a good sign. At least her boy might still be alive. If Senn had run, what were his chances? How far would he get before these demons caught up with him? Hopefully he'd get far enough to find help and protection.

What were her options? Escape was not likely, as she could barely move or focus a single magical thought. She could wait for help, which was almost certainly futile, and shortly be tortured. Then there was resistance and refusal, also sure to be countered with torture. Succeeding in the latter paths might end in death, and meeting Marek in the spirit world. Then there was acceptance—to give in, and let this otherworldly beast co-inhabit her body. Could she live with one whose ilk had slaughtered her people? If this demon Xipil were telling the truth about Marek, he wouldn't wish real harm to come to her. And honestly, it sounded like Marek. Maybe he had won over some of the spirits to his side and sought to regain control—on both sides of the curtain separating the worlds.

Her demon captor stalked back out of the darkness. Xipil stood leaning on the table, arms bent slightly. "And, Lieh Morel? What do you think of our proposal?"

Voice wavering, she asked, "Do I still retain my ... myself? If Tamesis were to leave me, would I return to being who I am now?" Lieh wasn't sure she'd believe the answer.

"Of course, you retain your mind, your senses, and your memories. All you lose is control."

"And what about magic, how does yours work with my own?"

"A reasonable question. We have only spirit magic, brought with us from the other side. Not very effective on most targets in your physical world, but every living being has a spirit of its own, and our magic can be used upon these. For example, binding our spirit to yours allows us to stay here indefinitely, without fading back to the other side." Xipil stroked his beard. "Spirit magic is also a bit similar to your earth magic, giving us a great advantage in augmenting healing spells and keeping our hosts healthy. So you see, we can use pain as a great tool for persuasion ... and heal our new body in no time." He set his jaw and fixed the unblinking pits of his eyes on hers.

Xipil's answers were not very satisfying, but seemed to be all she would get. "How do I know I can believe you about Marek?"

"You don't. You just have to trust us. But how else would we know all about you and your family?"

How else? There were so many ways. Torture, coercion, lies . . . to trust these demons would be folly. But she didn't have to trust them, she only had to play along for the time being. Lieh had to choose possession or death. The only sensible choice was to give in and enter this dark tunnel, paired with a demon. Maybe there would be a way out of it at the other end, and she could someday take vengeance for her butchered clan. Her voice trembled in fear, but Lieh finally agreed. "Yes. Then . . . I will submit."

Tamesis grinned like a madwoman, which she almost certainly was. Xipil even reapplied his artificial smile. "Excellent. Now I have a few last questions of my own. About your father, what was the source of his magical burst of spirit energy?"

Lieh avoided giving up the full truth. "I don't know. Like you, I thought he was dead. I found his body in his study in Islingin. Perhaps he was hiding in some magic trinket." Maybe Xipil was as bad at reading human expressions as he was at displaying them himself, and wouldn't see through her lie. There was always distraction, "You know, it might help your cause if you work on your facial expressions."

He briefly registered her barb, but ignored it. "And where might this magic trinket be now? In the hands of the other Magus whose art we observed? The one who killed the bear, and left absolutely no trace upon escaping this battleground?"

She had to keep Senn a secret. "Just a boy from the camp, who happens to have quite strong magic . . . his parents died in Islingin."

"So we are to believe. One of them, at least, is surely dead—Marek Seltin. And he told us that you were pregnant when he died. We shall assume your son has taken this talisman, wherein your father Talen Morel seems to be hiding. Your son's name?"

It seemed there was no concealing anything from Xipil. "Senn. His name is Senn Morel."

"Interesting, he shares your family name instead of Marek's? Our master never mentioned that your magic was stronger than his. Well, even those of us around for longer than recorded history learn something new each day. Despite Senn's power, we will find your son. I'm sure it will be a touching reunion. Now, enough questions. Please open your mind to Tamesis, and try to relax."

The wrinkled old woman leaned over the table and brought her eyes a hand's breadth from Lieh's. Relax ... was Xipil joking? She heard whispers, —*Let Tamesis in, quiet your fears, living one ... I will ease pain in few moments*— Lieh slowed her breathing and opened her mind. At least this was better than death, right? The old woman's black eyes started to clear, like storm clouds rolling past to show a blue sky behind them. After a moment they had changed completely to their natural blue color.

The eyes widened as the old woman realized she had control over herself again. She looked around at Lieh and Xipil, then at her bloody hands, raising them up and turning them over, looking from the palms to the backs. She leaned back her head and let out a bloodcurdling scream. It seemed as if she would never stop.

Xipil moved his head from side to side, maybe in annoyance. He reached over and pulled a knife from the woman's belt and quickly sliced the ropes that held Lieh, then offered her the knife, hilt-first. Was this her chance? Her ribs felt a bit better, maybe she should try it. Lieh reached for the knife and took it, holding it backhand. Wait, she hadn't meant to grip it that way—of course, it was Tamesis in control now. Lieh's eyes would have widened in horror, had she still been in charge of them. Instead, Tamesis twisted Lieh's mouth into that demonic grin, narrowed her eyes, and sank the blade deep into the old woman's throat. Her voice was cut off mid-shriek. As Tamesis pulled the knife free of her former host, blood sprayed out in warm, red spurts and the woman toppled over dead.

Lieh cried out, horrified that her own hands had just been used for murder, but it seemed only Tamesis could hear her scream. And her possessing demon just kept on smiling. Now she had to live with this monster ... maybe death would have been a better choice.

CHAPTER FOUR
Aftermath

After a hard walk in silence for the rest of the night, Jarel called for a break, although it was obvious to Senn that they could all use one. Dawn was just filtering through the trees, and he could see the others' weariness clearly. Wildon looked like a walking corpse, Lani was red from the exertion despite her tanned skin, and Jarel's roughly bandaged cut had started bleeding again. Only the four hounds seemed unfazed by their midnight trek. The party stopped near a fallen tree so they would have somewhere to lean their backs. They sat down heavily, the hounds laying by Jarel's feet.

Jarel said softly, "We're at least three or four leagues distant from the fight. If the kid's spell worked, we should be safe for a few hours. And if it didn't work, we'd know already. Lani, can ya give me some help with a healing spell here? I feel like I've got rocks in my head."

She chuckled. "You may have rocks in your head, but I still love ya. About the healing ... sorry honey, I'm really exhausted. Need at least a few hours of sleep before I can do anything more than spark a fire. Maybe this will help ..." She planted a big kiss on the side of his cheek.

He smiled weakly. "I wish. Senn, what about you, kid? Got anything left?"

After losing track of his mother, and keeping a concealing spell going for half the night? That reminded him: he could save himself the energy drain of that spell now that they had stopped to rest. The Orb signaled, —*Deactivated*— At least that burden was now lifted, but he still worried about Lieh.

Back to the problem at hand. "I might have enough energy for something simple. But only if you promise to stop calling me 'kid'. I'll be fifteen next week, and I've got more magic than the rest of our clan put together."

The warrior let out a hearty laugh that quickly turned to a cough. "Sorry lad, inhaled a bit too much smoked bear fur for my own good. Alright, I promise, you're 'little man' at least for the rest of the day." Then his smile faded and he looked down at his feet. "Ya know, the four of us, we probably are the entire clan now." They all looked at one another, the truth of the statement not sitting well with any of them. "Let's get this cut of mine taken care of, then rest up for a few hours. We can decide what to do after a bit of shut-eye." Lani put her head on his shoulder in unspoken agreement, and Wildon nodded slowly.

Senn lifted his head weakly. "Umm ... just one question. I haven't learned any earth magic or healing spells. How do I heal a cut?"

Wildon made no move to get up. "You don't fix the cut, exactly. You make a channel to it, and a matrix for the damaged area. Draw up and feed in the earth energy, while imagining how the damaged flesh will repair itself. The energy accelerates the body's own healing process. It is relative to the amount of energy you use. The earth magic takes direction from the thoughts you pour in with it, so make sure you visualize the cut closing and healing properly, with no infection." He waved his hand weakly toward Jarel. "Good luck. Lani can help you over there. If it doesn't work you're probably too tired, and we can try again later."

—*Go for it, Senn*— Talen sounded confident. —*I might have a healing trick or two up my sleeve, but you should be able to handle this without me*—

Senn dragged himself over to Jarel and sat down on the opposite side from Lani. She cradled the big man tenderly in her arms. It would be nice to have someone like her, with each partner providing mutual support in times of hardship. Lani, with her long, dark blond hair ... well, she was only a few years older than Senn, and the curvy shape of her body was fantastic. He stopped himself. Lani and Jarel were together; he shouldn't even be thinking about her that way.

The big man turned his head, and Lani peeled off the makeshift bandage. Underneath was a cut as long as Senn's forefinger, a mess of half-dried blood and matted hair. First Lani rinsed out the area with some water from a skin. She leaned over and touched Senn's hand, making him more than a little uncomfortable. "Alright, it's washed clean. Now just give it a try."

Senn pushed the mix of emotions out of his mind and focused on the spell. He did exactly as Wildon had explained—building a matrix, imagining the edges of the cut closing together and new flesh forming—as he drew on the earth energy. The feeling was different from the other types of energy, not like a tool, but as if life itself were flowing through him. So this was why some people put all their efforts into earth magic. Finally he channeled the energy, releasing it into the matrix around Jarel's cut. Within seconds, the bleeding stopped and the edges of the gash began to knit back together.

Jarel sighed, "Aaahh . . . that's good . . . I feel like a dozen."

"You mean, feel like a million?"

"Nah, I can't count that high. But definitely nice work, little man. I think you've got at least as much magic as your mother, and so far you've been damn good at using it."

A weary smile spread across Senn's face. "Thanks. I hope you'll be ready to go after a few hours' sleep. I think we'll be hungry, and someone will need to do the hunting." Senn scratched one of the hounds behind the ears, and it licked its chops in response. He lay down, activated the spirit alert spell, and fell asleep within seconds.

Midmorning sun greeted Senn, as he awoke to the aroma of bread and dried meat that Jarel was holding under his nose. He looked at the jerky with bleary eyes; what a strange way to be woken up. "I thought that might get ya moving, little man. But don't look horse jerky in the mouth, just eat it. My head feels great, by the way." Now that Senn smelled some food his stomach was rumbling, so he took a few strips of meat. The others were eating as well, and they leaned in to listen as Jarel continued.

"Here's the way I figure it, and I'm sorry it's not pretty. Our clan has probably been wiped out. It's too dangerous to go back there looking for anyone. We have to find another clan, see if we can join up with 'em. Shouldn't be too hard to persuade 'em with magic like Senn's on the table."

Senn shook his head forcefully. "No. We have to figure out why this is happening. Maybe we can stop it."

Wildon regarded him with a sly look in his eyes. "What makes you think we can do that? Something to do with your new toy?"

He didn't want to give away too much about the Orb yet. But he had to say something. "Yeah ... it ... contains some powerful spells that my mother told me about. There's a spirit warning spell, so we won't need to keep a watch at night. On top of it, I have her box of magic books and some items from Islingin." Senn took the box out of his pack and looked inside. Nothing there that he couldn't show Wildon: three small books written in some unknown language, a couple of ivory-and-bloodwood rings inset with different patterns, a silver knife with a bone handle, and a pair of identical wooden bracelets. He offered the box to Wildon, who looked through the items, touching each of them and frowning.

"These are magic items, but protected by a seal. One has to know how to unlock each one before it can be used—worthless until we find the key." He picked up the books and looked at the covers. "Ah, the ancient tongue!"

Senn looked up, "So, you can read them?"

"No. That is a study in which, sadly, I did not excel. Besides, those studies were at least thirty years before the fall of Islingin. But maybe I know someone who could help on both counts. We are even headed in the right direction, east toward Janklo. A few years back I went on some travels to gather news from other clans. I managed to find Aidan Alkar, and we spent many nights recounting our exploits."

Jarel nodded. "That's your Magus friend, the one you always told us about?"

Wildon continued, "Exactly. Aidan is fortunate enough to retain his magic, unlike myself with this cursed, fading power. Anyhow, I have heard since then that his clan has been able to imprison and send back a few demons, a skill we might find useful."

—*Senn*— Talen spoke in his mind. —*The imprisonment spell is something I cannot explain, as there were no demons on this side when I was alive. Aidan could fill in a lot of knowledge gaps. As for the magic items, those are my seals. Let's worry about that when we find a need for them. I have no idea what books your mother may have taken in her flight from Islingin, so we'll have to find someone skilled who can read them. I can't do that from in here—*

Senn took a deep breath and blew it out slowly. "Let's go find this Aidan. We owe it to the others in the clan who didn't make it. What do you think?" Lani and Jarel nodded in agreement, and they all started to pack up.

Senn took advantage of the break in discussion. Guilt had been gnawing at him more and more ever since they had fled in the darkness. —*Talen, I feel responsible. If I hadn't broken the seal on your Orb . . . none of this would have happened. Then we ran, abandoning everyone in the clan, even my mother—*

—*Well, son, I can understand your misgivings . . . but we both know, if there is any blame to lay around, it falls on me. You followed my instructions, to open my warding locks in the Orb. Also, remember what your big friend said: you have to know when it's not your fight. We had no chance of defeating the remaining demons, not alone, especially not with at least one of them using strong magic to the north of us—*

—*But I hate to think the clan was lost for nothing—*

—*As long as you remember your clansmen, they aren't lost. If their deaths drive you to bring an end to this demon scourge, you do honor to the sacrifice they have made. Keep them in your heart, Senn—* He sniffled and blinked back his tears, and resolved to do just that.

Noon had come to the forest, and it was as bright a day as there could be beneath such tall trees. Both Xipil and Tamesis ignored Lieh completely, and with Tamesis in control of her body, there was nothing she could do about it. In the meantime, she learned how Marek's minions had found her by listening to their conversations. They had gleaned information about Lieh's whereabouts from solo demons they had met in their travels. Then they had homed in on her based on these rumors. Her father's energy burst had pointed the way for the final few leagues.

The trio of demons had now set up a temporary base in the camp, trying to figure out which way Senn was heading. Shyama was out on constant patrols looking for traces, focusing to the east where there had been no attackers. Xipil had just returned from checking around the camp to see what, and who, was left.

"Tamesis, this is a mess. I have no idea how these people lived here so long without encountering any of these spirits before.

"The wolf told me he is here with friends: the roasted bear and the broken moose. They fought this same clan almost two years ago, and have searched for them ever since. How the fools could have taken so long to find them, I don't know. Maybe they spent too much time looking for those monstrous animals they inhabited. I suppose they didn't want to be killed a second time, but you can see all the good their monster forms did them. Regardless, maybe they can be of use to us. The wolf saw a small party escaping to the east, but was too busy here to give chase."

An awkward feeling came to Lieh, as Tamesis talked with her mouth in that strange, halting accent. "Yesss. Must be east. Shyama and wolf together could find boy . . . will wolf help us?"

"Mmm. I have been thinking about that. He would like to remain with his companions. Seems they have been here a long time, and knew each other even before coming to this side, which explains their cooperation. The moose is still alive, but beyond healing. The spirit from the bear has reassociated, and now he's looking for a live body. There are a few survivors of the clan laying around, barely alive. We could persuade a couple of them to host the two spirits. As payment, this trio would lend us their talents, however meager they might be."

"Ah-hah. Xipil always good at persuading by words. Just tell Tamesis, if need. I persuade by knife," she said, twisting Lieh's mouth into a wicked smile. She hoped it wouldn't come to blades; the last incident with Tamesis' knife, wielded in Lieh's own hand, was still replaying itself in her mind. The demon spoke again, "Who is left, what form can spirits have?"

Xipil assumed an unnatural frown, as if he were practicing human expressions. "There is no one a worthwhile spirit would want, but there are a young Minor Adept and a battered warrior who seems pretty good with a sword. Right now the warrior is half-crushed under the moose, so he shouldn't take much convincing." Lieh wasn't sure whether to feel joy or pity to find that some of her clan seemed still to be alive. "Probably the moose could persuade the warrior without help if it could move, but it can't get its head around to face the man, since its legs are all hacked or broken.

"The Adept is a young girl, badly burned from one of my fireballs. She said her name is Namee. If you can calm her a bit, she should be more open to the reassociated spirit from that bear. Perhaps Lieh Morel will help you, knowing that another of her clan might be spared a pointless death?" He raised his eyebrows on cue, testing out his new powers and looking pointedly at Lieh. The effect was as if he had glued on false eyebrows after his own had been burnt off.

"Of courssse. Will discuss with gracious host!"

"Excellent. You deal with the girl. I'll speak to the other two—the wolf is hanging around that bloody moose trying to figure out what they do next." Xipil turned and stalked off into the woods.

Tamesis talked directly inside their shared head. —*Sso Lieh. Would you help me persuade girl to live? Without magic, spirit magic, her burns kill so quickly*—

—*Listen, you ungrateful demon bitch. You haven't so much as acknowledged my presence in here all day, now you want me to help you?*—

—*Choice for Lieh, again. Prefer if Tamesis persuade by knife?*—

That was again no real choice, the worst outcome for both her and Namee. —*Alright. I'll do it*—

—*Goood! Then we visit girl. I talk to bear's spirit, then you get control for a minute, but only to talk. Tell her all fine. You know my other option, yess?*— Tamesis didn't wait for her answer, just started off to the north, which was fine with Lieh.

It was a short walk to the tree where Namee had been hiding while she lit up the northern battlefield. Tamesis surveyed the area, smirking at the bodies she and Xipil had left as they came down the northern path. The young woman was laying on her side next to a huge, blackened oak. Half of her body was covered with burns, and she was shivering in pain. The energy ball had hit the base of the tree trunk, and the enveloping blast had caught her as it fanned out behind the tree. She wouldn't last long in that condition.

There was a shimmer in the air where the reassociated spirit floated, and it spoke silently with Lieh's possessor. Sharing her body with Tamesis, Lieh was able to listen in.

—This scorched human won't let me in! Doesn't she realize she's dying?—

—Just wait. I am Tamesis, help you. This form, she is familiar to girl. Later you help us, pay back debt for giving you better form—

—Yes, yes, just hurry. My strength is already fading. Soon I'll have to find whatever form I can. Two years ago, I spent too long as a forest mouse after losing my Adept form, and I don't relish being a mouse again— This spirit must have been the demon woman from that prior attack. Lieh was at least glad it hadn't been an easy recovery.

Tamesis spoke to Lieh this time. *—Your turn. I give control for talking, only that—* A hole opened in the shell around Lieh, but just a small one, as promised.

"Namee. It's me, Lieh."

The girl opened her eyes, at least to the extent she could, and stared at Lieh. "I-i-is it you? A-are we dead?"

"No. At least, not yet." What could she say? "If you let this spirit in, at least you'll have a chance to survive. Otherwise it's death, and straight to the other side." She tried to reach out, to give Namee a reassuring touch on the cheek, but Tamesis wasn't moving.

"And . . . L-Lieh . . . what about y-you?" Her eyes were wide with fear.

Her voice was full of unexpected emotion. "I'm . . . hosting a spirit now. Still myself in here, but . . . just watching most of the time." *—Damn it, Tamesis, let me touch her—* A hand moved out and rested on Namee's less-burned arm. "But who knows, at least there is still hope this way, however small. You just have to open your mind and let the spirit in. Between its magic and yours, you'll heal quickly."

Namee sighed in resignation. She shuddered again with pain, and seemed to relax. It looked as if she weren't ready to give up on life just yet. Her eyes slowly clouded and became inky black, then her half-blackened lips slowly raised at the corners. "Tamesis, was it? Some earth magic wouldn't hurt, to speed this up a little."

Tamesis touched several of the worst-burned areas and applied a liberal dose of earth magic to speed up the healing. Lieh realized the hole in her prison was still open, and quickly took the time to explore its boundaries. It was a shell of spirit magic, locking her away from the controls of her own body, so to speak. The spirit magic felt much like earth magic, maybe that was a clue. There were jagged edges—maybe with enough mental force she could tear through and destroy the whole shell. Or she could push her consciousness through the hole, and somehow attack Tamesis from beyond the shell . . . but then it was too late. Her captor had closed up the hole. "Healing faster now, yess? Soon we start search. You help find this one's offspring. Boy has powerful magic, as you know already! Tamesis impressed, how boy burned your last form alive."

Lieh hoped fervently they wouldn't find Senn. She doubted he was a match for two Adepts and a Magus, all three battle-hardened.

Namee sat up painfully and turned her head, as soft footsteps padded up behind the two of them. The demon wolf bared its teeth in greeting. Xipil was there as well, and . . . damn it. It was just as she had feared. The warrior trapped under the moose had been Rikk, and there he stood grinning at her, limping a bit as his legs healed up. Xipil must have used the full power of his earth magic for Rikk to be walking already. The revived demon was fidgeting with his sword, testing its weight.

"Huh. It's a nice sword. I can see why it did such a number on my moose legs. An' come to think of it, this same sword ended my stint as a wolf some time back. It's only fair I git to try it now, huh?" He laughed and shook his head. "Well Mister Xipil, we'll honor our end o' the bargain. As long as yer huntin' them that killed me and her twice, at least. Call me Kert, that there's Darcy, an' the wolf—well, he was so long on th' other side he done forgot his name. He's so fond o' that wolf, he ain't never tried another form. We taken to callin' 'im Dolf, and it's not like he kin' complain."

The wolf growled deep in its throat, obviously not pleased with his new alias. Kert looked himself over and stretched his arms out. "Well, whoever this bastard was, I hope he kept these here muscles in good 'nough shape to make up fer havin' such a poor trace o' magic. I tell ya, if I'da known I'd end up in 'im, I wouldn'ta taken that chunk out of 'is leg as a wolf way back when."

Namee and Rikk were both under the power of the demon spirits inside them, just like Lieh, with no control over their actions. The irony of fate. It had stared them all down today: Lieh, Namee, and especially Rikk. As they fought their demon enemies all three of them had blinked, and ended up possessed instead of dead.

CHAPTER FIVE

Demon in Snake's Clothing

Xiuhcoatl relaxed on the warm stones in the foothills of the mountains. The long, gray-brown snake suited him perfectly and allowed him to enjoy all this world had to offer. In the spirit world there was no time for rest, no sun, and not a single warm stone. Yes, he could use his meager spirit magic to keep his snake body warm, but that magic didn't have much use over here—and snakes didn't have any magic of their own for him to draw on. Why exert himself by using spirit magic when the warm spring sun could have the same effect? Over the last few years, he'd certainly gotten used to this place. Hopefully Marek would keep him on permanently once the new council was active.

Resting in the sun on a warm rock, wearing a snakeskin body . . . this was the life. Xiuhcoatl recalled the events that had brought him here: like his comrade Xipil, the spirit had been persuaded by the young Marek Seltin to join his cause. Promises of power on the new council were all well and good, but being out in the sun was even better. Fortunately his task afforded plenty of time for relaxing outdoors.

Thinking back to his first moons in the physical world, he remembered fondly the discovery of his preferred form. Upon emerging he had taken up residence in a small fox. A cunning animal, but not too useful for the task of collecting Magi from around Kartus. To get around a bit faster, he first switched over to a hawk. That was exciting: as a fox, he lured in the bird of prey to what it thought was just another meal. Then he persuaded the hawk to let him inhabit it, which fortunately wasn't that difficult. At last he ate the fox, getting a final and tasty bit of use from it.

The hawk had taken him as far as the former region of Leikton in the south, where it was rumored there were several powerful Magi living in the area's wandering clans. During that time he also began to observe other spirit activity on the ground. Before Marek's leadership, a random assortment of spirits had come across the rift. Now that Marek controlled it from both sides, things were different. But back then in the beginning, most of the spirits which had come across were just angry, violent, hateful creatures. That mindset showed up clearly in their foolish actions in the physical world.

Xiuhcoatl saw these spirits in their animal forms, spending weeks stalking the woods and plains without finding anything but other animals. They became attached to their forms, only leaving a borrowed body when it died or upon finding a more suitable specimen of the same type. Worst of all, he had yet to find another spirit which had bothered to take to the air. Large beasts of the type spirits usually sought to inhabit tended to have no interest in birds—and vice versa. Since no accidental discovery of flight presented itself, they spent most of their time wandering aimlessly until they blundered into a clan by accident. Xiuhcoatl was different: working within a framework of logic and reason gave him a huge advantage.

After some weeks of scouting from the air he found a likely Magus, living in a clan on the plains to the west of Leikton, as his first target. This spellcaster was clearly in charge, and whenever magic was needed, he used it with abandon: whether hunting big game to restock their provisions or levitating himself to get a good overview of the route they traveled.

The clan was completely nomadic, moving every few weeks. As a bird, it was easy enough to observe them without drawing a second glance. Xiuhcoatl also studied the local wildlife to see what would be the most effective way to reach the Magus without being killed. After all, he had no desire to spend hours or days reassociating. That would only end with a rushed search to find a new form before his spirit leached back through to the other side. Eventually, he observed a type of dark colored snake with an inky black mouth, which had particularly strong venom. One bite would immobilize its victim in short order—quite a useful ability. He found a large specimen and approached it one day after it fed, easily persuading its tiny mind to let him in.

With such a strong persuasive element on his side, it was not hard to entrap the Magus that was his target. Xiuhcoatl simply slipped into his tent at night and bit long and hard, injecting a massive amount of venom. The man knew the snake, repeating "Black mamba!" over and over, but even his strong earth magic wasn't sufficiently fast or powerful to keep the venom's effects at bay. After fifteen minutes of struggling, the Magus finally realized it was hopeless, and gave in to possession. Once Xiuhcoatl took over, the powerful mix of spirit and human magics was more than enough to drive back the venom, and the body recovered. The very surprised snake was taken along in a thick bag, since Xiuhcoatl wished to inhabit it again when he handed over this Magus at Islingin. Of course, the Magus had a lot of questions and pleas, which he kept trying to communicate in their shared body. However, when one has spent hundreds of years blocking out the cacophony of the other side to retain one's individuality, ignoring a single voice is easy.

Next came the matter of getting from the south of the continent back to the north. Boats were hard to come by because there was no infrastructure left, and there was no one who could help sail one up the coast. Of course Xiuhcoatl couldn't go back the way he'd come, as a bird. In the end he took a fine horse from the clan and departed in his new Magus form. The old road from Leikton through Silville to Islingin was still there, and although not in good repair, the journey only took about six weeks. Along the deserted road he found plenty of places to feed both horse and snake.

Finally Xiuhcoatl arrived at Islingin, its city wall rising up right beside the riverbank. After entering through a deserted gate, he navigated the empty streets to Islingin Keep at the center, mamba bag in hand. The huge towers and battlements rose above him, not exactly a welcome sight to one who preferred the sun on his shoulders to a roof over his head. He walked down winding corridors deep into the Keep until he reached the entrance to the Spirit Chamber.

When Marek and his disciples had first created the passage to the spirit world in the chamber, there was prey aplenty for the spirits who came across. There were not only the humans themselves (foolish Magi anxious to taste the power promised by the spirits), but also animals living on their refuse in the Keep. After its residents' flight, however, the Keep had become a deserted maze of solid stone. Spirits could not travel fast or far in their non-corporeal forms, and recently most newcomers had leached back to the other side before they could find a host.

Now, with Marek in charge on the other side, everything had changed. One of his followers named Umkoome, who was fortunate (and clever) enough to have found a Major Adept's body to inhabit in the forests near Islingin, stood by the Spirit Chamber. The door she guarded was made of solid oak, the same as the new wooden interior of the room.

Xiuhcoatl entered the gateway chamber with his snake, and Umkoome closed the door behind him. The warding spell was now active: no out-of-body spirit could disturb him now. Only Marek's chosen spirits would be allowed through the rift. He walked to the pedestal marking the opening, and held his hand to it carefully. From the other side he felt the presence of Clayne, Marek's gatekeeper in the spirit world. —*Brother, I have found a candidate of just the type our master is seeking, and he is strong. Send over Marek's first Council member to take his new host!*—

There was a moment's pause. —*Of course. Prepare yourself, and have your next host ready. Tynan Maltus will come across shortly*—

Xiuhcoatl carefully opened the bag with the mamba, and loosed it on the floor. As it reared up to strike, he soothed it, spoke to it with his spirit magic as well as his voice. "If you let me in, your suffering will end. Out in the wild, you and I will travel together. Otherwise, it's back into the bag for you."

He felt another pressing on his consciousness. —*Xiuhcoatl. I am Tynan, here to claim what Marek promised*— As Xiuhcoatl started his transfer into the snake, Tynan gracefully took his place inside the Magus. For a second he could hear the helpless man's wailing in the background, but it faded as he slipped fully back into the beautiful, sleek, and deadly black mamba.

The thrill of that first capture was long behind him, but the excitement came anew with each additional Magus he found for the growing

Council led by Tynan. Sometimes Xiuhcoatl switched bodies for his journey and found a new mamba in the plains of the south. Other times he coerced a fellow spirit to carry him to his destination, with the promise of bloodshed at the other end (which was of course delivered). He had brought Magi from every corner of Kartus, and now had fond memories of each hunt. The western coast, the southern plains, the eastern deltas, the mountains and forests—they all called to him.

Now he was on his way back to Silville, having heard rumors of a strong Magus there. The trip had become a little complicated. Xiuhcoatl had hitched a ride with a spirit in wolf form thus far. But the imbecile was too lost in the form, listening to the wolf's desires, and had run off into the high mountains one night. It seemed that now Xiuhcoatl was on his own in mamba form to weave his way through the rocky mountain foothills leading to Silville. It would take time, but that was one thing he had in plenty. His master Marek might not be happy about it, but the master wasn't here—and the warm sun was.

CHAPTER SIX

The Chase

Senn couldn't believe it was finally happening. He was laying in his bedroll after a long day's hike, a bit apart from the others so he could study the Orb's spells in peace with Talen. That was when Lani approached him.

"You look cold out here all alone, so far from the fire! Can I join you and warm you up?" She crouched down and slid her hand under the blanket onto his leg, sending a tingling all the way up his body from his crotch to his tongue.

At first he was flustered, but he'd been feeling that way around her all the time lately. "Uhmm . . . I guess you can . . . I mean of course!"

The next moment, she was lying beside him naked. He rolled over toward her. Lani reached down and grabbed his member, but for some reason her hand was icy cold. Just a second ago it had been so warm on his thigh? There was a crunching noise and . . .

He woke up as a shirt dropped from above and covered up his nethers. Jarel was standing in the leaves next to him, eyes averted. "Shit, the early bird always sees the worm. Better keep that thing under wraps, kid. You're lucky it was me walking back from a piss and not the girl."

Had Senn ever been so embarrassed? Probably not. The blood rushed to his cheeks as he quickly pulled the bedroll back over himself. "Oh sh . . . I'm sorry. My blanket must have slipped off, and . . . well . . ." Come on, think up a story. Who was another girl in the clan besides Lani? Ah, the young Adept who had been lighting up the sky just north of him during the last attack. "Namee . . . I was thinking about her lately, er, sometimes. I wonder if she might have made it out alive somehow."

Jarel smiled. "I can see you're hoping so. Well, maybe she did, and if not you can always look 'er up in the afterlife." He paused. "You know kid, it's tough not having a dad when these desires come up for the first time. And now your mom's probly gone too. Need any advice, you just lemme know, alright?" Senn nodded mutely, and Jarel walked back toward the others.

Shortly Senn joined them by the fire for a breakfast of leftover roasted deer and some roots. Jarel and the hounds had made out well on their hunt the day before, and they had risked a fire to roast some of the meat and dry the rest. Now they had filled up their packs with strips of tasty venison. That was good, because they had been running low on supplies. The last few days they had moved at a grueling pace to stay ahead of any pursuers that might be following. They had turned north yesterday, and Wildon thought that today would be their last push to the river Fayn. He was convinced there were pursuers; no concealing magic could hide them from seven demons. At the river, Senn and the others would cut logs and make a raft that would carry them swiftly toward Janklo.

"Good morning." He nodded at Wildon, and the blush returned to his cheeks as he looked at Jarel and Lani, sitting side by side. The big warrior winked at him reassuringly. Huh, he wouldn't be doing that if he knew Senn had really been dreaming about his partner.

Wildon beckoned him over. "Come on, my boy. While you eat let's discuss something: you need to learn how to hunt. We can't give all that responsibility to Jarel while you scour the forest for nuts and mushrooms." Senn sighed, looking down at the deer meat, and wondered if he'd be the one replenishing their supply the next time. "And hurry up, will you?" Wildon appeared anxious to move out. "I'll explain the theory of hunting with magic while we walk. Those demons may be hot on our tail!"

As the party walked through the forest, Senn kept his eyes open for game as Wildon had instructed. He ran through the hunting spells again, keeping them fresh in his mind. One option was to make a noose of solid magic tightened around the neck of one's proposed dinner, but that noose could be hard to control once the animal started jerking around. Best save that for another time once he had more experience. A channel of solid magic sharpened to a knife edge could work, but unlike a tree, the animal wasn't likely to hold still. If he weren't fast or accurate enough to sever its head, he'd end up with the wounded quarry escaping into the woods, or a big bloody mess of chopped meat.

The more likely scenarios involved projectiles. He could launch a real projectile like a spear or rock, and use a magic channel to guide it. Then there was the option of a magic projectile. For that, solid magic alone worked the best, and in a small enough quantity just to knock out or kill the prey. Too much solid magic would mash the quarry to a pulp, making it hard to pick out the meat from the bones and entrails. Heat magic would cook the poor creature a little earlier than planned (organs, hair, and all). Earth magic was too slow—what would he do, persuade a bush to grow around the animal and trap it? Finally there was cold magic: actually a viable option, but it would leave him with a solid lump of an animal that would have to be carefully unfrozen (with yet more magic) before it could be cleaned and cooked.

Senn walked to the front where Jarel was setting the pace with his hounds, leaving Lani and Wildon to bring up the rear. "Jarel . . . I've been meaning to ask you . . ."

The big man glanced back, and let Senn catch up with him. "Sure, what's eating ya?"

"Do you feel guilty that we left the others behind?"

"Nope. We had no choice," he answered without hesitation. "It seemed to me, that fight was about as easy for those demons as boiling fish in a barrel. We were lucky to get away at all, the same as in Islingin. Guess I've been real lucky twice now."

Senn perked up. "Maybe you can tell me what life was like in Islingin, and what happened at the end? My mother never really said much."

"Yeah, I can tell you about Islingin. My pop was a soldier. He didn't have much magic either, but was big the way I am now and good with a sword. We lived on the west side of town, by the river, there was a barracks there. I used to play on the docks with a bunch of other kids. There were lots of 'em who lived on boats. I learned a good bit about sailing and fishing, those kinda skills. But when I was about nine, that's when the demons came. I guess some of 'em possessed some Magi from the Conclave, then they started going wild, killing whomever they could. More spirits were coming, ended up possessing people's dogs and tearing around like mad, biting everything in sight.

"Some of the guards from the Keep came back with freaky black eyes and started fighting. One of 'em killed my pop. Rikk was there, good young soldier, he spitted that one with his sword right in front of me. Then he grabbed me, and Lani who was about three or four, the daughter of a friend of his. Rikk threw a pack together, just a couple blankets, food, and some weapons, and we got the hell out of there. We met up with your mom on the road out: she was getting a group together to go south of the mountains and away from Islingin. Now Rikk isn't the biggest of men, but he's got a lot of muscles and he knows the tools of the trade. Seeing all those weapons sticking out of his pack, Lieh said 'hell yeah' ... or something like that." Jarel grinned, though Senn seriously doubted those exact words had ever come out of his mother's mouth. "In fact, this axe is one of Rikk's, he gave it to me when I was old enough to swing it. It's served me well 'nough ever since."

Interesting that now Jarel was the rescuer. "But," Senn frowned, "what about your mother?"

Jarel snorted, and spit on the ground. "She was a whore when my pop met 'er. Nine moons later she left me at the barracks for him to take care of, I guess she had more important tricks in mind than raising a kid. But my pop was a good man. He always joked that he got a lot more out of 'er than he expected for five coppers. Some of the lads like Rikk helped raise me when Pop was on duty ... 'til I was old enough to look after myself on the docks." He sighed and nodded his head up and down. "Those were the days, huh? Well, maybe we'll get 'em back someday."

"Yeah, I hope so. Uhm ... one other question ..."

Jarel looked down at him. "What's that? Oh, your face is getting all red, I guess ya wanna ask about this morning?" Senn nodded. "Look, it happens to everyone, 'specially at your age. No harm in dreaming about

Namee. You have no idea how long I spent thinking about Lani, 'til a couple years ago when she got old enough we could be together."

Senn looked down at his feet. He felt even worse knowing that his fantasy was Jarel's lover. "Oh. Well, thanks, I 'spose. Just don't tell anyone, please."

"Course not. Hey, piece of advice for ya, if we ever meet up with Namee or some other girl ya fancy. I think an older kid told me once when I was younger."

"What's that?" Senn raised his eyebrows skeptically.

"Well, when you're getting close up with a girl, ya know . . . how does it go . . . her hand on your bird is worth two in her bush."

The party hiked hard all morning, stopping briefly for a lunch of venison strips and some mushrooms Lani had picked. Senn was walking at the front again with Jarel, finally getting used to the double strain of maintaining the concealment spell and walking at a fast pace. It was getting on toward dusk when he spotted the forest hare up ahead on the left. He whispered and pointed it out, "It's almost time to break for the night. Are you getting hungry?"

Jarel stopped short, keeping his voice low. "Good eyes, little man." He waved the dogs behind him, to avoid catching their prey's attention. "First, catch your hare. Then I'll stew it up nice. Let's see whatcha got, can ya do that magic Wildon told ya 'bout this morning?"

"Sure. Just give me a minute." What would be the best option? It would be good not to botch his first attempt, so Senn chose a simple projectile of solid magic. He built a matrix about the size of his fist, a channel to guide the ball, and a ram to launch it. Finally he drew up the required magic energy and fired the projectile on its way with gusto. The ball of solid energy hit the rabbit squarely in the head and knocked it sideways into the nearest tree with a crunch. "Yeah! Hare's on the menu tonight."

Talen chimed in with a word of encouragement. —Nicely done, Senn! I wasn't gearing up for time in the wild when creating this Orb, or I might have included something like that in my repertoire—

Wildon and Lani finally caught up with them, the old Sabi struggling a little with the pace today. "Looks like your first day of hunting was a success. There's nothing like seeing my best pupil advancing so fast! Though, boy, you might try a little less velocity next time. And you don't need such a big lump of magic for something that small."

Jarel walked over to the lifeless prey and pulled it loose, leaving half its head embedded in the tree trunk. The half still attached to the body was mashed flat, oozing blood and looking rather unsavory. "The part we wanna eat is still intact, but it's a messy kill. We'll lash it on *your* pack until we find a good place to stop." He winked as he tied the dripping hare to Senn's rucksack.

Wildon raised his hand to his ear. Senn had the impression he was using a spell of some kind. "Won't be long. I can hear the river, probably half a league from here. We'll be there before dark."

True to his word, they arrived at the river shortly afterward. It was about twenty strides across, looked too deep to ford, and was flowing far too fast to safely swim across. Wildon took charge, anxious to be on the water. "Jarel and Lani, can you cook up that hare? I'm starving. No fires though, I don't want to leave any trace at the site where we go into the river—just use magic. Senn, get started on our raft. Use only deadwood, and scatter the trimmed branches in the river. Find some ivy or other vines, and weave them in between the trunks. I'll give you a hand with finding the materials, but your magic will have to do the heavy lifting."

That reminded him of the Orb in his pocket. —*Talen! Any ideas on making a raft?*—

—*Nothing comes to mind. I've got a few more spells to show you when we find a quiet moment and some privacy, but none of them tie knots. Sorry, Senn*—

The raft took a lot longer to construct than expected. Trimming and moving the deadwood they found scattered about wasn't so difficult, at least not with his magic, but there was no spell to tie the thin, woody vines they scavenged. Manipulating them magically would require complex and continuously moving matrices, so the tedious work had to be done by hand instead. Eventually Senn and Wildon paused for a hurried meal of stewed hare and foraged plants, before the cooks joined them to finish weaving vines through the heavy logs. It was midnight before the raft was done.

Senn used a heavy lifting spell to move the raft to the very edge of the riverbank. He had wanted to wait until morning, but Wildon was insistent. "If we're going to sleep here on land tonight, instead of on the raft, we must be ready to go at a moment's notice. We were lucky to have two years demon-free, but this latest group still worries me. They can't be far back. Speaking of which, why don't you fire up that concealing trinket of yours, and do a good cleaning job on this whole area. If they realize we went into the river here, they'll do the same and be right behind us." Senn sighed and wiped his forehead with the back of his hand. Today it seemed there was always one more task, and he did it without much enthusiasm. Did he even have enough magic energy left to do it right? Time would tell.

After climbing into his bedroll, he fed energy into the spirit alarm, as he had every night so far. Talen's voice echoed from the Orb, —*Goodnight, son. Sweet dreams*— Senn's cheeks blushed again: with Talen's sphere of awareness, he probably knew about this morning's embarrassing moment. Great. At least that wouldn't be a problem tonight, now that Wildon's paranoia had Senn all anxious about another attack.

Lieh was becoming more worried about Senn each day. The search Xipil had organized was magical, methodical, and wide. He and Tamesis were casting about with magic for any traces, and had so far found a few areas where mushrooms or roots had been foraged. They were still moving east, but at least there was no clear trail, meaning Senn had done a good job with the concealing spell. Meanwhile, Shyama and Dolf ranged wide to the north and south. Kert and Darcy were somewhere nearby, hunting and foraging to keep up the group's energy. Apparently demons still had to eat to maintain their possessed bodies. Their relegation to victual duty suggested those two lacked any useful tracking skills. The fact they had been unable to find Lieh's clan for two years proved it.

Riding along with Tamesis' spirit in her mind and controlling her body gave Lieh plenty of time to think. Mainly she'd been wondering about Marek. He'd sent these three demons after her, knowing they would find his child as well. After seeing what Xipil and Tamesis did with their power at Marek's command, she wondered if her husband might be abusing the notion just a touch. Together they'd always wanted to find the roots of magic, understand it fully, and use it to the maximum. But they had always meant to do good with it, hadn't they? Now she wasn't sure. Maybe he'd just become a power-hungry maniac. She was traveling with six examples of what the other side did to people. Kert, Darcy, Xipil, and especially Tamesis were not exactly shining examples of normalcy. To the contrary, they were clearly all of them lunatics. What if Marek had become one too?

At that point Shyama came racing up from ahead, her lithe lynx body flowing between the trees like a flash of magic. She spoke to Tamesis and Xipil in her straightforward fashion. —*Found something. To the north of here. They must have turned! There was a hunt, a kill, it was a deer. Tasty bits of the carcass left. It was recent, and they were in a hurry. But they made a fire I could smell hundreds of strides away. Perhaps to cook and dry the meat. Call the wolf, now we go north!—*

Xipil replied, "Excellent work, Shyama! My guess is they are heading for the river. Perhaps they intend to cross it and throw us off their trail, or follow its banks east or west. Seems they aren't hiding as well as they might like to think." He turned away and whistled loudly, calling to Kert, Darcy, and Dolf.

The group convened shortly. "My fellow spirits, Shyama has found some traces of our quarry to the north. We turn toward the Fayn river. When we get there, scour the banks for traces of them! We can't be far behind now. You three," Xipil said, pointing toward the newcomers, "make sure you don't kill the boy who has the strong magic. He's invaluable to our leader Marek. You definitely want to stay on Marek's good side, lest he make your life rather miserable."

Kert obviously did the talking for the trio, as Darcy had hardly said a word since taking over Namee's body. "Yeh, we got ya, old man. Yer leader Marek'll kick our arses if we don't lick 'is. We'll try not to kill the damn kid, no promises 'bout th' others, though."

Xipil gestured with his hands, palms out in offering. "The others are all yours, however many and whoever they are." He looked at Tamesis, but it seemed he was talking to Lieh now. "Come now, Lieh Morel." Xipil looked as if he were trying to raise just one eyebrow, but it seemed his host body lacked that independent control. The result was that his whole fore-head contorted in a mass of twitching wrinkles as he attempted to force the issue. "Aren't you looking forward to a nice family reunion? Just think how pleased Marek will be when I arrive not only with you, but also with the son he's never met."

A foggy dawn was just breaking as Senn woke to the Orb's warning. —*Alert, spirits near. The number is unknown*— Obviously Wildon's paranoia was justified. It must have been harder to hide their trail than Senn had thought.

He crawled out of bed and shook the others awake. "Hey! I got an alert about demons nearby from my mother's magic item. It wasn't clear how many, but they are definitely still following us!" Wildon awoke in a flash. The dogs looked up and started sniffing the air. Lani and Jarel were snuggled up together; what had they been doing? From the parts sticking out from under the blankets, it looked as if Lani might be naked. But for once, Senn was too scared to give it another thought.

Jarel's head poked out from under the blankets. "Shit, they've found us? Alright, we're getting up. Two minutes and we'll be ready to go." Even the big strongman had fear in his voice.

They readied their packs quickly, and Senn and Wildon cast a careful eye around for any traces of their presence. With the help of the Orb's concealing spell, Senn gave the area a final quick cleaning. The imbued controls took care of all the details—leaves were blown around to cover tracks. Smells were broken down with earth magic. Footprints were smoothed over with solid magic. The warm spots under their bedrolls were equalized with the surrounding earth using cold energy. Waste they left behind was hidden under leaves and quickly degraded with earth magic.

Talen chimed in with some ideas. —*They're still likely to find this place, with the amount of building work done here last night. We can just hope they don't figure out that we made a raft. Maybe they'll cross to the other side, or continue following us downriver on foot. It might be a good idea to leave a few traces some distance inland from the riverbank farther downstream, to keep them from following after us by raft*—

—*Good idea. Thanks, Talen. I'll let the others know once we're on the water and see what we can figure out*—

In a few more minutes, Senn had the raft lifted up with magic and dropped in the water. The party climbed on, with the dogs looking forward to a new adventure and the rest of them feeling sleepy and scared. After one final sweep of the Orb's concealment spell to tidy up the bank, they were off.

The demons had fanned out traveling north toward the river, searching for any traces that might indicate where Senn and his companions had gone. Lieh hoped her boy had found some way to mislead Xipil and his henchmen in order to gain some distance. There was more good news, in that Kert, Darcy, and Dolf seemed to be rocking the boat. After a few heated outbursts, it was obvious that they were not pleased with their instructions to leave Senn alive. After all, he had roasted Darcy pretty thoroughly in her bear form. But so far, their fear of Marek had kept them in line.

Finally they reached the river and regrouped. Shyama rejoined from the west and Dolf from the east, both having covered a lot more ground on four paws than the rest of them had on two feet.

—*Xipil. No traces to the west for many leagues. Perhaps they crossed the river or turned east*—

"What about you, Dolf. Did you find anything in the territory you covered?"

—*Yes. Faint, stale traces by the river a league east, where I think they made camp. But wolf and I can't smell which way they went. Maybe we need some more time scenting farther to the east, or on the other side*—

Tamesis had ideas too. "Could be someone made raft, floated away!"

"Possible. Or maybe they are waiting for us to try going downstream, then will backtrack around us. Then, if we didn't find them downriver, we'd lose the trail cold." Xipil was no idiot. But it was clear he was at a bit of a disadvantage in trying to track this group of clever clansmen. "We will check down the river for five leagues, then cross it and search the far banks. If we find nothing, we have to assume they are traveling by raft. Shyama, Dolf, get moving. I'd like Dolf by the bank and Shyama farther inland." Shyama took off at once, but Dolf was a little slower. He

exchanged hard looks with Kert and Darcy before finally turning and loping off to the east.

"The rest of you, let's head a league east and check out the camp Dolf
found. We've been up all night and need a few hours' sleep anyway.
There'll be time for that while the other two search." Lieh was thankful
for that: the demons had to rest, or their host bodies would suffer the consequences.

They arrived at the area where Senn's party had camped. Tamesis
found the traces with Lieh's magic, just as Dolf had said. There was not
much to be seen, just a few scraps of decomposed dog crap and a few areas
where the leaves were strewn about a little differently. The signs were
subtle, but the longer one spent in an area, the harder it was to do a perfect
cleanup. Lieh also noticed that some of the trees had recently had vines
removed, and there wasn't as much deadwood around as she expected—it
looked as if they had made a raft! She kept that information to herself,
hoping that the others wouldn't notice.

Xipil returned from checking out the riverbank. "No signs they went
into the water here. But with the magic we've seen from the boy so far,
they could easily have concealed their entry. Let's see what news comes
back with our furred friends in a few hours."

Kert broke out some rations from his pack, mostly food he'd scavenged or meat that Darcy had caught and cooked. She had made good use
of Namee's magic, hunting some small game and then drying the meat
with heat magic so it would keep longer. Lieh could feel the tension as
Kert handed the food to Tamesis and Xipil. He received one wicked smile
and one stony glare for his efforts. After a brief pause to eat, they lay down
for a few hours' rest.

Shyama and Dolf returned about midday with mixed news. It seemed
they had found some more clues, but weren't in agreement over how to
interpret them. There were vague traces fifty to a hundred strides from the
riverbank, maybe a bit too obvious to be accidental, but clearly Senn was
still covering their tracks. Dolf said straightaway that he wanted to build a
raft, then the lynx said her piece. —*Xipil. They're either on land, or coming
on land to throw us off. If we go by river and they are on foot, we could lose
them. We could too easily pass them in the night—*

Of course, Kert was more inclined to agree with Dolf, and was ready to argue. "Dammit, we gotta go by river. Probly they got a raft, we'll lose days on 'em if we stay behind followin' the banks. Gotta be a week's walk to the sea from 'ere, and only two, three days by water."

Xipil attempted a frown, although it ended up looking as if his mouth were melting into his beard. "We will walk east for two days. If there is no assurance they are on foot, we'll make a raft the day after tomorrow at noon. We *cannot* afford to lose them by floating past in the dark. Any complaints, and Tamesis will hear them after reducing you to the form of a forest mouse."

CHAPTER SEVEN

The Perils of Possession

Meanwhile, Xiuhcoatl despaired of completing his journey to Silville before the mamba died of old age. The snake could move lightning-fast on flat ground, and moved well enough through grasslands. But, here in the foothills to the west of the mountains, travel was taking forever. Nights he had to find shelter underground, or exhaust himself using his meager spirit magic to keep the snake warm. By day, he wasted countless hours trying to weave around tall outcroppings of rock and small mountain-runoff lakes. Probably it was another thirty leagues or so before he would get out of the foothills and forests and reach the road that led south into Silville. Why had that wolf insisted on staying so far up in the mountains?

He had almost resigned himself to giving up the mamba for a faster-moving animal when he spotted the man. This could be his ticket out of here, with the snake in hand for re-use later. Walking fast by the edge of the forest, the man was carrying a pack fully loaded with gear and seemed to be moving with purpose. At that speed, it would take him less than a week to reach the main road. Dusk was falling, and probably the man would stop soon for the night.

Following the trail was slow going, but not too difficult. The man was not making any attempts to cover his tracks, and was following the course of a small valley. Darkness fell, and Xiuhcoatl started to feel the cold, but kept going. Normally by this time of night in these foothills, he was coiled up and warm. Now he was using what little spirit magic he could muster to keep the cold-blooded mamba alive. Soon he was going to have to call it a night and find someplace warmer and underground, or risk freezing to death.

Just in time, he came upon the embers of a dying fire with the man asleep beside it, his blankets thrown back. Xiuhcoatl took a few moments by the coals to warm up while observing his target. The man looked to be a rugged outdoorsman in his mid thirties. He was average height, looked well-muscled and fit, and carried a rather large pack. If there were enough food in there to make it to Silville, even better. It meant Xiuhcoatl wouldn't have to stop to hunt.

Invigorated by the glowing embers, he finally made his move, feeling alive with excitement. The mamba struck twice on the man's lower arm, and his victim awoke immediately. "Aaaaggh! What . . . did something bite me . . ." He jumped up from the blankets and shook himself off. That was when he noticed the snake. Xiuhcoatl reared up a little, hissed and opened his inky black mouth. The man whispered to himself, "Oh shit. A . . . mamba? How could it be, this far north?" He looked closer, then started shaking. "I'm gonna die, shit . . . !"

—*Why don't you tell me your name, human, and then I'll explain*—

His eyes widened as he realized what had happened, then he shook his head in fear. "Damn demons. Why the hell don't you just stay where you belong with the rest of the spirits!"

—*It's much more pleasant here than in the spirit world. In fact I'd enjoy living as a snake for a time, but this form is not so convenient for traveling, and I have tasks to do. So you see, I'll be borrowing your body for now. What did you say your name was?*—

"I didn't, but it's Rylan. Now, since you just bit me, that gives me a couple of hours maximum. What do you plan to do with my body before I die?"

—*You don't have to die. Just let me in, and take me to Silville. It's much faster than traveling as a snake*—

Rylan arched his brows, his voice trembling as hope crept back in. "Let me get this straight. You possess me, and you can heal this snakebite?"

—Yes—

"Then what happens when we get to Silville?"

—I'll return to the snake. What happens to you, we'll have to see once we arrive. I won't have any use for you, so you might be lucky. I'm not a senseless killer like most of my brethren that came here before me. I am just an out-doorsman like yourself, who happens to be stuck in the wrong body in the wrong place—

Rylan was starting to sweat a little; beads of perspiration were building up on his forehead despite the cold. He worked his mouth and spat on the ground, then spat again. "Shit. I'm already seeing two of you. Alright, let's do it. Anything is better than death by mamba bite."

—Just relax and open your mind— Xiuhcoatl looked into Rylan's eyes and transferred over from the snake, locking the outdoorsman away in his own little prison made of spirit magic. Now to get to work on that poison. He called up the man's earth magic, and ... nothing happened. The spark of magic he could draw wasn't enough to heal a pinprick. Maybe he was doing something wrong, or Rylan had exhausted his magic supply and would recover shortly. He waited a few moments and tried again ... nothing more than before.

—Rylan, in order to neutralize the poison, I need your earth magic to mix with my spirit magic. But it seems that nothing is available. What can you tell me about this—

He could detect a combination of amusement and fear in the response. *—What magic? I'm only a Medi. I can barely even light a fire with my worthless magic!—*

Xiuhcoatl tried to wrap his mind around how this could have happened. In the past he had possessed animals that needed little convincing, or Magus-level humans who needed a lot. Back in the time when he'd been alive, he'd been a Major Adept, with no lack of magic. It just hadn't occurred to him that anyone could have so little. He'd been desperate, and had simply made a mistake.

—Alright Rylan, here's how it's going to work. I'll do my best with what I have, my spirit magic mixed with your whit of earth magic. Most likely you'll end up dead, but don't give up on me yet— At this point his belly started to cramp, and shortly he almost fell over from the pain. Xiuhcoatl ignored it and pushed his spirit magic as far as it could go, trying to neutralize the toxins. However, without any substantial amount of earth magic, it was hopeless. He dropped to his knees and vomited on the ground. Maybe he should try to find the snake and transfer back before it was too late? He tried to move ... no, there was too much pain; Xiuhcoatl had never experienced agony like this before. He couldn't see very well anymore. Who knew where the snake had slithered off to ... no chance there.

After an uncertain time crumpled in pain, seemingly more time than he'd spent in the spirit world, his borrowed body started giving up. The magic was barely even slowing down the process. He started convulsing wildly, but soon the pain-wracked jerking stopped.

Just before the body lost consciousness, Rylan got in a parting shot. *—I was just on my way between clans, finally found where my sister has been all these years. Now I'll never see her again, you worthless demon bastard. If I meet you on the other side you can be sure you'll get a pounding!—* Xiuhcoatl doubted that, but still, he felt bad for this man. Rylan had done nothing wrong, nothing deserving of this end. Besides, the man must be quite the skilled outdoorsman to survive out here alone; he was just the kind of person Xiuhcoatl could get along with. Maybe next time, he should consider talking to his target first.

—I haven't said this in hundreds of years, but I'm sorry. For what it's worth—

—Not worth your venomous hide, demon—

Vision gone, most of its senses gone, the body finally gave up. Rylan's spirit had a pathway to the spirit world, a natural channel from the dying body. But Xiuhcoatl's spirit, here against the rules of nature, could not follow despite being bound to Rylan's. As the man's spirit separated from his dying physical form, Xiuhcoatl was ripped out of the body. He was ejected in shards in every direction, an explosion of pain even worse than the snake poison had felt at its peak. For the first time since he himself had died countless years before, Xiuhcoatl lost consciousness.

CHAPTER EIGHT

Aidan Alkar's Plan

S o far, so good, thought Senn. There were no signs of pursuit as they meandered down the river toward Janklo. Every few hours, they had brought the raft to shore and taken a short break on land, much to the appreciation of the dogs. In order to keep their pursuers on land, Senn had purposely done a poor job of concealing their tracks during these breaks, instructing the Orb's spell to leave a few traces of their passage.

While they made their way downstream, Talen gave him more instruction on the spells imbued into the Orb. There was a healing spell, made for curing general ailments. The trick of healing spells was that one had to know the way the wound would heal naturally. Therefore one had to understand the injury or ailment first. The imbued spell contained a general knowledge of the body, and could handle simple wounds like cuts, broken bones, and damaged muscles just fine. However, serious internal injuries and wasting diseases were too advanced; they required a more personal touch from someone with training in medical knowledge and magic.

Another spell that Talen deemed immediately useful was one that cast and guided energy balls. Relying on this spell, the user did not have to track the target and re-route the ball along its path. He only needed to give the target, the type of energy (hot, cold, or solid), and the size of the projectile, then the spell handled the rest. This way the spellcaster could throw more than just one or two energy balls at a time, limited only by his available power draw. Finally, there was a spell for wind, which would call upon air magic to redirect the air currents around the user. Fog could be blown into an area to obscure it, or could conversely be blown away. Leaves or dust could be swirled up around one's enemies, or a steady breeze could be summoned to help fan the flames of a bonfire.

Unfortunately, there was no chance for Senn to try out most of these new spells without calling attention to himself. At least he could play a bit with the winds, calling up breezes to scatter the leaves on the riverbank or to cool his friends off as the noon sun climbed overhead. The Orb had some nice enhanced spells, and probably there would be a need for them soon enough.

The others were enjoying a quiet reprieve from the events of the last days. Wildon slept a lot to recover from the unaccustomed strain of so much walking. He also gave a few brief lectures about magic to Senn between naps. Lani and Jarel spent the time relaxing in each others' arms, and Jarel occasionally entertained them all with tall tales remembered from his youth. Senn tried to avoid any more untoward thoughts about Lani, but sometimes they slipped in anyway. The way she smiled, her laugh ... well, there were always other women; best to put Lani out of his mind.

Finally, after two full days of travel down the river, the following dawn brought with it changes in the landscape. The trees became a bit thinner and the river widened. Upon waking from a damp and fitful night, Wildon noticed the new scenery and perked up immediately.

"We need to leave the river soon. Aidan Alkar's clan should be north of the Fayn somewhere near Janklo, although they may have moved since my visit. Let's stop here, and I'll try a locater spell. Maybe we're close enough that I can find Aidan." Senn used solid magic channels to bring the raft to the bank, and Wildon climbed off. "This might be useful for you to learn, Senn. It works better on dry land, where the earth magic can flow smoothly through the ground. You think of a person you know well, and try to open a magical link to them. The distance the earth magic searches depends on the amount of energy you draw, and as you reach farther the energy required goes up steeply. If the target is close enough for your earth magic to reach, that person will know your location. The spell only speaks to the target, and you only learn their location if they respond in kind with their own magic. We can't try it on anyone from our own clan because it's too risky—they may have been possessed. But I trust Aidan's survival skills enough to take the risk."

Wildon put his palms down in the dirt a few strides from the river-bank and closed his eyes. Senn could see the strain as the old Sabi drew up as much earth magic as he could muster. Then he waited a few moments for a response. Finally he stood up with a smile and walked back to the raft. "Good news—Aidan responded. They're quite close to the coast, and I know the place well. We travel a few more leagues down the river, then after passing the next creek running into the main branch, we leave the raft and turn northeast for about three leagues."

The party resumed their ride down the river, and within an hour came to a fork where a smaller channel joined in from the north. Senn latched onto a tree on the bank with a solid magic channel and pulled the raft to a small pebbled beach just downstream of the join. "Here we are!" They all clambered off, and Senn sent the raft on downstream so as not to leave any trace for their pursuers to find. The dogs seemed especially relieved to see it go; they had not enjoyed being cooped up on a floating square of wet trees a few strides across. Everyone stretched their legs and gathered up their packs. Then they turned and headed up into the gentle hills north of the Fayn.

Over the past few days, Lieh had amused herself watching the antics of the two factions of demons. After a day and a half of following the spurious trail on land, Dolf had found a few marks on the riverbank fifty strides from one of the inland clues, just before dusk. Kert had persuaded Xipil that their quarry was trying to trick them into staying on land, and the demon group had started building a raft of their own.

Xipil and Tamesis obviously didn't know much about raft-building, as they'd just used magic to cut fresh trees. They wouldn't float well, and required a lot more effort to prepare than deadwood. It was a long and arduous task to strip the trees of their limbs, and the effort lasted well into darkness. After expending so much magic energy, the two of them had gone to sleep to replenish their power. Kert and Darcy had orders to tie the logs together with vines and wake the others when the job was completed.

Marek's henchmen awoke to Shyama's snarling, with sunlight already beaming through the trees. Shyama had just returned from patrolling to the east. Lieh saw immediately why the demon lynx was upset. The raft, which had been laid out for assembly by the riverside, was gone.

—Xipil! Your fool lackeys. They've taken your raft. I saw them, downstream on the river. That angry man made some unsavory gestures. It seems they dropped the wolf off to patrol on the north side of the river. I can't get to him there!— The frustrated lynx twitched her head from side to side.

The demon Adept rose slowly from his blankets and stroked his beard. He reapplied his dripping frown. "Damn it. I should not have trusted those three. Probably they aim to kill the lot of the clansmen, Marek's boy included. Tamesis! We're going to need another raft." Lieh smiled as they got back to work, felling more trees. With the two groups separated, it gave Senn a chance—especially against the three idiots who were heading toward him now.

After walking several hours northeast from the Fayn, Senn and the others started looking for signs of habitation. There was nothing but the sparse forest they had traveled through since leaving the river on a slow uphill climb. Finally, they came upon a big man sitting high up in a tree, smiling broadly. He had a graying beard and a ring of wispy hair encircling his bald, red pate.

"Ah, my scouts told me true. Wildon Herst, back again after all these years! No black cloud in your eyes, they said. So it's you, and you're not possessed by a demon from the other side?"

Senn was aghast. Scouts had been close enough to see the color of their eyes without them knowing it? This clan knew what they were about.

Wildon stepped forward. "Aidan Alkar! Come on down and say hello. I'd come up and greet you, but since we last met my magic's become as useless as my father's was at the end." He grinned and added, "I've brought a boy you'll be interested to meet. He is the son of Lieh Morel, and his magic has bloomed at last."

Aidan clapped his hands, "Marvelous. Let's see what we have here." He leaped out from the tree, but instead of falling, floated softly to the ground, landing just in front of Senn. "You must be Lieh's son, as this well-muscled lad with the axe looks a little old to be him. What's your name?"

"I'm Senn Morel. These are my friends, Jarel and Lani. We all escaped together after an attack on our clan by seven demons, and . . ." he paused, downcast, "we may be the only survivors."

"Well, Senn, you cast a sobering mood over my excitement at seeing Wildon again. I'm glad to meet you all the same, and you're welcome to our hospitality." He greeted them each with a hearty handshake. Wildon received a bear hug, and a slap on the back that looked as if it would knock the wind out of the old man. "So," Aidan frowned at his old friend, "what kind of demon scum have you brought my way?"

The old tutor looked a little sheepish, an expression Senn had never seen on the man's face before. "I suppose I have to apologize this time, Aidan. We barely escaped with our lives. So far we've survived with the help of the young boy's magic, and some spells in an imbued item he carries. It looks as if some of the demons are following us. They must be clever ones to do that despite the concealing spell we've used. Hopefully we threw them off the track by coming down the river, but there's no guarantee. Actually, we were hoping you could teach us a little something about sending demons back. Well, teach Senn, actually; he's the most powerful Magus I've met, even including the old Conclave members."

Suddenly Senn realized something, his face reddening. "Uhm . . . Wildon? I just remembered . . . ah . . . that concealing spell. I didn't have it on during the trip down the river, and forgot to reactivate it when we headed north." With that, Wildon sat down hard on his pack and blew out a long breath.

Aidan held a finger over his pursed lips. "So, we have up to seven demons on the way here. Two Magi among us, plus my clan and your two friends . . . and I see Jarel here carries a mean-looking axe."

Jarel nodded. "Lani can throw up a good shield in battle, she's a Minor Adept."

"We'll need more than Minor Adepts if there are really seven of these monsters coming. But let's see what we can arrange. Any idea when they'll arrive?"

Wildon shook his head. "I guess they could be right behind us, if they also built a raft at the river. But we took great pains to throw them off by leaving a false trail on the south bank."

"If there's enough time, we could follow the same route back toward the river a ways and conceal your tracks as we go. Then we could set up an ambush for these demons—that would even up the odds a bit!"

Jarel nodded at that idea. "Every attack I've experienced so far, they came straight for our camp's center. We didn't have much time to prepare, and they knew exactly where we'd be. But this time, we can lead 'em to water and make 'em drink their own medicine!"

Their host looked puzzled. "What exactly are you trying to say? Never mind. I have an idea, but we'd better move fast since we don't know how much time we have. Wildon, you and Senn come along with me. Jarel, Lani, I'll send you back south with some of my strongmen and Adepts. You can help them set up the ambush about a league from the river, and they'll use magic to cover your tracks from here back to the ambush point." He whistled, and a few men appeared from behind nearby trees. How long had they been there? "You heard me, let's clean up those tracks and get a trap ready. Jarel here will show you the way. Let's get ready to take down some demons!"

The young warrior smiled. "Yeah! I'll take that bull by the horns, and stick my axe up its arse!"

With Senn following along, the two old friends caught up on the news, Aidan telling Wildon about his clan's exploits. "Apparently I'm known as 'Aidan Demonkiller' among some of the clans, because of all those I've managed to send back to the other side. What do you think of that, eh?"

Wildon looked fascinated. "Fantastic! I remember we spoke about the possibility when I visited you several years ago. Since then I've heard rumors from others that you were successful. How does the spell work?"

"Well, I have a special warded coffin that is rather large. When the strongmen and their magic counterparts wound a demon badly enough, but don't kill it, we put it inside. Eventually the body dies, and then the warding runes come into play. They took me moons to complete, and they're the trickiest part. The runes trap the spirit inside the coffin until it fades back to the other side."

Senn spoke up, anxious to see this masterpiece of magic. "When can you show it to us?"

"We're going to get it now, boy, to bring the coffin to the ambush. We have to move our camp less often when we can send some of these demons back to the spirit world. And with this set up as a trap, I want to put them in the coffin on site, right after the attack. It's too dangerous to carry a live demon back to my camp on a stretcher to box it up, don't you think?" He chuckled.

"Aah, I see. But, one question: is there any way to keep the possessed person alive?"

"Hmm. Most demons we have encountered are possessing animals. The few that possessed people, we figured those folks had been driven crazy. Why, have you got some ideas?"

"Well, at least one of the demons that attacked us was possessing an Adept, right, Wildon?" The old tutor nodded his confirmation. "If we could free that person from possession, we might learn a lot about the demons and their plans. If we have enough magic to trap them, couldn't we find a way to force the spirit back to the other side while keeping the person alive?"

Aidan ruminated on that as they walked. "Interesting idea, Senn, but it seems to me it's usually the person's death that drives out the demon. How would you achieve that while saving the possessed victim?"

"Is there a way to simulate death, so that the demon spirit would be forced out? I know some people in our clan who almost died during attacks. One or two talked about a tunnel and a light before recovering and waking up, once our Adepts healed them. If we could manage to put them in that place near death, but then keep the person alive with magic, the demon might be forced back to the spirit world." It seemed a little foolish thinking up such an idea—after all, who was he, anyway? Maybe he had magic, but for sure he knew nothing about inventing new spells.

Aidan stopped walking and turned toward him, nodding his head up and down. "There's more to you than meets the eye, boy. There is a fish that lives off the coast, very poisonous," he said, shaking his finger vigorously. "When someone eats it, they lose their senses and usually die. But a few of them come out of it, with the help of magic. They also talked about this tunnel with a light at the end."

Wildon smiled. "Excellent. To think my student is coming up with all this! Maybe we can try it out and trap that Adept demon. If we can rid him of the spirit, we could find out from the Adept himself what these demons are up to—if he's still sane. Aidan, let's make a plan to poison these demons, and you can teach Senn all the particulars of the magic."

Aidan nodded and turned back toward the camp, walking with even more enthusiasm than before. "We're almost there. I'll have a few of my boys hunt up some of those fish down by the ocean and bring them to our ambush site."

As they walked, Senn couldn't help but wonder about the demons following them. Besides the demon Adept who had attacked the camp, were any of his fellow clansmen now among the possessed? Where was his mother, and could she have escaped to safety? He could only wait and hope she was alive.

Soon the camp sprawled before them. With so many tents, there must be well over a hundred people living here ... roughly twice the size of Senn's old clan. Their host led them to a large tent in the center of camp. "Here's where I keep the gear. Nic, Piet! Come meet our guests, Wildon and Senn." Two young men walked out, and they all greeted one another. Nic was an archer, a tall, strong Medi with a bow slung across his back, who was in charge of weapons. Piet was a lanky Major Adept, responsible for magic tasks for Aidan, and he was in charge of the coffin.

"Senn is quite a resourceful young Magus. He just came up with an idea to poison a demon, to expel the spirit from its host. Let's show him our coffin, eh Piet?" The gangly young Adept nodded vigorously, and led them into the large, dark tent that held the weapons and magic gear.

Inside the tent were racks of high-quality weapons, the likes of which Senn had seen in his clan among the older weapons made in Islingin. Aidan assured him that at least some portion had been made by his own clan: swords, arrowheads, axes, spears, and maces. Others were procured during expeditions into Janklo, but with the risk of being found by demons who prowled in and around the now-deserted city. Some new wooden shields hung on the wall, as well as a few pieces of leather and metal armor.

Finally Senn spied the pièce de résistance: a massive hinged wooden coffin, a full stride wide and two tall, almost big enough to hold the body of that bear he and Jarel had killed. Aidan beamed with pride and gestured toward his masterpiece. "Go ahead, take a look, touch the wood and tell me what you feel."

Wildon was already poking around the sides of the massive piece of woodwork. Senn walked up and looked inside it. There were no markings visible, only dark stains on the gray wood—blood. This box was surely a coffin for both the spirit and the victim who were trapped inside together. The slats interlocked, and there was a lip around the lid, so there would be no crack where a spirit could slip through. He touched the wood with his hand and probed it with magic. A web of details opened up to him, as intricate as the spells in the Orb, but spread thinly throughout the entire wooden piece. The whole coffin was one massive imbued item, but what powered it? "Aidan, what exactly keeps the spirit inside?"

The Magus peered over their shoulders as they studied his work. "Well, these spirit forms are souls, held together by spirit energy. That energy is very volatile in this world, and can't keep them here for long before it dissipates and they fade back." He slid his hand down the side of the coffin. "Imbued in the wood are something called warding runes, made with earth magic, which don't need magic input from a spellcaster to work. They are activated by the very energy they ward against. In this case, they draw power from the spirit energy holding a demon's soul here in our world. A bodiless spirit can't pass through the wards, because the spell would absorb all the energy holding it here. So the spirit remains trapped in the coffin until its energy dissipates, and then it fades back to the other side. Hah! What do you think of that?"

Wildon nodded. "Ah yes ... the old studies of warding runes ... I remember vaguely from my schooling in Islingin. I didn't quite have the power to try out such sorcery, and back then it was far more theoretical than nowadays, wasn't it." Wildon pointed to Senn, "You've got to learn this, boy. Study what's imbued in that wood, and when we have some free time, we'll learn to copy it."

Talen spoke to him as well. *—Senn, I'll help you recreate this if needed. Now I've felt it as well, and will study the complexities during our journey—*

Aidan clapped his hands together. "All well and good. Now, let's get down to tacks. Piet, gather a few men to move the coffin. Then round up a few boys, tell them to go down by the sea and catch a couple of those poison fish—we'll need them for what we have planned. Nic, round up twenty of our best fighters and Adepts, and a couple of archers. There are demons on the way, and for once we know exactly where these demons are going to be. Let's greet them the *one* way they're not expecting!"

CHAPTER NINE

Old Friends

By late afternoon, their plans at the ambush site were coming together. Jarel and the scouts had made a couple of camouflaged areas out of deadwood and vines to hide the strongmen and spellcasters. They had set up toward the south, where their unconcealed trail led. Aidan's strongmen and Adepts had arrived, and were settling in with warm blankets and hot tea to wait. The demon coffin was hidden behind an ancient monster of a tree a bit farther north, ready for use if they managed to take some of the attackers alive. Nic had arrived with two additional archers, who were preparing tree perches for themselves overlooking the southern ambush point.

Most importantly to Senn, some of the boys from Aidan's clan had finally returned with their catch of poisonous fish. These were brought over to a headquarters area in a clearing near the coffin, where Aidan was coordinating the preparations with help from Wildon and Senn. The big clan leader was delighted and his voice boomed in thanks. "Excellent work, lads! Now, get on back to camp and make sure everyone is ready in the event the demons get past us. They should be packed up in case we have to move." The boys scampered off with all haste, probably anxious not to be around when a pack of demons descended.

Aidan turned to Senn and Wildon. "Now, let's get to work. I'm thinking about using darts to deliver the poison. That way if a demon escapes after we dart him, at least the spirit can't stay in the host for long. Sound good?" The magic tutor nodded, and Senn just watched. "Then, we'll carve them out of sticks like so ..." A twig levitated in air, and shavings flew off it until a straight dart with one sharp, pointed end was left. "Senn, I'll let you make these. We need about forty."

He grimaced at the thought of making forty darts; it was tedious work. "But ... there are only seven demons at the most! Do we need so many darts? And is there enough poison for forty of them?"

"Full of questions, aren't you. We need at least a dozen poison-tipped darts. The rest are for you to practice with."

"You mean I get to shoot these?" Now that sounded more like it!

"It's either you or me, and we both have to be prepared in case something happens to the other. I've fired thousands of arrows and darts with my magic, how about you?"

"None, yet."

"Well, by the end of the day it'll be at least two dozen. That is, if we have until the end of the day." Aidan scratched the side of his face and paced back and forth across the clearing. Senn could understand his worry, as Aidan had committed everything to this fight: his demon coffin, the best warriors in his clan, and their leader.

Senn blurted out, "I guess I should tell you, we'll have at least a little warning. Maybe a half hour or more, if the demons are people on foot. I have a ... magic item ... from my mother, which gives me an alarm when spirits are getting near. There are a few more spells it can do, too."

Aidan started slicing up the fish on a split piece of deadwood. "That's helpful, for sure. It'll be good to know in advance when they're coming, that'll keep us from getting too jumpy and will make sure they don't catch us dozing. When we have some time later I'd like to see this talisman of yours, to find out what you've got there."

—That shouldn't hurt, Senn. Aidan's reputation is good, and I heard his name long ago ... he was one of the best known Magi from Janklo when I was alive. He should be trustworthy, although let's not let him know that I'm in here. Perhaps he could also take a look at my magic items, the ones in your wooden box, so it's no surprise if you unlock them later—

Senn nodded a quiet agreement. "Sure Aidan, we can look at my Orb when we have some free time. I'm hoping it can help keep us safe on this journey, along with some other books and magic items I have from my mother."

Aidan said, "That brings me to another point. Your journey . . . where is it you are planning to go, anyway?" Wildon looked at Senn, and they both raised their eyebrows. The two of them looked back to the clan leader, who smiled. "You don't know."

Wildon looked sheepish. "To tell you the truth, we only thought as far as coming here to find you. It seemed like a good idea to learn how to capture demons and send them back to the other side."

"And I've been thinking too . . ." Senn wanted to point the group in the right direction. "After what happened to our clan, we owe it to them to stop the demon invasion once and for all. If we combine our efforts and our magic, maybe we can figure out how to do it."

Aidan spoke again, "I've got some plans of my own, which could fit well with yours. A few men in my clan used to sail, back before the demons burned or sank all the ships in Janklo's harbor. None of them are shipwrights, to be sure, but some have done shipbuilding labor or seafaring, including myself. I've got a decent size boat that we've assembled in a secret cove, some leagues north of Janklo. It holds about twenty people, mostly crew. I've been planning a voyage east across the sea to Hyanto, to find out if any demons have made it over there. If not, it would give us a safe place to do further studies on how to stop them, without fear for our survival."

Wildon nodded. "Good idea, we could join you. If we find a way to combat these demons, we could eventually take the fight to Islingin, and stop this blasted invasion at the source. When do you plan to leave?"

"As soon as possible. In fact I was planning to head off as soon as I picked a few more good strongmen and Adepts to fill out my crew. But now that you're here . . . well, you can fill those spots. We'll leave as soon as this nasty business is done."

Senn smiled, and said, "Sounds like a great idea!"

"Alright, then. As it's decided, I'll send someone back to camp and have the crew prepare the ship for departure. But first . . ." Aidan scooped up a pile of dark, smelly fish guts on his knife. "Here's the most toxic part of these fish." He laid it carefully on a big leaf and continued, "This isn't fast acting, but it'll do the trick and will put these demons near death, given time. That should exorcise the spirits from their hosts, and the demon coffin will send 'em back to the other side. Now, let's poison ourselves some darts!"

Aidan's ambush team had everything prepared as twilight came. The sky started to cloud up, and night fell early. The darkness helped to hide the strongmen, archers, spellcasters, and coffin under a gloomy blanket of flat light, but the sky threatened rain as well.

At the makeshift headquarters, Senn was practicing with the extra darts he'd made. To fire a dart, he created a guide channel aimed at the target and a ram of solid energy to launch it. He picked up a dart and dropped it in the air, where the solid energy held it in place. It appeared to be floating in mid-air. Then he drew up energy and pulsed it into the ram, flicking the dart forward along the channel. It smashed into the target marked on a nearby tree.

"Good, Senn . . . you're doing fine, but it's not so hard firing at a tree. Let's see how you do against a moving target." Aidan was tireless in his pursuit of perfection, and that applied to training others as well. Wildon had been a much more lenient tutor. But with their survival at stake Senn had no qualms about giving it his all.

Now Aidan levitated a scrap of wood and moved it across the clearing. Senn had to recalculate his trajectory, making the channel swing around to follow the target as he launched the dart. At the last minute Aidan upped the speed of the target, forcing Senn to re-aim the channel as the dart was in flight. But he wasn't fast enough, and the dart flew wide of the target. "Argh!"

"Right, boy, but this is why we practice. We'll keep at it until you can hit every shot. You need to anticipate what movements the target might make, and be ready to adjust the direction of the guide channel at an instant's notice."

They continued practicing until all the extra darts were used. By that time Senn's marksmanship had improved dramatically. The last three shots had hit the mark despite Aidan's random and swift movements of the target. After the long day the group had experienced, especially among Senn's party which had arrived by raft early in the morning, Aidan called an end to the preparations and had his men set a watch. Since shelters would call attention to their presence, they had to sleep out in the open with nothing but the trees and their blankets to cover them. Senn refreshed the spirit alert and fell quickly into a deep sleep.

Dreams riddled with a strange combination of excitement and fear wracked the boy all night. He feared being awakened by the Orb's warning or a bloody surprise attack at any moment. Simultaneously, he was thrilled by the idea of putting his idea in action: catching a demon and freeing the possessed victim from the spirit's clutches. Before dawn he was dreaming of a grateful Lani thanking him for saving them all. She was just moving to show her gratitude, her hands slipping under the sheets toward his manhood, when he awoke to a pattering sound. The rain had finally come, and the timing could not have been worse.

Senn spent the rest of the night in a sodden state somewhere between waking and sleeping. Eventually he and the others woke up to the gray dawn and ate a cold breakfast, not wishing to light a fire and risk giving away the ambush. Aidan and Wildon approached him after the meal to begin a day of research and training while they waited. There was more target practice, then a discussion about the Orb's powers.

Aidan was particularly interested, and turned the Orb over in his hands as he examined the markings and felt out the imbued magic spells. "Hmm, seems some of the spells aren't active ... mmm ... but these others, works of art. So, Lieh Morel brought this out of Islingin? Quite fascinating, it really looks like the work of a master, perhaps your grandfather? Here in Janklo I always heard a lot about the great Talen Morel."

Senn found no reason to hide the Orb's origins, but had to cover for the remaining spells that Talen hadn't yet explained and activated. "Yes, I think so. However some of the spells seem to be locked, or maybe unfinished. Once we have more time I'll try to get them working."

Aidan handed the Orb back. "Maybe once we're on the open ocean there will be time for that." The big man looked around at the wet, restless warriors and Adepts. "But for now we need to stay ready. I'm going to give a little reassurance to the men, to remind them we'll have some warning. Right?" He looked at Senn expectantly.

"Ah, yes, of course . . . the warning spell is charged up. The Orb will notify me the demons are coming before they arrive." Hopefully that would be soon, as his nerves were starting to fray. The spitting rain wasn't helping his state of mind either.

All afternoon they waited; Senn's legs were cramped from sitting around in the cold and damp. Jarel came by at some point to see how he was doing, and the warrior seemed just as anxious about their situation. "Aidan came by to say it's just a question for time, or something like that. I never asked time for anything myself. But I wish it'd hurry up, I'd rather not sit all day getting soaked by this rain. How're ya holding up, Senn?"

"Nervous, the same as you. I guess most of your past fights were pretty unexpected?"

"Yeah, always starting from the blast of the horn, that early warning from Lieh. Even that short hour of waiting was bad enough, but this? I'd take two fights right away, rather than do this much waiting for one." Senn nodded in agreement. "Well, I guess I'll get back to the front where a couple others from Aidan's clan are waiting. I'll hunker down there with Lani." He winked and trudged back toward the south.

Just as the sky began to darken, Lani came by his post. "Hey Senn!" She gave him a big smile and touched his arm in greeting, lightening the tension that was thick in the air. "Just stretching my legs. No warning yet?"

He looked at his feet nervously. "No, nothing."

"Let's hope we don't have to wait another day. But you did such a good job throwing them off track . . ." she winked and looked him in the eye. "For all we know, it could take another week! Or maybe we lost them when we went down the river?" Was she flirting with him? No, she couldn't be; she was just being friendly. Don't think about Lani and her beautiful smile, her taut body . . . no. Even she wasn't enough of a distraction today, because his thoughts soon reverted to demons: bears, moose, and fireball-wielding Adepts.

"Senn? You alright?" He was startled out of his reverie. She must think he was an idiot kid, drifting off when she was in the middle of a conversation with him.

"Sure Lani, just got a lot to think about, you know? I'll be heading to wherever they strike first, probably where you are in the south. I have to be ready with energy balls and these poison darts."

"Energy balls, incoming!" Lani threw a playful punch and Senn flinched. "Just don't hit me with one?" She flashed that wide, gorgeous smile again.

"I'll try not to." He finally managed a weak grin as she turned to walk back to her post. Now Senn was worried about incoming energy balls as he tried to ignore the cold rain trickling across his face.

They were all unrolling soggy blankets to turn in for a second night of waiting when the warning finally came. —*Alert, spirits near. The number is three*—

Senn raced to Aidan's side. "They're coming! Three demons!"

The clan leader looked around quickly. "What timing, when it's dark and wet. It's hard to tell if that will help them or us more. Piet!" The skinny Adept looked up from preparing his bedroll by the demon coffin. "Make a round of the posts and let them know we have company, coming any time now! Once the battle is met, I want you to light up the area around the fight. Make sure our men can see these demons. It's only three of them, so I expect with the strength we have lined up we won't have too much trouble." Piet nodded and headed off to quietly warn the others.

"Alright Senn, are you ready with those darts?" The boy nodded. Aidan had taken half a dozen of the poisoned darts, and given Senn the other half dozen, each batch carefully wrapped in thick leaves to avoid pricking the spellcasters. "We want to take them alive, so that means no massive energy balls or falling trees. First try solid energy, to knock them out. And remember, the poison will take time to affect them, maybe hours —don't count on it during the battle!"

Wildon finally emerged from his damp cocoon of blankets, shivering and blue. "Senn, I'll go with you and set up a shield. Aidan, I suppose you'll stay here with your imbued coffin?"

Aidan gave his old friend a grim smile. "Absolutely, Herst. You two and the others do what you can, then bring any captives here once they're weakened. I'll save my strength and keep a dozen men here as backup."

Together, Senn and Wildon walked quietly to their hiding place behind a tree, their eyes peering out around the trunk to watch the likely entry point twenty strides south. As they settled in to wait, Wildon whispered, "It should be any time now, how about trying to hear them coming? You can use air magic to extend your hearing. Visualize a matrix to magnify the sound traveling through the air from the direction which you want to monitor. Catch the incoming sound and aim it into your ear like so . . ." He cupped his hand to his ear. Senn did the same, and then created a tube-shaped matrix aimed toward the darkness off to the south. As he fed in a steady trickle of air magic, his hearing was suddenly amplified. He could hear every distant raindrop.

After a few minutes, footfalls and voices materialized out of the distance. Senn heard panting, as if from a dog, and the careless crashing of human footsteps as well. There was a crunching noise of breaking sticks, then a familiar female voice he couldn't quite place. "Ow . . . Damn it, Kert . . . we should stop for the night before one of us breaks a leg. Now we've got little enough magic, no sense wasting it on healing ourselves."

"Come on, Darcy . . . ain't no problem. Besides, this trail's gettin' stale, and I don't wanna risk losin' 'em just 'cuz it gets washed out with rain. Anyways we're damn lucky, seems they didn't bother with concealin' their tracks, thinkin' they done lost us on the river!" The man's voice was also familiar, but with that strange accent, Senn couldn't identify it.

There was a low growl, then the woman's voice again. "Then why not send Dolf ahead while we get some rest?"

"Look, like I done told ya, I'd rather not have 'im go alone into a poss'ble fight. B'sides, if we stick together we 'kin surprise 'em all at once in the dark while they's sleepin', and knock the piss out of 'em once an' fer all!" The footsteps were drawing close enough that he could almost hear them without the spell. The archers twenty strides to the south were probably just drawing their bowstrings tight. Senn released the spell and nodded at Wildon. They left their hiding place behind the tree, each readying his planned spell as they moved into attack position. Wildon put up a shield while Senn sighted in the darkness for their targets.

Twang! Twang! "Shit, somethin' hit me!" The man sounded angry, whoever he was. There was a snarl and the sound of heavy paws racing across wet leaves. The sky lit up with Piet's contribution, and they could see Jarel and a dozen others at the front. They were hiding behind the two big shelters of deadwood they'd propped against trees, one on the left side of the incoming trail and the other on the right. Two solid energy balls raced out toward the demons, who tumbled out of the way as the missiles splintered trees behind them. "Dammit Darcy, there's a buncha people attackin' ... send some of them fireballs that way!"

The woman's voice again ... "Alright Kert! As soon as we're close enough I'll let loose with whatever strength this girl's got!" The pair came closer and Senn recognized who they were. He couldn't believe his eyes—what a horrible sight! It was his own clansmen, Rikk and Namee, sprinting the short distance that separated them from Jarel and his fighters. The two of them must have been possessed after the last attack by the demons the clan had managed to kill. Rikk drew his sword, the sound ringing out loudly across the glade as the blade came clear of its scabbard. With his left hand he ripped an arrow out of his sword arm, a battle cry loud in his throat as he ran forward. Would Senn's companions be able to fight against these possessed friends? Jarel answered Senn's question by loosing his dogs, who raced across the space toward the sprinting attackers.

Senn watched, frozen, as a black wolf the size of two strongmen barreled around the rightmost tree into his companions' hiding place. It hit the first energy shield with a whimper and thrashed around for a few seconds until it found a way between the energy shields, just as one of the Adepts launched an energy ball at it. The blast of flame hit the wolf in the hindquarters, knocking it halfway around, but that didn't stop it from sinking its teeth into someone's leg. Screams of pain filled the air.

Wildon's voice was loud in his ear. "Come on son, hit them with some energy! That's what we're here for!" Right ... fight the fear, it was no different from the attack on his clan, except that this time they *had* to win. There was nowhere left to run. Senn launched the solid energy ball he'd prepared, taking aim at ... Namee. As he let it fly, she launched a flaming energy ball of her own at the defenders nearest the wolf. It slammed into an energy shield, taking it out ... but the shield had served its purpose and protected those behind it. Now Senn's ball hit her in the shoulder, spinning her around just as an arrow thunked into her side. Besides that, two of Jarel's dogs were slowing her down, until she flung an energy ball at them, scattering the hounds in a whimper of pain.

Rikk had reached the hiding place now, having dodged another energy ball from one of Aidan's Adepts. His sword cut deep into another one of the dogs, which fell to the ground, whimpering loudly. Rikk ducked around the energy shields protecting the tree on the left, where Jarel was waiting. The possessed man shouted a battle cry, sword held high, and slashed down toward Jarel. The big warrior knocked the sword aside with the head of his axe, then backed away a step, clearly thrown by this face-off with his once friend and mentor. Senn took careful aim and released another solid energy ball, aiming downward toward Rikk's head with a high arc. He used enough energy for a hard hit that would stun but not kill. As it arced through the air, Rikk took a powerful, wild swing at one of the Adepts who was trying to get out of the middle of the action. The young Adept was slashed deeply across the ribs and fell over with a gurgling sound. Lani tried to catch him as he crashed to the wet ground with a thud. At that moment Senn's energy ball arrived, knocking Rikk hard on the head and sending him to his knees, dazed. The sword tumbled out of his hands, and Jarel pulled it out of his reach, while glancing sideways at Senn.

Now that the opportunity presented itself, Senn reached for one of the poisoned darts. He carefully constructed the guide channel and launched it on its way, aiming at Rikk's exposed neck. As the dart dug into his flesh, the demon seemed to be startled back awake, and tried to regain his footing. But Jarel was ready, and smacked the side of Rikk's head with the flat of his axe. This time Rikk didn't get back up.

With one of the three demons out of the way, Senn looked to see what the other two were doing. The wolf was riddled with several arrows and bleeding from a few deep cuts. It turned, looking for an escape route, and eyed the lone boy and old man. Senn and Wildon must have looked like easy targets, because the wolf charged toward them. Hopefully the shield would hold ... but Senn didn't want to take any chances. No point in holding back and getting hurt. He constructed a huge ball of heat energy and flung it toward the charging animal. The massive black wolf turned its face from the oncoming blast and took it on the shoulder, changing colors briefly as its fur lit up in flickering hues of blue and orange. Bits of flesh and blood splattered Wildon's shield, bouncing off its shimmering surface and ricocheting away into the darkness. Somehow that didn't stop the wolf, although now it was slowed and badly limping. It veered wide and continued past the pair toward the location where Aidan and the other half of the defenders were waiting. Senn guessed his fellow Magus could handle the wolf now without any problem.

He tried to peer through the haze of smoke that remained from the burned wolf fur and vaporized leaves—no good. Dashing out around the shield, he skirted the smoking patch of ground where his energy ball had hit. Ah, there was Namee. She had picked herself up from the last pair of hits, and now strode toward Jarel purposefully, one arm hanging limp. Another arrow sprouted from her side as Jarel hefted his axe and turned toward her. He bellowed, "Nic! I'm gonna try and bean 'er the way I did this other one, take 'er alive!" Senn prepared another solid energy ball, but he was too late. Namee launched a fiery blast at Jarel, just as he risked stepping out from behind Lani's shield in order to get in a good swing. He caught the burst of heat energy straight in the chest, and it exploded upward into his face, throwing him backward as if hit by a boulder. From his tree perch, the archer Nic let out a cry of anger. As Jarel flew backward, Senn let loose his energy ball, perhaps with a bit too much gusto. The solid energy ball cracked into Namee's shoulder, knocking her down and back. As she fell, Nic's next arrow skewered her in the throat.

Senn ran forward. Was there anything he could do to help? It looked as if one warrior had been badly mauled by the wolf. Several Adepts were working to staunch the blood flow and bind his cuts. Behind the opposite shelter, the slashed Adept was lying still and lifeless. Nic clambered down from his archery post, yelling to Senn about Namee. "Damn, I was aiming low to avoid killing her, bad luck that your energy ball spun her like that!"

Meanwhile Lani was focusing her attention on Jarel. "Senn, get over here! I need your help! He's fading..."

The tunic Jarel wore had been mostly vaporized. His chest and face were a mass of red and black skin, and he could barely move his lips. Drips of rain from the trees above were pattering gently on his wounds, making them glisten in Piet's artificial light. "Good shot, Nic... but a hair too late to be the Nic of time. Senn..." Jarel lifted his arm and waved him over, "I was trying to go easy on 'er. I know how much Namee must've meant to ya." Senn was embarrassed again, hoping that Jarel hadn't taken the risk just for him. But it was too late now to dispel any myths about his interest in Namee.

Lani's eyes were tearing up a little. "Quiet now, my big brute. We're going to get you through this. Senn, try to repair the skin, especially where he's bleeding!" Senn felt with his earth magic to see which areas needed the most repair.

But Jarel waved him away. "Save it," he coughed, and spat out blood. "Too much damage inside. The world . . . it's spinning . . . take care of it for me. That, and my hounds." Senn didn't have the heart to tell him none of the dogs had survived the attack. Jarel stopped breathing and his eyes glazed over. The eyes, that must be it . . . the moment the spirit detaches and goes its own way. Lani sniffled, tears streaming down her face along with the raindrops, as she hugged Jarel's lifeless body one last time.

The group had a lot to do before they could proceed with the next step of their journey. There were three dead including Jarel, and four if they counted Namee, which Senn certainly did. A team quickly set about digging graves for all of them, as Piet kept his lighting spell going strong. Rikk was still unconscious, and a pair of strongmen dragged him by the armpits toward Aidan's group and the demon coffin. Senn went with them to see his old clansman into his (hopefully temporary) resting place. In addition he created a ball of glowing heat energy above them, to better see where they were going.

Aidan was waiting for them, a smoking and snarling lump at his feet with two darts sticking out of its snout. He was yelling to several Adepts from the group. "Lay the coffin flat, and throw this smoldering mess of a black wolf in it, post haste! We need it in there with the lid shut before it dies." He nodded to Senn and the others who were dragging Rikk. "Put him in the coffin too! Senn, did you stick him already?"

He nodded. "Got a good hit in just before Jarel knocked his lights out, see there on his neck?"

"Excellent shot, boy. Let's get ready to load him up. We'll dose him with our double strength Magus-level earth magic just before we close the lid, to help keep him alive for the next few days."

As Aidan and Senn followed the trio to the coffin, Rikk started to wake, obviously not yet feeling the full effects of the poison. They laid him inside, and he weakly moved his arms to protest, while the warriors held him down. "You ... damn humans ... where's Darcy?" He noticed the charred wolf panting weakly beside him. "Shit Dolf, what'd they do to ya?" Senn's possessed comrade stared at his captors and narrowed his eyes. "Maybe we don't got what it took, but Xipil will. He's damn powerful, 'long with that Magus woman Lieh they possessed back at the camp. She'll kick yer arses right into the spirit world, her an' Xipil, before ya know what hit 'cha!" He showed a wide, evil grin that was quite out of place on Rikk's normally kind face.

Senn glanced at Aidan, catching his eye. His mother had been captured by these ruthless animals? His lip trembled as anger and fear coursed through him. Any way you looked at it, there would be a lot more than three casualties if this demon Xipil and a possessed Lieh Morel caught up with them. Tears welled up, but Senn tried not to cry. Aidan looked down at the demon with a frown, drips of water glistening as they ran down his bald head and dripped off his nose. "Let's see how long you keep thinking that way, demon bastard. It seems to me you'll soon be contemplating that question from the other side yourself, along with your wolf friend here. Senn! Let's dose him up. A powerful shot of earth magic—concentrate on sustaining the body, but don't do anything against the poison. We want it in full effect to force the spirit out."

The two Magi each reached down and laid a hand on the weakly struggling demon, working their earth magic spells to keep Rikk alive. "What're ya doin? Whatcha mean back to th' other side?" Senn and Aidan stood back, and the big clan leader took hold of the coffin's hinged lid. "What the hell ya mean 'bout poison, anyw—?" The lid swung shut with a crash, and Aidan slid the warded locks into place. It was done.

CHAPTER TEN

The Spirit Trap

Xiuhcoatl chittered, and chewed on the tasty nuts he'd found cached where his host had hidden them last fall. The red squirrel wouldn't exactly have been his first choice, but it was his last chance before fading back to the other side. After several hours of senselessness, he had finally reassociated above the dead body of Rylan, the outdoorsman. His black mamba was nowhere to be found, and unfortunately he couldn't move fast or far enough in his spirit form to find it. In the end he had thought it better to settle for the squirrel than to return to the spirit world in disgrace.

Now with a meal in his belly, he had time to look for the snake. Where would it go? With this weather, it would have stayed by the embers of the fire through the night, and gone in search of more natural warmth once the sun came up. Xiuhcoatl scampered along the path, tail twitching left and right as he surveyed the valley for sunny patches. Through this terrain, he could move faster than the snake, and was certain he could catch up with it.

After an hour or so the terrain became a bit more rocky, and he spotted some pools of sun where the snake could be warming itself. Xiuhcoatl started investigating these one by one. Sure enough, he eventually found

the mamba curled up on a sun-drenched rock ... almost as if it were waiting for his return. Perfect! He looked left, then right, twitched his tail a
few times for good measure, and approached the snake slowly.

As he moved in, the mamba saw him and reared up in striking position, opening its dark black mouth. Was it hungry? The last few days
Xiuhcoatl had been working it hard, covering many leagues with little rest
or food. He hoped he could persuade the snake before it decided to make
a meal of him.

—*Let me in, together we can escape this cold place. Back to the warm
lands of long ago*— But it didn't seem that the snake was interested this
time; maybe the cold and hunger had made it ornery. When the snake
struck out at him, Xiuhcoatl dodged left. He ran right to avoid another
strike, then scurried left again. Apparently he should have picked a direction and stuck with it, because this time the snake's fangs made contact
and bit hard. The snake backed off, leaving the squirrel alone briefly as it
quickly lost functions. Xiuhcoatl tried hopelessly to communicate again,
but it seemed the mamba's base survival needs were tuning him out.

Soon the now-familiar pain caused by the mamba's venom was shooting through the body of the squirrel. After a few moments in paralysis the
snake decided it was safe to eat its prey. Xiuhcoatl was studying the inside
of the mamba's throat when the squirrel's body finally gave up its tiny soul,
once more wracking him with intense pain as his spirit was fragmented
and thrown about the rocky clearing.

For the second time in one day, Xiuhcoatl slowly became conscious of his
surroundings. The sun was behind the mountain peaks, illuminating the
sparse cloud cover and making it glow a brilliant mixture of red and
orange.

It seemed that the mamba had left, and most likely it was searching
out a warm hollow in a tree to shelter for the night. Better to give up on
the snake, since it had eaten him as a squirrel—there was always the option
to find another mamba in the southern plains one day. Looking around,
Xiuhcoatl searched for other possibilities. There! High up in a dense
stand of trees near the edge of the rocky clearing, he spotted a nest of
sticks that was well within range of his barely-motive spirit form.

After a few minutes of work with his weak spirit magic, he made his way up to the nest. An old female hawk was arranging sticks, perhaps preparing to lay a clutch of eggs. It would be a shame if they didn't have a chance at life because of Xiuhcoatl's intervention, but that was a risk he had to take. He could not turn down such a sure-fire and quick mode of transport to Silville.

Quietly he spoke into the hawk's mind with simple persuasions. —*Let me in, you will not be cold or hungry. With my help your brood will prosper*— Just a little white lie, no harm there. The eyes defocused and the tiny creature's will relaxed, opening up to him. Xiuhcoatl flowed inside and took control, feeling at home in the creature already. This hawk was not a young one, for sure—but she felt comfortable and familiar like a well-worn pair of shoes. Thankfully, he did not think she was carrying any eggs yet. This had been quite a trying day, so he decided it was time to rest. Xiuhcoatl gave in to the bird's instincts and fell asleep.

Eventually the sun climbed above the mountains and began to warm the air, producing the thermals that would carry him southward. Now, to find Silville. Up into the air … the beating of wings churned the air around him and he took off, lifting higher and higher until he could see far along the western mountain range. Silville should be around fifty leagues south, giving him a travel time of only two or three days. After this ordeal it would be good to finally reach his destination, even if he then had to find another way besides mamba venom to persuade his target to let him in.

Xiuhcoatl followed the thermals higher, allowing the natural tendencies of the bird to find the best route to his destination. He really had to get this bird's-eye view more often in the future, as it was a truly amazing way to see the landscape of Kartus. Snow-capped mountains, rolling forests, wide runoff lakes, and deep canyons spread out below him like masterful works of art. In fact right now he was high over a wide lake, looking down at the ripples in the water caused by the blowing wind. The hawk's spectacular vision was able to pick out jumping fish and floating waterfowl, even from this distance.

But then something went wrong. His host seemed to be flying more weakly, her wings not keeping them as high up as planned. The aged hawk's breathing became shallower, and Xiuhcoatl tried to strengthen the body with his meager spirit magic. Unfortunately the bird, like the hapless outdoorsman Rylan, had no earth magic to promote fast healing—and there was no time for spirit magic alone to do much of anything. His host's mind was fading out of consciousness, and the wings just wouldn't respond anymore. Soon the poor hawk plummeted toward the water at a frightful pace, with Xiuhcoatl trapped inside.

Finally the water came up to greet them, and at that speed it was about as forgiving as the solid stone of the nearby mountains. The hawk died instantly and her fluttering soul vanished, splattering Xiuhcoatl's spirit across the lake in droplets among a cloud of damp feathers.

Reassociating like this for the third time in under two days was not pleasant. If it were possible for a formless being to ache with full-body pain, this is what it would feel like. And what a predicament: Xiuhcoatl was stuck in the middle of a lake, too far away to reach the shore in any direction in spirit form. Above was nearly nothing, just the occasional bird moving far too fast for him to catch. On the lake itself the waterfowl were mostly clustered by the shore, again out of reach. Below the surface there were sure to be thousands of fish and other such water creatures, basically useless to him. Trying to jump from a fish to a duck or any other land-bound animal would be as fruitless as his previous attempt at persuading the hungry mamba as a squirrel.

It seemed that sometimes existence presented one with little or no choice. He could only choose between several bad options, and hope that circumstances worked themselves out in the end. Xiuhcoatl moved toward the nearest waterfowl floating on the lake, trying to reach one before his spirit energy dissipated, which would send him back to the spirit world. If those birds turned the right direction . . . if his magic energy held out long enough and he could make it that far . . . quite a few conditions, there.

In the end, Xiuhcoatl's energy was totally depleted. Despite his efforts to pull more spirit energy from the other side, the amount required to hold his spirit here far outweighed the incoming trickle. There was not enough magic for him to stay in the physical world, which he had come to think of as home. His spirit faded back through the thin veil separating the worlds, and he returned to the dark place that was all he had known for countless years.

Immediately Xiuhcoatl was aware that the area around the rift looked different than when he had left. He looked down at his glowing, floating form—at least that was the same. But instead of the usual wide swath of darkness with other glowing forms scattered about in groups, he saw only three forms. One he knew instantly as Marek, while the other two were unknown. All of them were surrounded by a circle of glowing runes floating in the air, warding the whole area against any spirits entering or leaving. This was usually a practice reserved for the most powerful and least savory of this world's residents who were trying to control some of their lesser competitors. How had he reappeared in his own master's prison?

Marek floated over to him, leaving the other two alone. —*Xiuhcoatl. I see you've finally had your first setback in the task I gave you?*—

—*Yes, Master Seltin. I made an . . . unfortunate choice, and the following unlucky circumstances brought me here*—

—*One makes one's own luck by controlling all the circumstances. But I can forgive this failure, because you've already achieved more than I had expected, and in a shorter time. In fact it's fortunate you've returned at this moment, because I have a new task for you in the physical world*—

Interesting . . . at least that meant Xiuhcoatl would get to go back. —*Many thanks for the further opportunity to serve you. May I ask first: how is it that I ended up here in your prison?*—

—*Ah, yes. This is not a prison, but instead a spirit trap. When one of the clans found a way to send our kind back, I realized that they appear in this spirit world very close to where they left it. As all the spirits left through that opening*— He pointed to a column of glowing runes in the center of the circle, —*they all reappear within my net, whether they are sent back by magic, or simply fail to find a host in time*—

Xiuhcoatl recognized the column in which Clayne, Marek's gatekeeper, admitted spirits to the fissure between the worlds. That was newly constructed when he had left on his mission. —*Very clever of you, Master. This way you find out news of the physical world, with reports coming in from all across Kartus*—

Marek's rough-shaped figure glinted, the spirit equivalent of a smile. *—Exactly, and these two here have brought me invaluable information. You must hear it firsthand. It is uncanny the timing of it all, with you arriving here at almost the same moment. It seems that these two fools, Kert and Dolf, were actually traveling with my wife. When they went their own way on a foolhardy attack, they were mortally wounded and then sent back here . . . by my son!—*

Xiuhcoatl listened patiently as Kert repeated his tale, with the ex-wolf Dolf looking on and nodding. Clearly Dolf wasn't used to saying a lot, while Kert unfortunately was.

—They was the same clan that did in me an' Darcy, couple o' years back. We found 'em when there was some pulse o' spirit magic. We could feel it leagues away! Three of us, we attacked 'em from all sides, tryin' to get the jump, an' there was other demons there too. Some woman an' a scrawny kid had a lotta magic, one killed me and th' other killed Darcy. Dolf ended up fightin' near these demons Xipil an' Tamesis, he made it through, 'cuz Xipil had some nice magic power—

What a mess. Trying to understand this idiot's story was like trying to make sense of a madman's ramblings. In fact, the tale probably was a madman's ramblings . . . albeit marginally based on reality. *—Cut to the chase, will you—*

Kert continued, *—Yeah, right. Me an' Darcy got these nice forms o' some dying humans, an' Tamesis got this Magus form, I guess 'er form is Marek's woman—*

Xiuhcoatl saw his master's glowing form twitch at that. Kert continued, explaining that Senn and his companions had escaped, and later ambushed the spirits with poison and an imbued box.

Marek spoke up, *—Let's hear some more details. Can you describe the ambush location to us? We'll need to get back there to find out what happened to the party after they killed you—*

Xiuhcoatl listened as Kert described the river with a tributary entering from the north, the raft laid up on shore, and the direction they had walked following Marek's son. Finally he had heard enough and nodded to Marek, who jumped back in.

—Gentlemen. Many thanks for your fascinating tale, but I think we won't be needing anything more from you. May I ask you to escort yourselves out of here—

This didn't seem to make Kert too happy. *—Ey, you said if we told ya what we knew, we'd get to go back to th' other world!—*

—No, I said I'd consider sending you back if I thought you might be of use to my cause. Then you told me you disobeyed my servant Xipil, and tried to kill my son. If you don't get the hell out of here, I might overlook your generosity in providing me information, and consider those other facts instead— Marek raised the glowing shape of an arm, and it brightened noticeably as he gathered up spirit magic as if for a blow.

—Alright, you bastard, just send us back out in the slums o' this dark hellhole. We're goin' already— Marek opened up an exit in the runes surrounding them, and Kert and Dolf left the magical cage. The doorway sealed up behind them.

—So, Xiuhcoatl, you can see I'm a little upset by what's been going on out there. Xipil's instructions were to find Lieh and keep her safe and compliant. He should have persuaded her to join our cause, but instead he's had Tamesis possess her. That murderous, psychopathic bitch, controlling my wife? She'll think I've turned into some kind of monster! And then he teams up with these morons, who try to kill my son?— Marek's form grew brighter.

—I can see how this could upset you. But look on the positive side, your son seems very capable of protecting himself. It looks as if now he's even found a way to send our spirits back here—

—Absolutely true. Fighting these fools may have been a useful test of his skills. Furthermore, if he's teamed up with another Magus near Janklo . . . who could be Aidan Alkar . . . he would certainly be safe. We just need to make sure he stays out of the way of my plans for the new Spirit Council. In addition, I've decided that the current number is enough. With the eight Magi you've already brought in, we'll be able to handle affairs over there.

—To your tasks: First, keep an eye on the boy, and make sure he doesn't become an obstacle to our plans. In addition I need you to find Xipil and inform him of my desires for Lieh and my son. Help him to track down the boy, and bring him to Islingin with Lieh. Maybe you can persuade my kin of our cause, where Xipil could not. Lastly, I want you to bring one more Magus, as I need a form for myself. Someone powerful enough to be worthy of

my ambitions! If you do run across Alkar in the region of Janklo, he would be perfect.

—*I trust you can handle all that without ending up back here again?*—

Xiuhcoatl's heart was already warming at the thought of escaping the dismal spirit world and returning back home to the sunlight. —*Of course, I shall not fail you. As you said, it was fortuitous that I ended up here*—

Marek had calmed down, and his spirit form was now an even, dull orange glow. —*Excellent. Now, what will you require for this task? I will have Clayne instruct Umkoome on what form to bring you*—

To travel from Islingin to Janklo and observe the humans? With the right bird he could be there in just a few days, and find out anything he needed to know without them realizing he was there. But he couldn't trust Umkoome to find him the perfect form. And this time he had to make sure he picked a feathered creature that wasn't about to succumb to old age. —*Just bring me a Minor Adept, and I'll take care of the rest from there. I will find Xipil and your son within two weeks. Of course I can't yet give you a timetable for bringing you a powerful Magus . . . but I will keep my eyes open for this Aidan Alkar*—

—*Perfect, then I will have Umkoome find you an Adept with all haste*—

What a wonderful opportunity. Xiuhcoatl would return to the living world where he belonged, and would soar through the clouds once more. When he completed this task, there were always the southern plains and their gorgeous black mambas to consider.

CHAPTER ELEVEN

Maiden Voyage

The rain and lack of sleep wore on Senn, along with the Orb's concealing spell. They had been walking for hours in the dark of night, and were supposedly getting near the rocky cove where the boat was anchored. Aidan said most of the ship's crew was already there preparing for departure. The last crew members and the remaining supplies for their voyage to Hyanto were on the way from the clan's camp. Time was of the essence if they were to embark before their pursuers caught up.

Wildon dropped back in the column to Senn, who was bringing up the rear with his concealment spell. Both had been excused from their turns carrying the demon coffin because of all the magic and energy they had expended in the evening's battle. "It just occurred to me, boy. I should congratulate you on turning fifteen today."

Senn scratched his head wearily. "I haven't been watching the moon, but I think you're right." Wildon slapped him on the back, and he smiled wearily. "I don't much feel like celebrating without my mother here. I guess she's still alive, so there's at least some chance I'll be able to celebrate with her next year."

"Absolutely, Senn. With the magic techniques that you and Aidan have developed, we may be able to free her of any possessing spirit. Keep your chin up, and don't stop thinking up those good ideas."

Finally they reached the rocky cove north of Janklo where the ship was waiting at anchor. Between the rain and the mist they couldn't see a thing, but Aidan promised it was floating there about fifty strides from the jagged shoreline. The clan leader gathered everyone around. "Listen up. We'll depart in the morning, as soon as the others arrive from the camp with the last of our supplies.

"The crew list is as follows: myself, Senn, Wildon, and Lani, for starters. Nic, you're on lookout duty and responsible for weapons and defense. Piet, you know your duties with the coffin and magic supplies. Keegan, I'd like you to join us, providing your magic skills. On this trip we can't have enough Major Adepts. Ten of my sailors are on the boat now, and another three should be arriving from the camp by morning. That makes an even twenty, and if we manage to get your friend Rikk out of the coffin alive, we'll have a lucky twenty-one, eh?" He winked at them. "Until then let's get some sleep. Those pine trees should provide some shelter from the rain."

After the long, wet day and the loss of two friends, it would be good to at least have a dry night's sleep. Senn selected a pine tree on a small rise where no water would pool. Then he used a knife-edge channel of solid energy to slice off branches from a nearby tree to build up a nice shelter. The thatch of branches was dense enough that no rain would disturb him for the remainder of the night. Finally he gave it a slow roast of heat energy for a few minutes to dry off the ground and the boughs before stowing his pack and crawling in.

As he clambered inside and lit up the shelter with a bit of magical light, a wet and miserable Lani wandered up, her dark blond hair sodden and dripping. "Hey Senn." She was shivering, probably from a combination of cold and grief. "Would you mind if I join you? I ... really don't want to be alone right now."

How could he turn away a woman in need ... especially when she was the girl of his dreams? Just a few years older, without such powerful magic as Senn had, and alone in the wild. "Sure ... of course. It's warmer here ... I just made a little shelter and dried it out. We, I, that is ... it was a hard enough day. Especially for us, and . . . I just wanted to be warm and dry after all that." She kneeled down and stepped through the opening, and he closed it up behind her with spare branches. "Here, let me warm us up a bit." Despite his exhaustion, there was always a bit of magic left in Senn's arsenal to cheer up such a beautiful woman. He measured out a bit of heat magic to warm up the air around them.

Lani dropped her pack opposite Senn's and threw her arms around him, sobbing gently into the back of his neck. He returned the gesture and gave her a strong hug, trying to be of some comfort. "I'm here, Lani."

"Jarel and Rikk were all I had, ever since Rikk rescued us from the demons in Islingin. I was so young I don't even remember it. Now they're both gone!"

"I know . . . my mother's probably possessed now, just like Rikk. But hopefully my spell works so we can save Rikk, and maybe others someday too. About Jarel . . . well, we both lost him. I was really happy to have found a good friend, someone to whom I could relate and who would give me some advice, even though half the time I didn't really understand it." Lani's cheek perked up against his neck as she smiled a little through her tears.

"Yeah, he did have a strange way with words. He was always trying to remember something clever from those days back in Islingin." They stayed there for several moments, kneeling down on a blanket of pine needles, holding each other tightly and sharing their sorrow. Eventually they broke off the embrace and leaned back on their packs. "Jarel told me you had some special feelings for someone too. I'm really sorry about what happened to Namee . . . we did everything we could after seeing who those two demons were."

What could he say that wouldn't be an outright lie? He couldn't admit that he'd really been daydreaming about Lani all this time. His cheeks were getting red just at the thought. "Namee was . . . special, and I wish I'd been able to get to know her. I just have so many feelings bottled up, and . . . I don't know, I'm just unlucky." Senn looked away.

"Aww, don't talk that way." Lani leaned forward and put a hand on his knee. "You're a pretty amazing person! I mean, I'd love to be able to do *any* of the magic that you've been throwing around so easily in the last few days. I'd barely have had the physical energy to set up this little lean-to tonight, much less the power to do it with magic in five minutes! And warm it up?" She started to smile a bit more, and caught his gaze again. The glow of Senn's magical light globe highlighted the beautiful hazel color of Lani's eyes—they glistened at him like jewels. Senn caught himself staring and smiled timidly, looking down at her hand on his knee.

"I guess I have only had magic for a few moons, but you're right, I'm lucky there." How nerve-wracking. This morning he would never have expected to be alone in a private shelter with Lani. It was even more embarrassing that he was aroused despite today's horrible events.

"Damn right, you're lucky." Lani looked down, then started to blush a little herself, and took her hand off his knee. "I'm sorry. I just realized, I'm getting all close with you, maybe it's a little strange ..."

Had she noticed the lump growing in his pants? "Uhm, sorry. It's just ... well, I've never been with anyone before. Like that. I mean ... and I've been thinking about ... this girl, so much lately, and ..."

She smiled slyly. "Don't worry about it. I remember when Jarel had this one-track mind for ..." Lani began to get choked up again. She sniffled and cradled her head in her hands. "I'm sorry. Maybe I should just go, I'm such a mess."

"No, please ... it's just ..." Aah, where were the right words. "I don't want be alone tonight either, after all I've lost in the last week."

Lani wiped the tears from her face. "Alright. Then let's get these blankets set up." She smiled again as she pulled the bedroll from her pack. "Maybe you can warm them up a little?" There was that cute wink ... Senn would do anything for a woman that could make him feel that way by just moving one eyelid.

As he unrolled the bedroll from his pack, she slid her blankets over directly next to his. Senn warmed them up to dry off the remaining moisture. They lay down next to each other, and Lani snuggled her back up to his chest. "Please, hold me ..." He put his arm over her, not sure exactly where to rest it, and settled on her shoulder. How could he be so close to her and not be aroused? There ... he gave just enough distance so she couldn't feel anything, er, untoward.

Lani placed one hand on top of his and squeezed. "Thank you, Senn. You have no idea what this means to me tonight." She rolled over toward him and gave him a quick kiss on the cheek before returning to her previous position. Soon she fell asleep, although in Senn's case it took much longer. He could barely believe that the woman of his dreams was here next to him, considering the frightful affairs that had brought them together. Eventually he drifted off into a fitful sleep fraught half with nightmares and half with beautiful thoughts of Lani.

Lips pressed softly against Senn's throat, and fingers ran gently down his thigh. He was laying on his back with Lani pressed against his side. Senn could feel the swelling in his pants, which he'd left on when climbing under the blankets. Lani was looking at him with a deliberate intensity as he met her eyes. Was he dreaming again? His smile must have belied his pleasure at the thought, because her hand moved over to his crotch, caressing his member through his pants.

Senn blinked, looking around his pine bough shelter, and made a small globe of magical light. No, he was definitely awake. Lani's lips pressed against his mouth and her tongue flicked about his lips. "You've never kissed anyone before?"

"Uh, no ... but ... please don't stop." She kissed him harder, and he opened his mouth in turn, tongues meeting there in the space between their teeth. When she paused for a moment, he asked, "What is this about? I thought ..."

She laid one hand against the side of his face. "I just need to feel alive. It's so warm here, and you're so close ... with what we both lost in the last days, why not live for this moment ..." Her hand was on his chest now, unbuttoning his tunic. He sat up and pulled it off over his head, then did the same with hers. What a perfect body she had! Within another minute they had shed the rest of their clothes and were laying beside each other naked, lips locked together. What was that advice about the bird ... he slid his hand between her legs and, feeling a wet patch there, rubbed gently. "Ooh!" That must have been a good spot. Lani reached over and put her hand around his member, massaging it softly in return.

After a few minutes she slid down his body, taking him in her mouth, and licked him wetly. "Senn, are you ready?" He nodded, unable to speak. "Put it inside me." Lani moved over onto her knees, perfect arse staring up at him. "Just make sure to get the right one ... you know?"

"Oh yes ..." Senn moved up behind her. He was more than a little nervous. A few of the older boys in the clan had explained this to him. From this angle, it would be the pink flower down below. He carefully guided his member to the right spot, and slid it in.

"Wait, Senn, higher up ... it should be the ... ooh!" He pushed his member completely inside Lani, and she moaned with pleasure. "Aaah ... slowly in and out ... there ..." It was too much, and he couldn't hold on any longer. "Yes, there, come on ... oh!" Her back arched, and he exploded inside her, both of them collapsing with gasps of pleasure. After a moment they separated and lay on the blankets beside each other, breathing heavily.

"That was amazing, Lani ... is it always like this?"

She turned to him, a contented smile on her face, and laid a hand on his breast. "To tell you the truth, that was different than what I'm used to. I ... I learned that where babies come out, nothing goes in. Usually it should be ... the other place." Slowly she shook her head, eyes unfocused. "Now I'm not so sure. Maybe I should have asked for a second opinion."

"What?" That didn't make any sense. "That's ridiculous. Who told you that?"

Lani looked down, and a stray lock of hair fell across her face. "Um, Jarel. He learned it from some soldiers by the docks in Islingin." She looked Senn right in the eyes. "Do you think that's why Jarel and I could never have any babies?"

Lieh sensed the rain was starting to annoy Tamesis, who shifted constantly on the raft trying to find a comfortable position. Judging by Xipil's twisted brow, he was also not enjoying the bad weather. Either that or he'd just had a stroke—but at least he'd managed to make a facial expression.

There seemed to be news, as Shyama mentally called to them from the shore with spirit magic. —*Xipil, Tamesis. I've found where Kert and Darcy left the river, right near a fork. A battle took place about a league from there. It was only a few short hours ago. We can be there by noon. There are fresh graves, no other bodies. No dead wolf—*

The leader called back, —*Fine, wait for us by the bank where we should exit the river. You can take us to the site of the battle. If you find anything to eat along the way, that wouldn't hurt either*— Shyama growled in approval and took off into the woods. They had been going hungry the past day or so, as Kert had been carrying most of their food supplies. Hopefully Shyama would have found food for them when they finally got off this damn raft.

Because of the green wood and its tiny size, the surface of the raft barely floated above water. Between the rain falling from above and the river sloshing up from below, neither of the demons had been dry since they had heaved this miserable excuse for a watercraft into the river. As poorly as the vines were tied, Lieh was surprised it hadn't fallen apart yet.

Soon they arrived at the fork in the river, and there was Shyama signaling to them. Tamesis used magic to pull the raft to the bank, where they spotted the other raft dragged up in the mud. It was clearly better constructed than the worthless craft on which they had floated downriver. At least one thing could be said for Kert: he was a better outdoorsman than Xipil. Thankfully, Shyama had caught a hare for them. Tamesis flashed her knife and grinned. Lieh had never seen anyone quite so skilled with a blade. Within minutes the hare was frying with magic heat on a flat stone.

As they ate, Xipil laid down some ground rules for Tamesis and the big lynx. "If we find Kert, Darcy, or Dolf, we get what information we can —and then kill them. There is no point in having them around to interfere with our plans again. As for the humans, if we catch up with them we'll have to see what kind of reception we get. Maybe Tamesis' form will be of some use in capturing the boy. Of course, we should have the element of surprise. They won't be expecting us now that they've encountered those three idiots." He licked his fingers and stood up. "Now, let's move out! There's no time to waste!" Just beyond the rafts, wolf prints mixed with Shyama's lynx tracks, leaving an obvious trail to follow.

After a few short hours following Shyama, they came to the site of the battle. There were scorch marks and broken shafts everywhere, and a lot of blood slowly rinsing away in the rain. Besides that evidence, there were graves. Tamesis licked her lips in anticipation. "Should find who's buried here, Xipil? Underground? Tamesis wants to know!" She grinned and pressed a finger to her mouth.

"Absolutely. Just be discrete. After all, each of us was human once, although sometimes in your case I wonder." Xipil scrunched up one eyelid in what might have been a wink; or had a bug had flown into his eye? He turned and stalked off to examine the rest of the battlefield, littered with scorch marks, bloody bits of flesh, and the occasional arrow.

Tamesis looked sideways at the mounds of fresh earth, then called up digging scoops made of solid magic. Within minutes she had uncovered the four bodies within. A bit of air magic brought a funneled blast of wind, which blew clear the last bits of soil. Lieh saw two men she didn't recognize, but was dismayed to find that the other two were Jarel and Namee. It seemed Darcy hadn't been careful enough. Perhaps her spirit had reassociated and found a new form to possess by now. But what of the other demons? They were nowhere to be found. Maybe they had fled into the woods.

As if in answer to Lieh's question about Darcy, Xipil returned from his rounds carrying a scraggly, wet raccoon by the scruff of its neck. "Tamesis, make sure Darcy tells us *everything* we'd like to know." He tossed the raccoon roughly to the ground between them.

"Yessss . . . very good. No use to run, little one. Unless . . . want to test aim of my energy balls?" The raccoon backed away slowly, its pitiful gaze flitting back and forth between the two demons. "The bodies! Xipil can see, one was Darcy's. Others, three unknown!" Tamesis crouched down and locked her black eyes on the miserable-looking animal. "What can you tell, worthless one? Want to gain back respect you spoiled?"

The raccoon chittered nervously before Darcy finally managed to get a thought through to the two demons. —*We ran into an ambush. They must have known they were being followed! Among all three of us, we only killed three of them. There were some archers and half a dozen spellcasters, with shields, arrows, and energy balls everywhere. Kert was knocked out shortly before I took a shaft in the throat. Dolf was nearly fried when he tried to charge the boy, then he headed off toward the north. I have no idea what happened to him after that*— The animal sat up a little higher on its haunches. —*At least I took out that big warrior with the axe, the one who killed my bear form! I used up just about all the magic I could draw to roast him alive*—

Tamesis twisted her face into that evil sneer, the one that made Lieh feel sick inside. "So, Darcy likes idea to roast alive?" She gestured with her wrist, and a ring of flame leaped up from the damp leaves around the raccoon. Well, at least this time Lieh agreed with what Tamesis was doing, even if she might have chosen a more humane way to go about it. As the circle of flames slowly constricted, the smell of burning raccoon fur filled the air. The animal's cries of pain echoed through the forest, mixed with Tamesis' cackling laughter.

Eventually the morning became bright enough that Senn and Lani decided to drag themselves out of the shelter and back into a rainy reality. Senn was afire with conflicting emotions, and from Lani's aloofness as they repacked their bedrolls, she probably felt more grief than happiness at that moment. And . . . how had she not known the difference between the right and wrong place to put his manhood? Apparently misunderstandings can happen when two children grow up in a small clan without parents, then end up learning about sex together. Especially when one of them was Jarel.

The pair of them picked up their packs and left the shelter. As they weaved their way clear of the dripping trees, they could see clear sky out toward the ocean; auspicious conditions for the start of their journey. The earthy smell of damp leaves was quickly replaced by a salty sea breeze as they walked. Soon they arrived at the stony beach, where Aidan's ship rode slowly up and down on the cove's moderate swells. It was beautiful to behold, especially for Senn who had never even seen the ocean before. Waves bobbed the ship gently up and down, and softly broke against pebbles where the water met the edge of Kartus. The ocean faded into sky many leagues away, more distant than any view Senn had ever seen in the forests. He tried to gauge the size of the ship—ten men laying head-to-toe would just barely cover the length of it—about ten strides. What about those massive wooden posts sticking up from the ship, what were they for?

Aidan wandered over and clapped the awestruck pair on the back. "Amazing, isn't she? I call her *Janklo's Pride,* as she's the most beautiful achievement to come out of this region in fifteen years." He was beaming as he pointed out the features of the ship. "Two sails, very maneuverable, and look at that beautiful main-mast standing tall. See the upper deck in the stern there?"

Stern . . . that must mean the back. There was so much to learn!

"The wheel is on the upper deck behind the mizzen-mast, and below that are two small aft cabins. You two and Wildon will share one cabin, and I'll share the other with my Adepts. Let's take the longboat out and get you situated! We're just about ready to depart."

Senn looked warily at the narrow boat that would take them out to the *Pride*. It was only a stride across and three long, carrying men who were holding long handles that dipped into the water. They climbed in, and Aidan motioned for Senn to take hold of one of the free handles as he took another one. Finally the clan leader pushed the boat free from shore and said, "Alright, grab your oar and start rowing! You've got to learn a bit about oceangoing ways if you're going to survive on the water for the next moon or so." A moon was a long time, but hopefully very little of it would be spent in this tiny boat. Senn watched the others at their oars, dipping the ends in the water and pulling the boat along with the strength of their arms. It took him a little while to get the hang of it, and more than once he caught Lani giggling at his awkward movements as his oar splashed around in the water. After a few minutes he found the right motion and rhythm. It was a bit like the night before . . . but better leave that thought for another time when he was alone with Lani.

At last they reached the *Pride* and climbed up a rope ladder that hung down the side of the big ship. "Now, here we are on the main deck. The longboat sits forward on the deck there . . ." Forward must be the front; finally, a word that made sense. " . . . and down that hatchway is the berth deck, where Nic and the sailors will sleep. That's also where the supplies are kept." Senn watched a few of the sailors carrying casks and boxes below. "Now let's show you to your quarters in the port cabin. I'm on the starboard side with the Adepts. Wildon's already in your cabin arranging his belongings." They walked to the back of the ship where the upper deck stood barely a stride above the main deck. Aidan opened the rightmost of two small doors, leaned down, and poked his head into a tiny room. "Wildon, visitors for you!" He guffawed loudly. "I hope you're not bothered by small spaces, because this is the best we could do."

The ship wasn't nearly so big up close as Senn had imagined it to be from the shore. Ten strides was a lot, but most of that space was filled with coils of rope, ladders going between the decks, the longboat's cradle, the wheel, and much more that he didn't have the words for just yet.

Lani ducked inside the tiny cabin, and Senn followed her in. Even though he wasn't full grown yet, he still had to stoop down to get through the door and could barely stand up straight inside. It looked to be a little under two by two strides, and was maybe a stride tall. The right and back walls each had a small round window looking out over the water. There were two pairs of bunk beds along the left and right walls, with tiny chests for the contents of their packs at either end. The chests seemed to double as seats, as Wildon was sitting awkwardly on one of them. He greeted them with a smile that looked out of place on his pasty face. "Welcome to the most luxurious ship in all Kartus! I suppose that's not saying much, as it's likely the only ship in all Kartus. At least we're not below decks like the others." The old tutor burped and swallowed, one hand on his belly, looking more than a little sick.

Aidan looked in on them again. "Unpack your gear and relax. We're going to run up the sails and set out within the hour. After we're underway I'll show you more, but for now you three would only get in the way. If you're hungry, just give a shout and I'll have one of the sailors bring something up." He left the diminutive door open for them to observe the preparations, and stomped off across the main deck.

Senn wasn't about to be shy, as he wanted to learn whatever he could about ships. "Wildon, what are sails?" Lani cocked her head, obviously wondering the same thing.

Wildon scratched his short beard and pursed his lips. "That's right . . . neither of you from our inland clan has ever seen a boat. It's simple, really. The sails are big pieces of cloth that are aimed to catch the wind, so we can travel without expending much physical effort." That was a relief; at least it meant they wouldn't be rowing the big ship anywhere. Wildon thought for a moment and held up his finger. "An especially interesting note for you, Senn, is that powerful spellcasters can call up air magic to control or intensify the wind. This way we would never end up becalmed, stuck in an area with no wind."

It was all so confusing. "Thanks for the explanations . . . I guess we'll need more as we go." The Orb might be of help in the wind department—he had to discuss this with Talen later. It would be a lot easier to sustain a wind spell for a long period with the Orb's optimized use of magic. The wind spell he'd played with on the raft would likely be perfect for moving this sailing ship.

Out on the deck there was a lot of activity. Nic, Piet, Keegan, and Aidan's sailors were busy loading supplies, including the big demon coffin. That last piece needed the strength of several men, and just barely fit down the hatchway to the lower deck. At least it wasn't being stowed too close to Senn's bunk! He turned his attention back to the cabin, and began unpacking his belongings into the chest. For once in his life there would be no need to run from the place where he slept. Or to look at it another way, there would be nowhere to run if anything *did* go wrong.

After arranging the contents of his pack in the chest, Senn looked back to the deck. Once the loading was complete, the crew's activities turned to ropes and canvas instead. The sailors hoisted giant sheets of fabric that hung from slanted wooden poles. Soon the sails were up and filling with wind. Aidan stomped around on the deck just above their cabin, and a loud "Weigh anchor!" echoed the length of the ship.

Wildon stood up shakily and made for the door. "That means they're bringing up the anchor and rope which have been holding the ship in place. We'll be moving soon! Let's see if we can find a place to watch." Senn and Lani followed him out the door. The trio climbed up a steep and narrow ladder to the upper deck, where Aidan was giving orders. The ship was alive with activity as sailors tightened and secured ropes, and several men raised a big chunk of curved, pointy metal up on the front of the boat. That must be the anchor.

Aidan greeted them as they approached his position at the wheel. "So my friends, welcome to the first sea voyage aboard the *Janklo's Pride!* We've done a few short tests, but nothing out on the open ocean. What better time than now to start, and what better weather?" It was true. The sky was almost completely clear, with the few remaining clouds rapidly disappearing from above them. "Find a place out of the way by the rail there . . . just don't fall overboard!" Aidan laughed, full of life as he steered his boat clear of the cove on her maiden voyage.

The land slowly slipped away behind them as the ship angled into the wind. Aidan explained a bit more about sailing. "The wind's coming from the east, the same direction we want to sail toward. So we sail at an angle to the wind, going southeast, then tack to go northeast, beating a zig-zag path. I'll watch the stars and the sun to make sure we're heading in the right direction." The big man turned back to the wheel and yelled back and forth with the crew again, double checking that all the lines and sails were properly set.

After a while Wildon turned back toward the ladder, looking a little green. "Looks as if we're well under way. I'm going to . . ." Quickly he held a hand to his mouth and paused. "Yes. Going down to the main deck for a minute. Then maybe for a nap in the cabin." He made his way slowly down the steep staircase, looking as if he might lose his breakfast at any second.

Lani turned to Senn, the two of them leaning on the starboard railing and watching the land fade from view. "How's your stomach? I'm feeling fine so far . . . no seasickness for this girl yet."

He grinned. "Me neither. To be honest . . ." He glanced around, finding that they were about as alone as one could get on this ship. No one was paying them any attention; the crew were all busy with their own tasks. Senn moved closer and put his hand on her arm. "I've been thinking about last night. Lani, it was so . . ."

"Amazing." She smiled shyly, and glanced at him with a distant look in her eyes. "But here . . . Senn, I don't know what will happen, and there are so many people around constantly." She glanced away. "I'd rather not attract too much attention right now. And you know it will take a while before I can really get over what I lost when . . ." She started shaking.

Senn gave her arm a squeeze. "Well, you know I'm here whenever you need anything." They stood in awkward silence. What else could he say? And where did their relationship stand?

After some time, Aidan bellowed from the wheel. "Jann, take the helm! Steady as she goes."

A short, stocky seaman walked over and nodded, then took the wheel. "Right, steady as she goes, Captain."

Aidan approached them, eyes sparkling. "Seems you're both better off than Wildon. Apparently he doesn't take too well to the sea. I'll give him some tips later." His eyes turned to the hatch in the main deck. "Now here's the interesting question, Senn. What do we do about your friend in the demon coffin? And how long do we wait to open it?"

In the excitement of their departure, Senn had nearly forgotten about their spirit prisoners. "I suppose we need to find out if the spirits are still there, or if they've faded back to the other side." How could they possibly do that?

"What about that talisman you were mentioning, some kind of Orb? Could you use the spirit warning spell?"

Senn pondered that for a moment. —*Talen! What do you think?*—

—*It's hard to say, Senn. The spell detects traces of spirit energy nearby, and it could be that the runes on the coffin absorb all those traces. But I suspect there would be some leakage, allowing the spirit warning to tell us if the spirits are still there or not. Try resetting the spell right next to the warded box*—

"Aidan, I think it should work. Can you take us to the coffin?"

The Magus thought about it, fingering the gray beard on his chin. "Instead let's bring the coffin on deck. That way if there's any trouble, we have more space to fight the demons back into the coffin or leave them behind us in the ocean." He turned to his crew, who were now busy on deck checking over the running of the ship. "Merle, Uri! Grab a couple of men and bring my demon coffin up on deck, fore." He looked back to Senn and grinned. "Now, let's find out if we need an energy ball or a healing spell once we open the box."

They climbed down the ladder and walked forward, where several seamen were bringing the demon coffin up from below. It took four men to get it through the main hatch to the deck, where they set it down with a resounding thunk. Senn brought out the Orb and delved into the spell, which was still active. Come to think of it, there should be no risk of demons finding them out at sea. After this extraordinary use, he wouldn't need to keep the spirit warning refreshed anymore. He switched the spell off, and then reset it. The magical voice spoke in his mind.

—*You will be warned if spirits come near. Refresh this spell each day*—

That was good news. He walked slowly around the coffin, holding the Orb close to the cracks where the wood joined and the lid closed. "Nothing. The spell doesn't detect anything!"

"Excellent, then let's crack open the lid and see what's inside. Be ready for anything." Aidan looked around at the sailors and spellcasters, making sure everyone was prepared with their weapons and magic. The sailors and Adepts were all standing ready, each with hands or weapons raised nervously. Was anything alive inside the coffin? Were two spirits floating around in there, looking for hosts? Aidan touched the warded locks, sliding them open, and raised the lid a fraction. "Anything now?"

Senn held the Orb close. "Still nothing!" The big man heaved the lid open with one hand, the other held up in front of his body as protection. What greeted the party was neither a spiritual nor a physical reaction, but a stupendous, overpowering stench. "Aaagghh! Something died in there!"

Aidan quickly called up a measure of air magic, blowing the foul smell out of the casket. "That's for sure, lad." He held his hand to the wolf. "Cold. And from the sludge in the bottom of the casket, we can see this beast lost a lot of blood after we put it in here. No surprise it's dead." Next he touched Rikk's body, closing his eyes in concentration. "We're in luck, he's still alive." He reached to the eyelids, opening them one at a time and checking underneath. The irises were hazel green, no sign of the normal inky blackness that would indicate possession. A wide grin spread across his face as he looked to Senn. "It seems your idea may have worked. Now let's try to wake him up, before we risk moving him out of the coffin. Shall we?"

Senn placed his hand on Rikk's chest next to Aidan's. Through the torn and bloody tunic he could feel barely any sign of life and no breathing movements to speak of, but a slow heartbeat was still evident. "What should I do? How do we fight the poison and wake Rikk?"

"The poison is affecting his body's functions, especially in the brain. Send in earth magic to root out the poison and break it down. This is something the body can't do well on its own. Then feed the magic to his head, bringing a sense of energy and vitality." Aidan closed his eyes, and Senn could feel the earth magic flowing. He did the same, adding his own power to result in a virtual river of earth magic.

Soon Rikk's pulse quickened, and they could observe his breathing once again. After several moments his eyelids fluttered open and his pupils responded to the flood of light. He took in a huge gulp of air and tried to sit upright, grabbing the two arms pressed against his chest. "I can move! By the stars, I'm free!" He focused on Aidan, then on Senn, and glanced around at the ship. "How . . . where am I? Is this a boat?" He put a hand to his head, then laid back down. "Damn does my head hurt. And my arm . . ." There was still a mass of scabbed skin on the half-healed wound where the arrow had struck early in the previous night's battle.

Aidan gripped Rikk's left shoulder earnestly. "Welcome back to the free world, my friend! You're aboard the *Janklo's Pride,* rest assured there are no spirits here. I'm Aidan Alkar, Magus and ship's captain." Rikk nodded slowly as Aidan continued, "We look forward to hearing your story, but first you need some rest." The captain arched his eyebrows at the grizzled warrior and his pained expression. "I'll bet you could use some real sleep, not this drug-induced haze we had you in as a demon."

Rikk nodded gently. "That sounds good. I'd probably do well with a week of sleep. But I'll try to collect my thoughts and give you a good report a bit sooner than that."

The big clan leader turned to Senn. "I'll let you take care of these wounds with Lani, it'll be good practice. I'm going to check in on Wildon." The clan leader rose and stomped off toward the aft cabins, where the old magic tutor was presumably busy inventing new shades of green.

Senn hadn't had a chance to try out the healing spell in the Orb. That could be useful in situations where someone was banged up pretty badly the way Rikk was. —*Talen, I'd like to try out the healing spell*—

—*Sounds good, Senn. Just allow it to determine the extent of your friend's injuries, then apply energy and allow the Orb to do its work. The wider the energy channel you open, the faster he will heal, up to a point. Remember you are just augmenting the body's own processes, so there is a limit. The spell will only draw as much energy as it can use. Any way you look at it, your friend should be feeling a lot better by tomorrow*—

He explained to Rikk and Lani that he was going to utilize the talisman's spell, then he brought out the Orb. First he fed in some power to the right sector to activate the spell.

—*Bring the Orb close to the injured person*— Senn held the talisman next to Rikk's head. —*Several wounds found, please apply energy*— He let the magic flow through him, allowing it a wide pathway. The wounds must have been bad; there was a heavy drain as the Orb sucked in energy and funneled earth magic to Rikk. The warrior closed his eyes and let out a deep breath.

"Thanks, Senn. I feel a hair farther from the edge now, and the pain's subsided enough that I'd prefer to avoid the grave rather than embrace it." He sat up painfully, with more success than his last attempt, a smile playing around the corners of his lips. "Speaking of which, how about helping me out of this pool of decaying wolf bits?"

Lani rested a hand on one of Rikk's shoulders. "Sure, Rikk. We can move you to the fourth bed in our cabin, where you and Wildon can look after each other. He's pretty seasick. Then I'll see if I can find you some clean clothes from one of the sailors." Senn walked around to support the stocky strongman on the other side, and the two of them raised him slowly back to his feet. Lani joked, "Not bad, considering you've been unconscious for the better part of a day."

"I've been out a day, huh? Well, I guess it could have been worse." As they walked him into the cabin, Rikk exclaimed, "You know what? I just realized I'm starving. That idiot demon was so keen to find you, he hardly ate anything all day yesterday. Any chance to rustle up some grub?"

Senn chuckled. Anyone who had been stuck with an arrow, smashed with an energy ball, broadsided in the head by a sword, poisoned, and then locked in a coffin splattered with wolf guts . . . well, he must be feeling a lot better to be thinking about food. "Aidan said to ask any of the sailors if we got hungry. I'll see what we can find for you."

"Alright. Just one request . . . no dried moose or wolf, please . . . ?"

CHAPTER TWELVE

Flight of the Valkyrie

Xiuhcoatl was pleased. It had taken only about a day for Umkoome to find him a new human host, with the help of the Spirit Council Magi. Clayne let him through from the spirit world to the wooden chamber of runes, where Tynan Maltus was holding a young man in shackles. Amusing that now their roles had reversed. Many years before, Xiuhcoatl had brought Tynan's Magus form from the plains near Leikton.

"Brother Xiuhcoatl! I am happy to welcome you here, as you once did for me."

—*Excellent, Tynan. I look forward to getting back to work after this minor setback*—

The Magus nodded. "You've survived in your dangerous line of work longer than anyone expected. But sometimes fate has a way of showing you who's in charge. Take your new Adept body, for one . . . I've persuaded him he's better off hosting you than dying."

—*In that case, he may be fortunate, since I won't need him for long. I'll just be scouting out the right form for long-distance travel and surveillance, on Marek's orders*—

The spirit drifted over in front of his new host. After a moment of fear from the young Adept, Xiuhcoatl flowed inside and took control. He was a Minor Adept in his twenties, named Kenzie Merril, and was quite anxious about what would happen to him. —*No worry, young one. You've caught me in a generous mood; I have a short-lived need for you and no reason to do you harm*—

Umkoome let Tynan and Xiuhcoatl out of the chamber, giving her greetings to the hunter as he passed. Tynan was as anxious to show his hospitality as Xiuhcoatl was to return to his appointed task. "Brother, can I show you around the restored Keep? We've made great strides forward in preparing the way for Marek. You really should see the Council Chamber; it's been renovated to its former glory in keeping with Marek's wishes."

Time to see how this new form sounded ... Xiuhcoatl cleared his throat. "I'm on a tight schedule as demanded by our master, but perhaps I could spare a few moments. Just the Council Chamber, then I'll take some provisions and be on my way." As Tynan led him to the council room, Xiuhcoatl wondered briefly what his Adept form Kenzie thought about his temporary inhabitant. Surely his voice must now sound a lot more direct and confident than when this timid, fearful Minor Adept had used it himself. Fortunately, Kenzie was not jabbering incessantly inside their shared mind, as some of Xiuhcoatl's past hosts had done.

They walked up from the bowels of Islingin Keep, following several long corridors and winding staircases until they reached ground level. Sunlight filtered in through the barred windows, and they made their way from the base of the southwest tower to the spacious main courtyard. The Keep was built on a simple square plan with towers at all corners, but the southwest tower which led to the cellars was by far the tallest and most solid. Its gray stone exterior, liberally coated with bird excrement, testified to the Keep's lack of upkeep in recent years. On the north side of the courtyard was the entrance leading to the Council Chamber. They climbed several ornate, carpeted staircases until they reached a beautiful corridor ornamented with newly-cleaned weapons and shiny suits of armor.

Finally they came to the Council Chamber itself. Wide, stained oak doors opened into a majestic hall lined with dark wood paneling. The chamber's tall windows looked north over the ocean through iron-grilled bars. A long, polished mahogany table sat at the center, surrounded by a dozen chairs. It was an inspiring testament to the achievements of the civilization the spirits had sacked that the room had been restored almost perfectly to its previous state. Or perhaps it was just pompous extravagance on the part of their master, who would soon be ruling from this chamber. Marek would need some way to keep the human population in line, and what better way to do that than to appear as ruling royalty and to live among its trappings? "Tynan, some guidance from Marek: events are moving faster now. You'll only need nine chairs. On this journey I hope to fetch one last form, for Marek himself."

Tynan nodded. "Thanks for this advance information. I'm sure we'll get more detail at our next briefing with Marek in the Spirit Chamber, but we can already prepare for your return and the arrival of our final Council member." He put his hand on Xiuhcoatl's shoulder and looked him in the eyes, black glinting into inky black. "You know, you'll have an important place in our new rule. Resourceful people like yourself are hard to find."

"I'll keep that in mind." Xiuhcoatl could not help but think that what he really wanted was to explore the land in any and every beautiful body that nature could provide. Fortunately his current position allowed him to do exactly that, so he had no complaint. "Now, I'm off to find a new form for my hunt."

The Magus took his hand in a tight grip. "Take care, Xiuhcoatl. The next time I see you should be the day Marek comes across, so I hope for both our sakes we are well prepared with his Keep and his new Magus form."

High on the rocky cliffs southwest of Islingin, the morning sun was warming the rocks nicely. Xiuhcoatl found himself imagining where the best atmospheric thermals would form. He scouted for a worthy host, and it wasn't too long before he spotted the falcon scraping out her nest below a small overhang near a cliff top. The bird had nice, clean plumage, and didn't look so old as his last fateful fowl . . . this one was the way to go. The next time the falcon left its nest-in-progress, Xiuhcoatl slowly made his way closer and scrambled down a small wash of rocks toward the ledge with the scrape. The last bit of vertical distance was precarious, as he had to climb hand-over-hand down the rough face. At last he reached the ledge and hid underneath the overhang to wait for the falcon's return.

While waiting, Xiuhcoatl thought of what he would do with his current form. Kenzie Merril didn't have too much magic, and didn't seem to be any threat to Marek's plans. The man hadn't seen too much anyway, so there would be no harm in letting him survive. —*Kenzie, you should know I am grateful for your loan of this form. After I cross over to the falcon, you can have your body back*—

The young Adept answered back, —*I know it wasn't you who kidnapped me from my camp in the dead of night. No one appreciates being treated like this. But I'm thankful you're at least letting me live*—

—*You know, not all spirits are hell-bent on destroying your society. Those of us you met in the past day are actually working to restore some order to this world. Though you don't appreciate our methods, you should give us the benefit of the doubt. Soon enough, you'll see*—

After a short wait the falcon flew back to its scrape, and Xiuhcoatl reached out with his thoughts to comfort it. —*What a beautiful nest. We'll go for a hunt together, and feast on a fresh kill! Just let me in*— It wasn't difficult with such animals. Within moments he transferred to the falcon, flexing his newfound wings and feeling more alive than he had in a long time. A new task, a fresh start in a beautiful creature . . . he was ready. Xiuhcoatl took one last look at Kenzie Merril and flashed a quick thought his way. —*Good luck, young man. If someday you meet another spirit as charitable as myself, I hope you'll remember what happened today*— The falcon turned, spread its wings, and leaped off the edge of the cliff, soaring away.

Back in the air again, Xiuhcoatl surveyed his surroundings as he climbed on the thermals. He had to cross the river, then pass over Islingin. According to his information, Senn Morel and his companions were in the region of Janklo, directly on the eastern horn of Kartus. It was a journey of a bit under two hundred leagues, which should take four or five days. Xiuhcoatl would fly just inland of the coastline, because there were no good thermals over the water. Upon reaching Janklo he would turn inland. Once he arrived in the immediate area described by the spirit Kert, there should be no problem in locating his quarry—it would be easy to spot human activity from this altitude.

Below him the landscape passed by swiftly. The high ground gave way to the valley, followed by the river, then Islingin at the river's mouth. Where the city's northern boundary met the rocky coast, Islingin Keep rose up sharply, a proud monument to man's achievements against the elements. Nevertheless, Xiuhcoatl had a feeling that given enough time, nature would win all battles. After all, he could see no remnant of the civilization that had been here when he'd been alive, and his people had been quite the builders in their ancient time.

Far below him, a seagull crossed his path. The falcon's instincts kicked in, reminding him that he was hungry. Xiuhcoatl was never one to pass up a good meal or a new experience. What would this be like? His form was perhaps the fastest animal alive. He gave in to instinct, and the falcon dove down toward the hapless sea bird. At this speed, any miscalculation could mean instant death. But if the falcon hit its mark of the prey's wing, the target would be out of action and perhaps dead, while the hunter would be unhurt. The pressure increased with the speed of Xiuhcoatl's dive, and he smiled to himself in anticipation of the upcoming fresh meal.

Lieh was beginning to get worried. Shyama didn't seem to have any trouble following the trail of the large group that had left the battleground. Despite their quarry's use of a concealing spell, there had been quite a lot of people tramping through these woods, and Shyama was one of the best trackers that Lieh had ever seen. The three demons stayed close together, to have as strong a response as possible in case of another ambush. The sun had broken through the clouds, and was drying the sodden forest floor. They moved quickly; hopefully Senn and the others were prepared for another fight in short order.

After several hours on the move, they finally reached the shoreline and found something totally unexpected. The trail ended in a well-worn clearing next to a cove. There were a lot of tools and construction leavings around, but otherwise no buildings or people to be seen.

While Shyama sniffed around the clearing, Xipil surveyed the scene. He pointed to several small skiffs which were pulled up on the rocky shore. "Damn! It looks as though they may have found the only possible way to keep us from following." He shook his head and shifted his gaze to

Tamesis. "From the tools and jigs in this clearing, it's obvious someone's been building a ship here. They may have escaped with the Morel boy."

At last Lieh's spirits started to lift. This way Senn would have a chance, but the big question was: where were they going? Xipil obviously had the same thought. "There must be a clan nearby. They can't *all* have left on that ship with such short notice. If we find the remaining clansmen, they can tell us where the ship is headed."

"Yesss! Let Tamesis loose on clansmen, I find answers quickly. We have enough magic, you think Xipil?" Lieh's spirit inhabitant was getting agitated at the thought of killing again. This was quite disturbing; every time they got into a pinch Lieh ended up with blood on her hands. How long could she go on like this?

—*Xipil. I have another idea*— Shyama was done with her search of the area, and for once had some ideas to contribute. —*We saw this clan is powerful. They captured two of our kind, killed the third. No need for us to risk death. I picked up traces, maybe leading to a camp. It is well hidden, but the trail is too worn to hide it from me. I can find them. Let me observe and bring back information*—

The Adept stroked his pointy beard and considered for a moment. "Sounds good, Shyama. Your plan is much less risky than a direct assault, especially if this clan is as strong in magic as it appears. If we'd had Kert and his idiot friends as a distraction, we might have been able to take out the clan—but now we are only three." He attempted a smile, his expression looking as if someone had just served him rotten honeyed fruit. "I'm sure Lieh Morel is happy with that decision, yes?"

Aboard the *Janklo's Pride,* time moved in slow motion. Rikk was asleep on one lower bunk, with Wildon shivering and retching on the other one. Senn kept stealing glances at Lani, who smiled and blushed. They had no place to be alone on the entire ship, and Lani's desire to keep their relationship under wraps didn't help matters. They couldn't even talk about what had happened. But it was all he could think of—well, that and how long before they could be together again.

Eventually the day wore on until evening, and the warm sun on the deck tempted them to eat outdoors. Senn and Lani joined Aidan on deck, along with his Adepts Keegan and Piet, for an evening meal of crusty bread, stew, and vegetables. "Not bad, eh? Get your fill of these vegetables, lads. What fresh food we brought won't last long, and then we're eating dried rations and limes until we arrive in Hyanto." The group talked long into the night. Piet specialized in fire and ice magic, and knew all that Aidan's clan had learned so far about the magic of the demon spirits. Keegan was an expert in earth magic and its various uses, from healing to communication to speeding crop growth. She explained to Senn that the latter was invaluable for the clans as they moved often, and had to plant new fields and manipulate their harvest based on demon attacks. There would be nothing worse than having to abandon gardens right before winter, and being unable to stock up enough food to survive through the cold season.

Finally, after a long discussion about spirit magic, the conversation wound down. Senn had the distinct feeling that Keegan was flirting with him, unaware that he was already taken with someone else. Keegan was attractive in her own way, too: a short, passionate young woman with fiery red hair who constantly smiled and joked with everyone. Senn smiled back, hoping she wouldn't get the wrong idea. Eventually he and Lani retreated to their cabin, sneaking in quietly so as not to wake their injured and sick comrades. Senn bade his new amour a wistful goodnight, wishing to the stars that they could be alone with a real bed instead of sharing a four-bunk cabin.

The next morning, Rikk was up and about again. Apparently the magic that Senn had worked with the Orb had boosted his body's healing processes into overdrive. The old warrior dragged himself out of his bunk and walked stiffly out of the cabin, hassling the nearest sailor on deck for some breakfast. Soon the sailor brought a tray laden with bowls of porridge to their cabin, and even Wildon attempted to eat a bit.

Shortly thereafter Aidan knocked on their door. "Ho there, all! It seems that our sleeping beauty is just about recovered. None the worse for wear, I take it?"

Rikk shook his head slowly. "I feel as though I've lived through two lifetimes of pain in just the last week."

"Well, if you're up to it, we'd love to hear about it. Your story might help us to determine our next step." Aidan gestured wildly with his right hand, as if he were wielding a sword. "We need some ideas to devise the right weapons to fight these demons."

"Alright," Rikk began between mouthfuls of porridge. "First off . . ." he glanced apologetically at Senn, ". . . your mother is possessed by a pretty bloodthirsty spirit. Sorry." Senn winced and cradled his head in his hands. He already knew his mother was possessed, but now he had to hope she was strong enough to hold out against an obviously evil inhabitant. Rikk continued, "Also, it seems that Marek Seltin is now something of a demon leader on the other side." Senn's eyes widened at that—even in death his father was a bit off his rocker. "Marek's sent several demons over here, I think to prepare for him to cross back over to this world. There were three demons searching for Lieh, and one of them is the crazy one possessing her. It seems they knew about Senn, too." That was interesting. So, his father knew about him, and had sent minions to possess or kill him. Which one was it? Senn shivered at the thought.

Rikk regaled them with the rest of his story, giving as much detail as he could about their pursuers. He finished with the run-up to the fateful battle two days before, when Kert, Darcy, and Dolf had disobeyed Xipil's orders and pressed ahead alone.

Most interesting to Aidan, Senn, and Wildon was the interaction of the invading spirit Kert with Rikk's own soul. Aidan called in his Adepts from the other cabin to hear about those details. The lanky young Piet was anxious to learn what it was like directly from someone who'd escaped possession, while Keegan kept stealing sidelong glances at Senn. Piet took Rikk's hand and shook it firmly in greeting, and immediately started with his agitated questioning. "How did it happen in the first place? How long did it take? What did it feel like? What kind of magic . . ."

Aidan cut him off with a wave of his hand. "Let our strongman speak, already. Rikk, just start at the beginning and tell us everything you can about this demon spirit, Kert, who possessed you. If something's missing we can clarify as we go."

Rikk breathed in deeply, and slowly let it out. "Sure, I'll do my best. Well . . . at first the leader Xipil came over to my side, when I was trapped under the moose. Xipil used his magic to move it off my crushed legs. Then he turned its head around to face me, and it talked directly into my mind. I was in a lot of pain, probably dying. They were going to kill me if I didn't let this spirit in, so in the end I agreed." He paused and rubbed his forehead with his hand.

Piet took advantage of the pause. "What was this transfer like?"

Rikk looked up for a moment, thinking. "It's hard to remember, I was in so much pain. The spirit ... it flowed in through my eyes, and the moose's eyes changed from dark black to brown. After that, the moose died quickly. As for me, I was trapped by some kind of weird energy, and I couldn't control my own body. I was just along for the ride, with Kert in charge."

"So they use their spirit magic to create a cage for your soul. Interesting. What about your injuries? How fast did you heal after the spirit possessed you?"

"Oh, that's the other amazing point. My legs were hurt pretty bad, I had some broken bones and a lot of pain. Then this demon used his magic, and mixed it with mine. I don't have much, but I could feel him drawing up earth magic. Combined with whatever magic he had, I mended faster than I would with Lieh's full strength spells!"

Piet looked excited about this new information. "So spirit magic heals quickly, similar to earth magic!" Keegan paid more attention too, now that the story had entered her realm of expertise.

"Yeah, it was fast! Within a couple of minutes I was walking. It was painful for a while, but the demon ignored it and kept going."

"And this communication with the mind, how about that?"

Rikk nodded. "Uhm ... I think the demons could direct thoughts to people with their minds. Usually they just talked normally, although there were a wolf and a big cat who couldn't speak. They always used this thought projection. I don't think that just anyone could hear it, only the people or demons they wanted to. I could hear everything that Kert heard, although I couldn't talk to anyone but him. We couldn't really read each other's thoughts—but we could talk to each other mentally."

Keegan spoke up, "It sounds similar to the earth magic spell for location! That spell also targets the chosen person, and others can't detect it. This spirit magic really does seem close to earth magic."

Senn said, "Why not just use earth magic to trap these spirits when they try to possess one of us? An Adept or Magus might be able to build a cage the way the demons did, only with earth magic. Then when a demon enters through the spellcaster's eyes, it ends up trapped in a magical cage itself."

Piet bobbed his head up and down. "Fantastic! We'll have to try it out. How would that work . . . ?"

Aidan had been watching them all debate, and now had a big grin on his face. "I think we're having a good discussion here. But don't get too excited about letting a demon in. If you fail, you end up possessed. And if you succeed, you have a constant drain on your earth magic to maintain a barrier around the spirit. Then how do you get rid of it?" He looked at Senn. "This young man has a lot of ideas. His last one freed Rikk here from his possession. Maybe we can figure a way to combine these ideas to catch spirits and send them back. I can imagine trapping a spirit in this earth magic prison, then climbing in the demon coffin and forcing it out. Then it would have no physical power, and would eventually fade back. However, we should only try this kind of tactic as a last resort, because failure would be too much of a risk. Just imagine if Senn or I were to be possessed, alongside Lieh and Xipil . . . it could be bad news."

They talked a bit more about the options, but Senn was fixated on this new idea to trap a demon spirit in an earth magic prison. It seemed that the others were intrigued by it as well. A 'last resort' situation such as Aidan had mentioned was always a possibility. Hopefully Senn wouldn't be the first to try it—the consequences of failure would be dire. He just had to picture Namee throwing energy balls at his friends, and then imagine her as a high-level Magus.

Xipil's crew was not having much luck discovering what had happened to their quarry, or which direction they had gone. Shyama had found the clan's camp quickly. Lieh realized that the clansmen must not have any kind of spirit warning spell like the one in the Orb, otherwise they would have detected Shyama stealing about the camp and climbing among the trees. Although the big lynx had been spying for several days, there just wasn't much gossip around the camp.

One detail they had found out was that it was indeed Aidan Alkar's clan. This was actually quite a relief to Lieh. Aidan was a well-known and respected Magus, and Senn would be safe with him—at least insofar as that was possible in these times. Perhaps the clansmen avoided idle talk about their plans at Aidan's instruction, knowing that a demon could be lurking anywhere. The normal demons that the clans encountered usually didn't sneak about, but just attacked straight on. In this case, the clansmen had unwittingly foiled Xipil (the first demon Lieh had ever encountered who had tried anything clever).

It was morning, and Shyama had just returned from her latest patrol, prowling around between tents and huts at night to listen to whispers within families. She growled to wake them up, looking around their little campsite half a league from the cove. Relations were increasingly tense, and this morning was the worst so far.

—*Xipil, I have returned*— Their leader was just waking up from the night's sleep, as was Tamesis. He tried to arrange his pointed beard, which was sticking out to one side where he'd slept on it.

"Aah, another night of listening. What have you heard this time?"

—*Nothing useful that we didn't already know. A few people were talking about those who left on the ship. I learned a few names. Piet, Keegan, others. A few Adepts, and many crewmen. No specifics on where they went or what they are doing*—

Tamesis finally climbed out of her bedroll, bringing Lieh into the center of what was sure to become an argument. "Uselesss! What we don't know, won't find by waiting. Let Tamesis persuade!" She put her hand on the knife in her belt, fingering the handle anxiously, eager to be let off her leash once again.

—*That would be a bad idea. I have observed they have many spellcasters. Not as strong as Tamesis in Magus form. But combined, the clan is much stronger than we three*—

Once again Xipil made an expression of anger, and he would have had it almost right if it weren't for the comical sideways jut of his beard. "Damn it all! Why don't these clansmen just let it slip."

The knife slid free, and Tamesis made a gesture across her throat. "No need for clansmen to let slip. After you let Tamesis slit, survivors will tell all!"

"No. We can't attack the camp and risk that one or all of us get killed; Marek would never let us hear the end of it."

"We can find someone ... take one quietly from woods! Late at night, when no one sees. With my magic, no one hears, then ... prisoners!" She grinned wide like a madwoman. "Then let Tamesis find what they know. One hour, all secrets revealed!"

—*The clan would soon discover someone was missing. Within hours of the capture, they would be looking for the missing person. If we are quick, it might be possible. We must be wary*—

Xipil shook his head, perhaps in astonishment that the other two had agreed on something. "I didn't want to resort to violence and risk these spellcasters attacking us. However, it seems they are so tight-lipped that we'll never find out what we need to know any other way." He stroked his beard slowly, curling it back straight. "Tamesis, we'll do it tonight. You have to find someone who is alone, though—I don't want to risk alerting the clan until we have the information we want. Shyama will go with you as backup. Go after dark. We'll be ready to leave in case they follow us. Afterward, we'll need to find a secluded area by the coast to build some kind of boat, maybe a big raft with a sail. We can power it with air magic."

If Lieh had been in control of her own voice, she would have groaned. Just the thought of climbing on another makeshift raft constructed by these three landlubbers was bad enough. Then consider that they had to add a sail, propel it with magic, and chase down a *real* ship on the open seas ... a better recipe for disaster had never been concocted.

High over the coast, Xiuhcoatl homed in on his target. The journey had gone even faster than he'd hoped, with excellent weather providing good thermals. All the wildlife was out in force, providing bountiful avian prey for the falcon. In fact he wasn't sure how many different varieties of bird he'd tasted in the last few days, but each kill was a new and exciting thrill. Hopefully this form would carry him for a long time.

Eventually he found the area that Kert had described, where a tributary joined the river, and saw two rafts on shore. They must be one from Kert's crew and one from Xipil's. After a few more hours of flying, he spotted several interesting targets below. First, there was a large camp, bustling with clansmen. It seemed unlikely that Marek's son would be there, given that he was on the run from Xipil. Next he spotted a cove a few leagues from the clan, which had remnants of shipbuilding activity but no ship. Now *that* was interesting. Not far from the shipyard was an isolated camp with two bedrolls. He flew closer to get a better look. One man, one woman, and a giant cat—that must be Xipil and his companions.

Flying down into the camp, he settled on a tree limb a few strides up. —*Xipil?*— The man looked around for the source of the greeting. He was middle aged, with a strange looking beard. —*Up here*—

The man looked up, motioning to his companions. "Tamesis, Shyama! We have company!" He spread his arms and asked, "So you know my name. Can I ask how? And what is your business?"

Xiuhcoatl flexed his wings, folding them properly back into place. —*It's me, Xiuhcoatl. Marek sent me to assist you, since you've obviously had some trouble completing a simple task on your own*—

Xipil shook his head furiously. "You've no idea what you're talking about! This boy Senn Morel, Marek's son, is immensely powerful. He has found companions from a nearby clan, who killed all three of the other demons that were with us! They sailed off in a ship four or five days ago, darkness only knows where."

—*The boy bears her name? This means the mother is even more powerful than Marek? No matter. It seems she is in your power now. Is that Lieh?*—

The woman responded, "Yess! Lieh here, with Tamesis. However, Tamesis in charge!" She rubbed the handle of a long knife that was tucked into her belt.

—*That's another problem. You were supposed to keep her in control, not possess her. Marek was glowing with fury over that. Lieh, I apologize for your treatment. When an opportunity presents itself, perhaps we can remedy that. You understand we would need assurances you won't blast us all the second you have your own form again*— He knew she couldn't respond, but at least she could think about it. The crazed spirit Tamesis, however, was certainly not holding her tongue. In fact she held up her knife and gestured wildly at Xiuhcoatl. Hopefully she didn't plan to throw it.

"Baaah! Find another form, just as good, won't give up this one before!"

—*Have no fear, you won't be forced into a Medi*— He flexed his wings once more, then turned his head quickly to face the leader. One must establish the chain of command in such situations. —*Xipil, let's recount. In the attempt to bring Lieh to our side, you killed nearly her whole clan and allowed Tamesis to possess her. Then you hunted her son, after bringing several* dogs *on board to help*— The words came out as an epithet, as Xiuhcoatl remembered Kert's blabbering during their brief meeting on the other side. —*Let me tell you what happens when you work with dogs and let them off their leashes. They spoil your best laid plans every time! Without those fools, I suspect you three would have caught up to Senn Morel already, and handled the encounter more smoothly*— Xiuhcoatl paused to let that sink in, then continued.

—*This is why I always work alone. It's also how I successfully delivered the eight Magi for the Spirit Council over the past few years. Now, where have the boy and his friends run off to? And why are you sitting here in the afternoon instead of finding some way to follow them?*—

His head bowed, Xipil's demeanor was a bit humbled compared to his earlier attitude. Good, that was one step in the right direction. "You're right. It was a failure of my judgment to use those three fool spirits to aid us. The reason we haven't found the boy—well, he's joined up with Aidan Alkar, and it seems they've taken a ship out to sea, as I said. The clansmen are too tight-lipped for us to overhear anything about Alkar's plan, so we're going to torture the information out of one of them tonight."

Aidan Alkar out at sea? Interesting. Torturing innocent clansmen to obtain such trivial information as his destination? That was too much. —*You'll do no such thing. There's no need for that, I'll just find them myself. It shouldn't take long; this falcon is a marvelous creature. Just wait here, and try not to antagonize our master's wife any more than you have already. He wants her on our side. In addition, he wants Aidan Alkar as his own form: the ninth and last Magus I am to collect for the Council*—

Opening his wings, Xiuhcoatl prepared to return to the sky. —*I'll be back in a few days. I suggest you start planning how you'll follow them on the open ocean*— Xipil started to speak, but apparently thought better of it. Tamesis was stewing; it seemed she had been looking forward to questioning some clansmen in her own sadistic way. Then Xiuhcoatl noticed the lynx Shyama stretched out lazily, obviously taking less objection to his plans. Interesting . . . he'd have to remember that.

The falcon took to the air, leaving the land bound spirits behind, and made good speed back to the shipyard. Where would Senn Morel and his companions go? Were they heading north to Islingin, or south to Leikton? Neither direction made sense. For such a journey it wasn't any faster or safer by ship, and they could just walk. It certainly wouldn't justify moons spent building a boat of the size he could estimate based on the large shipyard. The boat must have been built already by Aidan Alkar, who decided it was as good a time as any to launch when Senn and company showed up with Xipil in hot pursuit.

The only possibility that made any sense was that they were headed for another land. Nafril, to the north, was a frozen wasteland. Who would want to go there and survive by eating whale fat all winter? Hyanto wasn't so far away to the east, and the weather was much more comfortable there. Perhaps that was their destination, though he had no idea why. Well, there was only one way to find out. As the shipyard passed beneath him, Xiuhcoatl caught one last thermal from the afternoon sun and spiraled high above the earth. Then he turned, and with his falcon form raced eastward over the sea toward Hyanto.

CHAPTER THIRTEEN

Gale Force

The *Janklo's Pride* had been at sea for just over a week. Senn and Lani still hadn't managed to arrange any time alone, as Wildon or Rikk had been laid up in the cabin for most of that time. At least Rikk had started practicing his swordplay on the deck with some of the other strongmen-turned-sailors. In the meantime, Senn was busy practicing his magic. He had called up a small blast of fresh, salty wind to keep them on a straighter course eastward. First he had experimented with the wind spell on his own, but now he was using the Orb's spell. It figured out all the factors to give them the optimal forward boost for the least magic energy expended.

Besides practicing spells, Senn had approached Aidan with his magical books and artifacts to find out more about them. The books were related to powerful solid and earth magics, probably the type Marek had used to open the rift that led to the other side. The spells worked on the very fabric of the physical world, creating sharp channels and forcing them through to the spirit world with earth magic. Aidan had borrowed the books to read, in order to find out more about the rift. Hopefully that would aid him in finding a way to close it permanently.

As for the magic items, Senn wanted to know how to use them. In order to avoid revealing too much to Aidan and Wildon, he asked his grandfather for help. Carrying the wooden box with him, Senn found a secluded spot on deck behind the longboat, silent except for the creaking of the lines overhead. —*Talen, what have I got here?*—

—*Ah, yes . . . I had almost forgotten about those items your mother took from Islingin. What's in there again?*—

Looking in the box, he pulled out the items one by one and held them close to the Orb. —*Two ivory-and-bloodwood rings with some kind of interwoven pattern around the edge, a bone-handled knife with a silver blade, and a pair of carved wooden bracelets*—

—*Mmm . . . very useful! The silver knife has a spell imbued so that it will burn as it cuts. If you use enough magic energy, you can do a tremendous amount of damage*—

That might be useful. —*Do you think it would slow down the healing processes of the demons compared to a normal weapon?*—

—*Absolutely. It requires a lot more earth magic to heal from a bad burn wound than from a simple cut. Next, the bracelets . . . those are for communication. They use a spell similar to the location spell that Wildon cast to find Aidan. They don't work over such a long distance, maybe up to a league away. The bracelets can be used between the two wearers to talk privately, the way we're doing right now. You and I can only do this without a powerful magic device because there's spirit magic involved on my side of the equation. The bracelets use quite a lot of earth magic to accomplish the same task, between spellcasters with no spirit magic*—

Senn grinned. —*That could come in handy in a pinch! Now, what about the rings?*—

—*Ahh, the rings*— Senn could detect a hint of a smile in Talen's voice. —*Those are the wedding bands that your grandmother and I wore. I always told Lieh they were magic, because I wanted to impress upon her the value of love in our lives. She missed the point, and took my words quite literally. After your grandmother's death I kept them on my desk as a reminder, and it seems that Lieh gathered them up in her flight*—

—*You know, it means a lot to have something from you and my grandmother. I guess there isn't much history left besides the few items people carry with them*— He gripped the rings tightly in his hand.

—*True, boy. So you keep those rings safe, and maybe someday you'll have a special woman to give one of them to. You'll know the time. Now, I'm going to unlock these magic items. If the time comes to use one of them, you tell the others you figured out a secret way past the seals, based on some stories your mother told you about me*—

—*Great! Uhm, Talen . . . would I have been able to unlock these without your help if I had tried?*—

Talen chuckled, the laughter bouncing around in the back of Senn's mind. —*No chance, boy. When it comes to locks and secrets, I'm the best!*—

As the day wore on, the wind shifted until it was coming more from the south, bringing tall, puffy clouds with it. Wildon ventured outside to chat with Aidan and Rikk, who were sitting on the upper deck. Finally, the perfect opportunity to be alone! He relaxed his artificial wind spell and found Lani, who was by the rail watching the clouds.

"Hey, the cabin's empty, we could have it all to ourselves for a bit!"

Lani turned and smiled shyly, a twinkle in her eye. "You want to . . . do that again?" Senn nodded. She rested her hand on his, glancing around at the others on deck as the wind played with her hair. "Do you think they'll stay on the upper deck with Aidan for a while?"

A gale of laughter erupted from the upper deck, probably Aidan laughing at his own jokes. The big man was definitely glad to have Wildon up and about again. "I would say so. Aidan and Wildon haven't talked much in days, with one stuck captaining and the other hunched over a bucket or the rail. We should have plenty of time for . . ." His eyes met hers, and they both turned toward the cabin. Senn raced for the door, and Lani waited a few seconds before following him inside.

Once in the cabin, Senn used solid magic to seal off the cracks around the door and windows, to keep any . . . sounds . . . from escaping. He wedged a scrap of wood under the door so no one could walk in and surprise them. Lani tugged on the back of his tunic, and then they turned to each other, tearing off pieces of clothing as if they were on fire. They fell onto one of the bottom bunks together, lips locked and hands searching busily.

"Oh, Senn, touch me here ... and there ... oh!" Lani rolled over on top of him, leaning backward and gripping him with her thighs as he searched for her flower. She was so excited that she nearly cracked her head on the upper bunk. Then their bodies were together once more, moving in a beautiful rhythm of pleasure. Senn wanted it to last forever, but of course it couldn't ... and he couldn't. At least he lasted a lot longer than he had on that rainy night by the cove. When they finally stopped, Lani had almost bitten through her lip trying to keep quiet. They collapsed next to each other, the tiny bunk barely wide enough for their bodies side-by-side.

Senn didn't know what to say, but he tried anyway. "Lani ... I feel so good here with you. It's ... well, it feels right, you know?"

She turned, and he took in her entire face, even reveling in the little wrinkles by the corners of her eyes when she smiled. "Yes ... it's fantastic this way! I never would have thought, before, when I used to do it ... well, that other way with Jarel. I'm so glad you knew about this!"

That wasn't quite the answer he'd expected. "But it's because of me, too, right? I mean ... we're so good together. Just imagine if we stopped the demons, we could live in a real house someday ..."

Lani sighed and looked away. "Yeah, that would be something. But Senn, I don't want to think so far ahead. I guess ... well, I'm still upset about what's happened in the past weeks. These ... moments ... are wonderful, and it feels amazing, helps to heal the pain. I just can't get get over what I've lost so fast. Can you understand? I need to take it slower, at least when it comes to our feelings."

That wasn't how this was supposed to go at all. But what other choice did he have? Certainly he didn't want to lose her. "Well, I suppose we can go slower on that count. Does that mean we can't ..." He paused nervously.

She smiled. "Of course we can. You're not the only one who's been thinking about this all week." Lani reached over and grabbed his thigh, rolling him up on top of her for a second round. This was turning out to be his best day on the ship so far, and it seemed that the fun was just beginning.

Eventually, Senn and Lani made their way out of the cabin, hoping that their companions on the voyage were none the wiser. At least no one had tried to open the door in the last hour, and Senn's spells had held up solidly. When they emerged onto the deck, the scene was altogether different than it had been. The distant, puffy clouds had grown into looming, black-bottomed thunderheads of the worst kind. Aidan was shouting to his men, who were bringing down the sails. The boat was starting to roll from the waves—how had they not noticed that before? Then Senn remembered . . . he probably wouldn't have heard an energy ball crashing into the cabin door during the last hour.

"Senn, up here! Help us get Wildon into the cabin!" Aidan was calling him. Wildon's seasickness was back with a vengeance, and he was white as linen. Senn scrambled to aid the others in hoisting him down from the upper deck.

The old tutor didn't look well, and turned away as he burped loudly. "Sorry, boy. Thanks for the help. I'll . . . just be laying down here until this is all over." They guided him into the cabin, where he lay on the bed and promptly reached for his bucket.

Lani poked her head in the door. "I think I'll keep Wildon company to make sure he's alright. Let me know if you need any help on deck?"

Aidan grunted. "Will do. I think it's better if you stay safely in here, anyway. I'm going to get everything tied down. There's no time to waste!"

As Senn followed Aidan back onto the deck, he noticed the winds had picked up even more just in the last few minutes. The captain's voice boomed, "Ahoy, Jann!" Up on the deck the stocky seaman waved back. "Keep her bow with the wind as much as you can, ride down the waves, but try not to slam us into any!" Jann nodded to Aidan in response, now keeping both hands on the wheel as the seas got rougher. Senn saw that the helmsman had a tether around his waist, tied off to a post—he guessed it wouldn't be good if the crewman steering the ship got dumped in the sea during the height of the storm.

At that point, the activity on deck got confusing for the non-seaman. The crew was running everywhere closing hatches, tightening lines, and stowing everything that could move. Anyone not essential was sent below decks or into the cabins, and that included Senn. He'd asked Aidan if magic could be of any help. The big man had just smiled and responded,

"Our magic is but a mote in the eye of mother nature. Even ten Magi couldn't do anything to slow a storm this powerful. Just get in there and hope for the best."

Back in the cabin, Senn watched through the portholes with Rikk and Lani, all of them now feeling a bit uneasy in the stomach. Wildon was curled up in a shivering ball on his bunk, not even daring to stand, much less to look outside. Lightning strikes in the distance grew nearer as the rain intensified, and soon Senn could barely separate each flash from the thunderclap that followed. What would happen if they were struck by a bolt of lightning? None of the others huddling around the portholes knew, and Wildon wasn't capable of speech to answer the question.

The ship was riding down the back of each wave, propelled from behind by the wind despite having her sails furled. Clearly Jann had experience at the helm from before the demons' time. Even so, the bow still slammed the water hard on occasion as they came off a wave and headed up the next one. Soon they were crouched low and holding on to the sturdy bunk posts to avoid being knocked about the cabin. How long the ship could survive this kind of beating was anybody's guess, but no one really wanted to think about that.

Before long Senn's question about lightning was answered. They heard the crackling strike and saw the flash simultaneously, and it was deafening. A few screams from the deck penetrated their door over the crashing of the waves. Senn wondered if someone had been injured and might need help. Carefully he made his way over to the door, holding on to something sturdy with at least one hand at all times. When he cracked the door open, the scene was not pretty. The mainmast had been splintered, and part of it was gone. Several small fires were burning out thanks to the wind-driven rain, so at least there was no risk of the ship burning. Two injured sailors were being carried below decks. It looked as though one was burned and the other had been hit by splinters from the exploding mast. Aidan went below as well, probably to do some earth magic healing. Senn, Lani, and Rikk huddled around Wildon to check on him, while they all hoped they'd seen the last of the lightning up close.

Hope and reality are two clearly different animals. That truth was reinforced shortly afterward, when a second lightning strike hit the mizzen-mast that ran down between the two aft cabins. If possible, the thunderclap was louder than the previous one had been. It appeared as if fire were running down the wall of their cabin for a second, and there was a strange taste in Senn's mouth. A nail had been ripped out of the ceiling, and lay smoking on the deck. Senn looked around in a daze, noticing a strange buzzing sound in his ears. Lani and Rikk were talking to him frantically, but they couldn't hear each other. Somehow, the cabin wasn't on fire and no one was hurt, perhaps because they had all been clustered around Wildon. The old man had chosen the correct bunk, on the outside wall of the ship rather than on the inner wall by the mast.

Slowly their hearing came back. Aidan crashed through the door, shouting, "Who's hurt! What do we need in here!" The captain rushed toward Wildon, the worst looking of the bunch. "Did he get hit by the blast?" As he cradled his old friend's head, Wildon opened his eyes.

"No, Aidan . . . I'm fine. Rather. Still . . ." He burped, "still seasick." He closed his eyes again, clenching his jaw as the ship pitched over another wave, forcing Aidan to grab for a bunk post.

"You're all lucky no one was hurt. In that first strike, two sailors were injured. I sent my Adepts below to tend to their wounds after I gave them a first shot of earth magic." He looked around for a moment, surveying the cabin, which looked remarkably unscathed. "Going below probably saved Piet and Keegan, because that second strike did a lot more damage to our cabin than to this one." The nail caught Aidan's eye, resting in the shallow impression it had scorched into the floor. He pointed at it and grinned. "Just imagine the energy nature has command of, to do all this on a whim. We should be thankful she doesn't take sides!"

After three days on the wing, covering a wide swath of the ocean to the east of Janklo, Xiuhcoatl encountered the remnants of a storm moving away to the north. Turbulent winds buffeted him as he got near the cool, dense clouds. He skirted a bit south to avoid the tallest thunderheads, at the same time trying not to disturb his search pattern too much. If the ship had really left at the time Xipil had told him, his falcon form should reach it soon. That was, if he were flying in the right direction, and if their ship had been built well enough to withstand the storm. That was a lot of ifs, and truth be told, he was feeling less and less optimistic about actually finding Senn Morel alive.

Then he spotted the ship. It was several leagues south of the receding weather, and had been badly damaged by the storm. Xiuhcoatl dove down for a closer look, hoping that no one would take much notice of a lone bird circling. The rush of wind in his ears as he approached the ship was thrilling, until it receded as he slowed down to get a better view. *Janklo's Pride* was stenciled on the side in neat letters, but that was the only tidy-looking element about the vessel. Both masts had been struck by lightning, resulting in severe damage. Scorched splinters of mast and scraps of sail littered the deck. That didn't bode well for a long journey. With the winds now steady out of the east, she'd be pushed back toward Kartus if her crew couldn't repair the masts.

Now, to see who was on board. There should be at least two Magi, and probably some Adepts as well. If he were going to get closer and find out any useful information, he'd have to be careful not to alert them that he was anything other than a falcon migrating home in the spring. Come to think of it, he was rather hungry. There was not a surplus of birds out at sea for him to prey upon. Maybe he could find some rats or food scraps on board; that could be his cover. Xiuhcoatl slowly winged down for a landing atop the splintered mainmast, giving him a good vantage point to see and hear what was going on below.

A big, balding man with a gray beard called out orders to the crew, who were cleaning up the deck. Near the rear cabins he saw an awkward-looking youth, a beautiful young woman, and a strongman with one scarred leg. The trio was trying to help with the cleanup, but they obviously didn't know what they were doing. Maybe they were the newcomers to the expedition; the awkward boy certainly fit the description of Senn Morel.

The strongman said loudly, "Aidan, are you sure there's nothing more we can do to help?"

On the main deck, the balding man replied. "Thanks Rikk, but we've got it under control. After we clean up we'll have to think about our next steps. It doesn't look good."

That cinched it: he'd found Aidan Alkar. He'd have to wait to overhear their plans, and would look for a meal in the meantime.

After several hours, Xiuhcoatl was nervous: a few sailors had noticed him up on the mast, but fortunately they were only curious and not suspicious. At last the conversation he was waiting for took place. Aidan Alkar gathered together a couple of Adepts and the trio of non-seamen he'd seen earlier, along with an older man who looked quite seasick. They met on the upper deck, standing around the wheel to survey the damage.

The leader, Alkar, spoke first. "Here's the short of it. We got unlucky, and that storm pounded us badly—lightning took out both masts. Normally a hit on the mast isn't too bad because we can patch it back together. However, we've lost substantial pieces of both masts, and don't have enough spare timber on board to repair all the damage. Then there are the sails, which were rolled up but still got burned. There's some fabric for patches, but we don't have a full spare set. The best we can do won't be enough to get us to Hyanto."

Now the boy looked agitated. "But what about magic? Isn't there something we can do to put the masts back in order?"

"Sorry, Senn, but magic won't help. It can't meld wood together unless you use earth magic on live trees. We can't create big timbers from thin air, and the same goes for sailcloth. The only use we'll have for magic will be to strengthen the wind, but I figure we'll end up with a third of our previous sail at best—very slow going. In those circumstances, another storm like this one could be the death of us."

The strongman interjected, "Uhm, if we can't get to Hyanto, then what should we do?"

Alkar rubbed his beard and shook his head. "Good question, Rikk. I think the only option we have left is to go back to Kartus. Probably we shouldn't land at Janklo, because of those demons that are chasing Senn. Besides, with so little sail, the current would take us southward, and we might not even make Janklo if we tried."

The strongman nodded. "So, Leikton? Or as close as we can get to it, at least. Is that what you're thinking?"

"Leikton wouldn't be a bad idea, as I know a few people in those parts. We'd have to put ashore and travel about thirty leagues inland on foot. Going south by sea we'd lose these pursuers of yours, and at least have some time to develop a plan without demons hot on our heels."

Xiuhcoatl chuckled to himself—if only they knew! Though it was good they didn't; as the only bird for leagues around, he'd be an easy target.

The boy shrugged and nodded at Alkar. "As long as we end up in Islingin, it's fine by me! That place is the root of this whole demon infestation."

That could be a problem for Xiuhcoatl. He was supposed to bring Aidan Alkar and the boy to Islingin, but they shouldn't arrive with a whole pack of Adepts and strongmen out for vengeance. No, Xiuhcoatl must subdue the boy and persuade him of his father's cause, and possess Alkar himself. At least he would have plenty of time to arrange that as he followed their progress to the southeastern coast of Kartus. His first order of business would be to rendezvous with Xipil and get his group moving southward toward Leikton. They would need a lot longer to arrive there on foot than their quarry would take by sea. At least with Xiuhcoatl's aerial observations they would know exactly where to intercept Alkar's party.

The group below was starting to break up, preparing their repair strategy. Had the boy just looked at him? He thought so, but it wasn't unheard of to see a migrating bird at sea. He stretched his wings cautiously and looked back toward the western horizon. Less than two days of straight-line flight and he'd reach Xipil. Wait, there on the deck ... he spotted a rat scrambling along the fore decking. Normally the falcon didn't go for that kind of game, but this was an exceptional situation. There was definitely time for a meal before he started back to shore. With a few well-timed wing beats and a short dive, the falcon snatched up its prey unawares. The animal's neck was broken in seconds, and as its soul departed, the raptor carried its remains skyward for a meal in flight.

As he returned to the open sky, Xiuhcoatl beat his wings powerfully to gain altitude, his heart beating faster from both the effort and the excitement. What would he do after this whole business was through? Should he take on more tasks for Marek? Or strike out on his own, perhaps to another land? It would depend on what happened with the party on that ship. It wasn't likely they would cause enough trouble to spoil Marek's plans, was it?

Less than two days later, just as dawn was breaking over the forest, Xiuh-coatl reached the shipbuilding cove and returned to the clearing where Xipil had made camp. The lynx Shyama was nowhere to be seen, and Tamesis was squared off with Xipil across their small fire pit. Had she been sulking the whole time about her torture plan being canceled? That woman was one he'd have to keep an eye on.

The pair looked up as he landed on a nearby tree limb. Anger radiated from Tamesis as if she were burning with it. Xipil looked less combative, although it was hard to tell much from his stony expression. The leader of the trio broke the silence first. "Welcome back, Xiuhcoatl! Have you found them by wing? A tiny ship on the wide ocean?"

—*Greetings. I take it by your tone you don't have much faith. Believe it or not, using deductive reasoning and my own unique skill set, yes, I've found them*—

Xipil let out a gasp, and his face went from stony-neutral to a mask of livid horror. Obviously the man was having trouble getting accustomed to human responses after so long in the spirit world. "You found them? Where are they, and did you ascertain where they are headed?"

—*They were headed for Hyanto, as I expected*— Xiuhcoatl told his comrades about the storm and Alkar's new plan to meet up with friends near Leikton, then flexed his wings and cocked his head from side to side. —*I think they may be in for a surprise, though. One of the strongest Magi in the area disappeared without a trace several years back, thanks to some of my earliest work here. You know him as Tynan Maltus now*—

Hopefully that would spark a little more respect from his sarcastic associate. Xipil nodded, "The first member of the Spirit Council. Yes, that's something." He looked back to Xiuhcoatl. "Well then, I suppose our next move would be to journey to Leikton, would it not?"

—*Yes. I'll fly out every few days and check on Alkar's progress. I may not make it back more than once a week to inform you on their location, but rest assured, you will hear from me. Meanwhile we should find another form for Tamesis, and free our Master's dear Lieh Morel. That is, if she promises to behave*— He hoped Lieh was paying attention on that count. It would be a shame to have to hunt her down again; at least Xipil had managed to do that much. He did have a few redeeming qualities to offset his defiance and his dreadful facial expressions.

Tamesis finally spoke, spitting words as if they were acid. "Leikton, very far. By road three hundred leagues! Six weeks on foot, not so pleasant, you know."

—*That is true, but I can arrive there in only three or four days. Your problem is merely a limitation of your form. I suggest you look for some horses if you want to cut the journey in half. By my estimate, Senn and Aidan's party will be at Leikton in four weeks*—

Xipil said, "My dear Xiuhcoatl. You must have seen from the air just how few horses there are in these parts. They require far too much effort for these wanderers to maintain, and leave too obvious a trail for them to disguise. Therefore the clansmen don't have any horses. So we couldn't even steal them if we wanted to." The trio's leader was still trying to assert some shred of authority.

—*Well then, you two and your cat had better get walking, wouldn't you say?*—

Chapter 14
Parting Ways

Senn was beginning to long for landfall. His only experience outside the normal routine of shipboard life had been in the aftermath of the storm, when a migrating falcon had perched on the broken mast. In fact it had carried a rat away when it took off toward shore. He had thought that falcons mostly ate other birds, but it seemed this one was an exception. Ever since then, it had been a week of monotony.

The storm cleanup in particular had been a huge and tedious chore: the sailors had to manually fasten together the remaining pieces of the masts, after Senn and the other spellcasters had carved out interlocking joints using solid energy channels. Then the whole crew had taken turns patching up the holes in the sails, after having cut them down to a size that would fit on the pitifully shortened masts they'd reconstructed. Aidan had remarked halfway through the endeavor, "There's one lesson I've learned from all this. The next time I head out to sea, I'll bring a load of spare timbers and an extra set of sails!"

Besides these chores, Senn had spent time with Talen talking about the remaining spells in the Orb. Now almost all the spells were unlocked. There was a wall of fire, several air magic spells, and many solid magic spells—some of which could create sound as a weapon or a distraction. A blast of solid energy balls would be useful for offense, while for defense, the spellcaster could attach a magical shield to a strongman to deflect energy attacks or real weapons. The final spell Talen described was an interesting one that created a solid energy prison in the shape of a sphere to trap one's target. Due to the inherent strength of a sphere, this prison could contain almost any type of magical attack.

Senn wanted to learn more about these spells, to be able to cast them on his own without needing the Orb. Unfortunately the storm had knocked Wildon a step backward in his recovery from seasickness. The magic tutor currently spent a great deal of time staring at the horizon and vomiting over the rails. So Aidan had agreed to teach Senn about the more advanced spells that were imbued in the Orb.

The two of them met on the upper deck, sitting near Jann, who was at the helm enjoying the warm and sunny weather.

"So, my boy, up for our magic lesson?" Aidan was in good spirits as usual, not letting the comically short masts and miniature sails of the *Janklo's Pride* detract from his mood.

"Absolutely. I've been waiting for it all day, actually. You know, it's pretty boring at sea." He fiddled with the Orb, turning it over in his hands and running his fingers over the different sections like a peeled orange.

"That's true. You've got to make your own entertainment. The first sea voyage I was on, I learned more games with cards and dice than I would have thought existed. But we didn't have any women aboard! You're the lucky young one on this voyage."

"Hmm, that's true." Did Aidan suspect anything? Senn had 'made a bit of his own entertainment' with Lani lately—the few times they'd found a free hour to lock themselves in the cabin alone. That required quite some planning to make sure Rikk and Wildon were both occupied elsewhere. Senn was still getting signals from Keegan as well, although not as pronounced as before—had she heard anything from the cabin next door? He wasn't quite sure what to do about her, since Lani was adamant that they keep their romance secret.

Aidan cracked his knuckles and asked, "Well then, what do you need me to explain there in your magic Orb?"

Senn shook off his thoughts of young women. He closed his eyes and felt each spell in turn. "There are the fire wall, the air blast, and those sound related spells I told you about."

Aidan pursed his lips and thought for a moment. "Alright. Let's start with the fire wall. That one's easy to practice here." Senn was puzzled by that, furrowing his brows. But Aidan just pointed at the ocean. "Don't look so surprised, just glance around you. We're surrounded by the perfect practice ground for fire-based spells." Suddenly it all made sense. He could cast the spell over water, with no worry about burning up a forest or anything else important.

The smiling Magus scratched his sunburned pate and continued, "So, you ask, how does a wall of fire work? It's simple, really. Think of an energy ball: it has a thin closed matrix of solid energy containing the heat energy. For the fire wall, you're making a narrow, *open* matrix to contain your heat energy. Sort of like a long, shallow ditch dug in the dirt. Route the magic there with a closed channel, and when it reaches the open ditch, pump up the heat energy flow until it ignites in flames. Then you just have to keep feeding in energy at a steady rate. Let me warn you, this is not a spell for the faint-hearted. You'll need to draw a lot of energy, and even you or I will tire fast from such magic. Now, try it out there on the starboard side downwind of us, far from the ship."

It seemed simple enough. Senn created the matrix, opened channels to it, and poured in the heat energy. At first there were just a few tiny flickers above the waves like the flames of a campfire, so he turned up the power until he could feel the magic flowing through him freely. Now the flames sprang up a full stride tall, causing alarm from several crew members who were leaning on the main deck rail. As Senn glanced toward them, his matrix dropped beneath the crest of a swell and the whole spell fizzled out in an explosion of steam.

Aidan burst out in laughter, "Ah-hahaha! We've found one drawback to practicing in the ocean. I think you've got that spell down, you can fine tune it at your leisure. What's next? Blast of wind?" Senn nodded. "That's an interesting one. You've already brought up gusts of wind, and made a constant breeze to speed up the ship. How would you make a stronger gust?"

Senn scratched his head and thought. "You don't just add more power?"

"Nope. That would take a *lot* more power to get the response you want, and would be as difficult as lifting a hundred-stone weight with your own two arms. A much more efficient way to do it is to build a funnel-shaped channel that directs the wind to a smaller point, while increasing its speed at the same time. See if you can blow this wood scrap from the top of the mast." Aidan levitated a chunk of wood leftover from the wreckage and perched it atop the mizzenmast several strides up.

Senn's first attempt didn't do much, as he didn't use enough wind. Then he found the mouth of his funnel was too far away from the top of the mast. Finally on the third try, Senn got the right combination of funnel design and air magic, blasting the scrap of wood clean out into the ocean. "Alright! That'll be helpful in a fight."

"Especially if your opponent is levitating." Aidan winked. "You'd be surprised how often I've used that. Plenty of demon animals attack from the trees, and once we had a possessed Adept sneak into camp to attack us by levitating from above."

"Thanks, I'll have to remember that. I guess if you knock someone out of the air you're using gravity to do the damage, and not using so much magic energy." The big Magus inclined his head in agreement. "So what about the last spells, those related to sound?"

"Ah, yes. Those are the tricky ones. Well, sound travels in air, so you'd expect to use air magic to generate sound. But that's not the case, because it takes too much power to move the air back and forth fast enough to make a sound. What you do is use a plate of solid energy, and vibrate it back and forth at the right speed to create the sound. This is difficult, because you have to link the vibrations very closely to your mind, imagining the correct speed. Especially in the beginning, you will have to speak out loud and link the plate to your voice. Try it." Aidan pointed to a spot opposite Jann a few strides away. When he spoke, the sound was coming from there . . . "Like this. My throat isn't really making any sound, but I'm imagining my own voice, and linking the moving plate to it."

Jann turned to the pair with his brows arched. "Damn cap'n, is that why I could always hear ya on deck, even in the middle of that storm?"

"No, Jann, I've just got a loud mouth. Although, now that you mention it, that's a good idea if we get in trouble with the weather again." He gestured for Senn to try out the spell.

This time he had no luck, no matter how hard he tried. He could get clicks and a few random tones to come from his plate of solid energy, but nothing more. "Aidan, I just can't seem to do it." This was frustrating—it was the first time he hadn't been able to figure out a spell.

Aidan grunted. "Hrm. Well, there's always something that's tough for a spellcaster to learn, even a talented Magus. Keep at it in your spare time, that one really takes a lot of work. You can practice with the Orb's spell and attempt to duplicate it, after feeling where and how the magic flows, you see?"

Senn nodded in disappointment. "Alright, I'll do that. Thanks for the lesson!"

"No problem, that's why I'm here. In my clan I give all the advanced lessons, and I can tell you, it's a pleasure to have such a talented student. I just hope that after all this, you put your magic to good use. Don't abuse it."

What did that mean? Did Aidan know about Marek's failed experiments that had caused the rift between the worlds?

"One other thing, Senn. I've been reading those magic books of yours, and they describe arcane methods to reach the spirit world from this one. However, after studying them, I can't deduce any way to re-seal the rift. I think our best chance is to gain control of this tear, and to prevent any other demons that come through from finding a host." He stood and clapped Senn on the shoulder. "I'm off to make my rounds. If you need some help with that last spell, try asking Keegan for some suggestions. She mastered it early on in her studies." Aidan headed down from the upper deck, giving Jann a friendly salute on the way by.

Senn was left with a head full of thoughts about his father, and wondered who might know what details about him. Then there was his first real failure at casting a magical spell; his inability to make sounds at a distance. And there was Keegan . . . how could he ask her about that voice spell without making a fool of himself, after all her advances? It was probably easier to avoid her; after all, he could just use the spell in the Orb if he needed to throw his voice. He stood up, and decided instead to see what

Lani was up to. She'd be able to put him in a better mood, especially if they could sneak into the cabin for some time alone.

Walking. All they had been doing for days was walking. And, of course, arguing. Lieh was sick to death of the constant squabbling within Xipil's band of demons, but at the same time, she was glad for anything that might bring them a step closer to failure. Her thoughts on Marek had turned from sour to rancid, after seeing the types he employed. The falcon, Xiuhcoatl, was the most intelligent of them all—but he still treated his supposed comrades with little to no respect. Had Lieh herself behaved that poorly in recent years, when she was trying to live up to Marek's standards?

It was nearing nightfall when Shyama bounded out of the woods, carrying a few hares limply between her jaws. —*Xipil. Here's your supper. I'll eat mine as-is. I assume you want a fire*—

"Ah. Thank you. Tamesis, let's set up camp here for the night. I think we've come a good six or seven leagues, and it wouldn't be wise to push much more than that. Can you please arrange a fire?"

Tamesis hissed, reminding Lieh once again of the misuse her voice and body had been put through in the last few weeks. "Of coursse, Xipil. Anything you like, your servant Tamesis does. Much like Xipil, now servant of Marek's pet bird, isn't it!"

"That's enough! I've heard enough of your complaining today! Just because you don't like Xiuhcoatl's methods doesn't mean we can ignore the requests he delivers from Marek."

"But Xipil. You roll over, play nice, so much different from following orders. Days lost, could have learned more, faster, using blade! Marek wants not to waste time. Only weak human-loving bird said to spare clansmen." Tamesis had gathered logs together, using no tinder and making a pile of wood far bigger than that needed to cook two hares. She had been taking out her frustrations by finding new, interesting ways to irritate Xipil. If Lieh was right, tonight would be no exception. At least this was amusing, a bright spot in her otherwise dreary days.

Xipil was cleaning the hares and preparing them for roasting. He tried to contain Tamesis' methods where he could, in this case by doing the butchering himself. "Xiuhcoatl is obviously in a better position than we are at the moment. Remember why Marek chose each of us! I'm the expert in politics, and you're the blunt instrument. That's the reason I'm in charge here, Tamesis."

Shyama looked up from her own meal, the hare almost devoured already. —*Maybe Marek made a poor choice in leaders. Think if he had another Xiuhcoatl. More clever and more kind. Lieh would be on our side instead of being our prisoner. Marek wants to rule these humans, not destroy them. So he needs their respect. You two have no intent or ability to gain it—*

Now the hares were prepared, trussed up on stakes that would hold them over the fire. Xipil handed them off to Tamesis. "Their respect? Shyama, do you really think these people are going to willingly follow Marek after the hell they've been put through by our kind? No, the only way is to rule with an iron fist. That's why Tamesis and I will be so important in maintaining the peace after the Spirit Council takes over."

—*And has Marek explained this to you? I think not, he just gave you a simple task. The same as all the rest. None of us knows his plans in detail. Perhaps not even the Spirit Council. One point is certain: Xiuhcoatl is more trusted than you. Maybe his methods are better—*

"Irrelevant. Marek's plan has to account for the facts, and I say there's no way to persuade the humans to follow willingly. We could ask Lieh what she thinks if you don't agree."

Tamesis was clearly tiring of this esoteric argument. She buried the stakes in the dirt, hares leaning over the tall stack of boughs she had piled for the fire. "Lieh stays inside, no talking today. We go south, yess? Capture Senn Morel, possess Aidan Alkar, bring all to Master. Glory us all! Next task, maybe Tamesis goes alone. More blood, blade, fire! Less talk!" With that she started on the spell to light the fire. Lieh saw where this was going, and smiled inside. There was a shallow matrix, a bowl underneath the fire. Tamesis filled it with heat energy, then opened the floodgates wide. A column of fire two strides tall burst forth among the stacked logs, instantly charring the hares to a blackened crisp and sending a plume of sparks high into the treetops.

A life on the open ocean was not one that Senn relished, for time passed too slowly. With the repaired masts, it was too dangerous to fill the sails with magical wind for fear the creaking timbers would snap. That meant the ship had traveled at a crawl for the last three weeks while Senn honed his magic skills. Now he could cast all the unlocked spells in the Orb by himself with the exception of the sound-related ones. So far, he had avoided approaching Keegan to ask her advice about those spells, somehow unable to summon the courage.

His relationship with Lani was stagnating as well. She still wouldn't share any deep secrets or put an arm around him at the ship's rail. Now a chance presented itself for Senn to ask her thoughts. Lani was sitting alone on the fore deck trying her hand at fishing, something they had learned from Jann. Senn approached and sat down beside her, provoking that amazing shy grin. "Hey there Senn, how's the magic practice going? I haven't seen any whirlwinds or geysers of flame shooting from the waters today."

"Very funny. Honestly, I've just been thinking a lot today, feeling a little strange about us." Would she come around and show more interest with time? He looked down at his bare feet, uncertain how to phrase the question.

Lani's face took a darker cast, as though a shadow had come over her thoughts as well. "Thinking? Me too. What . . . where are your thoughts headed?"

"I'm not sure. I just, well, don't know what to feel about it all. We should be sharing more, you know? And let everyone know about us. I mean, they're bound to find out eventually, right? Even if it's just by accident?"

Now it was Lani's turn to look at her bare toes. "Senn, I'm sorry. Maybe . . . could be it wasn't such a good idea, all this. I think I'm still not over my past, and . . ." She briefly flicked her eyes at his, a short, guilty glance. "I can't stop thinking about Jarel. He really meant everything to me, and it was a mistake to think I could ever replace him. Maybe it isn't our fate to be together, you and I."

A chill raced through Senn as his heart started beating faster. "You mean . . . this is nothing, what's going on between us?" He didn't know how he was supposed to feel, but it definitely wasn't pleasant.

"Well ... no, it's not *nothing*, please don't think *that* ... it's just ..."
She sighed. "I should never have come to you the way I did. We had both
lost someone special, and I thought we could both take comfort somehow." She looked at him with her eyes wide, "I really didn't mean for you
to fall for me."

A cold feeling had settled in Senn's stomach. He couldn't think of anything that would change Lani's mind. She really wasn't interested in *him*,
only in a comforting shoulder on which to wipe away her tears. "So that's
all? It's over between us, because you mean too much to me?"

At least she looked him in the eye, her chin quivering a little as she
said it. "Yes. I'm sorry ... I didn't expect ..."

Senn didn't want to listen to anything more. He stood up and walked
away, wanting to get as far away from her as he could. Unfortunately on
this ship, that meant about ten strides away on the upper deck. He leaned
against the stern rail, tears coming to his eyes. All this time, he'd thought
there was something special between him and Lani. Especially the way she
reacted to his touch ... but he didn't want to think about that. It was all
over, gone forever, his fantasies and dreams for their future.

Lani was always talking about fate. Maybe *this* was meant to be, maybe
this was the price fate had made him pay for thinking about his friend
Jarel's girl. No matter—Senn wasn't sure he believed in fate, anyway. He
would have to make his own luck the next time, although that thought
didn't comfort him much now. Hot tears rolled silently down his cheeks.
Was Lani really worth all this pain? She was the first woman he'd ever
been with, but his circle of acquaintances *was* rather limited. Senn could
count the eligible women in his former clan on one hand. He looked starboard to the horizon, glowing red-orange where the sun was just starting
to go down.

Wait a minute. There, where the sun was shining off the horizon.
What was that? He wiped the tears away. "Jann! Look there ..." He
caught the attention of the helmsman and pointed. "Could that be land?"

"Let's take a look." Jann pulled a long tube from the pocket of his
tunic and sighted off to the right of the setting sun. "Aye, lad, good eyes.
Run below an' fetch the cap'n, he's taking stock of our stores." The sailor
cupped his hands and shouted the length of the ship, "Land ahoy! All
hands, land ahoy!"

Now there was a reason to put his worries behind him, at least for today. They would soon be on solid ground again. Wildon would be ecstatic! Senn raced down the ladder to the main deck on his way to the hatch below.

As he ran, he noticed a familiar shape perched atop the mainmast— was that the same falcon? It was looking at him, and immediately turned its head toward the sunset. Why would it be back? If the bird was migrating, it could have flown the length of Kartus twice since Senn had last seen it . . . maybe it was a different falcon?

Xiuhcoatl primed his wings nervously as he noticed the boy looking at him. Quickly the falcon cocked its head around toward the sunset and the approaching coast. He was surprised it had taken so long for the humans to notice landfall, but then again they didn't exactly have his sight. Besides that, they were a bit nervous about climbing up their jury-rigged, albeit short, mainmast. At least that made his spying perch a bit safer.

Beneath him, Aidan Alkar came up on deck, followed by a steady flow of crewmen who were eager to spot the first land they'd seen in weeks. They passed around a spyglass and cheered amongst themselves, as the helmsman steered the ship directly toward shore. After an hour or so, they were close enough to see the flat plains of the southern savannas, dotted with occasional oases of trees.

Aidan gathered several of the crew around, including a few Adepts and Senn Morel's group. Xiuhcoatl listened closely to find out the details of their plan. "Judging from the terrain we're still a bit north of Leikton. We can't be too far away, as we've already left the forests behind. Now, I have a map that shows a nice cove to the east of Leikton. We should be able to reach it with a day or two of sailing down the coast. We'll leave the ship in the cove and hike to meet my friends in Leikton." He looked around, noting no objections from anyone.

"Furthermore, I don't plan to give up my ship so easily. Most of the sailors will stay on board, under Jann's leadership." The stocky helmsman nodded. "You and the crew will be responsible for building new masts and repairing the rest of the damage to the *Janklo's Pride*. We'll try to send more fabric back for sails, if they can spare any at Leikton. After that we'll have to see what happens. Maybe we can rustle up some horses and ride north to Islingin. I don't want to chance another storm at sea right now, and it's a long way to Hyanto."

That was enough for Xiuhcoatl. He knew where the party would be heading when they arrived on shore, and their likely plan after making contact with the clans near Leikton. Besides, he had to make sure Xipil and his company were still on track to get to the savanna in one piece. Their bickering had been so bad the last time he'd checked in that he was halfway expecting one of the trio to be dead upon his return, most likely Xipil. The falcon looked skyward and started beating its wings; Xiuhcoatl took to the air once more, leaving the ship and its occupants far behind.

After a day and a half of flight, Xiuhcoatl spotted his comrades from the air. They were near a cutoff from the road where a small trail headed south into the forest. As he settled down on a nearby tree limb, he heard the familiar sounds of an argument brewing between Tamesis and Xipil. This one sounded as if it were going to be good.

"Damn it, you crazy bitch. We are not taking some unknown path into the woods. If we get lost or the trail fades away and we have to bush-whack, we'll lose time. It's much better to stay on the road."

Tamesis gestured with her knife. "Main road goes far west, then south-east. Waste much time! Follow this trail, clear our path with magic, much faster!" Were they arguing over a shortcut?

Shyama growled at the pair, interrupting their angry staring contest. She was right below the tree where Xiuhcoatl had settled. How had she gotten there without him hearing? —*Both of you, stop your fighting. This is pointless, you gain nothing. Anyway, Xiuhcoatl is back*— They glanced around for a moment, then finally saw him in the tree above Shyama. —*Why don't you ask him. He could tell you what the trail looks like from above*—

Xipil walked a few steps closer and looked up into the tree. "Ahh, returned already from another trip over the water. So, my feathered friend, what news from the skies? Should we stick to the road?"

—*Greetings, Xipil. I would recommend taking the trail. It follows a direct path south, and as it's visible from the air for quite some way, it should be relatively clear. You might save three or four days' walking that way*—

For once it was Tamesis' turn to gloat. She bared her teeth and cackled loudly. "See, Xipil? Shyama not only one, who knows outdoors."

Embarrassed, Xipil put on a magnanimous air, probably trying to impress Xiuhcoatl. "Fine. We'll take the path. With this additional information, it's clear that your choice is better." Despite his soft words, his face didn't match and looked more like the expression of someone who had just eaten rancid meat. "What other news have you brought from shipboard?"

—*They have sighted land*— Xiuhcoatl related Aidan's plan to find his friends. —*Since you can't beat them to Leikton, I propose to prepare an ambush farther north at the edge of the forest, where the trees give way to the plains. Capture them as they depart from Leikton. I warn you, they may be ahorse. If it seems that they might go by ship, I'll find a way to delay them. Regardless, I should have Alkar by then, leaving you only the boy and some assorted Adepts to deal with*—

"What do you mean, 'only the boy?' He's remarkably strong! Perhaps you can use Aidan's Magus form to help us capture them. That would guarantee success instead of just giving us a good chance. Surely Marek would rather have his wife and boy as well, not just his new form?"

Xiuhcoatl considered for a moment. For once Xipil had suggested a worthwhile idea. —*Excellent, then we shall meet back at the ambush point after I have taken Alkar. You should head there with all haste, as we will need thorough preparations. I'll keep my eyes open for a new form for Tamesis as well, in case Lieh Morel is willing to work with us. We'll talk about that on my return*—

"Marvelous!" Xipil was stone-faced, but confidence radiated in his voice. "Then we will await your return on the road where the forest meets the plain." Xiuhcoatl was anxious to escape from this tension before Tamesis could chime in again about losing her powerful Magus form. Even in an Adept form, she would provide enough muscle to aid in capturing Senn. With a few quick wing beats the falcon was aloft once more.

—*Xiuhcoatl*— A last farewell, oddly enough from Shyama. —*Be safe. Do what is right*— He wasn't sure, but it seemed that the big cat was worried about him.

He directed a last thought at the lynx as well, for her ears only. —*The same to you, my friend. Keep these two in line, and we shall meet again soon*— With that, he winged his way aloft to find Senn's party, and his next target: Aidan Alkar.

At long last, here it was—land! They were only a bow's shot away, five minutes by longboat from those golden plains glowing in the noonday sun. Senn waited anxiously with his companions and the boat's crew on the main deck, as Aidan prepared to address the crowd from the upper deck. There was a buzz of low conversation running through the assembled crewmen as they anticipated the end of this ill-fated leg of the voyage. Aidan's trusted helmsman Jann stood by on the upper deck.

"All hands, listen up! Jann is in charge of repairing the ship and captaining the return journey. Four weeks from now you sail back to Janklo. Don't wait any longer, as we're planning to travel by horse to Islingin."

Aidan glanced around at the worried stares and grinned. "Look, men. We're going to have two Magi, three Adepts, and several strongmen with us. And we're meeting friends in Leikton . . . so we'll be fine. Just take care of the ship and my demon coffin. Now, make ready the longboat and let's get our feet on solid ground!" A few cheers went up at that remark.

He motioned to Jann, who came forward for a few words. "Men, let's give a cheer for our cap'n and chief, for bringin' us all through alive! Including one that was possessed, and lives free again!" There was a much bigger cheer that time. Senn saw that even the two men injured in the lightning strike were cheering, now almost completely healed. On that high note, Aidan and Jann stepped back, and the crew moved to prepare the longboat.

Senn saw Aidan pull Jann aside, and he worked a quick spell to hear what they were saying at a distance—the same spell he had used when they had ambushed the possessed Rikk and Namee. "I've no idea what'll happen on this leg of the expedition. This is a large group to be traveling across the whole of Kartus, even by horse. I expect we may attract the wrong kind of attention. At the end of our journey we're going after the source of this demon scourge, which won't be easy to root out. If we're not back by midsummer, you and the clan must organize an expedition to Hyanto. Carry on without me, you hear?"

Jann inclined his head. "I don't like it, Aidan. But I suppose you're right. The ship and our survival is more important."

The clan leader clapped him on the shoulder. "Right. Think of it this way: if we don't succeed, it means Marek's plans, whatever they are, will be moving ahead full steam. If that happens, you'd better warn those in Hyanto of what's coming, if it's not there already."

"Aye aye, sir." The two shook hands and Aidan climbed down the ladder to retrieve his pack from the cabin. Senn furtively released his spell, then made his way to the neighboring cabin to pick up his own pack. He had been ready to disembark since early morning. As he entered the cabin, Rikk was on his way out, pack in hand. Inside, Lani avoided eye contact as was usual nowadays. Wildon looked more sprightly than he had in weeks.

"So my boy, what do you think? Are you ready to disembark this floating heap of timbers? I'm anxious to be done with my first, and hopefully last, sea voyage."

"It's been interesting, Wildon. I think I really enjoyed it, despite the storm, and . . ." What else could he say? His favorite moments of the journey were in the past, they were based on a woman's lie, and he longed to forget them. "I learned a lot from Aidan about magic. He says I'm progressing fast in all the disciplines. Plus I can use most of the spells in the Orb now, as well as cast them unaided."

Wildon raised his bushy eyebrows. "Nice work. Accomplishing that would have been hard to do while on the trail. It's much easier to study and learn magic when you have hours at a time to concentrate." He stood up and hefted his pack. "Well, I'm off to the longboat. I never would have thought I'd be so glad to get back on the trail. Maybe soon I'll be able to think about food without turning green." He headed out the door, leaving Senn alone with Lani.

As Senn was about to lift his own pack, Lani finally broke the silence. "Senn ... I'm sorry, again. But thank you for keeping ... what happened ... a secret. I don't want to cause any more tension than necessary, you know?"

Huh. He didn't want to be mean, but this didn't seem fair. "Right. You mean, you don't want everyone else in the group to look down on you for using me." Lani turned away, looking guilty, and Senn knew he was right. "Don't worry. I won't tell the others." He sighed, knowing she must have had her reasons. "With what happened to Jarel, I guess I can understand needing comfort, somehow. Just give me some space, alright? I don't want to be reminded about this all the time . . ." He was still so attracted to her, even as annoyed as he was. Maybe it was just her body that set him off?

Lani stood up, tears in the corners of her eyes. "Thanks. I really appreciate it." She threw her arms around him, burying her chin in his shoulder and dripping tears down his neck. He awkwardly put his arms around her back to return the hug. Why did she feel the need . . . oh well. Senn gave in to the sorrowful embrace, trying not to be aroused by the closeness of this woman for whom he had such strong desire. It seemed that he would never understand women.

CHAPTER 15

A Bird in the Hand

Arriving on shore in the longboat was one of the most crisp and clear experiences of the journey so far. Everything was memorable to Senn: clear water lapped over fine, white sand of a type he had never seen before. Dunes climbed up from the beach, ending in scrub grass that transitioned to wide, rolling plains with occasional stands of trees. Here it was much warmer than it had been on shipboard with an ocean breeze. The heat of the southland baked him like bread in a brick oven; it was merciless compared to the cool, shady forests of his northland home. Small animals that Wildon called crabs scuttled across the sand, evading Senn's footsteps as he walked across the beach. "They're good eating, especially if you catch their larger cousins in the water offshore!"

They had bade farewell to Jann and most of the crew on board, and now said their final goodbyes to the men who would row the longboat back to the *Janklo's Pride*. Anxious to be underway, Aidan set off at a furious pace through the dunes toward the plains. The small group was quickly strung out in a long line: Aidan, Senn, and Rikk up front, followed by Piet, Nic, and Keegan, with Wildon and Lani bringing up the rear. Aidan said it was a perfectly sized group and an excellent distribution of skills for such a trip, with the two Magi and their battle spells easily making up for the scarcity of strongmen.

As they walked, Rikk gave him a firm clap on the shoulder. "How are you feeling, Senn?"

"Well enough, I suppose. We're on the way to Islingin, where I wanted to go in the first place. Plus we've developed some ideas on the capture of demon spirits, in the event one tries to possess one of us spellcasters."

"Sure, but that's not how I meant it. How are you feeling about your girl troubles?"

Senn looked behind them quickly, making sure the others were far enough back that they couldn't hear. "How do you know about that? I haven't told anyone, and I'm pretty sure she hasn't either."

Aidan chuckled and shook his head as Rikk continued. "It was obvious something was going on, the way you two were looking at each other the past few weeks. Now she's avoiding you as if you were a demon, so it must have gone wrong. Besides, she looks guilty as hell."

"Yeah, I guess. I feel pretty down. It seems she was just lonely after Jarel was killed, and there I was, with a warm shelter from the rain." He kept his eyes on the trail in front of him, trying to put a quick end to the conversation.

"Sorry kid, it sucks to be the next guy, you know?"

"What do you mean?"

"Err, when someone is just with you to help themselves get through that tough time after they've lost their last partner." Rikk raised one eyebrow. "Guess you learned that the hard way, huh? Don't worry, it's happened to most of us at some point. Though in my case it was way back in Islingin."

Aidan chimed in, "Don't feel too bad, Senn. I've seen the way Keegan looks at you, and she talked about you all the time in our cabin. If you're lucky maybe she'll ignore your past with Lani." He looked intensely at Senn, "But make sure you don't do the same to her as was just done to you. We're all like family in my clan, and no one takes kindly to recklessness with matters of the heart." That said, they trekked in silence for some time, none of them sure how to follow Aidan's stern admonition.

The rest of the day passed slowly as they wound westward through the heat of the plains. The grass of the savanna parted smoothly as they walked through it. Despite the ease of walking, Senn was sweating more than he ever had in his life from the heat. Eventually he fished a hat from his pack to protect his forehead from the sun, and noticed that most of the others had done the same.

Aidan called a halt late in the afternoon at an isolated stand of trees; it was a perfect clearing in which to set up camp for the night. "Alright, folks. The good news is, the spring rainy season seems to be over, so I don't expect any storms. On the other hand, that means it'll be hot like this all the time."

Senn heard a few sighs of disappointment, though Wildon muttered, "As long as the ground doesn't move under my feet!"

Aidan continued, "I'm expecting some demon attacks along the way, as we're a pretty obvious target. Senn, will you set up that spirit alarm?"

He'd completely forgotten about that. While at sea, he hadn't activated the Orb's warning spell because there wouldn't be any spirits aboard the *Janklo's Pride*. But it was important now that they were back on land. "Absolutely, I'll do it right away."

"Great. Now, it's about three more days to Leikton. I'm going to use a locater spell to find exactly where we should be headed. Hopefully I can get in touch with my old friend Chelan Lang, a Magus in this area. He was a well-known leader here before the demons came, the way I was in Janklo. I'm guessing he's in charge of a clan now."

Nic spoke up with a question that was on all their minds. "Aidan, what about dinner? I've been thinking about a fresh roast ever since we left the cove at Janklo."

"Good point! I think you just volunteered to go hunting. I'm not sure exactly what lives on these plains, but I'm sure you can find something tasty. Hare, antelope, ostrich . . . bring it back and I'll tell you the best way to cook it. Take Piet with you, he could benefit from some hunting experience. Use solid energy balls, so we don't start any fires."

Nic pulled the bow and quiver from his pack and smiled. "Sounds like fun. We'll see what we can find before the sun goes down." He and Piet took off with a surprising amount of energy, the prospect of roasting meat clearly giving them a second wind.

The rest of the party started gathering wood scraps and clearing a safe place for the cooking fire. With all that grass and no rain on the horizon, it was definitely a good idea to avoid setting the plains ablaze. Senn bumped into Keegan while they scavenged on the northern side of the stand of trees. "Hey there, Senn! Pretty sparse landscape around here, wouldn't you say?"

He paused and set down the small bundle of sticks he'd collected so far. "Hey yourself. Sure, with seasonal rains it makes a lot of sense."

"That's why it's all the more important to have some Adepts that are strong in earth magic. I bet way more people focus on that down here than on heat energy spells."

"Yeah, and they probably use solid energy spells to defend against attacks, to avoid starting a brushfire. It would be pretty hard to flee after a demon attack if a sea of fire covered the plains."

"Just keep that in mind if any demons attack us, young Magus . . ." She winked at him and turned toward the clearing.

"Wait . . ." Might as well give it a try. "Aidan said you might be able to help me with a spell that gives me trouble: making sound at a distance?" Keegan looked back and smiled, the left side of her mouth turning up a little more than the right, giving her a sense of mystery. What was she thinking to cause that smile?

"Oh, yes, Aidan mentioned that. I wondered how long it would take you to ask. Of course I'll give you a hand."

"Thanks, that would be great. I even have the spell imbued in a magic item, but I just can't duplicate it on my own."

"Then let's take a walk after dinner and work on it. For that spell it's better to have some privacy so you can really concentrate." Keegan winked at him once more, then turned again and continued back to the clearing. Had Senn just put himself in a tight spot? Although he wasn't with Lani anymore, he certainly wasn't ready to jump into something new quite yet.

Back at their camp, Rikk had cleared a safe area and laid wood for a fire. His magic was just enough to light it. Nic and Piet had returned with some kind of small deer and a brace of hares. The deer-like animal still had an arrow in its throat. For some reason the hares looked similar to the one Senn had bagged as his first hunting experience, and the archer wasted no time in telling the story.

"We spotted these hares in an open area, and Piet let loose with a barrage of small energy balls. It probably would've been fine, but he gave 'em about the same power as that lightning that struck the *Pride*," Nic laughed. "These damn hares tumbled a good two strides from the force of the hit. I tell ya, don't get in the way of this one in a fight!"

Piet smiled modestly. "I only hunted once before, and that was for much larger game."

"Right. Anyway, when it came to the big kill, this little deer moved like a flash when it got spooked. But nothing outruns my arrows... so we'll eat well tonight." He grinned and dropped the bow and quiver on his pack.

Aidan whistled. "Two hares and a gazelle. That's a good afternoon's work, boys. Rikk can probably help you clean those, if that fire is any measure of his outdoorsman skills." Already the twigs and logs Rikk had arranged were crackling loudly on their way to becoming cooking coals.

The clan leader sat down on the sandy earth, wiping his sweaty forehead with one hand. "While you crowd were conjuring up the fire and catching the roast, I tried to reach my old friend. I didn't get any response from Chelan Lang, but it's possible something has happened to him. I did get a response from his son Darin, who gave me a fix on their location—several leagues north of Leikton. So, now we have a destination! We'll leave early tomorrow so we can make good progress before it gets too hot. It wouldn't hurt to take a long midday break; my bald dome won't take too much more of this sun." That drew a few chuckles from around the fire. Senn had to admire a leader who put his people at ease by poking fun at himself.

—Alert, spirits near. The number is one— What was this? A spirit alert, after less than one day on solid ground? That was just their luck. Senn glanced around hurriedly, but all he saw was a lone falcon diving down to perch on a nearby tree. It carried a dead bird, probably its own evening meal. Somehow that falcon looked familiar ... same size, same colors ... yes. Definitely the same one he had seen aboard the *Janklo's Pride.* That explained the spirit warning—a demon spy was following them!

Only eight members remained in the group. This pleased Xiuhcoatl, as it was excellent news for the planned ambush. Hopefully they wouldn't collect many more companions when they met the clan near Leikton. He turned to his meal, doing his best to appear innocuous and blend in with the savanna landscape.

Suddenly the air shimmered around him. The colors of the world changed a fraction—something was wrong. Everything had grown very silent. He dropped a bit of birdflesh from his beak to look around, then stopped short as it landed in mid-air and slid down toward his feet. This was not good! Xiuhcoatl extended the falcon's wings, but spread them only halfway before they touched the solid globe that surrounded him. The falcon was trapped—how could this be? He'd been so careful . . . but then again, the boy had spotted him on the ship.

Below, Senn Morel talked excitedly with the others. They raced back and forth around the clearing, collecting boughs and scraps of wood. A few headed off into the cluster of trees, looking for something. Then Xiuhcoatl's glass prison levitated, snapping the branch he was standing on. This left him floundering in the bottom of the sphere among entrails of his supper and fragments of the loose branch. Quickly the sphere dropped to ground level, and he was face-to-face with Aidan Alkar. The grin on the large man's red face was a bit unsettling up close. Would they kill the falcon, with Xiuhcoatl ending up a dissociated spirit again? Before long, the others returned from the trees with further supplies: sticky sap and several long vines. They used a combination of magic and more conventional means to construct a birdcage around him.

Finally the globe of magic energy disappeared, and Xiuhcoatl fell to the floor of his new prison. "Well, well." Aidan stood over him, and a menacing, tight-lipped stare replaced his grin. "Two hares, a gazelle, *and* a falcon." He turned to the boy. "Senn, I'd say you have the best catch of the day here. Don't stick your finger in the cage, he just might bite." The Magus looked back to the cage, and Xiuhcoatl met his stare. "So, birdie, care to tell me why you're following us?"

Xiuhcoatl let out a long, shrill cry. Wasn't it obvious that birds can't talk? But Aidan didn't give up. "No, no, no. I know you can understand me. And I know you can talk to me without speaking aloud. Why don't you start with your name."

That game was finished, then. What could it hurt to reveal his name? The question was, how much was safe to tell them? And how would he slowly give out that information while he bought time to escape? —*I am Xiuhcoatl. Not that you'll gain anything from knowing that—*

"You never know, Xiuhcoatl. A name in itself can sometimes be very powerful. My name is Aidan Alkar, though I expect you already know that." Aidan smiled, as the falcon's head twitched involuntarily. Xiuhcoatl had to get a handle on his reactions, lest he give away any secrets unintentionally. "So, shall we discuss why you're following us, or would you prefer that I start plucking feathers?"

—*Certainly that won't be necessary. I merely enjoy learning about the new society that's sprung up in the centuries since I was last alive. Not all of us spirits are solely interested in your destruction—*

Senn's expression indicated he was not convinced. "Then why are you following *us*? Our group is too unique for it to be a coincidence that you picked us. Two Magi traveling together on an expedition must be pretty rare."

—*If you hadn't noticed, I'm inhabiting a falcon. With this form I can travel over fifty leagues in a day. What could be more interesting than to follow the travels of two such powerful men?—*

"There's something you're hiding, and it's clear you don't want to tell us. Though I think we can persuade you. Aidan, we still have those poison darts. How long would it take to build a warded box just big enough to send him back?"

Send ... back? What did the boy mean by that—ah, he meant an imbued box like they'd used on Kert! That would be a disaster. He could *not* let them send him back, as Marek was unlikely to give him a third chance. Xiuhcoatl would be stuck in the spirit world forever. Would there be enough time to work out an escape plan before they finished this box?

"That's a good question, Senn. The big coffin took me many moons, but you remember the massive size of it. Between the two of us, we could imbue a small box in one or two weeks." He turned to Xiuhcoatl and came close to the cage bars, keeping his nose just out of reach of the falcon's beak. "You think about that, birdie. Better start talking soon, or we *will* send you back to the other side."

Where was Keegan leading him? She and Senn had walked north out of the camp, then turned west for another ten minutes. Soon they reached another stand of trees, this one a small oasis surrounding a tiny pool of fresh water fed by a spring. "Keegan, how did you know this was here?"

She danced around the grassy clearing by the pool with short, graceful steps, red hair bouncing. "Earth magic. I sent out feelers to find natural sources of water, and there happened to be one right near us. We won't go thirsty on this trip, not while I'm around."

"Impressive. There's so much to learn about magic!" Senn sat on a big rock in the clearing, opposite the pool.

"It's not all about magic—cleverness counts too. How did you know that bird was a demon, anyway?"

"Well, the spirit alarm told me a demon was near, and I'd seen that same falcon several times aboard the ship."

Keegan tiptoed over and sat next to him. "Well, let me show you a little something magical." She rested her hand on Senn's arm, and he turned, not sure what to expect next. "How about you join me over here," her voice called from behind him. How could she be there as well . . . oh, of course. Senn was caught up in the excitement of Keegan's touch, and had forgotten the whole reason they came to this secluded glade. He wiped the look of surprise off his face.

"Right. You've got to show me how to throw my voice like that!" Senn shook his head in frustration. "I can cast the spell using my magic Orb, where it's imbued into the wood. But I can't for the life of me make it work on my own."

"Alright, so you know the basic principle of the moving plate?"

"Sure. I can create the plate, but all I can produce is some random sounds and tones."

"Then I know exactly where your problem lies. You need to connect to the vibrations of the human voice. Here, use your earth magic to feel inside me as I talk. Imagine that you connect that magic to the vocal area in my throat, and let the vibrations travel directly to your mind." She placed his fingers on her throat, and Senn closed his eyes, letting the earth magic flow. "Do you feel the vibrations?" The words echoed in his mind.

"Yeah, I think I do!"

"Just concentrate on my voice. Think about those vibrations, and make a moving plate somewhere over there." Keegan waved her hand toward the pool. "I'll just keep talking, and you focus on the vibrations, linking them to the plate. Your mind, the vibrations of my voice, and the plate: they move together as a connected triangle." He worked the spell as she continued. "What do you feel? Can you bring it all together? Aah, congratulations ..." He realized her voice echoed back from the pool. "Now you've taken the first step."

Senn moved his hand away. "Amazing. I felt such a synergy in my mind—it was the perfect melding of magics."

"Well done. This time try it with your own voice. Then instead of matching the plate with your actual voice, just imagine yourself speaking inside your mind. You'll find that you can duplicate almost any sound you can think of."

A loud animal roar came from the other side of the oasis, and Senn started with alarm. Keegan giggled. "Just kidding. I heard that sound in the distance earlier today. Now it's your turn ..."

"I'll just start talking, and form the triangle with my voice, my mind, and the plate ..." It was working. "Here's my voice coming from the pool." After a few minutes of practice he stopped talking out loud and just imagined himself speaking. "It's still working, are you proud of your new student?" Senn's voice called out from the other side of the clearing.

"Absolutely. It feels so good to help out a fellow spellcaster. Even you Magi need a helping hand from an Adept now and again!" She gave him a playful push, almost knocking him off the rock where they were seated.

"Hey, now, watch it there. Do that again and I might have to escape where you can't follow." Senn concentrated for a moment, working the spell, and then levitated a stride up in the air. Keegan laughed, reaching up and grabbing hold of his toes. What a great time they were having—she was really an impressive woman. Perhaps his feelings for Lani hadn't been as strong as he'd thought, if Senn was already falling for Keegan.

Fortunately, she had pulled him almost down to ground level, because he lost his concentration and actually did fall on her. They collapsed on the ground together laughing. "Senn, I thought Magi were more careful with their powers!"

"Usually we are. I was distracted . . ." He looked into her eyes, took in that enigmatic smile with one upturned corner, and forgot all about his recent heartbreak. Keegan giggled and closed in, kissing him briefly on the lips before standing up again and striding off toward the east. He raced after her. "Wait, what was that? Don't you want to . . ." To what? Certainly he didn't expect or even want the same kind of wild night he'd had with Lani at the cove. Keegan was so much smarter, funnier, more *alive* . . .

Keegan called back, "You've got a lot to learn about women, Senn. Don't you want to get to know me first, before you . . . ahem . . . get to know *all* about me?" Her sweet laughter echoed off the trees as she cavorted back toward camp, leaving Senn rushing to catch up.

After three full days of trekking, the expedition had almost reached its destination near Leikton. Senn was glad for that, because it had been a stressful journey so far. Aidan was convinced that the only motivation strong enough to pry information from Xiuhcoatl was the threat of sending him back. The first evening, Aidan had put Senn to work making planks. The second night when they camped on the open plains, they joined the box together and began to imbue it. Aidan and Senn took turns, impregnating the wood with earth magic runes that would absorb all traces of spirit magic. They had made progress, but it would take a long time to complete the box.

Senn and Rikk were tasked with carrying the demon falcon's cage. Aidan wanted Senn nearby the whole time in case anything went wrong and they needed to fight or recapture the demon. Since Rikk had mentioned the demons' ability to jump to another body through the eyes, the cage was covered in thick cloth at all times. Maybe once they reached their destination, Chelan Lang and his clan could take a turn guarding this troublesome bird.

All that lifted his spirits was Keegan's companionship during each day's walk. He was beginning to really appreciate her witticisms and intellect. Though only a couple years older than Senn, she had already been practicing magic for almost five years. She had explained a lot about magic, especially earth magic, that he hadn't known. One time when they had been running low on water, Keegan had shown him the spell to search for water sources. Now whenever she walked up beside him as they hiked, his heart would beat faster with excitement. It felt much more real than his several weeks' infatuation with Lani. Senn was a little over-wrought by the prospects, unsure of what to do next. He would have to wait until they could be alone again, and that wasn't possible when he was up late every night working on the new bird-sized spirit coffin with Aidan.

As the day wore on toward afternoon, Aidan halted to let everyone catch up. "Alright, folks. From the location Darin Lang gave me, the stand of trees up there should be the right spot for their camp." He pointed to the southwest, where a large grove stood on top of a hill overlooking the plains. "Let's be careful, because I've no idea what to expect. It's been a long time since I met Chelan, and I only met Darin once in Leikton, a good twenty years ago. Let me do the talking, and I expect we'll be fast friends in no time."

They struck off toward the trees at a good clip; Senn was anxious to set down his pack and rest for the night. After twenty minutes they reached the crest of the hill, only to be surprised by how thick and shady the grove was. It was so dense they could not see very far into it, and Senn was reminded a bit of the forests back home. He called out, "Aidan! Any ideas where the camp might be? This grove looks bigger than I thought."

"No idea, the spell's not that specific." He led them into the grove, searching for signs of habitation. "Let's see if we can't press ahead and find Darin Lang."

Just then a loud whistle echoed among the trees, and before their eyes a dozen armed men stepped out from the shadows. They carried the biggest assortment of bows, spears, swords, and axes that Senn had ever seen in one place, and all those weapons were pointed at him.

CHAPTER 16

The Escape

At long last, Xipil's band arrived at their destination. Lieh was relieved that they would finally have a break, as she felt her body's weariness even if Tamesis seemed not to. The shortcut through the forest had taken several days off their journey, and now they camped at the ambush point where the road met the plains. From this vantage point they would be able to see Senn and Aidan's party coming from half a league away.

The preparations made Lieh quite nervous, as she wondered how Senn and company could possibly escape unscathed. Tamesis was all for scorching the earth, leaving no one alive but Senn, and this time Xipil was in agreement. The only one of the three demons who had doubts about this plan was Shyama. She, like Lieh, expressed concern that they might kill Senn instead of taking him alive. But as usual, Xipil ignored the big cat's objections and carried on.

After sleeping well for the first time in weeks, the trio woke early to begin their preparations. Xipil, of course, assigned something for everyone to do. "Tamesis, you've got the strongest magic, so you get the detail of digging pits across the road, there . . ." He pointed to a spot where the overgrown path narrowed between several tall trees. "I'll figure out how to undermine some of the larger trees, there, so we can easily knock them over with magic to block the path. Shyama, you collect straight pieces of deadwood that we can use as stakes or arrows."

—*Lovely, Xipil. Fetching sticks is a task for dogs. I will do it, though. You know green wood is better for this. I can't cut branches from living trees. I have no magic, and these teeth are meant for flesh*— Shyama stalked around in a circle, clearly unhappy with Xipil's recent decisions. Could that help Lieh somehow? Maybe Shyama had a conscience after all, and could be persuaded to desert. But Lieh couldn't think of any way to talk to the lynx from her magical prison.

Xipil shook his head. "If we had enough time, Tamesis and I could cut fresh branches. However, our quarry could arrive here at any moment. And I'm not convinced that Xiuhcoatl will be able to possess Alkar so easily. Since we may not get much if any warning from him, we have to be prepared for anything." Xipil stroked his beard, "In fact, maybe you can use those teeth of yours to sharpen the deadwood you collect?"

—*Don't push it. I'll find your deadwood. Then I'll be out patrolling the road. Maybe I can give you a few hours' warning of any approach*— Shyama took off, loping away into the forest to the north.

"Xipil, should be careful! Shyama has doubts. Ssee? Any problem, let Tamesis take care." As usual, the demoness unsheathed her knife at the appropriate moment. "Magic, blade, no one immune. Make sure we deliver to Master. He rewards with glory!"

The seeds of foment were sprouting. Lieh could only hope they bloomed soon, before it was too late for Senn and his friends. Was there anything she could do to ease fate onto the right path? It didn't seem so; at the moment Lieh was powerless. Even with warning from the Orb's spirit alert spell, Senn's company would have no choice but to continue along the road with caution, where they would inevitably spring Xipil's trap. In the bloody battle that loomed, the deranged Tamesis might hold all the cards.

Aidan Alkar stared down the shafts and blades of a dozen weapons, and eyed the taut bowstrings with particular care. With no preparation, he couldn't think of a way to protect all eight of those in his party. Was this only a precaution on the part of the clan, or did they make a habit of executing strangers? "I'm here to speak with Darin Lang. We don't mean any harm."

A tall man with dark hair and a clean-shaven face stepped forward, brandishing a well-used longsword. "If you're looking for Darin, you've found him. Now, tell me who you really are, and why you're here." The bowstrings remained tight, and Aidan hoped the archers would keep their cool. If even one arrow were loosed, he could guess the reaction from Senn, Rikk, and the others standing behind him.

"Look, Darin. I'm Aidan Alkar, an old friend of your father's. You might remember me, as we met once in Leikton long ago." A bead of sweat trickled down Aidan's forehead into one eye. He tried to blink it away without moving, his eye burning from the salt.

"Yes, I met a Magus named Alkar as a boy. But my father disappeared without a trace some years back, and now I'm in charge. We've seen a lot of demon tricks, so there's little reason to trust someone I barely remember. How about a little proof you're no demon?" He flicked his sword point and stepped forward slightly.

"My eyes are clear of possession. You can check all my companions as well."

Darin eyed the party coolly and said nothing; probably he was weighing his options.

It wouldn't bode well if Darin were to discover the caged falcon by surprise, its irises black as night. Aidan added, "Just be careful, because we have a captured demon with us—and we plan to send it back to the other side."

Darin gestured with his sword. "A captured demon, eh. At least you're forthright." His gaze flicked up for a moment, then returned to look directly at Aidan. "If everything you say is true, then we can talk. First let's take a look at your eyes. Helder!" A massive bowman with a shaggy beard and shoulder-length brown hair stepped forward. He relaxed his bow and slung it across his back, trading it for a long, flat knife from his belt. First he approached Aidan himself, examining his eyes closely.

"Looks clean, Darin!" Helder continued around to the rest of the party, checking everyone in turn. "They're all clean, least as far as I kin' see."

"Good. Next, I want to see this demon of yours, and learn how you plan to send it back. We've heard something of that on the wind, and if you can explain it, you might really be Aidan Alkar."

Aidan motioned Senn forward. "Senn here is carrying the birdcage for a falcon we trapped a few days ago." The boy brought the cage forward and took off the blanket. Inside, the bird was still in good enough health, as they'd been feeding it scraps every night. None of them wanted it to die, which would release the spirit to search for another host. "It followed us for weeks as we traveled here by ship."

Darin stepped forward to inspect the occupant of the cage. "I see you keep it covered up, I suppose to make sure the spirit can't transfer to another animal." Aidan nodded. "Now tell me, how do you plan to send this demon back?"

"Allow me. I have to retrieve something from my pack." Slowly Aidan lowered his pack and removed the wooden box, offering it to Darin. "Take a look at this, and feel for the runes. If you're heir to your father's magic, you'll be able to understand just how I plan to send this demon back."

The clan leader took the box, and spent a few minutes delving into its magic. "Runes activated by spirit energy. Why didn't I think of that? But it's not finished!"

"Why do you think this demon is still here?"

Darin smiled at that, and handed back the unfinished box. "No demon thrall would be walking around with a runed item like this. Men, lower your weapons! Aidan, let me greet you the way you deserve." He held out his hand, and Aidan grasped it warmly. "I only wish my father were still here to see you. He always talked about you and your clever uses of magic; I see he was right."

Aidan sighed in relief. "You had me worried, Darin. I haven't stared down that many weapons at once since before we united under the Conclave, back in my youth. Now, let's talk about the ways we can help each other. I can teach you how to imbue these magic runes, and perhaps you can provide some horses for our journey to Islingin."

"Let's discuss it over supper. Our stable is well-stocked, and I'd gladly trade horses for the magic to send demons back. You may share our camp tonight, and we'll do what we can to help you. I have a feeling there's an interesting story behind your demon prisoner."

That night was one of relaxation and enjoyment for their group, weary from long weeks of travel. They could continue their work on the runes another day. Darin explained that his clan was nomadic, then led them through the trees to a marvelous tent city on the western side of the grove. For supper, Senn and Wildon joined Aidan, Darin, and his strong-man Helder Stowe around the fire, where they exchanged stories long into the night. At the end of the evening, Darin showed them to their tents. It would be a pleasure to sleep under cover again, and Aidan looked forward to waking without a sheen of dew covering him and his blankets. As the leader of their party, Aidan was lucky enough to be offered a private tent. A good meal, new friends, and a full night's sleep—these were the things a man should cherish in such tough times.

Xiuhcoatl worried more by the minute. He was so close to Alkar, yet he could neither escape his cage nor find a new form. Soon they would force him to either give up what he knew, one piece at a time, or return to the spirit world in failure. His only bargaining chip was that if they sent him back to the spirit world he could tell Marek about their plans. But surely they would never free him—and what would be the result? He would spend days or weeks in a cage, only to be carried into the jaws of an ambush he had arranged. The only option was to wait and let fate sweep him along on its current. Or was it? Xiuhcoatl remembered what Marek had said about making one's own luck.

Looking around the cage in the near-darkness, no easy way out presented itself. Over the past days he'd tested the supple boughs and tied vines, finding them all either too strong or too well-protected by dried sap for him to chew or claw through. His falcon form wouldn't fit between any of the bars. No other reasonable form had presented itself, as mice and other small animals tended to avoid falcons. His captors had fed him only dead rodents and table scraps. What were his other choices? Remain here to betray his master, or be sent back in shame? Perhaps he should try taking a radical form, one that none of his kind would ever consider. A mosquito buzzed its way across the cage looking for a way to escape. He'd never heard of a spirit possessing an insect; was it even possible? It might not work, but given the alternatives, it could be worth the risk. Xiuhcoatl made his choice. Unsure how to influence the mind of such a simple creature, he tried his best.

—*Blood. Fresh, dripping red blood, yours for the taking. Let me in*— It worked! Xiuhcoatl transferred over to the insect, hoping it wouldn't expire before he was finished with its fragile form. He was immediately taken by the strange sensations of his new form: odd vision through eyes that composited thousands of tiny images, a strange sense similar to smell from long antennae, and stabilizing vibrations from a pair of knobs behind his wings. No matter, he could still get around, and he was confident he'd find a better host shortly. That is, if he survived long enough.

Now to escape. The falcon, fortunately, kept silent and relaxed—perhaps not yet aware it had regained its own faculties. With Xiuhcoatl's help, the mosquito was able to quickly find its way out of the cage under the edge of the covering. Senn and Rikk were sleeping in the tent, and gave off a . . . delicious? . . . smell as they breathed. It took sheer force of will to overcome the mosquito's attraction to them, but he could not afford to be swatted to death. He steered clear of the humans and flew outside.

The most important question: where would Xiuhcoatl find a black mamba? There were large numbers of them in these savanna plains. Having studied them and lived as one for quite some time, he judged the most likely place to find one nearby would be a tree hollow. Steering the mosquito using the newly learned wing and stabilizer senses, Xiuhcoatl headed for the forest and began to check the nooks and crannies of the grove's trees. The task was not an easy one, and it took half the night before he found his target: an olive-green snake, giving off a small amount of sweet-smelling vapor in its breath as it rested.

Having found the coiled-up mamba, it was easy to gain entrance. The snake took little notice of mosquitoes, and ignored Xiuhcoatl completely until he began speaking to it. —*Let me in, strength and power will be yours. Together we will never go hungry*— He transferred over to the black mamba, feeling out the sleek, familiar form as the mosquito buzzed away in search of easier prey.

It was time for the next step in his mission. The anticipation before the hunt was building, and Xiuhcoatl used his weak spirit magic to warm up the snake in preparation. Then he uncoiled and slithered out of the tree, taking off quickly across the dewy ground toward the camp. One by one, he poked his head inside the tents until he found Alkar's, and in black mamba form he made his way inside. Xiuhcoatl's target was fast asleep with one leg free from the blankets, snoring gently, unaware ... until the mamba reared back and struck the man's leg three times, injecting a massive dose of venom that could kill a horse.

"Gaaaahhh!" Aidan Alkar sprang awake as though he'd been shot by an arrow. In fact, that's probably what the Magus thought had happened. "What the hell, my leg ... aah!"

—Hello my target, my prize. Don't bother to fight so hard, the venom is already working its way through your bloodstream. Even your powers as a Magus can't heal it—

Alkar breathed heavily, trying to get through the pain. "Who are you, how did you find us?" He was concentrating as if he were trying to work a spell, though Xiuhcoatl knew there was no hope of his victim healing himself. Eight Magi had tried that and failed; the mamba's venom was just too strong.

—You brought me along in a cage, remember? But you weren't quick enough completing your box of runes, and no mere birdcage will hold me for long. I make my own fate, and meeting my master in shame isn't part of the plan—

A wan smile crossed the Magus' face. "Xiuhcoatl. So, what *is* your plan? You kill me first, and then who's next?"

—No such game, my friend. Just let me in, and I'll tell you all about it. The venom dose and bite location don't give you long to decide. Once I'm inside, my spirit magic combined with your earth magic will make a potent mixture. You'll be healed in no time—

Sweat already dotted Alkar's brow, and he shook feverishly. "What makes you think ... why would I give over to you rather than die ..." His breath was already becoming ragged. Xiuhcoatl must have struck very close to the blood vessels. This wouldn't even take twenty minutes.

—It all depends how you prefer to meet Marek Seltin. On your own two feet here in this world, or as a shimmering spirit on the other side. You can choose to either let me in, or die. Judging from your breathing, one of those will be occurring within a few short minutes—

The Magus leaned forward and peered into the snake's eyes. "Alright. I'm ready ... don't want to die today ... come inside." It was strange how little fear Alkar had, as if he were already prepared. No matter, all that was important now was the form. The man inside would soon be a prisoner, just as he had made Xiuhcoatl his prisoner. Only Alkar would never again be free as long as he lived. Their eyes met, and the spirit slipped inside.

—*We're going to have fun together, you and I. Before I deliver you to the Spirit Council as Marek's new host, we'll capture your friends in a little ambush I planned where the road meets the forest.*— Let the overconfident Magus chew on that for a while, now that he would be powerless for the rest of his days.

Xiuhcoatl felt out his new form and began to take control. He drew up the earth magic to begin healing Alkar's body, but startlingly, nothing happened. For a moment he flashed back to his brief time with the unfortunate outdoorsman Rylan, but there was certainly no lack of magic here.

"A little strange . . . isn't it?" Wait! Xiuhcoatl hadn't said that, but it was definitely vocalized. He turned his head to check for someone else in the tent. But his head didn't move. "Sorry to break it to you," Alkar wheezed, "but your plans just changed. You made it into a Magus all right, but as prisoner this time instead of jailer." His breath was still becoming more ragged by the minute. "Now . . . let's see how this . . . spirit magic works." Xiuhcoatl could feel his meager spirit magic being drawn up and mixed with his host's earth magic. The spell wasn't that difficult, almost identical to a straight earth magic one. His host had no problem fighting back the venom with the potent mixture of magics.

Still unsure exactly how this could have happened, Xiuhcoatl investigated his surroundings. Every pathway to control Alkar's form was blocked in a way he had never experienced. His spirit was trapped inside a shell of earth magic, similar to the way he would have contained the body's rightful inhabitant. Xiuhcoatl had certainly possessed more Magi than any other spirit, but even he had never heard of this before. —*Very clever, Alkar*—

"Just call me Aidan. I have a feeling we'll get to know each other quite well in the next few weeks. By the way, thanks for telling me about your plans. Spirit Council? Hah. I'll show them what I think about having a committee of demons in charge."

—*Just wait, Alkar. I make my own fate, and in the long run, you're not going to change that*—

"Aah, where would we be without fate leading us by the nose. Isn't it a paradox to say one *makes* fate? Either we have free will and make our own choices, *or* we're predestined to make them. Based on what I've seen, I'll go with free will."

Xiuhcoatl thought for a moment. Isn't that what he had meant? Unfortunately it seemed he'd have plenty of time to ponder. The trapped spirit settled into his earth magic prison and tried to calm his rage, as his plans slithered away under the tent flap along with his mamba.

What to do now? Aidan wasn't sure how to proceed, but he knew one detail he had to find out right away. Rifling through his pack, he found a small mirror. Sure enough, his irises were black as night. Talking to Darin again with his eyes looking like that could prove fatal. However, Senn would trust him, as this was exactly the plan they'd talked about should one of them face possession. He could steal away in the night, and Senn could explain it to Darin after Aidan was long gone.

Climbing quietly out of his own tent, he located the one where Senn slept and snuck in. Quietly he shook the boy awake, and Senn rubbed the sleep from his eyes. Hearing movement, Rikk sprang awake as well. "Shh, it's just me, Aidan!" Rikk relaxed his grip on the knife he kept next to his bedroll and sat up slowly. Aidan whispered, "Senn, do you remember how we talked about capturing a spirit with earth magic?"

"Sure, Aidan. Last resort, you said." The boy sat up, leaning back on his arms.

"Yes, well, take a look in your cage there. Our prisoner escaped somehow." Looking suddenly flustered, Senn reached for the cage and threw back its cover. Then he conjured a glowing ball of heat energy in his hand, lighting up the whole tent. The falcon was still there, but its eyes were clear. "Don't be alarmed, because the earth magic spirit cage worked. Look at my eyes."

Senn and Rikk both crowded closer to peer into Aidan's dark black eyes. They gasped, and Rikk's hand strayed back toward the knife. "How can we be sure you're Aidan?"

"Ask me anything. Rikk, you know firsthand how little the spirit would know of its captive host's thoughts."

"That's true. Then what did you warn Senn about on our first day of hiking?"

Clever that Rikk would ask that, of all questions. It was just about the last piece of information that Xiuhcoatl would care to know. "I told him to be careful with Keegan's feelings, because in my clan we watch out for one another."

Rikk smiled, while Senn looked a bit sheepish. Was something already going on between Keegan and the boy? At least now they were both reassured that Aidan was still in control of himself.

Senn blew out a long breath and asked, "What next?"

Aidan stroked his beard. "Here's what I figure. If Darin sees me with these black eyes it won't be very easy to explain. Instead, I'll take a horse from the stable and be gone under the cover of night." Senn nodded, and Aidan continued. "In the morning you explain everything, and show him all about the magic runes. You can leave him the small box as a gesture of good will; we certainly don't need it any more."

"Alright. Then where should we meet up with you? A few leagues up the road?"

"That's not how we'll play this. I have another idea, which results in us splitting up so that I go on alone." Senn met his eyes with a questioning look, and Aidan smiled. "Xiuhcoatl let slip two interesting pieces of information: first, there's an ambush up the road, where the plains meet the forest. It's probably Xipil and your mother. You'll want to avoid them, possibly skirt wide around that area. Second, my body is destined for Marek, and something called the 'Spirit Council.' Marek needs a Magus to possess . . . and apparently I fit the bill."

Senn drew in a sharp breath. "You don't mean to . . . trade spirits and imprison my father instead?"

A wicked grin spread across Aidan's face, and he felt Xiuhcoatl's spirit grow uncomfortable at the very thought of it. "Absolutely. I will become king of the demons, and in reality we'll have one of us humans running the Spirit Council."

CHAPTER 17
Saddle Sore

Senn awoke feeling surprisingly refreshed. Maybe it was because for once, he knew what was going to happen next. He and Rikk climbed out of the tent, taking the bird cage with them. They found Darin waiting for them, along with a hearty breakfast of bacon, eggs, and something called grits. Senn set the birdcage on the ground and got right to the point.

"Darin, something happened last night."

The clan leader's unwavering eyes met his, "Tell me."

"Somehow the spirit escaped from the falcon. It tried to possess Aidan." Senn took a deep breath, and showed Darin the falcon's clear eyes. "But we had planned for something like this. In case it happened to one of our Adepts or Magi, the host would make a cage of earth magic to trap the spirit, before it could do the same to him."

"And did Aidan succeed in trapping this demon?" Darin's fist was clenched, his knuckles white.

"Yes. He came to us last night, Rikk and me. We made sure we were really talking to Aidan, and not to a demon."

"So where is he now?"

Senn exchanged a glance with Rikk. "Aidan thought it would be better . . . that is, he didn't want to scare anyone . . . so he took a horse and left last night." He went on, "We have a plan. This demon wanted to take Aidan directly to Marek Seltin, the leader of the spirits, to be his Magus form. Instead, Aidan will try to trap Marek, and cause some real trouble for the demons."

Darin relaxed a little, then pursed his lips and rubbed them with his finger. "And you plan to follow him—to put an end to this demon invasion, as you were saying last night?"

"That's about the gist of it." Senn smiled nervously, hoping that Darin wouldn't have any major objections and try to stop them.

"Alright," Darin said, reaching for a crispy slice of bacon. "I'll go along with your plan, on one condition. I'm coming with you. I'll take any opportunity to free our people from this scourge and return life to normal."

Rikk chuckled. "Well, no problems there. We were more worried you'd put the axe to our plans, but if you want to come along, all the better. How do we arrange our departure?"

"First, I'd like to leave the knowledge of your runes with the Adepts of my clan. I hope you can spare a day to show them how it works. Then we'll saddle up and ride north."

Darin's suggestion meshed well with Senn's plan, so he and Rikk informed the others. Wildon in particular seemed glad to increase the numbers of their little band. Senn brought out the half-completed demon box and taught the clan's Adepts how to imbue runes into the wood. In addition, he told them about the earth magic cage to prevent possession, hoping at the same time they would never need to use that knowledge. It was a little nerve-wracking to teach the older Adepts about these powerful spells—especially since Senn could measure his magic experience in moons, not years. Fortunately he knew what he was doing, and explaining magic came naturally to him.

When evening came, they sat down to a more modest meal than the previous night. Lani and Wildon sat away from the others, deep in discussion. Nic, Piet, and Keegan joined Senn and Rikk around the fire. Keegan in particular seemed worried about Aidan, and how they would get along without him. "Senn, did he look alright? Will he really be able to trap Marek?"

Senn scowled between bites of meat. "He looked fine, except for his black irises. I hope he succeeds. Otherwise I'm not sure how we'll manage to destroy this Spirit Council that Aidan mentioned. I don't even want to think about fighting against Aidan and my father, both sharing the same body."

Keegan briefly touched his arm. "That would be hard. But hopefully it won't come to that. Also ... how do we deal with this ambush Aidan mentioned?"

"I'd rather not attack my mother, either. The best plan would be to skirt a few leagues around them, through the woods. Darin said he knows a few game trails where we can take the horses. Then we're off toward Islingin. He said even with horses, it's about a six week journey."

She giggled. "Have you ever ridden a horse before?"

"No, our clan didn't have any up north."

"Same as our clan—I haven't ridden one either. But it looks like fun!"

Rikk laughed at that. "I guess I'm the only one here that's ever been ahorse. You tell me after the first day if you still think it's that much fun." He stood up and pointed off to the south. "I'm going to take a little walk. Feeling restless after too much sitting today. Anyone want to join me?" Senn was about to stand up with the others when Keegan subtly rested her hand on his leg, keeping him seated. Nic and Piet, however, took Rikk up on his offer.

What was Keegan up to ... "Don't you want to get a little exercise? We've been sitting all day explaining runes and spells. A walk might be nice."

"Sure, I'd like to go for a walk. But maybe just the two of us? And the opposite direction from the boys?" Senn noticed her sly grin, the lopsided smile intriguing him once again.

"Alright, then let's head north along the edge of the grove." They walked for several minutes without speaking, until they had left the camp area.

Finally, Keegan broke the silence. "What do you really think about all this, Senn?"

"What, you mean our trip to Islingin?"

"No, not that!" She took his hand in hers. "I mean, what's going on between us. How do you feel about it?"

That was a tricky question. Should he mention the reason he had ignored her advances on the ship? That hardly seemed relevant anymore, since Lani was completely out of the picture for him now. "Honestly, I wasn't interested at first." That was true, for sure. "But the more we talked, the more attracted I was. Then, when you taught me that voice throwing spell . . ." He smiled shyly, unable to say more.

"Yeah, I know what you mean. I'm glad you came around, Senn!" Keegan stopped and faced him. She threw her arms around his neck and planted her lips fully on his. Senn wasn't sure how long they stood there, lips locked and tongues playfully searching each other out. "Let's go!" His energetic little woman skipped along the edge of the grove, pulling him after her.

The sun was just disappearing below the horizon to the west, lighting up a smattering of thin clouds with bright hues of orange deepening to red. He pointed it out to Keegan. "I think that has to be the most beautiful sunset I've ever seen. How could we be so lucky?"

"Maybe this sunset is here just for us." Keegan stopped in a patch of lush grass on the edge of the prairie. The grass was deep green where it was screened by the overhanging trees of the grove. She pulled him down in the grass and climbed on top of him, kissing him again on the lips, and then continuing down his neck. "This little glade, I certainly picked it just for us!" Her wavy red hair was glowing from the orange sky behind it, framing her with a burst of fire that matched her energetic personality.

"One promise I can make to you, Keegan. I'm here only for you." She giggled as Senn kissed her, then she pulled her shirt off over her head.

"And these are here just for you too, Senn . . ." Keegan's tiny breasts were almost perfect in shape. He kissed her nipples gently, while slowly caressing her back. "Oooh!" Soon the rest of their clothes followed, and they made love together in a magical rhythm. Senn was amazed at the bond of closeness he felt between them as they climaxed, both crying out below the burnt-orange background of the evening sky.

At last they relaxed together and enjoyed a few moments of peace before heading back toward camp. This was something special. After Senn's last experience, he could tell the difference . . . the two of them had something real here. "Keegan, I want you to know. Whatever happens tomorrow, next week, or in Islingin ... I hope we're there together through it all."

She smiled, looking dreamily into his eyes. "Me too."

Dawn came early to the plains in the late spring. Senn squinted when Darin woke them up at first light, but the plains native said he wanted to get started before the day's heat was upon them. Since Senn and his companions all came from a culture where readiness was the key to survival, their packs were prepared for departure within minutes of waking. The only two packs missing were Lani's and Wildon's. Senn walked over to the tent the tutor and the Adept shared and stuck his head inside.

Both of them were up, and Wildon had a worried look on his face. Lani appeared rather upset, sniffling and wiping her red-rimmed eyes. Senn asked, "Hey, what's the matter?"

Wildon motioned him into the tent. "Alright Lani, I think it's about time you told him."

"Told me what?" Senn didn't like the sound of that.

She looked up, wide-eyed and sobbing softly. "I'm not coming with you and the others. This isn't my fight any more." What could she be so upset about? Maybe Lani had seen him with Keegan, and her feelings had changed? Then Wildon motioned for her to continue. "Senn ... I'm with child."

His jaw dropped. "You ... that is ... uhh, a baby?"

"Yes. I missed my cycle a few weeks ago, and now I can feel the life inside me by using earth magic. Here, you try." She took his hand and placed it on her belly, a place Senn had thought he'd certainly never be touching again. He opened a channel of earth magic and sensed inside. Sure enough, there was a tiny form inside her, growing slowly. "You know it can only be yours, because ..." Lani looked away shyly. Ah, yes: Jarel and his ... unusual method.

"Ooh. So, what do we do about this? I mean, you can't just stay here with strangers." Should Senn stay with Lani, to keep his child safe? But then he'd miss this opportunity to stop his *own* father and thwart the demons.

Wildon put up a hand. "Ahh, Senn . . . I'll be staying here with her as well. I've found that in the last years, traveling has agreed with me less and less. Now there's nothing left for me up north, with our old clan destroyed."

That was true, and now all the old clan mates were fragmenting further. If Lani and Wildon stayed here, Rikk would be the only one left on the expedition with Senn. "But . . . you've been helping us since the very start! What will we do without you along to guide us?"

"While I *have* been a part of this ever since that first attack, I feel that recently I haven't been able to do much. You learned about the more powerful magic spells from Aidan while I was laid up seasick. Now I'm sure Piet or Keegan can help you out if you have any questions, and that's even before mentioning Darin." Wildon leaned back against a pillow. "Besides, I've found that the warmth here feels much better to my old bones than the cold temperatures up north."

Senn would miss Wildon, who had tutored him in magic ever since he had shot his first pebble through the air. But maybe this wouldn't be all bad. If Wildon would take care of Lani for him, he'd be able to continue the expedition to Islingin. "So you'll both stay here. What about . . . the baby? He'll be a Morel?"

Lani finally perked up a little. "Well, that's he or she, and we won't know which for seven or eight moons!" Looking a little uncertain, she said, "As for the name, I haven't decided. It might be easier . . . if the baby were a Telus. I could just say it's Jarel's." That at least made one point clear, that Lani didn't want Senn back. It was just as well, because he wanted to be with someone else now, anyway. But what would he tell Keegan, now that he knew . . . that he would have a child?

Outside, Darin called, "Let's go! Time to ride out!" Senn stood up to leave, lifting the flap of the tent.

"I wish there were more time. Just promise me that you'll send word of how it goes for you two here in the south. Someday I want to come back and see . . . our child. But I need to make sure this baby will be born into a safe world. I don't want him growing up in fear the way I did. Goodbye . . . and good luck."

Lani smiled through her tears, then stood and gave him one last awkward hug. "You too."

Wildon shook Senn's hand firmly. "I'll take good care of her and the baby, don't you worry."

As Senn stepped out of the tent he ran straight into Keegan. She just stared at him, then turned and stormed off toward the row of horses that were waiting for them. "Wait, Keegan . . . !" Had she just walked up? Senn chased after her. "Hey, I can explain!"

She turned, her face almost as red as her hair. "No need to explain. I walked by and saw you coming out of the tent, and heard how you'd come back someday to visit your child. That says it all! I *thought* something was going on between you two on the ship, but I didn't realize how serious it was. Is that why you didn't want anything to do with me then? You were sleeping with *her?*"

"Look, Lani and I had something for a little while, but in the end it didn't amount to anything." He put his hand on her shoulder, trying to make contact. "You're the one I want to be with now."

Keegan brushed his hand away. "It didn't amount to anything? Sure it did, it amounts to her being pregnant with your child! Now leave me be." She kept on walking, with a pace that brooked no following. Senn sighed, suddenly alone with his thoughts, which had all just turned sour.

Aidan was pushing the horse too hard, but there was no other choice. He had to get past the ambush site quickly, in case Darin Lang decided to chase him down. Even in that worst-case scenario, he hoped Senn could convince Darin to turn back before encountering Xipil's ambush.

Then the real question became, what should Aidan do when *he* arrived at the ambush point? He couldn't go around it, because he didn't know the paths and would get lost. Besides, the trio of demons was expecting Xiuhcoatl in Aidan's body to help them with the ambush. He might be able to talk his way past them. So far he had not been able to pry any useful information out of his spirit prisoner, although they'd held a few interesting conversations. At a minimum, Aidan already knew the names of the demons he had to fool, thanks to Rikk's tale of his possession. He had gained some insight into the way Xiuhcoatl spoke, so he could use similar speech patterns. It seemed that Xiuhcoatl didn't think highly of his comrades, but that was not much to go on. Aidan would just have to see what happened, and to hope he didn't have to go head-to-head against the possessed Lieh Morel.

After two days of hard riding, the overgrown road met up with the river and ran parallel to it. Aidan refilled his water supply and rested his horse before continuing on. Another two days passed, and the character of the plains began to change. More trees dotted the prairie, signifying the ambush would be coming up soon. Aidan made a final late afternoon stop at the river, so the horse would be in top shape in case he had to make a run for it.

—*Alkar. You realize you might not even make it past my comrades. If they suspect anything, you're dead*—

That could be the opening he was looking for. Perhaps Xiuhcoatl didn't want to risk that Aidan might die; he could use that angle to extract a bit of information from the spirit. Aidan replied with his thoughts, —*True, but if I die, you'll have to reassociate and find a new host. Unless maybe this earth magic cage pulls you back to the other side with me when I go*— That scenario was unlikely, but maybe the spirit would believe it.

There was a long silence before Xiuhcoatl spoke. —*That would be unfortunate. I suppose I can't very well expect you to do what I would have done, which is to stay and fight your friends. What if I were to help you get past Xipil?*—

Aidan smiled. —*So your survival instinct isn't dead after all? If you help me, I might consider it a gesture of goodwill*—

—*You could find a way to let me go, to put me in an animal somewhere: release me back into the wild*—

—*Absolutely not. If I did that, there would be no way for me to entrap Marek. You'll just have to choose: risk a battle with your three compatriots if I'm found out, or live to fight another day*— At least Aidan was forcing Xiuhcoatl to think.

—*Fine. I shall help you get past, in the interest of self-preservation*—

—*Excellent! I knew you would come around. So what shall I do to persuade them that I am you?*—

There was another long pause before the spirit continued. —*They are expecting you, or rather me, to help them capture your friends. Tamesis and Xipil will be very upset if I don't, so we need a good excuse that holds water. Tell them that Tynan sent a spirit as a messenger bird to summon me with all haste to bring this Magus form. That should get you past them. If they ask for more details, you don't know any, as Marek is quite tight-lipped about his reasons—*

Aidan recorked his water skin and stood up. —*I think you've made a wise decision. We'll know soon enough, as we're almost there*— He remounted his horse and returned to the road.

Within an hour, the trees started closing in. As he slowly approached a narrow section of the road, a lynx the size of a strongman appeared in front of him. Xiuhcoatl advised him, —*That's Shyama, the most reasonable of the three*—

Time to give it a go, to see if he could fool them. "Greetings, Shyama. As you can see, I have been successful." How should he wrap up this first lie? "Marek will have his Magus in no time."

—*Welcome back, Xiuhcoatl. Congratulations on your capture. You'll want to avoid the spiked pits. Just follow me around them. The others are waiting on the far side*— She led the horse off the road. —*Be careful of these trees. The ground is dug up around them. When Senn Morel's party arrives, Tamesis and Xipil will topple the trees with magic*— It was a decent plan. Too bad for them that Senn and the others would be sneaking around their carefully prepared trap.

Beyond all the pitfalls, a middle-aged man was pacing back and forth, while an angry-looking woman sat on a log sharpening sticks with a wicked knife. Now for the second act. "Xipil. I have returned with news."

The stony-faced demon greeted Aidan as he climbed down from the horse. "Xiuhcoatl, how nice to see you again. Apparently you were successful in finding a human form, so this time we can both speak naturally. I take it this is Aidan Alkar?"

He smiled. "Absolutely. However, there's been a change of plans. Tynan sent me a spirit in bird form as a messenger, and I am summoned to Islingin immediately. Unfortunately you will be on your own here to capture the others."

Xipil's face twisted into a mask of pure agony, as if his beard were on fire. —*Don't be concerned,*— Xiuhcoatl said privately in Aidan's mind. —*My colleague has a few issues adjusting to life in the physical world, and facial expressions seem to be one of them*—

The spirit was right, as Xipil's words didn't match the harsh set of his brow. "How are we to capture a Magus and several Adepts without your help?"

"Ask Tamesis there. I'm sure she can figure something out." Knowing the ruthlessness of these demons, and how they would not even encounter Senn's party, he threw in a little something extra for good measure. "Just kill all of them except Senn Morel. That shouldn't be so hard, don't you think?"

Tamesis stood up and buried her knife point in the log where she'd been sitting. "Yesss! On that, Tamesis can agree! Kill all others!" Aah, poor Lieh. It was too bad she was stuck with such a monster, and couldn't do anything about it. Perhaps she would find a way to escape before too long.

Aidan's last comment had persuaded Tamesis, but Xipil didn't change his mind so easily. "Why would it be so important to get back to Islingin a few days sooner? Marek would never know the difference if you stayed to help us."

"Who knows the reasons of our master. I'm not one to question him. And I don't want Tynan's bird-messenger to report back that he spotted me fighting alongside you, after he delivered orders that I return immediately. No, I'll be on my way, as Marek doesn't like to be kept waiting." He remounted the horse. "Senn's party will be here soon; I can confirm they are headed to Islingin."

"Very well then. Among the three of us, we'll manage somehow. Ride safely, and take care of Marek's new form."

Aidan held up his hand in farewell. "Best of luck to you also." He turned and rode off northward along the road, with Shyama keeping pace beside him. Once they were well away from the others, the demon lynx spoke.

—Xiuhcoatl, this may all fall apart without your help—

How should he respond? —I know that, but what choice do I have? Marek has spoken—

—Clearly none. I just wanted to tell you. If the ambush goes wrong, I will stay out of the thick of it. Look for me. I will come find you. Perhaps you can vouch for me with Marek. I am only the brawn, but even I see the flaws in Xipil's every plan—

—Sure. I will watch for you. Do your best, and take care—

—You as well, friend Xiuhcoatl—

What an awkward conversation! But if Shyama and Xiuhcoatl were so unhappy with their leadership, maybe Aidan had a chance to win them over to *his* side. Finally the lynx turned back, and he picked up the pace. One more obstacle overcome; now he just had to get to Islingin. There were somewhat over three hundred leagues of open road for him to travel, with no one for company but Xiuhcoatl. He might as well make it more interesting.

—So, Xiuhcoatl, do you and your lynx girlfriend have plans together when this is all over?—

Burning hot, the sun beat down on Senn and his companions. They were now seven: Keegan, Nic, and Piet from Aidan's clan; Senn and Rikk remaining from Lieh Morel's; and Darin Lang with the towering Helder Stowe joining from the plains clan. Darin had brought Helder along to help with light spells and heavy fighting. They had a couple of spare horses, which had been meant for Lani and Wildon—but which were now just carrying extra supplies. The first day was grueling for Senn, if only because he'd never ridden a horse before. Their pace wasn't fast, and Darin said it would take five days or so before they reached the forest. When they finally stopped for the night, Senn's legs and buttocks throbbed with muscle pain. All he wanted was a little affection (and perhaps a dab of earth magic) from Keegan, but she was still not talking to him.

At least the evening's meal was good: one last cut of fresh meat brought from camp before they would have to revert to dried rations. The group sat around a small fire to eat and to discuss their plans to avoid Xipil and his demons. Darin spoke first, since he knew the area best. "I suggest we follow this road for about three or four days. After that we cross over the river Kell to the western bank at a ford I know, and bushwhack for a while." He laid out his plan to skirt the ambush.

Rikk nodded. "If we're across the water, it'll be much less likely they can scout us out as we go past. Besides, we're not in such a rush now. We want to give Aidan several days in Islingin before we arrive."

"Right," Senn added. "Aidan will be pushing hard to get there fast. This way he'll have enough time to take control of this Spirit Council, posing as Marek."

Darin continued. "After we make it into the forest, it'll be a little less than two weeks to Silville. It will be rough going when we get to the pass through the mountains, but it's the fastest way to Islingin. I might know some people near Silville. If they've survived this long, I expect we can find their clan and see how folks are faring in the mountainous regions." Everyone around the fire was in agreement. "So it's settled: our next goal is the northern plains ford!"

With the inexperienced riders among them, it took four more days to arrive at the ford. As they crossed the Kell, Senn delighted in the soothing cold of the mountain-fed river, which eased his aches and pains. After another half day of travel across the plains, more and more trees began to dot the landscape. Once the plains gave way to forest, the tough part began: clearing a path through the thick undergrowth where there was nothing but the occasional game trail. After almost a day of cutting through underbrush with swords and magic, Darin decided that they must be past the ambush. They angled back over to the river, and within a few hours, found a ford. After crossing over to the east side of the frigid Kell, they continued their journey north into the mountains.

During the long ride north, Keegan spoke to Senn as little as necessary. She was the one he most wanted to be with, to ride beside, and to hold close at night ... but apparently that wasn't going to happen. How could he get through to this woman he cared about so strongly?

Eventually, the fork toward Janklo came and went. The way became steep and rocky, devolving into a narrow trail laden with switchbacks. They rode more slowly to keep the horses from tiring as the trail wound upward. Late one morning, they finally came to the pass. An empty, crumbling tower, probably vacant since long before the fall of Islingin, overlooked the trails leading down to the east and to the west. Helder Stowe strode over to the tower to take a look inside, bow in hand. After a few moments he poked his head out from a few stories up, then returned to the group to give his gruff assessment.

"We've got some cause to worry. Someone's been squattin' there. From the looks of the leavin's, no one human, if ya know what I mean. I think we best get off this exposed chunk o' rock as soon as we can." Certainly no one had any objection to that.

Senn took one last look at the majestic surroundings before they headed down the westward trail, marveling at the snowy mountain peaks rising up on either side of the saddle. Several leagues ahead on the trail would be the abandoned town of Silville, rich with the ores that had given rise to the art of smithing. It had been known as the capital of weaponry—even the best smiths in Islingin would have trained there. But like Janklo, Leikton, and all the smaller towns scattered in between, it had been overrun by demons. Did the road pass close enough that he could catch a view into the town itself? Senn was dying to know what it was like to walk through a town, however ill-advised that might be. He had never strolled down a paved street or walked among stone dwellings.

The party continued along the trail leading westward from the pass. Once they left the exposed face for the relative safety of the rocky switchbacks, Darin stopped to search for his friends. "I was last here several years ago, when my father was still alive. We met with acquaintances of his from a clan near Silville, and I spent a good deal of time with a woman named Ziya Rell. Let's hope I can find her." Darin knelt down and worked a location spell, sending earth magic tendrils to search out Ziya Rell. After a few minutes, he received an echo back. "Good news! I've found them. Their location is just south of the trail, perhaps a half day's ride ahead. We should be there before nightfall, in time for a meal among friendly faces." There was a curious look on his face, and Senn wondered just how well Darin knew this woman. Maybe he and Ziya had made some kind of connection on his previous visit?

They continued onward, looking forward to a relaxing meal and some fresh news about life in the western mountains of Kartus. However, as the sun sank low in the sky, the spirit alarm sounded: an unknown number of spirits. "Darin! We've got spirits in the neighborhood. The Orb just warned me."

"Damn!" Darin reined in his horse. "Well, maybe it's not so bad. Down there on the left you can see the edge of Silville. Probably several demons are squatting in abandoned houses, so we might be able to avoid them. Doesn't that talisman get any more accurate about *where* they might be?"

"No, I'm afraid not. It only picks up traces of spirit energy nearby, so they could be anywhere." Senn looked anxiously where Darin had pointed, finally spotting the tops of a few stone houses peeking between trees that were growing thicker as they descended. Soon they came around a bend, switched back left, and there was the city, perched on a grassy mountainside overlooking steep cliffs and a distant valley floor. Silville was the biggest settlement Senn had ever seen. He wondered how many thousands had lived there during its height, and where those former residents might be now. Probably those who had survived, such as Ziya Rell, were living in the nearby forests. Or perhaps they had relocated to the lush, green valley downhill from the mountainside they now traversed.

Darin gazed at the town with furrowed brows. "Ziya's location is coming up soon. But I'm a little confused, because it should be there, about half a league ahead—where the road passes a hundred strides or so north of the city wall."

Helder snorted. "Makes no sense. That'd put 'em right on the border of the town itself. I'm nervous enough goin' by it like this on horses. But walkin' right up to the wall? Does Ziya know somethin' we don't?"

"Hopefully nothing's happened to her. Let's be prepared with spells and weapons anyway, just in case it's a trap." Darin looked worried, perhaps for Ziya's safety as well as their own. Helder and Nic unslung their bows, while the others drew swords or readied spells. Slowly they continued forward until they neared the town, with its two-stride-high stone wall visible on their left side. Darin held up a hand, and they halted while he searched for signs of life in the area he'd perceived as Ziya's location. Stone buildings with slate roofs stretched up the hillside, a few jumbled streets visible between them. Then off to the southwest, just below the setting sun, there was a furtive wave next to a gate through the wall. "She's there! And alone, I think." They left the road, angling toward the gate. As they drew nearer, Senn saw a tall, thin woman with brown hair crouched low next to the gateway. Darin rode out a dozen strides ahead. "Ziya! Are you sure it's safe here so close to the city?"

That was when Senn glanced behind them and saw the two men standing in the road with drawn bows. They must have been waiting in the trees by the cliff, hidden among the long shadows cast by the setting sun. "Look there!" As Senn's party reined in their horses, two more figures appeared on top of the city wall, also with bows drawn. Senn hoped this was just caution on the part of Ziya's clan, similar to their first encounter with Darin, but then he heard the twang of bowstrings letting go and the hiss of an energy ball. He swung around and threw up a wide shield in front of those nearest him, covering their left flank where he'd heard the energy ball. An arrow from the archers on the wall bounced off his shield, which also took the brunt of the energy ball that must have come from Ziya Rell. Darin cried out in pain as an arrow stuck in his left thigh.

To Senn's right, he heard the 'thup, thup' of shafts landing in the dirt, loosed by the men on the road. They weren't so accurate as the bowmen on the wall, because they had a much longer shot. While trying to maintain his shield, Senn made a cone-shaped matrix and brought a blast of wind to bear behind the archers on the wall. He toppled one of them to the ground; a crack of breaking bones and a shout of pain echoed off the wall. Darin turned his horse and returned to the group. Ziya must be possessed, and had gathered a group of like-minded demons to assault anyone traveling along this road.

More arrows were loosed, but this time by Nic and Helder, each of them taking a flank. Nic's arrow skewered the second man on the wall, catching him in the shoulder. Helder's missed its mark to the north, but it disoriented the men on the road, who hadn't been expecting such swift retaliation. Darin returned to the group, holding between Rikk and Senn, and brought his own magic to bear to their left. He, Piet, and Keegan all aimed energy balls at the attackers by the wall in an attempt to incinerate them before they could do any further damage.

Senn had good results so far keeping a shield active while casting an offensive spell. Now he shifted that shield around toward the threat on the right flank. How long could he keep this up? It had better be long enough to take out those demon archers. He tried a fire wall spell on the ones in the road, building a shallow channel filled with heat energy. As he increased the flow of magic, an inferno several strides high surrounded them. Even so, one archer leaped through the flames, clearly possessed and swinging a flaming bow above his head. Senn shouted, "Some help here?" Helder nocked another arrow and took careful aim at the half-charred demon running toward them, then let the shaft fly. It caught the toasted archer in the throat, throwing the man's upper body backward and knocking him flat on his back. It appeared that both demons on that side were down.

Senn dropped his shield and turned back to the left flank. The second archer from the top of the wall was now lying at the bottom of it, burned and broken with another arrow buried in his chest. At least no one had been hit besides Darin, and his wound didn't look too bad. Ziya Rell was hiding behind the gate, which looked rather charred and chipped after hits from various energy balls. Darin called out toward the gate, "Damn you, what have you done with my Ziya!"

A voice echoed back, "She's not *your* Ziya anymore, unless you care to host one of the spirits you've just killed! Then I might be able to arrange a little love affair for you ..."

Quietly, Senn whispered, "Darin—what do we do with her? I have some darts, they should paralyze her and force out the demon. But they need time to take effect, so we'd have to capture her alive!"

"Anything to free her. Do it!"

"Just shield us from her energy balls." Senn searched his pack until he found the darts, still wrapped in what was now a dry casing of protective leaves. He brought one out and levitated it slowly past Darin's shield, waiting for an opening. Splitting his focus, he made a plate of solid energy to distract Ziya. Then he called out from behind her, inside the town, "Aha! Bet you never thought I'd get back here, did ya?" As the demon shied away from the phony threat behind her, she was fully exposed. Senn let the dart fly, catching her right in the neck.

"Owww! What the hell ..." Ziya clapped the side of her neck, breaking off the tip of the dart. Now for the final touch: Senn built a solid energy prison around the demon, trapping her along with any magic she might try to throw at them.

"Yeah!" Senn shouted in celebration, as he heard one last 'thup' behind him. He turned to see Keegan slouch over in her saddle, an arrow lodged in her left side. No! Where had that come from? He followed her eyes to the two men lying below the wall. The one he'd blown down with that blast of wind hadn't been killed, and in the commotion had managed to loose a final arrow as he lay on the ground. Now Piet lobbed a solid energy ball at his head. As on his hunting expedition, the young Adept put a little too much gusto (and perhaps fury as well) into the spell. The hapless demon archer's head ended up as fragments splattered on the base of the wall behind him.

Victory forgotten, Senn slid off his horse just in time to catch Keegan as she toppled off her own mount. He switched the energy prison spell over to run through the Orb, so he could concentrate on Keegan. Darin and Piet rushed to his side, ready to help. "Senn," Darin started, "we need to find shelter. This wound won't be a quick or simple one to heal, if it's even possible to save her."

Keegan coughed, and there was blood on her lips now. "Senn, I didn't mean it to end . . . like this . . ." She tried to lift her head, barely able to move it. "I want so much . . . to hold you again . . ."

Senn cradled her head with his hands. "Just relax. I'm going to do everything I can. I'm not going to lose you!" He felt deep inside with earth magic, trying to judge the extent of the damage. Clearly the arrow had missed her heart, but its point had penetrated a lung. He closed his eyes and fed in a surge of earth magic, reinforcing the damaged area to slow the bleeding.

Darin said, "Let's move her inside the wall; we'll be less visible there. We have to get that arrow out before any healing spell can take effect, and the faster that happens, the better. Can you maintain that energy prison?"

"Yes. Have a few of the others stand watch by Ziya with weapons ready, just in case." Darin nodded, and motioned for Helder and Nic to keep watch. Rikk and Piet lifted Keegan and carried her through the gateway into Silville. Just across the narrow street inside the gate, they found an open door. Senn and Darin followed as the others laid Keegan down on the floor inside the house, with Darin limping badly from his own arrow wound. "Darin, what should we do?"

"We've got to get this arrow out of her. I know a trick I learned on the plains. Here, you three hold her down, and get ready with earth magic when I'm done." Senn knelt down and cradled Keegan's head between his knees, holding her arms with his hands, while Rikk and Piet held her legs. Darin closed his eyes. "I'm feeling for the arrow point and slicing it free from the shaft. Get ready, because next I'm going pull the shaft out. I'll spin the arrowhead around and guide it out the way it came in. That's the painful and dangerous part. We'll need to stop the bleeding with magic as fast as we can." Darin took a deep breath, "Here we go." He pulled the shaft out, and blood started dripping fast from Keegan's side. She struggled in pain, moaning weakly before she passed out entirely. Darin focused, furrowing his brows, and after a few seconds the arrowhead emerged tip-first from the wound. "Now!" All three spellcasters fed in healing earth magic, while Rikk pressed a cloth over the wound. After a few minutes Keegan seemed to be in less pain, and the bleeding slowed.

"Good job, men. Now we just have to wait it out and see if she comes around. If the lung heals up well, she might make it." He leaned back against a wall, then grasped the shaft of the arrow sticking out of his own thigh. "Senn, do you mind trying out the spell on me? I'm not about to die, but I'd walk a lot better without this shaft stuck in my leg."

The past few hours had been tense. Night had fallen, and the only light besides the moon was magical. Senn had a constant drain from the magic prison, as the Orb drew energy to keep Ziya trapped inside. He never left Keegan's side, waiting for her to regain consciousness while the others kept watch for any incoming demons. They were all worried that the fighting (and the presence of horses) could attract more unwanted attention from other demons in the area. When Senn had checked the Orb's spirit warning spell, it still indicated an unknown number of demons—possibly including the spirits from the archers who would eventually reassociate nearby. He and the others were anxious to be gone before that happened.

Finally, Keegan opened her eyes and spoke. "Senn? Am I ... is it alright?" She pointed to the blood-soaked bandage around her midsection, coughing gently.

"You're awake! Thank the stars!" He stroked her hair gently. "You're going to be just fine, thanks to several Adept- and Magus-sized doses of earth magic. Darin really has a knack for getting arrows out." He pointed to the bloody fragments in the corner of the empty room. "Want some water?" Keegan nodded, and Senn tipped a trickle of water into her mouth from his water skin.

"Thanks. Have you been here the whole time?" He nodded. "You know ... I really want to thank you ..." she coughed again, "I guess I've been a bit silly lately. About ... all this. Now I can see how you really feel." He squeezed her hand and gave her a kiss on the forehead.

Nic stuck his head in the doorway. "Senn, Ziya seems to be out cold. She was pounding on the walls for an hour or two, but now she's just laying there."

"Good. Look, Keegan's awake! Can you keep an eye on her while I deal with Ziya?" He exchanged one more look with Keegan, catching a hint of a smile on her lips, before heading out the door to the energy cage by the town gate. Darin stood at the edge of the magical shield looking at the woman imprisoned inside, who lay unconscious in the bottom of the sphere.

"Aah, Senn! So, you think this will work?"

"I hope so. The demon should have been thrown out, because her body is in a half-dead state from the poison on the dart. I'll release the energy prison, and you make sure she's not just faking it." Senn relaxed the spell, and Ziya dropped a hand's width to the flat ground. Darin reached forward and checked her signs, searching with earth magic.

"I don't feel anything . . . she's very relaxed." He pulled back her eyelids, "Senn! They're not black! Her eyes are blue, crystal blue the way I remember!"

"So it worked! The spirit was thrown out of her as soon as the poison took effect. Quick, let's bring her to the house where Keegan is recovering. My redhead is awake now, by the way. We just have to get them both moving, and escape from here before these spirits find new hosts." Senn took Ziya's legs while Darin lifted underneath her arms. Together they brought her into the house and laid her next to a startled Keegan.

Senn smiled at her. "Don't worry, she's not possessed any more." He explained to Darin how to heal the poison from the darts, and they both applied earth magic to break down the poison and help Ziya's mind reawaken. Within a few minutes she opened her eyes and lay silent.

Darin leaned over her. "Ziya? Can you hear me?"

Finally her lips moved, "Yes." She looked surprised by her ability to speak once again. "Was that me?" She shook her head slowly from side to side. "I'm free again!" She sat up and threw her arms around Darin, holding him tight. He gave in to the unexpected embrace, and held her as she started sobbing into his shoulder. "You have no idea . . . no idea what they did! The clan is gone, my little girl is . . . gone! What they made me do . . ." She was obviously disturbed by the experiences during her possession, which Senn could well understand after what he'd seen in recent weeks.

"Darin." Senn caught the clan leader's eye. "We need to leave. The farther away we are by the time these spirits find new hosts to possess, the better." He rested his hand on Keegan's arm, "Do you think you can ride?"

She sat up, wincing as she touched the bandage on her left side. "Give me a few minutes. And maybe another dose of that earth magic . . ." Her quick wink confirmed to Senn that she was recovering. It would still be a few days before they could ride at their previous speed, but at least they might get out of harm's way.

Shortly thereafter they made their way back to the horses, with the wounded among them limping and leaning on the shoulders of the others. Senn glanced back at the upward-sloping streets of Silville, bathed in soft moonlight. His first visit to a town, and it had almost ended in tragedy.

Darin had a more positive view of the evening's events as they rode slowly away. "This is the first time I've ever met demons in battle and ended up with *more* companions once the fight was done!"

CHAPTER 18

Two Ends of the Same Road

I t was almost sunset when Shyama returned from her latest foray to the south. Lieh was thankful that they hadn't seen anyone since Xiuh-coatl had ridden by days before. Conversely, this made the others furious. Xipil had been pacing the whole afternoon, and to say Tamesis was impatient was an understatement. It was all their esteemed leader could do to keep her from blasting the tops off trees with fireballs. Instead, she had made a sport of exploding any poor wildlife she saw with solid energy balls.

Shyama bounded out of the trees, skirting around the traps they had laid for the ambush. —*Xipil, I have news*—

The demon Adept stopped his nervous pacing and held up a hand to quiet Tamesis, who had been about to blast a squirrel into the spirit world. "What news?"

—*We've been outflanked. I don't know how. For the last day or so I have been ranging farther. We thought they should have been closer behind Xiuh-coatl, and they were. Today I found tracks leading up to a ford. They crossed the river days ago*—

Xipil smacked his hands together. "Damn it all! How did they know we were here? Are you sure it was them, and not some other humans on horseback?"

—*I recognized several scents. It is Senn Morel and his companions. Perhaps they were nervous after Aidan Alkar was abducted, and therefore chose to leave the road*—

The demon leader stroked his beard, thinking. "That must be the case. So, they have circled around us on the way to Islingin, to disrupt our master's plans." He eyed his two comrades. "Any ideas?"

Tamesis snarled and shook her head. "Too far to levitate. Walking, too slow. Need faster way!"

Shyama broke in again. —*Your solution might be readily at hand*— Xipil looked to the lynx expectantly. —*On my way back here I observed several men on horses. They are searching for a herd of buffalo to hunt. I would expect their clan is nearby. The men were looking for a place to camp in the wild. We could take their horses while they sleep*—

Tamesis, of course, unsheathed her knife and broke into her favorite wicked grin. "Could do more than that! When no one knows, no one follows . . ."

Xipil nodded approval. "Good ideas, both of you. Let's get moving! Shyama, lead the way." The big cat growled and started off through the woods, leaving them running to catch up.

The trio walked halfway through the night, with Shyama scouting ahead to make sure they didn't lose the element of surprise. At first they stayed on the road, but then turned off to walk through the tall, dewy grass of the prairies. It was several leagues before the lynx finally found the hunters and returned to report. —*Two hundred strides ahead. We are coming in from the west. They are sleeping beneath that tree. Three men, four horses, one man awake on watch. That one is facing east, opposite where we are now*—

The presence of a guard meant that stealth would be a priority. Xipil said, "Tamesis, you mentioned levitation. Go in first and take out the guard. We'll follow and give you a hand with the other two men."

Lieh winced, knowing what this meant: blades and blood. Before she knew it, Tamesis was off, sneaking through the grass like an animal. A hundred strides in, she stopped and worked the levitation spell, rising twenty strides in the air. Was Tamesis skilled enough to keep the spell going? After a few minutes it was clear that the demoness had prior experience with levitation, because despite the energy drain, she made it clear across to the lone tree. The sole man on watch was resting his back against it, just barely awake.

Slowly, Tamesis lowered herself down behind the tree, knife unsheathed. As her feet touched the ground, her arm—Lieh's arm—was already in motion, reaching around the tree and slicing through tendons, veins, and throat. "Wha ... gurrrgghh—" Tamesis quickly clamped her free hand over his mouth so the sound wouldn't wake the guard's companions. The two remaining men were sleeping in bedrolls out in the open, with only the tree sheltering them from the cold of the open sky. Lieh could feel Tamesis' pulse quicken as she planned their demise. Walking silently over to the second victim, blade still dripping from the first, she prepared to strike. At the same time, she conjured a ball of heat energy for the final man and let it fly. Just as he was engulfed in flame, she pounced on the second target, sinking her blade deep into his chest. "Aaaaghhhh!" His cry didn't last long, as Tamesis' next cut sliced his throat wide open. Lieh tried to block out the shrill screams of the man who was on fire, without much success. The shrieks of pain didn't last long, as the fireball had truly been Magus-strength.

Shyama arrived on the scene, bounding up to sniff around the burned jumble of bedding where one of the victims still smoldered. A smoking patch of grass to the east of them expanded slowly, about to start a wildfire on the open prairie. The big lynx did not deign to say anything just yet, and Lieh detected in Shyama a hint of dissatisfaction with the way the operation had gone. Xipil wrinkled his nose as he arrived a moment later, scrunching up his whole face like a rat in the process. "Congratulations, Tamesis. It's good we don't need to hide the evidence, as that might be difficult now." He pointed above them, where the tree had ignited from the recent conflagration beneath its branches.

—Shouldn't we put out this fire. There's no point to char the grassland in our wake—

Tamesis cackled, back in her element after weeks of restraint. "Let burn! Fire natural, here in prairies. Happens often, yess?"

However, there was a limit to Xipil's destructiveness. He shook his head, then combined a bit of cold energy with an air magic spell. The resulting icy blast came from the east, extinguishing the burning grass, and continued upward through the crackling tree branches. Soon there was nothing left burning, only a subsiding whirlwind that scattered flakes of ash around the clearing beneath the big tree. "That's all the damage we need to do for one night. Now, to the horses."

They walked south a few dozen strides, where four horses were tied to picket pins driven into the ground. Tamesis and Xipil untied all four horses, saddling up two of them and leading the remaining two. Xipil said, "The conflagration aside, that was nice work. Let's get going. With two horses apiece, we can do a bit of catching up. We'll ride back to the ambush point and rest there for a few hours. In the morning, we'll ride toward Silville!"

Back in pursuit of her son. Would Senn arrive in Islingin before they caught up? Regardless, Lieh had no idea what he could do when he arrived there. Strong magic aside, he didn't stand much chance alone against Marek and the eight Magi on his Spirit Council. She sighed and settled in for the ride, as Tamesis put her heels into the horse's flanks. All she could do for now was watch and wait.

Halfway there, Aidan thought. Just another few weeks of this monotonous riding, and he'd be at Islingin. At least there hadn't been any problems at Silville, though he hadn't allowed for any. After coming within view of the town, he had waited for nightfall and ridden the whole way past at a gallop. That had been over a week ago, and now he was well out of the mountains—nearly into the coastal forests of the western edge of Kartus.

While he was content with an uneventful journey, Aidan was a little bored with the company—his silent spirit prisoner. A few times each day he tried to coax his captive into conversation. The more he learned about Xiuhcoatl, the better he'd be able to impersonate him until it was time to trap Marek. On this day, he was finally successful.

—*Xiuhcoatl! What do you think, are you looking forward to passing near the coast and having a whiff of salty air as we go by?*—

After a long pause, the spirit spoke. *—Aidan, I've seen more of this land than any human possibly could. Besides that, I've done it in more different forms than most of my spirit brethren would ever dare inhabit. Did you know I even took the form of a mosquito, to escape your birdcage. Why do you think I'd be excited by a little whiff of salty air?—*

—Sorry. I thought the fresh smell might bring you out of this funk— How could he get him talking, to find out more about this secretive spirit? *—What about these different forms? Tell me of your latest adventures before you took flight in that falcon—*

—I suppose . . . what could it hurt to tell you now. I was on the way to Silville, to find a form for the next Council member. I was in black mamba form, and lost my mode of transportation through the forest. Then I met a woodsman traveling alone; in fact, it probably wasn't ten leagues from this very spot. Poor man, I think Rylan was his name. He didn't have enough magic to heal us after I inhabited him. After that I ended up in a squirrel and a hawk, before finally returning to the spirit world for new orders—

—Did you say, 'poor man?' It can't be that a demon like you feels guilty about a man's suffering?—

—What? Never. It is merely unfortunate to waste the life of another in vain. You will hopefully learn that not every spirit is a bloodthirsty monster like Tamesis, or a power-hungry fool like Xipil—

—That's interesting. So how would you classify yourself, Xiuhcoatl?—

There was another long pause before he replied. *—I am a lover of nature and freedom. That may sound a bit at odds with being a spirit in the physical world, considering I have to imprison my forms' souls. Still, better them than me—*

—You know, I'm starting to think that not all you spirits are evil. You just might persuade me yet— Aidan supposed it was possible . . . and even if not, the line of conversation was worthwhile to bring the spirit out of his shell, to get more information out of him. *—So my friend, what shall we do when we reach Islingin?—*

—What do you mean, what shall we do. It seems quite clear that I have no choice in the matter; you plan to exchange me for Marek and run the Spirit Council. But you won't maintain control of them for long. They'll soon see through your charade, and you won't live long in a room with eight angry Magi—

—Whether I succeed at impersonating Marek remains to be seen. But I think you should reconsider your allegiances. You seem to be a spirit with a bit of compassion . . . and maybe some motivation to repair your kind's reputation?— Xiuhcoatl said nothing. But at least he hadn't disagreed. *—If you side with me, there could be a place for you in the human world after this upheaval is over—*

—Why would I want to help you?—

Aidan narrowed his eyes and became deadly serious. *—Xiuhcoatl, I mean to rid the world of these demons who have destroyed our culture. Senn is hell-bent on achieving the same goal, and you know the two of us are a force to be reckoned with. If you can prove to me that you're different from the rest of the spirits, I might just overlook you when this business is all over—*

The spirit remained silent. Clearly he was thinking it over; Aidan might be able to strike a bargain with him yet.

Riding at night on a rocky trail is never the best idea. Fortunately for Senn and his companions, they could provide enough magical light to see the way. They rode for several hours in this unnatural brightness. Senn activated the concealment spell as well, in hopes of disguising their progress along the road. The path turned north, pointing them definitively toward Islingin, and eventually it flattened out to a gentle downhill. Sometime after midnight, Senn observed that Keegan and Ziya badly needed rest, and suggested that they make camp. They took their horses west off the trail into a sparsely forested area where they could walk without bushwhacking. At last they unpacked their bedrolls and lay down for the night.

Ziya took some extra blankets that had been in one of the spare horses' saddlebags. She lay down close to Darin, confirming Senn's suspicions that there was a romance brewing between them. But Darin wasn't the only one—Keegan had forgiven Senn for his recent and rocky past with Lani. She asked Senn to unroll her blankets right next to his, and for the first time, the two of them lay down to sleep with their arms around each other. He enjoyed her warm touch for a few minutes, then refreshed the spirit warning spell before drifting off to sleep in bliss.

The next morning, Senn was thankful to be awakened by the sun instead of by the spirit warning. Their attackers in Silville either hadn't found suitable animals or humans to possess, or hadn't deigned to give chase. He rose and prepared a simple breakfast from their dried stores, greeting the others one by one as the sun brought them out of their blankets. Ziya and Darin were among the last to wander over, with Ziya looking just as tense as she had the night before. Keegan, however, slept late into the morning while the others talked.

Rikk in particular was concerned for Ziya, having undergone some of the same experiences himself, albeit for a much shorter time. He welcomed her to the circle where the group sat. "How are you doing? I understand you've had a rough time lately."

Their new companion glanced around nervously, but Darin reassured her. "We're all friends here."

"Well . . ." she started, "it's been about two years since I was in control of myself. These demons . . . what I did . . ." She put her head down in her hands, the tears coming again. "I can't."

"That's alright," Rikk continued. "If it makes any difference, you're not the only one Senn has freed. I was only possessed for a couple of weeks, but I saw a lot of cruelty in that time. When the demon was controlling me, I attacked a man who had been like a son to me, just before he knocked me out. In the end he was killed in that fight—his blood is on these hands." Rikk held his hands up in front of him. "Eventually I realized: they weren't really *my* hands then. I had let the demon in, because at that moment I could only choose between possession or death. And that's no real choice at all, if you ask me. It's been hard to come to terms with how these hands were used, with what that demon made them do. It took a long time to get past the guilt. But I'm recovering from it, and you'll do the same, even if it takes a while."

Ziya nodded and curled up against Darin. "Right now all I can do is thank you for coming. Even knowing it could be a trap, Darin didn't give up on me, and all of you stuck by him. I wish I could do the same and help you on this expedition, but . . . I'm scared."

Keegan awakened and joined the group, with her blankets still wrapped around her. She sat by Senn's side and smiled at Ziya's last comments. "Good morning everyone! You know, Ziya, I think you must be someone special to Darin, after all this trouble he went through for you."

That brought a smile out of Ziya. "Yes, well ... we met several years ago, but couldn't be together. Both of us had obligations to our own clans. And I had my daughter, back then." Her eyes teared up again. "But I'm not sure I can go to Islingin with you. I need time."

Darin squeezed her shoulders. "Let's make a fresh start. We can be together now. And we could really use your magic on our side. The most important contribution we can make is to help Senn and his companions end this demon invasion once and for all."

After a moment, Ziya nodded agreement and wiped her eyes. "Alright. I'll come with you, and do what I can to help. If it means an end to all this ..."

Darin held her close. "That's the Ziya I remember. Now, to Islingin!"

Keegan stood up and brandished a strip of dried meat in the air. "Yes, to Islingin!"

With two horses apiece and Shyama bounding alongside, Xipil and Tamesis made quick progress northward. Already they had crested the pass, and Lieh could see Silville looming below. She wasn't sure how long their horses would last at this pace, but Xipil switched them out several times per day as they rode. This afternoon the animals seemed to be flagging, which might result in an early stop for the night.

Thinking back over the events of the past days, Lieh was increasingly worried about what might happen if they were to catch up to Senn and the others. When Xipil's group had abandoned the ambush point, Shyama had suggested to clear off the covered pits to prevent people and animals from unwittingly falling in. With only her wild grin in response, Tamesis had ignited the traps with flaming energy balls. As the grand finale, she had toppled all the trees they had undermined, adding to the conflagration. Xipil had been forced to repeat the previous night's firefighting spell to avoid burning down the whole forest. It frightened Lieh to imagine that firepower aimed at her son.

Eventually Shyama had found their quarry's trail again, some hours ride north of the ambush point. This had sparked arguments over how

Senn had known exactly where to cut around the trap. There was no logical answer forthcoming besides 'Xiuhcoatl told them,' but that made no sense.

By now, Tamesis' temper was hot enough to ignite a fire just with one look. As they arrived at Silville, Lieh was relieved to find that the houses were made of stone—there was no chance Tamesis could burn down the town. Xipil rode out ahead, with Shyama padding along between the spare horses. A soft 'thup' noise came from up ahead, and Xipil's horse reared up, nearly throwing him off. An arrow was sticking from the horse's side! Lieh cringed inside as Tamesis filled a massive energy ball with heat magic.

"Stop!" Xipil called out to the attackers, holding up his hand as he regained control of the horse. "Before we fight ..." he continued with mental communication, —*let's discuss our alternatives*— The question loomed: were these attackers humans out for demon blood, warned that demons were coming? Or were they demons who had mistaken this small party on horseback for humans? Lieh's query was answered swiftly, as a badly scarred bowman and two wolves emerged from the forest.

The bowman held his bow out in front of him in a gesture of peace. "I see you're one of us! Sorry 'bout your horse."

Xipil dismounted and pulled out the arrow as the horse bucked in pain, blood trickling down its side. Fortunately the shaft hadn't gone that deep. He calmed the mount and applied a bit of earth magic to the wound. "Think nothing of it." He gestured with the arrow, "Perhaps you can make up for this with information. We are looking for some humans, who should have come through here on horseback."

Shyama came forward and sniffed the wolves, greeting those who would traditionally be her enemies in the forest. Meanwhile the frightful-looking bowman related an interesting story. "We had a tight group, four of us Medi and a Major Adept. We tried to take out a party o' humans, but they were too strong in magic. Most of us got killed, I was th' only one to keep my form. We lost the Adept form, never found her body. They must have taken it with 'em."

"How long ago?"

"Musta been three, four days back. We're still looking for a couple forms that can fight, but at least we found these two wolves so far."

Lieh calculated in her head how fast they could catch up. Three days was a big lead—how could they possibly close the gap? For Senn's sake, it would be better if they didn't.

But Xipil hadn't given up on catching the demons' quarry. "Do you just plan to stay here waiting for more humans to pass by? Or do you want to chase down the group that killed your last forms?"

The archer scratched his peeling, scabby face. "We figured they were too strong for us, and probly would be too far away by the time we recovered. So, yeah, we'll wait and pick off the next humans who come by, and take their forms." He grinned, "Maybe there'll be another woman among 'em. Some magic wouldn't hurt, either."

Xipil stroked his beard. "How would you and your two wolf comrades like to come north with us? We could use your help. You see, we work for the spirit who's in charge of the tear between the worlds, and he sent us after those who just decimated you. If you join us, we'll offer you the chance to take revenge on them."

"But they were strong! What's to say we won't end up dead again."

"Because: we also have strong magic. We have horses. And we have the element of surprise." Xipil flicked his wrist and levitated the man up in the air, his arms and legs flailing as he dropped his bow. Tamesis looked on, laughing, as she juggled a pair of flaming energy balls in one hand.

"Aaah … enough! Just put me down." Xipil lowered him back to the ground. "Alright, I'll join you if I can have a horse."

"Of course, my friend. Only the wolves will have to walk. Now, do you mind sharing your names?"

"Sure. I'm Fynn, these here are Alina and Elias." Mental greetings were passed around among the non-speaking contingent, and Fynn untied one of the spare horses. "Would it help if our other two friends come along? Maybe they can inhabit your horses, until finding better forms."

"That's a fantastic idea, Fynn. Tamesis and I could use a bit of mettle in our steeds, and you can switch out between the remaining two horses to keep them fresh."

At Fynn's call, a fox and a squirrel scurried out of the forest. He lifted them up to eye level with the horses, and after a bit of persuasion, the spirits transferred over to their new forms. Lieh realized this wasn't good for

Senn's chances; three days' advantage didn't seem to be as much when they had two nearly tireless demon mounts among the horses.

Xipil spurred his new demon steed and led the way. "If we keep up a good pace, we should catch our quarry before they reach Islingin. With *these* horses we'll catch them faster, and with your help we'll double our chances of success. In two weeks, we should have them!"

After more than a moon on the trail, Aidan was almost there. In the morning he had captured a falcon on the cliffs for Xiuhcoatl to inhabit later. Then he had crossed the bridge over the river Brel. Now he walked along a straight stretch of road parallel to the river that led to Islingin. The tall cliffs where he'd trapped the falcon rose up eerily on the west bank of the Brel, with no explainable reason why they should be there. Rumors abounded about an ancient magical cataclysm that had created them, but that knowledge was now lost in the shifting sands of time. The same sands threatened to obscure Islingin and its builders from future generations if Aidan failed at impersonating Marek.

—*Once more, Xiuhcoatl. Let's go over it once more to be on the safe side*— During the long ride, Aidan had persuaded the spirit that it would be better to live as a clever god among men, than to live as a clever demon among a sea of other demons. The only remaining question was whether Xiuhcoatl would switch sides again, playing Aidan for a fool and revealing him. But as no better choice presented itself, Aidan would put his trust in Xiuhcoatl for now. Their plan was coming together nicely, although there were many names and details to remember. Aidan must add everything that Xiuhcoatl knew to his arsenal of trickery. Certainly Marek would know more, but with a touch of arrogance, Aidan could play off the information he was supposed to know and didn't.

—*Fine. I'll name the Council member, and you tell me what you know about him or her. Let's start with Tynan*—

—*Tynan Maltus, a Magus several hundred years ago, well known for his skills in combat. He destroyed legions of enemy soldiers for his King before traitors in his personal guard murdered him. Tynan watches keenly for intrigue ever since then*—

—*What about Jarl Meita?*—

—A master craftsman of imbuing magic items, he used his Magus power in ancient times to create fantastic weapons that could kill any living being. Marek would have him design weapons for use on spirits, to help control those who don't follow orders—

—That goes against my personal desires, but is the interest of our goal, so you should definitely have him work on that full-time. As long as you honor our bargain and don't use them on me—

Aidan laughed out loud. *—Sure, Xiuhcoatl. I won't, if you promise not to cause too much trouble. Who's next?—*

—Strago Seltin?—

—Aah . . . Marek's own grandfather. One of the trickiest Council members to mislead, because he tutored young Marek in magic for years before passing away. Strago was a ruthless and motivated man, not someone you'd want as an enemy—

They discussed the remaining Council members, elaborating on the few details that Xiuhcoatl knew about them. At the end the spirit said, *—I think you've got it all; at least everything I know. The problem will be if there's something missing that Marek would know, which you don't. Time will tell. Now we just have to orchestrate this transfer, and we'll take one step closer to freedom, both yours and mine—* That sounded good to Aidan, after fifteen years of running from demons.

Soon the River Gate came into view, its high arch and rusty fittings still impressive despite their lack of upkeep. Aidan remembered his last visit here, about two years before the demons had emerged. That had been another age, for sure: children used to play just inside the gate, while soldiers tried to keep them out from underfoot. Carts loaded with vegetables and animals for market would drive past on their way to the Market Gate. Colorful banners and flags once hung from the merlons where now vines and creepers grew. The outer pomery had been a wide stretch of empty ground outside the wall to see enemies approaching, but now thick brush and saplings sprouted there.

Stationed at the gate was a man with dark black eyes and a shiny spear, though his body had the soft look of an Adept. It seemed that Marek's Council had been hard at work recruiting new demon guards to join Umkoome in securing their city and Keep. Aidan walked up brazenly, in order to make the right impression. He recalled his long discussions with

Xiuhcoatl as he approached the guard, settling into the proper frame of mind to impersonate his spirit prisoner. The young man inclined his spear forward. "You wish to enter Islingin?"

"Yes, as a matter of fact. This is our master's new form, let's not delay its arrival to him."

"Let me see your eyes." He peered into Aidan's black irises and frowned. "Your name?"

Aidan stood up a bit straighter. "I am Xiuhcoatl, collector of Magi for the Spirit Council."

The demon guard stiffened slightly, and stepped aside. "Quite an honor to meet you, sir. Please pass my regards to the Council." He leaned forward slightly, "May I ask about the birdcage?"

"This is my next form, which I need after this human has been delivered to Marek." The guard's eyes widened in response, apparently surprised by the unique choice of form. Aidan nodded curtly as he walked past, making sure to keep in character. He was allowed none of his normal friendly grins, no jokes, and absolutely no bear-hugging his supposed comrades.

Past the gate, he followed the inner pomery north along the river, listening to the gentle flow of water just outside the walls. The fortifications went right up to the edge of the river, affording no space for an enemy to lay siege close to the wall. As Aidan remembered, the walls curved in from the river a bit farther north where the docks were built. Overall the city was well fortified, though its current fortifications had never been battle tested. The Magus Conclave had kept the peace quite well, and when the city had fallen, it was from the inside.

Islingin was built in the shape of a quarter-circle, resembling a pie wedge with its straight sides facing toward the sea and the river. Through the center of the city, a curved road ran from the river wall to the sea wall, parallel to the curving land wall. Aidan turned away from the inner pomery by the river and onto this curving central road, angling toward the center of the city. For the most part the city was intact, but he passed several collapsed jumbles of stone and the burned-out remains of a few wooden buildings. Structures and ruins alike were filled with animals, nests, and vermin. There was no trace of the demon inhabitants he had expected to find.

Xiuhcoatl clarified this: —*Those squatters were either recruited to Marek's cause or expelled from the city. Marek really does want a world where spirits and humans can coexist, so the city proper has to be habitable by civilized men and spirits*— Aidan suspected, however, that his vision leaned strongly toward the humans working for a ruling class of demons.

He passed the old Market Square on his right, a wide open area where grass and small trees now sprouted between the uneven flagstones. Here he made a final turn left toward Islingin Keep, its tall, simple towers jutting up against clouds forming out over the sea. The statue-lined promenade leading to the Keep had fallen into disrepair the same as the rest of the city, with tall grass edging most of the stones. Finally Aidan approached the Keep itself, an imposing square building with tall towers at all four corners. He identified himself as Xiuhcoatl to another guard, who allowed him inside and said, "Xiuhcoatl! Tynan told me to direct you his way as soon as you arrive. The Spirit Council is meeting right now in the Council Chamber. Do you know the way?"

Xiuhcoatl spoke softly inside Aidan's mind. —*You do know the way. Straight across the courtyard and then inside*—

"Yes, thank you very much. I can find the Council Chamber." He nodded curtly at the guard and made his way across the open courtyard in the middle of the Keep. After passing through the entranceway, he went up several staircases before reaching the grand, ornamented hallway. Aidan noted it looked quite good, almost as it had the last time he visited Islingin. Marek certainly hadn't relinquished his aristocratic aspirations. At last they reached the Council Chamber door, which boasted yet another guard. Three, so far ... and loyal demons were hard to come by. Aidan set down his pack and the birdcage before speaking briefly with the guard, who immediately opened the massive oak doors to admit him. He entered a chamber rich with wood paneling, the air heavy with the smell of freshly worked timbers.

Xiuhcoatl spoke in his mind, —*Aidan. Last time I was here I discussed with Tynan Maltus about finding you and bringing your form here. You can ask him about the preparations of the Keep. Tynan is there, the right hand seat by the head of the table*— Aidan surveyed the room quickly. The wide doors opened at the foot of a long table, placing him with a view directly down its polished length to his future seat as Marek, which was now empty. At the right hand of that seat was Tynan, presenting quite an imposing figure, but the others he couldn't identify. To avoid any awkwardness, Aidan spoke up first.

"Tynan! And of course, the remaining ladies and gentlemen of the new Spirit Council. I have brought Marek's new form as promised: Aidan Alkar, at our service."

Tynan rose and walked swiftly down the length of the room, grasping his hand warmly. "Welcome back, Xiuhcoatl! Well done, we couldn't have expected you any sooner."

Aidan shook his hand solidly and asked, "How are the preparations here at the Keep?"

"Almost complete, brother. The few remaining tasks can wait until after the Master has arrived. In our last briefing with Marek in the Spirit Chamber, he said he was anxious to physically cross over as soon as you returned with a host. Give me ten minutes, and I'll meet you in the courtyard." He returned to his seat to finish up a few more items of business.

Xiuhcoatl coached Aidan briefly on the names. —*There to Tynan's right is Marek's grandfather Strago Seltin, followed by the twin seductresses Raeta and Kelti Sul. On the opposite side of the table, Rook Valtis will sit on your left hand, followed by his wife Sel Spali. Finally we have the craftsman Jarl Meita, and the Hyanto expert Zin Wisner*—

Aidan took a quick look around. Appropriately, grandfather Strago had the oldest form, and was probably in his sixties. The spirit twins, even though no longer twins in body, were indeed the stunning blond beauties Xiuhcoatl had promised—if only Aidan were a decade or two younger. Rook Valtis and Sel Spali were a mismatched pair: Rook was a tall, handsome man, while Sel was a dumpy, stringy-haired, frightful woman. Well, dead spirits can't be choosy. Next was Jarl Meita, whose skinny form with bulging arm muscles gave him pause. The spirit must have added muscles on his bookish host's figure during his days spent in the smithy. Finally there was Zin Wisner, brought on to organize the eventual invasion of Hyanto. He exuded the mystery and strange customs of Hyanto through his downward-pointing mustache-ends and beard. That affectation looked a little strange on a possessed man who was clearly a Kartus native, but Aidan wasn't going to argue semantics with a possessing spirit.

—Alright, Aidan. Let's get out of here before your staring becomes too obvious. Strago is eying you a bit strangely. I'm supposed to know these people already— Xiuhcoatl had a good point. He turned and left the room as the Council members returned to their discussion. The guard closed the doors behind him, and Aidan collected his pack and the birdcage before walking back to the courtyard to await Tynan.

—Aidan, a few more details. Tynan will take you to the Spirit Chamber we talked about; memorize the route because Marek certainly knows it. As for your chambers, that's going to be tricky. I don't even know where they are located—

Aidan thought for a moment. He had met Marek in person the last time he'd been here in Islingin, but had not seen the man's chambers. Furthermore, it wasn't a given that Marek would have the same rooms as before. *—I'll see what I can find out—* Aidan prepared himself for the next step: swapping Xiuhcoatl for Marek in his earth magic prison. *—Are you ready for this?—*

—As long as you hold up your end of the bargain, I'll do my part as we agreed. Let's just hope that when I find your friends, they give me an opportunity to talk before they try to kill me—

He grunted in assent. That would be a timber in the cogs right there, if Xiuhcoatl were killed before he could inform Senn and the others about the situation in Islingin. All assuming, of course, that the spirit didn't flee, or worse, expose Aidan's deception to the Council.

Shortly thereafter, Tynan emerged from the entranceway at the north of the courtyard. "Xiuhcoatl, my friend. I see you've brought your form with you; very good. Are you expecting another long journey?"

"I never know what Marek has planned for me. Now that I have brought our Master's new form, I expect he'll want me to deal with this problem Xipil has created. He is still making a mess of his task, chasing Senn Morel all over Kartus. Lieh Morel has been possessed, and Senn is still on the loose . . . disgraceful." Hah, that should be a nice final touch. Taking Xiuhcoatl's not-so-esteemed colleagues down a notch would make it easier for the supposed Marek to deal with them if they showed up later.

Tynan shook his head. "Xipil and his cohorts have really botched the job. I don't know why Marek didn't select you for that task." He started toward the southwest tower, and Aidan followed.

"At the time I was busy building up the Spirit Council, which I suppose is a far more important task. Speaking of which, how is the mood in the Council? Is everything running smoothly?"

"Hah," Tynan grunted as they started down a winding staircase. "I think the twins have already slept with most of the men in the Council, including Rook Valtis and old Strago. Jarl Meita has all of us nervous, working to craft a weapon that could send any of us back. Zin Wisner is keen to invade Hyanto right off the bat, blithely ignoring the fact that we need to have Kartus under control first. And Sel Spali is miserable in that form you brought her—she may be a Magus, but she's ugly as a beast."

"So Marek will have his work cut out for him, keeping the Council in control." There was the perfect opening . . . "Are his quarters safe?"

"Absolutely. He's requested the top of the northeast tower, the old Conclave chairman's quarters—and he has two hand-picked Adept guards. From the outside, well . . . let's just say one would have to be a top-notch Magus to even think about breaking in. Levitating all that way and holding the spell while cutting through the window glass and the bars . . . that's not easy. Besides, by the time someone could get into the room, Marek would have made a cinder of them. Especially if this form you've brought him is as strong as we hear."

"Stronger. I wouldn't want to cross Aidan Alkar any other way than as a black mamba." Aidan allowed himself a restrained grin at that comment, feeling Xiuhcoatl's irritation at the reminder that he'd been outclassed.

The pair continued down dark passageways, their globe of magical light creeping into corners as they approached and scuttling back out of them as they passed. Aidan tried hard to remember all the twists and turns. Finally, they arrived at a heavy oak door guarded by a tall woman. Xiuhcoatl said, —*That's Umkoome, I've met her several times. Once you are in the room, you'll contact the gatekeeper, Clayne, on the other side—*

"Umkoome, nice to see you again." The demon sentry nodded back at Aidan, and opened the door for him and Tynan. As they entered the wood-shielded room, he sensed the warding runes all around them—almost exactly like the runes of his demon coffin. He wondered who had done these . . . perhaps Umkoome. It must have taken someone a *very* long time. In the center of the room was the pedestal that Xiuhcoatl had mentioned. He walked over and held his hand to it, sensing until he found the presence on the other side. —*Clayne, it's Xiuhcoatl. Is our Master ready? I have his new Magus form here. Aidan Alkar, as requested*—

—*Xiuhcoatl. Just a moment, I will fetch Marek. He is anxious and prepared to go at a moment's notice, so have your next form ready*—

Aidan set down the birdcage containing the falcon he had caught for Xiuhcoatl. Then he opened a passageway in the earth magic cage around his spirit prisoner, allowing Xiuhcoatl to speak to the bird in soothing tones. —*Let me in, and there will be no more cages. We will fly free, hunt, and soar back to the clifftops together*— Now Aidan felt Xiuhcoatl redirect the phantom voice to him. —*Here we go. After this, you're on your own*—

Suddenly something pressed on Aidan's consciousness, a dull force impinging on his mind. —*My servant Xiuhcoatl, I am here, and I proffer many thanks to you for another task well done*— Aidan opened the earth magic cage wide, feeling Xiuhcoatl flow out into the falcon. He carefully prepared the magic cage again as he had done before, this time to capture Marek. The spirit flowed over from the other side through Aidan's eyes, and directly into his trap.

Marek spoke, addressing everyone in the room: Tynan, Xiuhcoatl, and his new form. —*Excellent work, all of you. Aidan, I apologize for your current position as my prisoner. But you . . . wait a minute. Why don't I have control? You've tricked me!*—

Aidan allowed himself a little smile, for he was the only one who had heard this first proclamation of his supposed master. He repeated, "Excellent work, all of you. Aidan, I apologize immensely for your imprisonment. Perhaps you'll come to see how much good my reign can do for Kartus!"

Then, privately, he said, —*Nice work indeed, Marek. You've missed one critical point though, old boy. I'm in charge here, and you're the prisoner. Now let's see how good I am at impersonating you!*—

CHAPTER 19

Flickering Red and Orange

R iding north from Silville had been uneventful. However, Senn's time with Keegan was an absolute dream come true. They talked about everything under the sun, held each other close at night, and made love as if there were no tomorrow. Which might be true— depending on the way events played out, their days could very definitely be numbered. Darin and Ziya seemed to look at it the same way, as they were now as intimate as if they'd been together their whole lives.

As the road wound down from the foothills of the mountains, it took them toward the west coast of Kartus, near enough to smell the sea air but not to actually see the ocean. Then it curved back to the northeast, angling toward Islingin. Now they were traveling due east, only a few days from crossing the river Brel, although they couldn't see much of their sur- roundings through the heavy canopy of trees. Luckily those trees shaded them from the hot summer sun. None of them had ever been here before, and they were relying heavily on a rough map that Darin had found among his father's belongings to navigate the unknown terrain. Senn was- n't quite sure what they would do on arrival in Islingin. They didn't know how many demons they would find there. They had no idea if Aidan's plan to capture and impersonate Marek had worked. Perhaps most frustrating, they knew nothing about the city itself—for example, where Aidan and the Spirit Council could be found.

All this was running through Senn's head when the Orb's spirit warning sounded, interrupting his thoughts with the words that were far too frequent in the recent moons. —*Alert, spirits near*—

He called to the others in a panic, "Hey, Darin, everyone, I just got an alert from the Orb—there are spirits nearby. A *lot* of them!"

Rikk, riding directly in front of Senn, craned his head around. "How many are we talking about?"

He took a deep breath. "Eight." The last time he'd seen close to that many demons, they had butchered nearly his entire clan.

"Damn, Senn. You and your spirit warning ... talk about being the bearer of bad news! What the *hell* are we going to do about *eight demons?*"

"I'd say we should *run*. The problem is, I don't know which way. These demons could be approaching from either direction on the road, or it could just be a camp of them off in the woods somewhere. Maybe they don't even know we're here."

Darin, who was leading the line of horses, reined in and brought them to a halt. "Senn's right. We have no idea of their location or intentions. The question is, should we continue, or stop and hide in the woods somewhere?" The widely spaced trees and sparse ground cover didn't look as if they'd provide much camouflage.

Helder shook his head. "No use stoppin'. If it's a camp of 'em, we better move on past. And if they're comin' up on us from ahead or behind, they'd see the fresh hoofmarks of our horses. We ain't been concealin' our tracks."

"Good point," Darin said, his voice sounding troubled. "Should we keep on moving then? I don't see any other choice."

Senn replied, "I suppose. Let's be ready with shields in case they approach on the road." No one spoke, the tangible silence reflecting the fear they all shared. Darin continued onward again at a good pace, moving swiftly in the shade of the tall, ancient trees. If they *did* encounter eight demons, perhaps the number of powerful spellcasters in their group would help—but then again, it might not.

It was about an hour before the attack came. Out of nowhere, an arrow flew down and thunked into the rump of Helder's horse at the rear of the line. The horse neighed and jerked wildly, as a female voice called from the woods, "No! Kill *them*, not horses. First shot kill one of them!"

Senn yelled, "Watch out!" as he heard the hiss of an energy ball from the woods on their right. He threw a shield in front of Keegan and Nic, who were on the right side of the line, just in time for the fiery ball to smash into it and explode ineffectually. All around the line, the Adepts brought up their own shields to fend off any more attacks. Darin and Ziya took care of the front of the line, while Piet and Keegan protected the right side. Senn moved his shield over to the left flank in front of himself and Rikk. That left Helder in the rear, who dismounted from his wounded horse and traded it for the remaining spare. Helder was busy arranging a shield of his own when a solid energy ball struck Darin's shield in the front, nearly knocking him off his horse. But the shield held, and they continued to search for the enemy.

Before they could spot any sign of the attacking spellcasters, several dark shapes leaped out of the forest shadows. As they raced into the light, Senn recognized them as two wolves and a giant cat—animals that normally didn't get along so well. Here they worked in concert, all dodging the shields and leaping at Rikk's horse in the same moment. The warrior brought his sword up to slash at the attackers.

Rikk screamed, "Damn it, Shyama!" as the cat hit his horse's shoulder and the wolves bit at its legs.

Senn realized it must be Xipil, who had somehow caught up with them. He wasn't about to let these demons take Rikk down, not after all they'd put the strongman through already. This was no time to test his own strength, so Senn got out the Orb and called up several spells in quick succession. A volley of cold energy balls flew at the wolves, who were just in front of him. They took the hits and kept moving, albeit weakly. Meanwhile, Rikk clambered down from his wounded horse to deal with the forest cat.

More energy balls sizzled through the air, and Senn turned his shield toward them. Rikk would have to rely on one of the others now—Senn couldn't help anyone if he were toasted by an energy ball. He moved his shield to block a solid ball aimed straight at him and Helder, while on the right flank, Keegan and Piet defended against a fireball.

Helder was holding against the archer to the rear, but he couldn't shield and attack at the same time. Senn looked closely as the archer moved in for a better shot, and noticed his disfigured features. Maybe he was one of those who had been burned by the wall of fire in Silville? If so, ice was in order. Senn fired a quick trio of energy balls using the Orb, watching them pound the archer until he was almost frozen solid. Then he launched a powerful solid energy ball, smashing the hapless demon archer into frozen, bloody chunks.

Helder turned to him, "Nice shot, kid. What about those other two who are pummelin' *us* with energy balls?"

Senn relaxed the flow of magic through him except for that maintaining his shield. Around him was chaos: Darin fired solid energy balls blindly into the woods, while Nic and Ziya helped Rikk fend off the wolves and that massive cat. Both wolves were almost dead after being frozen, shot with arrows, and trampled by horses. The lynx backed away warily, feathered with several arrows, as Rikk brandished his sword at it. Finally the cat turned to the north and fled the fray, limping badly.

What to do next amidst all this confusion? They had to stop the energy balls fast, before one hit in their midst and did some real damage. Senn brought up the Orb again and cast the sound weapon spell to the south, toward the area from which the most fireballs had originated. He turned up the power and blasted the forest with a deafening mixture of high and mid tones that carried for a hundred strides or more.

After the echoes subsided, a continuous scream could be heard from the south. Was that ... his mother? Suddenly flames gushed up from the ground all around them—huge pillars of fire that could engulf any of them in a skin-crisping, muscle-melting inferno.

Senn cried, "Run! It's a wall of fire!" The whole line of them spurred their horses on, racing away down the path. Helder, on the last of the spare horses, pulled Rikk into the saddle behind him as he rode past. As the group raced down the path, more and more pillars of flame sprouted in the distance behind them. Fireballs flew through the forest in random directions, one of them igniting the treetops right above them and raining smoldering leaves among the horses. It was as if that Magus to the south (and it *had* to be a Magus) had just gone crazy.

Senn had never gone this fast on a horse before. He felt that he might bounce out of the saddle at any moment. Then, above the din of their own galloping horses, he heard another horse gaining on them from behind even faster. Was that possible? Darin had said their plains horses were among the best and fastest ever bred; but given its speed, perhaps the horse behind them was possessed. Senn called out a warning, "Behind us!"

Rikk glanced backward and screamed, "That's Xipil! Watch your backs!"

Senn surveyed the trees, made a few quick calculations in his head, and formed a channel with a cutting blade. If he had the right height, and the right angle . . . he fed in solid energy and quickly directed the cutting point back and forth, high above them, halfway up the tall trees lining the road. The impact of his cutting lance at the speed they were galloping was so strong that he could feel the resulting shocks thumping in his chest alongside his racing heart. Finally he relaxed the flow of magic, feeling exhausted from the effort, and looked back.

The timing was perfect despite the unbelievable speed of the demon horse. Xipil was a good thirty strides behind, and looked up just as the first of the tree trunks fell, angling down across the road. The tree crashed to the ground, catching the horse mid-body and stopping it short almost as well as a stone wall would have. Xipil was thrown off the horse, twisting in the air as the tree limbs snagged his arms. The next tree trunk hadn't hit the ground yet, and Xipil's body crashed into it in midair with a bone-splintering crunch. Several more trees fell in succession between the party and their pursuer, scattering pieces of flesh and bone as the demon rider and his horse came to a stop one chunk at a time. The demons' unearthly speed had been their undoing. "Yeah!" Senn's cry echoed off the few remaining unburnt, untopled trees around them.

Soon Darin deemed they were out of range of the fireballs, and they reined in their exhausted horses. He spoke between panting breaths, "Everyone still . . . still with us?" Nods went around the group, until they all looked in amusement at Helder. Rikk had his arms clamped tightly around the big man's waist, and Helder's long hair was stuck to Rikk's sweaty face like a spiderweb.

Helder said in his gruff voice, "Anyone more, uh, fem'nine care to share a horse with this strappin' man?" The group broke out in peals of laughter, all euphoric to find they were still alive.

Rikk released his grip on Helder's waist and wiped the strongman's long hair from his eyes. "Xipil was catching up so fast, for a second there, it felt as if we were standing still. Nice work, Senn!" He climbed down from the horse, looking around uncertainly.

An idea came to Senn. "Thanks. Why don't you take my horse, and I'll ride with Keegan? We're probably the lightest two here." Rikk agreed, and they changed horses. "Let's go a bit further, until the spirit warning reads clear again. Then we should rest the horses for the night." The group continued at a slow pace, eager to be farther from the scene of the battle, but not wanting to strain the horses much more.

One worry remained, looming in Senn's mind. Even at this distance from the fight, an acrid tang of smoke filled the air, reminding him of the fiery explosions they had just witnessed. Had the demon possessing his mother truly gone crazy? And was she still alive?

The demon horse's haunches quivered as a wailing, crackling sound ripped through the air. Its volume increased until Lieh thought her ears would explode, and it truly felt as if they did. Tamesis raised her hands to cover her ears, but that hardly helped at all. She was unable to stay on the horse as it bucked in agony, throwing her to the forest floor. The fall knocked the wind out of her, and she could hardly breathe. When the deafening noise finally stopped, Lieh realized that her hearing was temporarily dulled: she could see the horse galloping away, but she could barely hear it.

Tamesis wasn't handling this turn of events well. Fynn had missed his target, Shyama and the wolves had failed to bring anyone down, the efforts that Tamesis and Xipil had made with energy balls had all been beaten back, and now Tamesis' demon horse had run off. Lieh felt the rage building, and this time there was no stopping it. The demoness screamed at the top of her lungs, as if she wouldn't stop until she heard the wail in her own muted ears. She drew up fire magic in the widest channel possible. The horse, just barely in view, ignited when it ran straight through a gout of flame that billowed up from the ground. Tamesis looked toward Senn's party and the wicked grin returned. She unleashed the fire wall in their direction, fortunately not yet aiming to kill. Massive columns of flame leaped up at random.

Then Tamesis lost it. She reveled in the power of destruction. No longer content simply to scare their intended target, Tamesis decided it would be much more fun to ignite the entire forest around them. Trees lit up left and right as pillars of flame engulfed them; powerful balls of heat energy flew in random directions. The road, the nearby trees, forest animals . . . nothing was safe anymore, and Lieh hoped that Senn would avoid the swath of random destruction that Tamesis unleashed on the forest.

After several minutes at this pace, even a Magus' magic could be depleted. As the energy Tamesis could draw for fireballs decreased, she slowed her bombardment. Finally she sat on the ground among the flames, with burning leaves and twigs fluttering down around her. Maybe Lieh could reason with the demoness now. —*Tamesis! Use what's left of the magic to construct a dome shield above us. Otherwise the fire will kill us both!*— Her skin was already turning red from the heat of the blaze around them, and there were several small burns from the falling debris.

—*Destruction always good. Tamesis knows to save oneself, don't need Lieh's help!*— The demon was spent, the moments of annihilation having diffused her rage. —*We live to ignite another day!*— Tamesis created a dome of solid energy above them, which glimmered as burning leaves and branches bounced off it. The spell was set to continue drawing energy as long as there was some amount left to draw. As the demon lay down to rest, Lieh wondered if the shield would be enough to protect against the heat, smoke, and falling trees. Tamesis closed her eyes and drifted into a dreamless state of recovery.

Upon awakening Lieh had no idea how long Tamesis had slept, but it was enough time for the forest fire to burn itself out, at least in this area. Night had come, and thick, ash-laden clouds dominated the sky. Light rain was falling, perhaps even brought on by the fire-cloud above them. Most of the tree trunks were still standing, now blackened posts bare of leaves and smaller branches. Fortunately no boughs had fallen directly on them.

Curiously, Tamesis seemed to be incapable of proceeding alone. Xipil and Shyama were nowhere to be found, and all around them a barren wasteland steamed gently in the rain. Tamesis walked aimlessly for half an hour, unable even to find the road amid the destruction she had wrought. This gave Lieh an idea.

—*If you give me access to earth magic, I can locate my son and the others*—

Tamesis thought that over. —*Why Lieh help me? No sense for you*—

—*I want to find my son as much as you do. Remember, your mission is to bring him safely back to my husband. Besides, once Marek finds a new Magus form for you, I will be free again to rule by his side*—

—*Aahh, Lieh Morel, make good argument. Why Tamesis can't try spell?*—

The easy answer was that Tamesis probably could use the location spell to find Senn, *if* he responded. But Lieh had no intention to cast a location spell anyway, so she just made up a little lie. —*You need to have a personal connection with the one for whom you search. It wouldn't work for you to contact Senn*—

—*Hmm. Then Tamesis let you try. Only allow Lieh small flow, just earth magic!*—

Perfect! —*Then open up the shell and let me find him*— Lieh felt her prison of spirit magic open up a little at one corner. Now was the tricky part: she had to find a way out, fast, and do it on the first try before Tamesis shut her back inside. She probed the jagged edges of the cage's opening, testing the spirit magic carefully with her earth magic. The two types were very similar, as she had noticed long ago when Tamesis had let her talk to Namee.

Then it came to her all at once. She could make a prison for Tamesis, trapping the demon in earth magic! That should cut off Tamesis' control of the remaining spirit magic shell around Lieh. She worked quickly, before her captor could suspect anything. Drawing earth magic to the maximum extent Tamesis permitted, Lieh sent out tendrils deep into the section of their shared mind that Tamesis' spirit inhabited. Then, in one fell swoop, Lieh solidified that earth magic into a cage around the invading spirit. Within seconds, she felt the spirit magic that bound her fade away, and she was in control once again. Lieh lifted her own hand in front of her face for the first time in several moons, looking in wonder at the ash-flecked skin and the grubby fingernails as she flexed her fingers.

—*Lieh Morel! This not part of deal. Only small flow, earth magic!*—

"Ahem." Lieh took pleasure in clearing her throat and speaking with her own voice again. "Tamesis, you can take our deal and shove it up your demon arse. You're staying trapped in there until I find a way to send you back. That cackling laugh, the evil grin, *and* your bloody intentions ... you're going back to the spirit world, you hear me, bitch?"

—*Sssss!*— Tamesis only hissed and growled at her like an animal— that was fitting.

Lieh's eyes teared up for the first time in years. She had bottled up her feelings for too long. As the tears flowed freely, she cried for her dead clan mates, for her son's pain, for the possessed Aidan Alkar ... how would she atone for what Tamesis had done with these hands? Eventually the tears slowed and Lieh regained control over her emotions. She had to remain calm and find a way out of this predicament.

Now that the demon was caged, how would Lieh proceed? The demon horse was long gone, as was every other sign of life. It seemed the easiest way to reach Islingin would be on foot—she was only a few days away by now. There was no point to cast the location spell; Senn would just think it was another ruse on the part of the demons who had been chasing him for so long. Lieh would worry about how to find her boy and the others when she arrived in Islingin.

But then what? Lieh had just focused on escaping, and stopping these demons from hurting her son. What about Marek? He had chosen spirits who would follow orders, who would do anything in his name. Even Xiuhcoatl, the most civilized of them so far, lacked certain standards of human decency. He had rebuked his comrades, saying that Lieh should not have been possessed and treated so badly—but in the end, he had done nothing to rectify the situation. The last time Xiuhcoatl had been in their company, he hadn't given a whit about his demon comrades, much less about Lieh.

Who, then, would Marek have brought over to populate his supposed Spirit Council? What if those spirits were even more cold and ruthless than the minions she'd met so far? Lieh shuddered at the thought of humankind losing even more freedom than they already had. They would move from being hunted by disorganized, wild demons to being enslaved by a regime of intelligent ones . . . led by her onetime lover.

For once Lieh felt she had a real choice to make, instead of being forced into a decision by her circumstances. On one side, there was knowledge and power—the opportunity to achieve what she and Marek had always dreamed. But the price was high: her son, their clan, and the freedom of mankind. After pondering this for a while among the scorched remains of the forest, Lieh decided the other option felt better.

For the good of mankind, for her son, and for the memory of her clan, she would take up arms against Marek, even if it meant she had to kill him.

That decision made, Lieh hiked purposefully north through the burned devastation toward the road, which would lead her straight to Islingin.

Xiuhcoatl observed the area burned by the wildfire from many leagues away. An ashy fire-cloud was dissipating above it. Wisps of steam rose from the edges of the destroyed area, as if a light rain had put out the fire the night before. The question was, how had the blaze started? There were no thunderstorms in the area, and it hadn't been unusually dry of late. One easy answer sprang to mind that made him quite nervous: Tamesis may have gone wild and killed Senn and his party. Aidan had argued persuasively that a world run by demons was not in Xiuhcoatl's best interest, and Tamesis was a prime example. Senn Morel had better still be alive, because his talents would be the best catalyst they had to topple Marek's Spirit Council.

As Xiuhcoatl homed in on the source of the fire, he learned more. Several horses and a pair of wolves lay dead on a clear strip which must have once been the road. One dead human in the west lay scattered about in small, crispy pieces, with a charred bow next to him. A row of burned trees lay across the road, where another dead horse and a splintered body were intertwined among the blackened trunks and limbs. That one looked like Xipil . . . what were the chances? Xiuhcoatl flew closer and examined the body. Yes, definitely Xipil, meaning his spirit should be somewhere nearby looking for a new host. Then the falcon spotted a shimmer in the burned-out trees near the road.

—*Xiuhcoatl, is that you? Friend, any chance you can help me find a new form?*— The faint voice was barely audible in his mind, meaning Xipil was not much longer for this world.

—*Aah, Xipil. Have you seen Shyama?*—

—*That damn cat disappeared during the fight*—

What good news! If Shyama had survived, she might join his new cause.

Xipil continued, —*I was beginning to get a bad feeling from her. We should warn Marek against relying on her in the future*—

—*The worst failure I see here is yours, Xipil. Your latest scheme to catch Senn Morel apparently didn't go as planned, now did it? And you couldn't even maintain control of that beast-woman Tamesis. If Shyama saved herself after your worthless plan went awry, she at least managed to stay alive, which is more than you can say*—

—*Yes, Tamesis was out of control, that's true. She caused this fire. But . . .*— The strain of communication taxed what little spirit magic remained to hold Xipil's spirit here. —*Marek still needs me. I am sure he has use for someone of my talents. Can you find a form for me?*—

—*Regretfully, I cannot oblige. You've devastated the forest for leagues around, and I wouldn't be able to find so much as a mouse before you would fade back to the other side*—

—*Are you sure? Perhaps some forest animal has survived in a tree trunk or an underground burrow*—

—*I'm sorry, Xipil, but I fear you have failed Marek for the last time. And there will be no more free passes back from the spirit world now that your master is here in this one. Good luck back on the other side. I truly feel it's where you belong*— There was no response, and soon Xiuhcoatl could no longer detect the distinctive shimmer of an unattached spirit. Xipil was gone; one less problem to worry about.

Whom to search out next? Tamesis was either crisped in her own firestorm, or wandering around here aimlessly. It was better to leave her to her own devices, lest he be fried by her next bout of insanity. That left Shyama and Senn Morel, who would both be heading the same direction. Xiuhcoatl took to the air again, spiraling as high as he could below the dissipating fire-clouds. He headed off to the east, eyes keen for anything moving in the burned-out forest below. There was Tamesis, on the road not too far ahead—yes, just leave her alone. He kept on flying.

Eventually the edge of the burned area came and went, and the return of green treetops made the search more difficult. After several hours zig-zagging across the road, Xiuhcoatl spotted Shyama among the trees just north of the path. He dove down and landed in a tree above the lynx, who stopped quickly when she caught sight of him.

—*Xiuhcoatl?*—

—*Yes, it's me. I'm glad to see you survived*—

The lynx settled on its haunches and regarded him serenely. —*I'm glad to be free from Xipil's leadership. I saw his body in the road just before the fire reached it. How is Marek? Did you deliver Aidan Alkar to him?*—

—*Somehow, yes. But rather . . .*— How should he phrase this? He did-n't want Shyama to run to the Spirit Council and warn them that their leader was an impostor. —*What do you think about this whole operation of Marek's?*—

Shyama snorted softly and turned her head away. —*Poorly run. Half his henchmen are fools. There are no results*—

—*And what do you want from all this?*—

—*I want my freedom here in this world. Unfortunately, Marek is the only choice besides lawlessness*—

Xiuhcoatl opened his beak slightly, the closest this form could get to a smile. —*What if there were another choice?*—

The lynx cocked her head, obviously interested in his remark. —*Dear Xiuhcoatl. What are you saying. Do we have another way out of this mess?*— That was more like it. He could count on Shyama.

—*As a matter of fact, we do*— Carefully, he recounted the story of the last few weeks. Shyama was particularly impressed to learn that Aidan had impersonated Xiuhcoatl when they had met at the ambush site. There was hope yet that the Magus could double as Marek for long enough to take down the Spirit Council.

Finally, Shyama weighed in with her thoughts. —*Xiuhcoatl, we can't give up on the dream of being free. If we stay with Marek, we destroy that dream for all humans as well as for ourselves. We would end up chosen min-*

ions of Marek, always answering to him. If there is another choice, we should take it—

—Excellent, Shyama! I thought you might agree. Now, let me track down Senn Morel and see if I can't persuade him to believe me. There's a good chance of that, as long as he doesn't throw a fireball down my craw in greeting— The two spirits appointed to meet later along the road, where Xiuhcoatl could easily spot the lynx from the air. Then the falcon took to the skies again, following the road toward Islingin in search of Senn.

It was not long before Xiuhcoatl spotted his mark. He would have to be blind to miss seven horses traveling down the road, certainly a rare sight these days. The party was watching the woods warily, as if at any moment they expected a demon to jump out at them. Circling lower, the falcon alighted on a tree limb some hundred strides ahead of the group and waited until they drew closer.

At about twenty strides, Xiuhcoatl addressed all of them together with his spirit magic. *—Senn Morel, it is I, Xiuhcoatl—*

The boy shared a saddle with a young red-haired woman who clung to his waist. When Senn saw the falcon he immediately reined in his horse and raised his right arm, magic at the ready. "You! What are you doing here? I can build another cage, and keep it buttoned up with magic this time!"

—Wait. It's not as you think. I do not mean you harm, in fact I bring news from our friend Aidan Alkar— Xiuhcoatl could almost feel the solid magic cage spell that Senn must be preparing. *—Please listen before you imprison or kill me! Aidan has persuaded me to join your cause. I will help you bring down the Spirit Council and put humans back in power . . . in exchange for my freedom—*

Senn lowered his arm, but blew out his breath in indignation. "Hah. Why would we want to leave any of you demons roaming free? And why would Aidan possibly agree to that?"

—Because he needed my cooperation to trap Marek. If I didn't play along after he swapped Marek's spirit for mine, the Spirit Council would know he was an impostor. Furthermore, I am . . . different from most of the spirits you have encountered here—

"Different? How do you mean?"

At least now the boy was listening to him. —*I am not a bloodthirsty, savage killer like most of those who flooded here in earlier times. My desire is to travel the world and see it through the eyes of the wild creatures that inhabit it. This beautiful falcon, the deadly black mamba, even the tiny mosquito I used to escape your last birdcage ... seeing through their eyes is a delight to me. I have no desire to imprison, enslave, or rule your kind. I only want the same thing you do. Freedom!—*

"And how do you plan to prove that? It would be nice to take you at your word, but you might lead us directly into a trap. We have no reason to trust you."

Now there was a dilemma. —*I don't have some magic word to prove my new allegiances. However, I can arrange a demonstration: when you arrive at Islingin, I will kill the demon standing watch at the River Gate. It will look like an accident—*

"Are you telling me a falcon can take out a demon guard?"

Xiuhcoatl decided he had best tell the whole story, while he had his audience. —*You may remember the big lynx, Shyama. She is also weary of answering to a master whose goals would only restrict her freedom. I will enlist her to take out the sentry, who will have no idea what happened—*

The boy looked around at his companions. "Give us a moment."

—*Of course*— The group spoke amongst themselves in low tones, which Xiuhcoatl could have overheard if he had tried. But that was not his way, so he turned his concentration elsewhere to give them privacy. What should his next move be? To check in on Aidan Alkar ... to plot the sentry's demise ... to spy on the Spirit Council members ... there were so many options. Probably the best idea was to see how Aidan was progressing. If anything happened to him, Xiuhcoatl's plans would change dramatically.

Senn's voice called loudly from below. "Alright! We'll work with you, since we have nothing to lose. We'll meet again outside Islingin, and I expect you to keep your promise about that guard."

—*Excellent. I would shake hands on it, but as you can see ...*—

The boy smiled. "Right. We'll consider the bargain sealed, as well as it can be."

—*Then I'm on my way to make sure Aidan is still in charge of Marek, and not the other way around. If you do see my comrade Shyama, please show her the same courtesy you've extended to me—*

"Sure, we won't roast the big cat. Say hello to Aidan, and . . ." Senn pursed his lips and furrowed his brows. "*Good luck*, Xiuhcoatl. If what you've said is true, I mean that."

The falcon stretched its wings and took to the air again, following the thermals high among the clouds. The prospect of true freedom rang in Xiuhcoatl's ears . . . no master, no threat from humans or demons, just the open blue sky and a pair of wings.

CHAPTER 20

The Schemers

"Master Seltin! One hour until Council, just notifying you as requested." Aidan awoke slowly as the guard knocked on his door.

He sighed groggily. It had been a long couple of days working with the Spirit Council. Marek's idea had been to introduce the new Council as a positive change for the people of Kartus, ruling them while keeping rogue demons in check. But Aidan didn't care a whit about that plan, because he wanted to send the whole Council back to the spirit world before the scheme could go into effect. If he failed, these possessed Magi would dominate Kartus regardless of whether the Council itself stayed together.

—*Damn it, Alkar, how long do you think you'll be able to continue this charade?*—

Marek was still trying to worm his way out of the earth magic cage. —*Long enough, you pompous megalomaniac. Just long enough to see you all back to the other side and to free my people*—

—*They're my people too, Aidan! All I want is to bring them together under one peaceful rule*—

He shook his head. —*Right, your peaceful rule. It would only be peaceful so long as we humans did what you commanded. Among other directives, that would include invading Hyanto! Some peace that would be—* Marek didn't have any rebuttal to that. It had been an interesting few days discussing the pros and cons of spirit rule with his prisoner. Aidan had let Marek try to win him over, pretending that he might be persuasible, all for the purpose of studying the speech patterns and theories of the now-powerless ruler of the spirits. While Aidan hadn't stumbled across any informational gems, he had learned enough about Marek to express himself in the same arrogant and refined manner as his prisoner.

Aidan dressed quickly in a velvety red doublet and matching hose, the kind of exotic garb Marek probably would have chosen. "Guard! Breakfast." He stopped himself from adding a 'please,' something which Marek would definitely skip. This was tiring—every action or phrase was preceded by the thought, what would Marek do? He might as well have Jarl Meita make a brand with those words and burn it into the rump of his horse. At least Jarl's assigned task in the Council was moving swiftly. The smith was developing a magic weapon to use against the demons—wait, no spirit used that terminology; a weapon against rogue spirits. With it they could intimidate and control those rogues, or as a last resort, send them back to the spirit world.

How had the other Council members fared? In two days of Council meetings there had been little progress toward Marek's goals, which was a good thing. Kelti and Raeta's plan to lure nearby clans back to the city was to sleep with as many humans as they could, to prove that life with the spirits would be pleasurable. Tynan instead proposed to build a spirit army and take control by force. Zin Wisner constantly grumbled about the delayed invasion of Hyanto. When Aidan had asked him, "With what army?" the Magus had responded by talking in the tongue of Hyanto for the rest of the session—knowing full well that no one could understand him.

Rook and Sel forever bickered with each other, Sel seeming to have some notion that her husband had been unfaithful. Honestly, Aidan wasn't surprised about Rook's tryst with the twins. Sel looked like the child of a moose and a puffer fish, and her years in the spirit world had given her the same disposition as Xiuhcoatl's black mamba. The couple would wreak havoc across Kartus if the Council ever fell apart.

That left Strago Seltin, who often led the discussion to topics where Aidan knew he could be easily exposed. He didn't think the old man suspected him—Strago just enjoyed bringing up family matters and old memories. However, it wouldn't take much of a slip for Strago to realize that the Council's sovereign leader was not really his grandson.

All in all, it was a touchy situation. Aidan had no idea how to eliminate the Council, though Jarl Meita's weapon could be helpful. He sat down to the hearty breakfast that the guard had brought up. At least that was one facet of life these demons didn't want to change: eating. They relished every mealtime as if it were their last, because they'd all once enjoyed a final meal and then waited dozens, if not hundreds, of years before the next morsel passed their lips. Marek's cook must have been a culinary master in his previous life, as testified by the poached eggs, freshly smoked fish, exotic pastries, and fresh fruit that were spread out before Aidan.

After breakfast, he headed for the day's first Council session. He donned a gaudy sword that he'd found in the room, obviously a ceremonial touch on Marek's part considering that a Magus hardly needed a sword. He wound his way around the spiral stairs of the tower, which took him several flights down to the level of the Council Chamber. There was a hidden door through the rear wall of the chamber, opening just behind his chair. Although the chairman of the old Magus Conclave had not been a sovereign in his own right, the position had come with some advantages.

Just as planned, Aidan arrived last in the Council Chamber. The spirits' resplendent leader should not have to wait on his advisors. "Good morning. I expect you've all had enough time to further develop your plans since yesterday afternoon." The discussion around the table ceased and everyone turned to him, some looking more nervous than others. First he turned to the most restive among them, to get the day started on the right foot. That was, the wrong foot, if you looked at it from Marek's perspective. "Kelti, would you and Raeta begin? Our first order of business is to bring the local clans into the fold. Your reworked plan is of the utmost importance."

Kelti glanced around the table, looking a little timid. "Actually, Master Seltin, I . . . that is, we . . . spent some time working on our longer-term plans for Hyanto." Her gaze flicked across to Zin Wisner, then her focus returned to the tabletop in front of her where her fingers fidgeted.

Raeta was not quite so shy. "Yes. We have come to believe that Hyanto may be the future, because the natives there are ripe for our message. Whereas the humans here are already against us!" Zin was smiling at her as if she were some kind of goddess. "And besides, the native tongue of Hyanto is so . . . mmm . . ." Raeta smiled and caught Zin's eye. "Seductive!"

"Enough!" Strago pounded the table with his fist. "We are not here to discuss when to invade Hyanto. And I certainly don't want to hear about your latest debauchery."

Dead right—Strago didn't want to hear about the twins' revelry with someone else, when it just as well could have been with him. The old man looked to Aidan for backup. "My grandfather is right," he added in a loud but even tone. "There will be no more talk of abandoning Kartus. We shall begin a campaign to win over the local clans. This may involve bribes, favors, or trickery—but I want to see your strategy tomorrow! If there is no progress, I will throw you two off the Council and give your tasks to someone better suited."

"Marek!" Rook waved his writing quill with all the flourish of an imbued wand. "I am happy to aid the Sul twins, if you desire."

Rook's wife was not so enthusiastic about this idea. "Damn it, Rook, you'll do no such thing without me! I don't trust you with those two . . ."

Aidan didn't want his Council to get *too* out of hand in the first few minutes of the day. "For the last time! Keep your domestic disputes in your own chambers." He shot the quarreling pair a piercing stare, daring them to say anything more. "Now, the next order of business: increasing the city's spirit defenders. Right now they're spread thin, with just one man at each gate. Tynan, how are the arrangements coming along?"

"Ahem, yes." Marek's right hand man arranged his papers, looking carefully over the pages of notes. "Umkoome's Spirit Knights captured three more humans yesterday. Their forms have been taken over by three of our own, selected by our brother Clayne on the other side according to your directives."

Ah yes, the Spirit Knights . . . they were Tynan's most resourceful and dangerous demon guards, answering to Umkoome. Despite being mostly Medi and Minor Adepts, the Knights were very dangerous to small groups of clansmen caught alone in the forest. The irony was lost on everyone but Aidan: Tynan was in charge of kidnapping and possessing the very clansmen whom the twins needed to win over. A campaign of terror would only stagnate the Council's plan for gaining the clans' support. Therefore, it was something Aidan encouraged wholeheartedly.

"Very good," Aidan said. "That's a piece of positive news. Have the Knights continue their efforts, but do not take any unnecessary risks. They must keep a low profile." He might as well try to limit the influx of new spirit soldiers that he would eventually have to deal with. "Now, what should we do with those three new recruits? I open the table for suggestions."

Of course, Raeta spoke up first. "Well, the two of us could show them around town . . . give them a personal tour?"

Aidan bet they would give the recruits a *very* personal tour, and not of Islingin. "Noted. Any other ideas?"

Jarl Meita cleared his throat. "Ahm, Master Seltin. Not to jump ahead, but I could use some more help in the forge. It would accelerate my activities, especially if any of these men have use of magic." Aidan gestured in assent; that was perfect. In fact, Jarl's was the *only* area where he wanted to make progress.

"Anyone else?" He looked around the table expectantly. "Very good. The three recruits shall report to Jarl this afternoon in the forge." Raeta and Kelti appeared crestfallen, so he added, "If there is time, and if Jarl allows, the twins can show these men around town. It would be helpful for them to get their bearings in case they need to fight." That turned the twins' expressions into wicked grins. "Now, Jarl, how about your progress with our spirit killer weapon?"

The smith smiled. "Certainly. My plans are complete, and the sword is in the forging process. Having only one assistant slows me down. The new men can help keep the forge hot, hammer the metal, and do the grinding. Eventually, I'll need to . . . test the weapon's effectiveness." That sounded ominous. "Of course, the test subject . . . would be one of your choosing. Perhaps a rogue spirit, if the Knights round up any in the next few days?"

Aidan asked, "Tynan, can you please give those orders to the Spirit Knights? They should look for rogue spirits, and round up a few for . . . testing." He glanced around the room: did the others feel squeamish about the idea, the way Marek probably would? There was indeed a sense of discomfort all around. "When can we expect to view this demonstration?"

"Master Seltin, first I should explain: the process involves an infusion of several magics, including spirit magic, during the forging of the blade. With the additional men, the weapon should be ready in no more than three days. Not finished, mind you, no jewels and gold-leaf hilt—but ready for demonstration."

"Then please continue with all haste. We need that weapon against the rogues, and since *you're* making good progress, you have my full support." He slid his gaze pointedly to the twins.

But Jarl wasn't done yet. "There is one other matter, Master Seltin."

"Yes?"

"It's something I invented to control humans with strong magic, who resist us despite the inevitability of your rule." He produced a pair of locking metal cuffs and a tiny key from his coat pocket and passed them down the table to Aidan. "I call them Magus Manacles. It's an idea that I copied from your Spirit Chamber with its warding runes of earth magic. Now, the magics of the physical world can't ward against each other . . . but earth magic can ward against spirit magic. I thought that perhaps . . ." He paused to let Aidan finish the sentence. Quite the arse-licker, this one.

"Yes, you thought that spirit magic runes might ward against earth magic. Right?"

"Correct, Master! Not only do the runes work against earth magic, but they prevent all magics of this physical world from being called up. Clap these manacles on a spellcaster, and they completely lock out his magic."

Aidan picked up the manacles and examined them. They were simply constructed, with bone inlays in hammered iron, but he could feel powerful runes imbued in the bone. "Would anyone volunteer to demonstrate the effectiveness of these?"

Predictably, one of the twins was the first to speak up. "Marek, you can lock me up!" He beckoned, and Kelti walked around the table. He clamped on the manacles and waited expectantly.

Kelti smiled demurely. "Oh, of course. I'll try to get that key with levitation." She focused on the key, working a spell that was child's play for a Magus. It didn't move at all. "I can't do anything, Master. I'm helpless!"

"Alright, alright. Here." Aidan unlocked the manacles and Kelti scampered back to the other end of the table, giggling. These manacles could be very useful or very dangerous, depending on who had the keys. "How many pairs have you made?"

"Half a dozen so far, Master Seltin. All are ready for use, fully tested and working."

"Bring them to me tomorrow, all six pairs. I will hold onto these Magus Manacles for safekeeping, until we find a need for them."

The Council meeting continued for the next hour. Rook and Sel's bickering escalated until Aidan threatened to expel them from the chamber. The Spirit Council probably had as many—if not more—arguments and disputes than the old Magus Conclave in former times. Eventually they took a recess, planning to meet again later in the afternoon.

Strago approached Aidan after the others had left, just as he headed for the door. "You know, Marek, this isn't the way to run a Council. You're giving too much freedom, letting your subjects have too much rope. Where's the sense in that—they'll just use it to hang you! It may appear they're playing around, but they each have an agenda." The old man put a hand on his shoulder and gave it a squeeze. "Maybe it's a big shock to finally be back in the physical world. But we need your firm hand . . . nay, the iron fist . . . that I remember from the spirit world." Aidan stood a bit straighter. "I want to see my grandson, full of fire and vigor the way you were the day I taught you to cast energy balls! Remember that, eh? The look on their faces when that hare exploded?"

All it would take to reveal Aidan would be him nodding agreement to one story that Grandpa had falsified to catch him out. If the old man caught on to him, his ruse would be finished in a matter of minutes. "Yes . . . I miss those good old times. It even feels as if some of those memories are lost to me after the years I spent in the spirit world. Nevertheless, we forge onward."

"Just remember what matters. I'm here watching, making sure you do right by your promises in the spirit world. If you don't keep these Magi in line, Kartus will be faced with eight warlords striking out on their own!" Strago turned and strode toward the large double doors. Aidan clearly had some work to do. If the Council splintered, it would be nearly impossible to track them down one by one all across Kartus . . . and likely in Hyanto, as well.

Xiuhcoatl flew over the ocean toward Islingin Keep. Tynan had said that
Marek's quarters were in the northeast tower. His only question was,
which of the two Magi would be in charge when he arrived: Marek or
Aidan? It was early morning, so Aidan should not have left for his Council meeting yet. There, near the top of the tower, several windows were
glassed and barred. One had the glass angled open for air, and Xiuhcoatl
chose that window to alight. —*It's me, Xiuhcoatl. Are you awake?*— Inside,
Aidan (or was it Marek?) dragged himself out of bed. The red-faced leader
of the demons walked slowly over to the window and peered out at him.

—*Aah, Xiuhcoatl. I'm glad you made it back, hopefully you bear news
from Senn and the others. Come in*— He undid the window's catch and
swung it wide open, allowing the falcon to squeeze between the bars into
the room. —*It's been hellish here; I'm not sure how long I can hold this
Council together. Even if they don't discover my ploy, the Council might self
destruct at any time*—

Xiuhcoatl flexed his wings and straightened his feathers. Apparently
Aidan was still in charge. —*That's true. It's less work for us to deceive the
Council if there is foment within, but if each Magus struck out on his own, it
would be disastrous*—

Aidan rubbed his eyes with one hand, still waking up. —*What of
Senn? Did his party evade Xipil and the others?*—

—*Interestingly, yes and no. Although they slipped past the ambush, Xipil
discovered their ruse and pursued them. Then he made a mess of things
again: there was a battle, and Xipil was killed. He's gone now, back to the
other side. Tamesis is wandering around on foot, after starting a wildfire that
consumed leagues of forest before rain put it out. Shyama is on our side now;
Marek will be sorry to hear this, but his principles and methods don't even
ring true with some of his chosen spirits. Then there is Senn: his party fortunately survived the battle unscathed. I persuaded him to listen to me, and I
think I can win his trust*—

—*I'm glad you brought good news. The only positive development here is
that Jarl Meita will complete the spirit weapon in a few days. We have to
postpone any action until then, because it will be invaluable to have that
weapon. My question is: how do we get rid of the whole Council at once?
They are all powerful Magi, and if any one of them gets wind of what's hap-*

pening, all hell will break loose. These demons could wind up anywhere in Kartus, causing even more trouble than the Council would here in Islingin—

That was quite a quandary; Xiuhcoatl puzzled over it for a moment. *—What about that box you were making to send me back to the spirit world, when you captured me near Leikton. Could you make another one?—*

Aidan rubbed his beard. *—That's certainly an interesting idea! But it would take weeks to prepare a demon coffin big enough for even one or two Magi. If they started disappearing in small numbers, the others would become suspicious. We'd have to trap them all at once, and a coffin that big would take . . . who knows how long to make—*

Then Xiuhcoatl had a revelation. *—Aidan, you already have a coffin big enough for eight. The Spirit Chamber—*

The Magus pressed a finger to his lips, thinking. *—Yes, the Spirit Chamber! That's right. I would just need to orchestrate a way to gather the whole Council in there at once—*

—Right. You would need to seal them in the Chamber, and then . . . ahh, kill all of them?—

—I'd rather not kill eight of the finest Magi in the land if I can help it. I doubt we could accomplish that so easily, anyway. However, I've got a trick up my sleeve . . . some special poison darts, an idea of Senn's—

—Poison darts, to send spirits back? How does that work?—

—It's a slow-acting poison that puts the body in a near-dead state. Once it takes effect, the spirit magic can't bind the possessing spirit to the body's own soul anymore. The demon spirit is thrown out, just as if the body had died. The real problem is that I have only four darts left, and no means to make more of them here. We'll need to obtain the darts from Senn's supply as well, and hope it adds up to at least eight!—

—Good idea. I'll lead Senn here to Islingin and hide his party somewhere in the city, perhaps in the crumbling houses near Market Square. They should be fairly safe there for a few days. Once they are in Islingin, we'll exchange ideas again and come up with a more solid plan—

Aidan smiled in assent. *—Let me see what develops with Jarl's spirit weapon; I'll keep the Council resources focused in that direction. Give my greetings to Senn and the others—*

—That I will do. Take care of yourself, Aidan— Xiuhcoatl hopped up to the windowsill and slipped back between the bars. With a short leap

the falcon returned to the air, gliding away over the waves that crashed against the walls of the Keep. Would Aidan be able to maintain a balance: blocking the Council's progress while keeping its members together? If not, Xiuhcoatl might return to find a smoking crater instead of a Keep, and spirit Magi spread across the whole of Kartus.

CHAPTER 21

The Spirit Chamber

After two more days of riding, Senn and his companions were almost at Islingin. They crossed the river Brel in the late afternoon, marveling at the towering cliffs jutting up next to the western bank for no discernible reason. On this side of the river the forest thinned and the road turned north, following the water for the last few leagues to Islingin. Soon they passed through areas that had once been populated, but were now only clearings with rotting shacks and overgrown piles of stone. Dusk was coming, and Senn decided that arriving at this time would be to their benefit.

When they reached the edge of the forest, Darin reined in his horse. "Alright, folks. Let's wait just off the road here until we hear from that falcon. This is where he said to wait for him."

Senn hoped the wait would not be long, as he was anxious to see what the city was like inside the walls. Within the hour the spirit alarm warned him of a single demon nearby. Shortly the shadowy silhouette of a falcon swooped down through the twilight and landed on a bough just a few strides from Senn. Would Xiuhcoatl fulfill his promise to take out the guard?

—Good to see you again, Senn. No trouble with Spirit Knights or any-thing else along the way?—

"Spirit Knights?" Senn asked. "No, we certainly didn't see any of them."

—They are Tynan's best-trained spirit warriors, and recently they are out hunting for more human forms. The Council wants to increase the num-ber of loyal spirits in the physical world—

"We'll keep an eye out for these Knights once we're inside the city. Now, how about your promise?"

—Yes. I recommend that you come with me right to the edge of the trees to observe our demonstration of goodwill—

Senn nodded, ready with a shielding spell in case it was all a ruse to capture them. He walked forward cautiously, hiding among the trees, until he could see the demon guard across the cleared zone outside the wall. The city was in terrible disrepair: the cleared zone was overgrown, and vines sprouted from the crumbling mortar of the walls. The guard stood at what Senn supposed was the River Gate, surveying the road and the bushes with a bored look on his face. Xiuhcoatl gave a shrill shriek as a sig-nal, and cocked his head upward. High above the sentry at the top of the tower, a furry head poked around several loose stones, then disappeared back behind them. Senn saw the top corner of the tower's parapet give way, and the big stones fell, picking up speed. The lynx must have been strong to dislodge those big blocks. The guard looked up just in time to be hit in the face by a rain of building stones, even one of which could have killed a man. Within seconds he was half-buried and motionless.

—Now, let's bring your friends inside the gates, quickly! Leave the horses, you won't need them anymore. They would just bring unwanted attention from Tynan's spirits—

So far there was no sign of a double-cross by Xiuhcoatl; they might as well trust him. Senn raced back to the others. "Let's go! Leave the horses, bring only your packs and food." Quietly, the group gathered up their gear and followed Senn up the road. The falcon led them across the cleared area to the gate. The lynx Shyama was next to the guard, checking over the body.

—Greetings, Xiuhcoatl. Also to you, Senn Morel. The guard is dead, and won't be telling any tales. It will be a few hours before the spirit reassoci-

ates. He won't know the reason for the rock fall. But you'll want to be well hidden, because he may be suspicious. Best be on your way inside— Senn gaped at the enormous lynx up close. The last time they'd met, Shyama had been trying to take down Rikk's horse. In fact the strongman was understandably nervous as he walked by the big forest cat, keeping his hand on the pommel of his sword.

The falcon led them down darkening streets, first staying close to the city wall, then turning to follow a row of buildings along a big square. *—Keep silent now. The Market Gate, over there, has another sentry watching just outside the wall—* Sticking close to the buildings, the companions followed their guide in single file as he flew along from windowsill to flagpole. He led them down an alley off the square, and the group threaded their way through bones and wreckage that littered the narrow cobblestone path. Xiuhcoatl landed on the faded wooden sign of an inn, which bore the image of a coach and horse. *—Of all the derelict inns I've checked in the past few days, this one is in the best shape. It has several rooms in back, away from the road, where you should not be noticed or heard—* Senn led the others inside, where they crept up a set of creaking stairs to a windowless room at the back of the inn.

"We should take turns with a watch at the door," whispered Helder. "I'll take the first watch." Senn and Darin both agreed, and he headed back down the stairs.

Finally it felt safe enough for Senn to talk quietly. "Thanks for leading us here, Xiuhcoatl. Now we have to decide how to proceed. Does Aidan have anything in mind?"

—As a matter of fact, he does, but only a rough plan. He mentioned you have some poison darts?—

"Of course!" Senn fumbled in his pack and found the dry leaves holding his last four darts. "Four left. How about Aidan?"

—He also has four left. That would make just enough for all the Council members, assuming no missed shots—

"Let me think for a moment. This would be much easier if I could meet with Aidan somehow."

In the back of Senn's mind, another voice sprang up, long absent from his day-to-day conversations: Talen Morel. *—Senn, my boy. You've been doing quite well without me lately, so I've let you find your own path. One*

piece of advice, though: you might want to consider those magic items you've
been saving—

—Thanks, Talen ... I had almost forgotten about those— Now he
replied to Xiuhcoatl and the others, "I've got some magic items from my
mother, which I managed to unlock. Here ..." Fishing around in his pack
again, Senn brought out the wooden box and opened it up. He took out
the two bracelets and slipped one around his wrist, then held the other
out for the falcon. "Take this to Aidan. We'll be able to communicate
using earth magic."

Xiuhcoatl took the bracelet carefully in his beak. *—Of course. He
should be back in his chambers by now, and I'll advise him to contact you at
once—* The falcon moved carefully toward the steps, then took to the air,
swooping down the staircase and out a broken window.

While waiting for Aidan to contact him, Senn looked through the
other items in the box. He sat down next to Keegan, who was leaning up
against her pack relaxing her feet. "Hey there."

"Hey yourself, my big shot with all his magic items!" She smiled and
touched his nose.

"Keegan, I want you to have something. These used to belong to my
grandparents ..." Senn took out the ivory-and-bloodwood rings and held
them in the palm of his hand. "I'll wear one, if you will wear the other. It
would mean a lot to me, especially now that we're closing in on ... my
father. I don't know what will happen, but I want you to know how I feel
about you."

She looked at him with that lopsided grin as big as he'd ever seen it.
"Of course, Senn. I can hardly believe we ..." Her wide eyes glistened with
the beginnings of tears. "I feel the same way. I'd love to exchange rings
with you!" Keegan took one of the rings and slipped it on Senn's right
index finger, then he did the same with the other ring on hers. She intoned
playfully, "I now consider us ... bonded for life!" Senn put his hands
around Keegan's face and kissed her deeply.

Before long, a familiar voice sounded in Senn's mind via the bracelet.
—Hello, Senn! Can you hear me— It seemed that Xiuhcoatl had indeed
delivered the second bracelet as planned.

Senn opened a channel of earth magic and activated the communication spell. *—Aidan, it's good to hear your voice again! Though I have so*

many voices directed into my mind lately, I'm not always sure if they're real or imagined!—

—Ahaha, very true, my boy. How is everyone holding up?—

—Not too badly. Wildon and Lani opted to stay with the clan near Leikton, while Darin and Helder joined our expedition. We even added another companion along the way, an old Adept friend of Darin's—

—The more spellcasters on our side, the better. We're going to need them for what's coming. You see, the Spirit Chamber holding the rift to the other side is now surrounded by runes, just like the demon coffin. Between you and me, we have just enough darts to poison the entire Council. Then we could lure them to the Spirit Chamber and lock them up. Once the poison takes effect, their spirits will fade back to the other side. Do you have any idea how to make this happen?—

—As a matter of fact, I do— He smiled, and began outlining his plan to Aidan. There were a lot of details to consider; it was going to be a long night figuring them all out.

The last two days of Council meetings had grated excessively on Aidan's nerves. His supposed grandfather was less and less happy each day, and Aidan couldn't allay the old man's suspicions much longer. On top of it all, he'd hardly gotten any sleep while preparing the final elements for the plan he and Senn had conceived. Fortunately he'd been able to meet with Umkoome's Spirit Knights this morning, to hand over four sets of the Magus Manacles along with instructions to stay in the city during today's rounds.

Aidan entered the Council Chamber, the last one to take a seat as usual. He was nervous, counting on Jarl Meita to have the spirit killing sword finished. It was also risky wearing the magic bracelet, pushed high up on his right arm underneath his robe, but he'd need it to contact Senn.

"Greetings to you all. I expect that we shall see some advancement of our main strategies today?" Kelti and Raeta smiled and nodded for once. "Good. First, let's hear Jarl Meita's status. How is the spirit weapon coming along?"

"Aah, yes, Master Seltin. So good of you to ask. I have brought it today, in fact." Jarl reached under the table and brought out the sword, walking down the length of the table to hand it to his master personally. It was a rough-looking weapon, with just a solid steel hilt and a slapdash leather scabbard. Aidan pulled the length of the blade free, and gasps went up around the table. The finely polished steel blade itself was tinged blue-green, fading to black near the razor-sharp edge. It was a masterpiece compared to the quick and dirty job that Jarl had done on the hilt and scabbard.

"Marvelous. How does the magic work?"

"I impregnated spirit and earth magic into the blade during forging, and imbued two types of runes using human blood as the living component. When the edge cuts into flesh, runes of earth magic pull in the spirit magic binding the ... unnatural spirit ... that lives in the host. That drawn-up magic then powers the spirit magic runes, which further weaken the spirit's attachment to its host. The runes drain away all the spirit magic until the spirit is sent back to the other side." The smith smiled nervously. "I think it won't kill the host. The spell, that is. Of course with a mortal blow, the blade itself can kill."

"Does the sword merely require a nick to do its work? Or is a deep cut required, with extended contact? We must know how fast this magic works."

"Well ... it has not yet been tested. We need a subject. As I said before, that will be up to you."

Aidan studied the length of blue-green steel in his hand as Marek's spirit recoiled from the magic roiling inside it. If the sword worked, he could send back any demon at this table with one stroke. Still, he couldn't slash them all before they would overwhelm him with magic. And it would be tough to break into their well-secured chambers at night. Better stick with the Spirit Chamber plan. "Tynan, have the Knights found any rogue spirits?"

Tynan sighed and looked to his papers in chagrin. "Unfortunately, no ... they captured four more humans in the last few days, but no rogue demons. At least we can fortify the Keep's defenses as you requested." Marek's second held up one finger in the air. "One idea is to request a service from the Knights. If one were to submit to ... testing, we could save one of these captured human forms and bring the Knight back over from the other side after the test. Or he could have his original form back, if it survives."

Aidan mulled that over. "Sounds like a good idea. Agreed?" As the words left his mouth, he realized he'd made yet another character mistake. Aidan had been too nice in the past few days, and the criticism from Strago had been ramping up. He glanced at his purported grandfather, whose face was turning cherry red. The elder Seltin's annoyance would not be contained so easily this time.

"Damn it, Marek, maintain some damn authority around here. No wonder those *whores* at the end of the table make a mockery of our Council every day," he said, pointing an accusing finger at Kelti and Raeta.

By the stars, that man was trouble. How could he handle this without losing control of the others? The old man was testing him. What would Marek do? Aidan stood up, brandishing the spirit killing sword. "Hear me, Strago! You may be my kin, but that doesn't give *you* license to question *me*." How to give real force to this chewing-out? Aidan had no idea, but he had to try something. "What would my Grandmother say if she were here right now? She would demand you give me the respect I deserve!"

Strago's eyes narrowed. "Your grandmother? She was a damn whore, and you know it. I threw her out on the street and raised your father myself." He pointed, "What's that on your arm?"

Curses. Flourishing the sword had been a bad idea—Aidan's robe had slid back and revealed the wooden bracelet.

The old man continued, "Looks like an imbued bracelet that old Talen Morel had. Where did you find it?"

Down this path, Aidan could no longer explain himself with believable lies. His only recourse was swift action: he calculated the factors, drew up solid energy, and then cast the spell with his left hand. Strago was surrounded by a solid barrier that clamped him to his chair. Aidan stormed around the table and spun the chair so the old man was facing him.

Strago spat, "Damn you, I'll get to the bottom of this! Who the hell do you think you are . . ."

Aidan slapped him hard across the face. "I'll tell you. I am Marek Seltin, husband of Lieh Morel, uniter of the spirits, Master of both worlds! And you, who I brought here to protect me, are nothing but a bitter old man who is trying to rob me of my power. You will learn to respect my authority!" Swiftly he raised his right arm and slashed Strago across the cheek with the point of the sword. The man's eyes cleared immediately, changing from inky black to a natural brown. Aidan released the restraint spell, but the natural owner of Strago's former body only managed to babble incoherently for a few seconds before he fainted dead away.

"A successful test, I would say, by every measure. Thank you, Jarl, for this marvelous sword. Rook, Zin, clear this man out of here and find a cell for him below." He had to make this convincing. Pulling a pair of Magus Manacles from his robe pocket, he tossed them on the table. "Put these on him to keep him docile. We'll need his form, in case I decide to bring Strago back onto the Council." Aidan looked the table up and down, noting suspicious but frightened stares. That fear was good, considering the alternative. "If there are no questions, get moving!" Rook and Zin sprang out of their seats and hauled the unconscious Magus off toward the dungeons.

Aidan sat down in silence to await their return, letting the other five Council members stew in their fear. He laid the sword down on the table in front of him, and fed earth magic into the bracelet. —*Senn! Are you there*—

The response was mercifully swift. —*Yes, Aidan, here I am*—

—*Good. Everything is ready, in fact one target is already down. Put the wheels in motion*—

—*Then we'll see you shortly*—

That done, Aidan wiped a few beads of sweat off his brow. It was only a matter of time now. He could only hope that Senn's part of the plan went smoother than his had.

Lieh Morel had walked a long way. Senn and his companions on horseback had probably beaten her to Islingin by two days. She had hardly slept, and the aches and pains from the weeks spent on her demon horse had been replaced by sore feet. But here she was, after fifteen years, standing in front of her former home. Islingin: it was a little worse for the wear, but still there. From a distance, the River Gate looked a bit run down, and as she approached she saw there was a dead guard underneath a pile of stones. Hopefully Senn had done that as he entered the city; Marek must have been too short on manpower to replace the guard. She crept past the body and snuck inside through the gate.

With dark black eyes, she could impersonate Tamesis if needed, as long as she didn't have to gut anyone with the long knife she still carried. Even so, killing Marek would be easier if she could avoid drawing attention to herself. Slipping quietly along the streets she knew so well, Lieh thought it best to avoid Market Square. She was just passing by the open square one street to the west when the cries of a distant commotion reached her. Running stealthily to the nearest corner, she saw a half-dozen soldiers hauling off Senn, Rikk, and an unknown man in irons. What was happening? Those must be brutally powerful spellcasters to have subdued her boy. Perhaps he'd been betrayed or surprised.

But what about the others Senn had been with, those she hadn't recognized during the forest battle? They must have survived the firestorm in the forest, because she hadn't seen any bodies. If there had been a fight just now, they might have been killed. Well, there was no time to worry about that. How could she help Senn? A direct attack would be pointless against soldiers who had managed to subdue the most powerful Magus she'd ever known. There was always her original plan. She could kill Marek, and send his spirit floating free—without a Magus form he would no longer be so dangerous. The best way to stop a monster is to cut off its head, so that's exactly what she would do to the Spirit Council. She could track down Senn afterward.

Where would Marek be? Since he had created a new Council akin to the Conclave, they would have to be in Islingin Keep. Knowing her husband as she did, his were probably the best-secured, best-outfitted quarters in the entire Keep—with the best view. That would be the Conclave chairman's suite, at the top of the Keep's northeast tower. It was mid-afternoon, so the chances of him being in the suite now were slim. If she were right about Marek staying in the chairman's suite, it would be simple to hide there until he returned. Lieh headed back into the narrow streets west of the square and kept walking north toward the Keep.

Luckily there weren't many guards on the walls for her to contend with. Marek had obviously not expected anyone to attack him, or he would have thought out his defenses more carefully. Lieh walked all the way to Ship's Tower, where the river met the sea, without seeing a single soul. She climbed the tower stairs, exited onto the wall, and peeked out around the corner of the tower. A guard stood watch on the southwest tower of the Keep. It would arouse suspicion if she were caught slinking along the wall, when Tamesis would have gone in the front gate. Lieh edged around the tower to the merlons that crowned the wall, looking over them to the sea below. Not so bad. She prepared her spell and jumped over the edge.

Levitation could be tricky. Lieh was especially wary because the matrix supporting her was built on water. But she had practiced the spell often, walking above these very seas as a budding young Magus. Soon she reached the northeast tower, although the strain from holding a complex spell for so long was already wearing on her. Carefully she extended the matrix upward, widening its base at the same time so the solid magic construct would not tip over on the moving waves. She rose higher and higher, until at last she reached the barred, glassed windows near the top of the tower. Peering inside, Lieh couldn't see any sign of people or movement. She compartmentalized the levitation matrix in her mind, devoting one powerful magic flow to maintaining it. One mistake now would dash her on the rocks where the ocean met the wall. With the rest of her energy, she formed a powerful cutter made of two solid magic wedges. It took almost all she had left in her to shear through the window bars, but Lieh did it. She broke the lock, swung the window inward, and climbed into the chairman's suite.

The suite was just as grandiose as she had imagined. Everything was trimmed in handcrafted oak, obviously recently restored. Was it really Marek's room? She had to be sure, so she rifled through the closet. Flamboyant robes, ostentatious doublets, silk-trimmed hose ... that was Marek's style. How had she been attracted to this man? The more she learned about her husband, the less Lieh wanted anything to do with him. Her previous life in Islingin had been such a waste of resources, trying to learn the reasons behind her existence instead of just enjoying the fact that she was alive and well. Yes, Marek deserved whatever he got.

Lieh only felt bad for Aidan, whom she remembered as a decent fellow from an earlier meeting in Islingin. Could she go through with this, knowing that Aidan was alive and trapped in his own body? She shivered as a chill ran down her spine. But she didn't know any way to dissociate Marek without taking Aidan out of the picture as well. Lieh pulled out Tamesis' long knife and sat down on the bed to wait for Marek.

The morning's Council session had dragged on interminably, with most of the Council members too fearful of arousing their Master's ire to say anything disagreeable. That meant most of them had said nothing at all. Aidan had called an early halt, and they had resumed the sessions just after noon. They were hammering out the fine details of the Sul twins' new strategy for winning over the clans when the guard knocked and opened the chamber door.

"Master Seltin! My apologies for the interruption. The Spirit Knights are in the hallway. For some reason they've brought three new prisoners up here, and they say you'll want to see them at once."

"Bring them in." Aidan fingered the pommel of the spirit killing sword at his waist, which had replaced Marek's ceremonial sword. It was loose in the scabbard, just in case.

Six dirty and dusty Knights brought in the three men—Senn, Rikk, and Darin. Aidan eyed them down the length of the table, a feigned look of surprise on his face. "Who in hells are these men, and why are they important enough to be brought to the Council Chamber during our session?"

One of the Knights spoke, a thick man whose face appeared to have been hit with a board, and recently at that. "Master Seltin, they were found wandering within Islingin and using magic. This young man here," he said, pushing Senn forward, "claims to be your son."

"What reason do you have to believe this? Will you bring everyone here who claims to be some relative of mine?"

"Master, the level of magic he was using led us to believe he could be telling the truth. During his capture he exploded two entire buildings and uprooted several trees, which he threw at us as if they were children's toys. But once we put the Magus Manacles on him, he couldn't so much as hurt a fly." The Knight smiled a wicked grin, displaying a bloody mouth with several teeth missing. Perhaps he *had* stopped one of the trees with his face; that would explain his appearance. "The key, Master, was that he knew the name of your wife. Lieh Morel, the one that Xipil has been searching for these last few moons."

"Fine. We will get to the bottom of this. My thanks to the Spirit Knights for capturing these powerful spellcasters in the first place. What did they have on them?"

"Not much, Master. A sword, some dried meat, water skins, a packet of hunting darts, a few other sundries . . ."

Aidan nodded. "Just put it all on the table so we can see what's there." The guards spread the items out on the end of the table close to Zin Wisner and the twins. All Aidan cared about were those darts. Eight live ones and one dud, which Senn had prepared for Aidan himself. It wouldn't do if the traitor were the only one not shot, would it?

Kelti was looking at the pile of items spread out on the table when she said, "Master Seltin, look! One of them has the same bracelet as you!" She lifted the wooden bracelet from the table and stared at Aidan. Most of the Council members were lost in confusion. Unfortunately Tynan figured it out, and stared at Aidan with a look of realization.

One tiny error . . . just one omission . . . a single slip of the robe that had revealed his bracelet to Strago. Their whole plan had been reduced to a risky gambit with one unfortunate misstep. Hopefully Senn and Darin would have good aim with those darts. Then at least the two nights he'd spent deactivating the runes in the Manacles he'd given the Spirit Knights would pay off. Senn must have realized they were in trouble, too, because he gave the signal to Darin earlier than planned. "Now!"

Eight darts levitated from the table and shot toward the remaining Council members. Most hit home, including the dud that embedded itself in Aidan's own neck. But Tynan used magic to brush aside the one destined for him, and turned to Aidan. "Seltin! Or should I say Alkar? What is this . . . ?" The raging Magus looked a little surprised to see a dart sticking from his master's neck as well. Senn took the opportunity to send the last dart Tynan's way while he wasn't looking, scoring a hit on the back of his neck. "Ow!" He turned and pulled out the dart his hand. "What is this? And where is Marek!"

Jarl Meita was figuring it out now, too. "Why didn't the manacles stop them from shooting these darts? And what are these anyway! Are they poisoned?" He pulled out the dart from his neck and examined it.

No matter, Aidan thought: without knowing the action of the poison they wouldn't be able to neutralize it. The big problem was going to be surviving the next hour, waiting for the poison to take effect.

Jarl stood up, his face growing red in anger. "I tested those manacles myself! All six pairs were working perfectly!" He turned to Senn just as the boy launched a solid energy ball at him. But Jarl was prepared, and had a shield up already. The energy ball bounced off the angled shield, splintering the newly-restored ceiling of the Council Chamber. Plaster and bits of carved wood rained down on the elegant, polished table.

It was time to cut and run. Aidan and the others wouldn't survive a fight against seven Magi and six Spirit Knights if they stayed in this room. "Senn, get out of here!" The boy was already using magic to crack the manacles off the three of them, and a shield shimmered into place in front of them. Casting a shielding spell of his own, Aidan unsheathed the sword and took one last swipe at Tynan, hoping to get lucky in all the turmoil. But his second-in-command was no fool, and had a shield ready. The spirit killer just glanced off it, nearly flying out of Aidan's hand. Seven pairs of eyes looked to him, all finally realizing he had played them for fools. Kelti and Raeta appeared hurt, while the others just looked furious. Quickly, Aidan stepped backward to the chairman's door and threw a domed, curving shield up in front of him. He felt the shield draw a surge of power through him as energy balls of all varieties pummeled it. As he stepped through the door and closed it behind him, Aidan fervently hoped that Senn would take advantage of this distraction to escape. He took one last precaution, feeding in a pulse of heat energy to fuse the door mechanism solid. Aidan melted metal and stone alike; the obstacle would force his pursuers to either go the long way around or smash the whole wall down.

Racing up the spiral staircase to his chambers, Aidan stopped to speak with his guards. "Let no one in," he advised, completely out of breath from running up all those stairs. "We have a ... rebellion on our hands." He opened the door to his chambers and ran inside, trying to think how he could best escape alive and help Senn's trio at the same time. The sword was still hanging loose in his right hand, and he wondered if he should put it back in the scabbard.

Then Aidan noticed the woman sitting on his bed. Was that Lieh Morel? "Thank the stars, you're alive!"

Senn's solid magic spell cut through their manacles. They had to escape—there was no way he was prepared to take on seven Magi with just Darin and Rikk here to help him. Especially not when their plan was to save those Magi after sending their possessors back. At the other end of the table, Aidan took a swipe at the Magus closest to him with a greenish-blue sword. That must be the spirit killing sword he'd talked about. The Council's eyes all turned that way, aghast that their supposed leader was attacking one of their number. As the manacles dropped off, Senn took advantage of the distraction to grab his bracelet off the table. Rikk snatched his sword as well, while Darin seemed to be frozen, staring at the far end of the table.

"That's my father!" Darin started forward, but Senn grabbed his shoulder.

"We've got to get the hell out of here. He's your father, he's fighting my father, and my mother's wandering around in the forest looking for something to burn. Let's just try to survive this, and we can sort out the pieces later!" Around the table, all seven Magi were throwing energy balls at Aidan with a compulsion. Different sections of the wall around the Council leader's shield were burning, crumbling, and dripping with melting ice all at once. Fortunately the Spirit Knights whom Senn had let capture him were also distracted, and Treeface had only just noticed that his charges were no longer restrained.

"Hey! What're you do ... oofhh!" The Knight's cry was cut off as Rikk smashed his sword pommel into Treeface's open mouth, shattering his few remaining teeth and bloodying his already-ugly visage.

"Let's get out of here!" the strongman cried.

Darin snapped out of his daze and turned. "Alright. Quickly, down to the courtyard to find the others." The three of them pushed through the Knights and ran past the door sentry, as their captors cried out and drew their weapons.

As the trio ran, Senn turned and ignited a fountain of flame in the doorway. He walled off the area with a screen of solid magic, then extended the flames several strides until they were licking at the near end of the long table. Screams of the roasting Knights echoed down the hallway as Senn dropped the screen and fled down the stairs after Rikk and Darin.

They emerged into the courtyard at a dead run, hoping that their friends had succeeded in their part of the plan. Slowing their pace, they reached the main gate of the Keep, shields and energy balls ready. Senn broke into a grin at the sight: everyone was fine except the guard, who was lying inert on the ground feathered with arrows from Nic and Helder. On the southwest tower, he saw another guard slumped over the parapets, the victim of solid energy balls—thanks to Keegan, Ziya, and Piet. Darin greeted the others curtly, and then said, "We have problems!" When they looked at him quizzically, he shook his head. "Senn, you had better explain."

As Senn began, Xiuhcoatl flew down and perched on a stone carving by the gate. Shyama was not far behind, stealing up noiselessly from the south. "Change of plans," Senn said, addressing the group. "Aidan's been compromised, and the other Magi are all trying to kill him. Probably we're next. But they've all been darted—so we just have to stay out of the way for a while, until the poison can do its work. Only . . ." Senn paused, thinking. "If we want to avoid setting their spirits free in the open where they can possess again, we have to get them into the Spirit Chamber." He shook his head. "We had it all so well thought out . . ."

Helder gestured with his bow, "So lemme get this right. These Magi will be comin' down here any minute lookin' for us? *Seven* Magi? And ya want to lure 'em to the Spirit Chamber."

Senn cleared his throat. "Ahem, yes. And perhaps some assorted guards and Spirit Knights, depending on who survives the fire I started." There was already smoke rising above the northern wall of the Keep. Despite being made of stone, there was a huge amount of wood inside it.

The bowman shook his head. "Can't nothin' ever go accordin' to plan?"

Finally Xiuhcoatl spoke to the group, sharing his news from above. —*That's not our only problem. Four Knights were out on patrol, all Adepts, and saw the tower guard being hit by energy balls. They'll be here within minutes—*

"Alright," said Senn, "here's the new plan. Xiuhcoatl, you lead Rikk, Darin, Ziya, and Nic down below to deal with any guards and secure the Spirit Chamber. We'll need access there once we figure out what to do with the Magi. The rest of us will find a place to hide near here, so we can deal with these Knights. Try not to kill any of the Magi, since we can save their hosts after the poison kicks in." He drew a deep breath and let it out slowly before getting to the last part. "And . . . we have to get the Magi into the Spirit Chamber before the poison forces out the spirits. We don't want them escaping to find other hosts."

Talen whispered in Senn's mind. *—Once they're in the Spirit Chamber with you, I'll see if I can help. No guarantees, but I still have a few tricks up my sleeve—*

—Thanks, Talen. We'll figure out a way to lure them down into the cellars, and I'll draw them into the chamber—

Addressing the group again, Senn asked, "Shall we try it?"

Xiuhcoatl said, *—I don't like our chances, but I don't see any other choice—* The others murmured agreement.

"Let's do it. We don't have much time," Darin added. He motioned to Rikk, Ziya and Nic, all of whom Xiuhcoatl led through the gate back into the courtyard. "See you at the Spirit Chamber," he called out as they turned the corner.

Senn and the others selected a building outside the Keep but near the gates, where they would have a good shot at anyone who might approach. They spread out between two floors on a corner, where windows overlooked both the road going east-west along the Keep wall and the road north into the Keep itself. Senn and Keegan were on a lower floor with Shyama, while Piet and Helder went a few floors up. Before long the Spirit Knights came into view, their shimmering shields moving with them as they walked. One even had a personal armor spell in place, his glimmering form standing out against the stone of the Keep wall—he must be a Greater Adept.

"Now!" Senn yelled, and they all attacked at once. Helder shot arrows, while the other three launched energy balls. Senn concentrated on the Adept with the shimmering armor, blasting him with a volley of solid energy balls to throw him off balance. Piet called up a pillar of flame, but the Knights were clever: their shields extended under their feet to guard against such an attack. The flames just spurted up outside the shields, sapping energy but not doing any significant damage. Even though their magical power was no match for Senn's, these warriors were not easy targets.

One of the Adepts momentarily lowered his shield to fire a sequence of solid energy balls back at Senn. Keegan threw up a shield to protect the two of them, and the energy balls smashed harmlessly against it.

Keegan whispered in his ear, "I'll stand behind you and keep up the shield, while you stay on offense."

"Alright!" He turned back to the bombardment, loosing a few balls of heat energy, which did little more than scorch the earth around his target. Arrows and energy balls still flew from above, but Piet and Helder were not making much progress either.

Senn started curving his solid energy balls around, stepping up the power and slamming them into the Keep wall behind the Knights. He noticed one of the Knights trying the same tactic, but this building could surely withstand the one energy ball curving around to the left. He focused all his power on the Keep wall, and created a solid ram behind the merlons in an attempt to knock them down. Finally, a portion of the wall fell with a deafening crash, stones tumbling down on the unwitting Knights. Their shields were good, but not strong enough to withstand the crushing weight of all those stones. Screams and the noise of falling stones echoed across the road and even inside the room Senn was in, shaking the floor beneath his feet. The shimmering of shields and armor vanished as the last of the Knights expired. Once the stones stopped landing and the crackle of fireballs faded away, a sudden silence struck him. Where was Keegan?

—*Senn. Come over here quickly*— Shyama was a few strides behind him, licking at Keegan's form on the floor. —*She's not breathing*—

"No!" He noticed a damaged window on the left side of the room— the Knight's curving energy ball must have come through that window and hit Keegan while she protected Senn. He ran to her side, checking for injuries. She had been hit hard, and there was no sign of life left in her. "It can't be, no ... Keegan!" He shook her by the shoulders, as if that would bring her back.

—*My boy, listen ... take her ring*— Talen's voice said in his mind. —*Your grandmother and I did wear them, but they are more than what I explained to you before. See the bloodwood?*—

—*Yes, what does it do?*—

—*Just put her ring on next to yours and you'll see. I had a last few moments with your grandmother thanks to that ring, before she left for the other side*—

Senn removed the ring from Keegan's finger and slid it onto his own. Her voice echoed in his mind, —*Why am I here? Senn, I'm just barely aware of what is going on, but I think I'm dead!*— Her spirit was still here, caught by Talen's bloodwood ring!

He asked the Orb, —*Talen, does she have to go?*—

—*Hmm. Good question, boy. After the last few moons, I don't know what to say. She might be able to move from the ring into another form. Ask the lynx, why don't you*—

"Shyama! Look, Keegan's spirit is here, in the bloodwood ring. Could she move to another person or an animal like you?"

The lynx walked over, sniffing around the rings on Senn's hand. —*It might be possible. Let me find a form for her and try it out*— Shyama bounded away at full speed, and Senn saw her race down the street toward the Market Square.

Keegan said, —*Did I hear that right, there might be a chance for me to stay here? Senn, I just want to be with you, whatever I have to be. Please, I feel weak, and there's not much magic holding me here*—

"We're going to try. Just hold on, and let's hope Shyama is fast enough."

There was a commotion on the landing outside the door. Lieh levitated the knife and moved it through the air toward the doorway, holding it flat against the wall a stride or so away. Marek burst through the door, breathing hard and sweating profusely. He glanced down at a strange blue-green blade in his hand, then noticed her sitting on the bed with a bit of a shock.

"Thank the stars, you're alive!" Then Marek looked more closely. "Lieh, is it you, or Tamesis?"

"Lieh. Your little psycho pet is trapped inside." The knife shot out from the wall, propelled by her anger, and buried itself up to the hilt in Marek's chest.

"Aaah ..." Marek dropped the sword and fell to his knees, hunching over the protruding knife hilt. He tried to remove it, but there was too much blood dripping out around the blade, so he just left it.

"Marek, it wasn't supposed to go this way, but it has. I've come to realize we aren't right for each other after all. And, Aidan ... I'm sorry you were caught up in this!" Lieh turned away, tears in her eyes and bile rising in her throat.

The Magus wheezed softly, his voice a hoarse, bubbling sound in his throat. "Wait, Lieh ... damn. You don't see it ... I'm not Marek. He's ... trapped inside me, the same way you've trapped Tamesis."

Lieh turned, rising from the bed and taking an uncertain step toward ... Aidan? "So you're Aidan, you're in control of yourself?"

"Yes. And Senn and I, we've been ... communicating with these bracelets ..." He pointed to his arm.

She recognized the wooden bracelet from her father's belongings. Another one of the items she had never managed to unlock. "What can I do? We're two Magi, we can heal this! I'm so sorry ... I didn't know ..."

Aidan shook his head, looking at the pool of red beneath him. He lay down on his side, coughing up blood. "I don't think ... no chance for me. This sword ... made by a demon smith ... sends the spirits back. Cut me with it. Just a small cut."

Hesitantly, she picked up the sword. The grip seemed too crude for such an elegant blade. "Are you sure?"

Marek made one last appeal, —*No, Aidan! You're a fool if you go through with this. With our combined magic maybe you can be healed, then think of what we can achieve together!*—

"Do it, Lieh!" he said forcefully, bringing on another coughing fit. "Send Marek back before I die ... and he goes free in the air!" He held out his hand palm up, giving her a target. Lieh raised the sword and quickly slashed Aidan's hand. "Aaaagh! That stings." He blinked his eyes, "I think he's gone!"

"Your eyes are clear!" It was true—his irises had changed to a brilliant hazel.

"Thank the stars for that, at least. Now listen ... time is short. The whole Spirit Council ... they are after me. Get out of here, and ... take the sword. You can rebuild, gather the Magi ... send back as many ... demons as you can." Lieh laid a hand on Aidan's forehead, trying to comfort him. "Just go ... before they get here." Aidan's eyes started to lose focus, and his labored breathing slowed.

"I'm sorry, Aidan. Your valor will not be forgotten." In another moment he was gone. What had she done? Lieh closed his eyes gently as a tear ran down her cheek. This wasn't the way it should have gone ... but it was too late now, and she had to protect the sword. She took the scabbard from Aidan's belt and slid the sword back inside, clipping it to her own belt. As an afterthought, she took the bracelet from his limp arm and slipped it on her wrist.

Now she had to escape before a pack of angry Magi broke through that door. Lieh rebuilt her levitation matrix, climbed back through the window, and stepped out onto thin air. She didn't have to levitate far before she reached the point where the sea wall met the edge of the Keep. Once there, she clambered over the crenelations onto the walkway on top of the wall. Exhausted from both the magical and emotional stress of the last hour, she lay down in the middle of the walkway, sighing as if it were made of feathers.

The whispering and wailing hiss in the back of her mind reminded Lieh of one more task she must do without delay: get rid of Tamesis. She unsheathed the brilliant blue-green blade, glinting in the sunlight, and held the edge up to her own palm. She slid it along the skin until a line of blood appeared, the sharp blade cutting through with barely any pressure at all. —*Sssss! Noooo!*— In an instant, Tamesis was gone—back to the other side where she belonged. Lieh Morel was free again, completely free. Finally, the strange mixture of relief, exhaustion, and grief overcame her. She closed her eyes, letting the sun and the clouds pass over her the way waves roll across the ocean.

Senn looked up as Shyama ran down the street carrying a fox, which had evidently been patrolling the square for mice. He glanced to Piet and Helder, who had come down from above. They had some cuts and bruises from flying debris, but fortunately nothing more serious.

A moment later Shyama made her way up the stairs to the room where they sat huddled next to Keegan's body. The helpless fox was hanging from Shyama's mouth by the scruff of its neck, looking quite pitiful. —*Keegan, this may not be easy. You have little strength to persuade the fox to let you in, so I will inhabit the fox. If this works, you can transfer directly into my lynx form. Just visualize yourself crossing over from the ring. Make a channel of spirit magic to the lynx's eyes—*

Keegan's voice sounded faint. —*Alright, but quickly! The magic is fading fast—*

Senn took the fox in a magical grip, holding it in front of Shyama's eyes and just next to the rings on his hand. The fox's eyes turned cloudy and then black, but those of the lynx also stayed dark as night.

After a moment, Keegan's voice spoke in his mind again, but more clearly than before. —*Senn, I'm here. I can't believe this worked. Thank you, Shyama!*— Senn released the fox, which padded around the room calmly in the manner a lynx might. Shyama would have some adjusting to do in her new form, that was for sure.

The fox responded, speaking to all of them. —*No thanks necessary. After this is over, I plan to travel far from here. The lynx would not be of use to me then. She has served me well, and I have treated her well. If you do the same, you will have a long and happy life with her—*

Senn reached over and gave a big hug to his partner in her new lynx form. "I don't care what form you're in. As long as we're still together."

"Alright, young'uns." Helder stood up and pointed out the window at the northeast tower, where Aidan's quarters were. "We're gettin' short on time now. Hadn't we better get goin'?" They gaped in shock as the top half of the tower collapsed on itself with a tremendous crash, stones and mortar all disappearing out of view behind the Keep in a huge cloud of dust.

Standing up quickly, Senn made one more decision. "Shyama, I need you to lead us to the Spirit Chamber. Keegan, you should stay here. I don't think you'll be much help against these seven Magi." Keegan didn't seem too unhappy about that, given the debris cloud that now rose over the

Keep. He gave her one more caress down the back, as the rest of them started down the stairs. Senn took them two at a time, and followed his friends back through the gate into the courtyard of the Keep. They stopped there to decide what to do next. "I can't reach Aidan with the bracelet. Something must have happened to him. Let's just make sure we persuade those Magi to follow us into the Spirit Chamber! Shyama, where do we go?"

—*There, the southwest tower. There are stairs leading down*— The fox darted across the open courtyard, leading them toward the entrance.

"Come on!" The others followed Senn, stopping at the doorway leading down. "I guess they'll be here soon looking for us. Helder, take the lead with Shyama. Piet, I'll need your help with a shield in case the Magi shoot first without asking questions." The two of them crouched down and waited.

It was not long before the entire Spirit Council strode from the north entrance. All seven of them were there, which didn't bode well for any chance of Aidan still being alive. The imposing man in front, whom Darin had called his father, brushed his robes free of dust and flecks of stone as they emerged. The ugly one opened her mouth, "There they are!" Senn did his best to look surprised, and he threw up a shield next to Piet's as a volley of energy balls flew at them. Fortunately the shields held, and they had a brief respite while the Council members surveyed the damage.

The tall man in front said, "They're unhurt. Shield yourselves and follow me!"

Senn turned, speaking loudly to Piet, "Let's go! Where is this Spirit Chamber again?" They turned and ducked into the stairwell, quickly spiraling down it after Helder and Shyama. The little fox led them through a maze of corridors, which Senn brightened with a bit of magical light. At last they arrived at a massive wooden door, where their four companions awaited them with the falcon.

Darin smiled and spread his arms. "Glad to see you. May I present the Spirit Chamber, now open for one and all." He kicked a little dirt over the bloody stain by the door where Senn guessed Marek's gatekeeper had been standing. "Who's your guide here, a little fox? What happened to Shyama?"

—*I am* Shyama. *It's a long story, and we don't have time. Senn, we can't all fit in the chamber*—

"Right," Senn said, "since I'm the only one who has to go in there, the rest of you move further down the corridor and find somewhere to hide. Quickly!" It was an odd sight: three Adepts, two archers, and one strongman following a falcon and a fox down the dark corridors in the bowels of Islingin Keep. They weren't a moment too soon in hiding, because Senn could hear the Magi coming down the adjoining corridor already. He ducked inside the Spirit Chamber, looking around. The room was fully paneled with wood, and he could sense the warding runes all around him.

—*See the pedestal in the middle?*— asked Talen. Senn nodded. —*That must be the rift, I can sense it. Stand right behind it, and put up your strongest shield*— Senn moved to the spot Talen had described, and enclosed himself in a sphere of solid magic not unlike the cage he'd used to trap Ziya.

"What now?"

—*I hope they won't wreck this beautiful room*— Talen grumbled. —*There are a few more spells in the Orb that only I can use, as they need a bit of my spirit magic. They are based on some theories I had fifteen years ago about closing this rift. Two favors: first I need you to feed in earth magic and wind magic, all that you can. Give me an open channel of energy. Secondly, when I give the word, you have to cast a spell from the Orb. I have just unlocked it for your use. It's my self destruct, so to speak. When you use that spell, I'll be thrown out of the Orb*—

"Will you return to the other side?"

—*Yes. Let's just say life hasn't been too exciting for me during the past fifteen years, and I'd rather be among the spirit kind than live in the jungle of this world. Besides, the spells required to seal the tear between the worlds . . . well, they need to be carried into the gap somehow to plug the hole. I'll make sure the magic energy ends up where it needs to be. Just get ready*—

The door burst open, with the tall Magus in the lead, followed closely by the ugly one and then all the rest. One of the beauties at the back closed the door solidly after they were all inside, as if that would stop Senn from escaping. She looked a little pale—perhaps the poison was finally taking effect. The tall man spoke at last, "Senn Morel. I'm not sure where the rest of your friends have run off to, but I think you'll find there's only one way out of this room. And that's possessed by one of our fellow spirits." He flexed his fingers, and a ball of solid energy appeared there.

"No, thank you. I've already got my own soul inside, and one is enough for me."

"We'll see about that. Your father recruited me for my prowess in combat, so I'd be surprised if a mere boy can best me. Tynan Maltus has never been defeated in battle."

—Senn, keep them talking. I just need a minute more. Can you soften your shield so my spells can get out?— Senn modified the shield, realizing he could already feel Talen working his magic. The Orb was drawing energy through him at a frightening pace.

"There's no need for a fight, Tynan. You'll be beaten soon enough by the poison flowing through your veins. Did you think I would allow myself to be captured just to stick a harmless wooden needle in your neck?"

"Of course not. But your poison must not be so effective, when countered by the natural healing powers of spirit magic mixed with earth magic." Behind Tynan, the ugly woman looked rather unsteady on her feet.

"Tynn ... Gurrhggghh," she added, as she slumped over on a tall, handsome man who was trembling a bit himself.

"See?" said Senn. At that point he noticed a breeze in the closed chamber. Where could it be coming from? Aah ... Talen was drawing wind magic through him into the Orb.

—Alright, my vortex spell will soon break down their defenses. I'm using up what spirit magic I have left, mixed with a good dose of earth magic. Whether or not your poison works, they'll be ripped out of their forms. I'm starting the spells to seal the tear that Marek created. Once I do that there won't be much time, so here's goodbye. I wish you the best, my grandson!—

Senn had an idea to keep the others distracted. Taking out the Orb, he held it up for them to see. "Thanks, Talen. It's been good knowing you." He gestured to Tynan and the others, "Meet Talen Morel. He's been hiding for fifteen years, but today Talen has joined us in the Spirit Chamber!"

Tynan growled, squinting a bit and holding his stomach as if he were not feeling so well. "Talen Morel? Look here, boy. This is not a game, so you can cut that damn wind spell of yours. I'm ..." He wobbled a bit on his feet. "Uhh. I'm feeling ..." Tynan fell to his knees, looking around at the others, who were leaning heavily on each other or on the chamber walls. The whirlwind increased until it was beating on Senn's shield, which he released. Immediately the wind whipped wildly around his head, and he had the feeling it was going to tear his hair out. When he looked back to Tynan, the man's eyes were clear and he had a smile on his lips as he toppled to the ground. The others, similarly, had regained natural color in their eyes—bright blues, browns, and hazels.

That was when Senn noticed the voices. Spirits were clamoring on his consciousness, begging to be let in before they drowned.

—*Don't you want spirit magic?*—

—*I can teach you so much, you could rule these people*—

—*Imagine the wonders we could see traveling to Hyanto*—

—*I'll teach you how to forge fantastic weapons of legend*—

The whirlwind tightened, drawing the wraiths toward the tear between the worlds. It was a funnel of magic, pulling the spirits back to the other side. Finally the voices faded from his mind. —*Senn!*— This one he knew: it was Talen, still speaking from the Orb. —*Release me!*—

"Goodbye, Talen!" Quickly Senn found the spell to release Talen and fed in energy. A kind of lock opened, and he could feel a strange rush of spirit and earth energy escaping from the Orb. The whirlwind sucked this last vapor toward the rift, and as it went in, there was a loud clap like thunder.

The air in the room stopped whirling, and Senn broke out in a sweat. It was suddenly hot and dry in the chamber, despite being deep in the cold stone of the Keep. Across from him were seven sleeping Magi, piled in an awkward heap on the floor. He was still holding the Orb in his hand, but now it felt as cold as a lump of stone. Talen was gone, as were all the rest of the spirits in the chamber—but Senn was still there, heart beating and lungs drawing breath.

CHAPTER 22

Reunion

*A*idan. *Are you there? Damn it, Aidan!*— Lieh could not get the voice out of her head, and eventually it woke her. She was lying on the top of the wall in the fading sunlight, feeling guilty and wondering when she would stop dreaming about Aidan. Then she realized the voice was still there, and it was Senn's. —*We can't find you, and can only assume you are gone. Farewell, my friend*—

Lieh probed the bracelet, and it responded with a familiar pattern. —*Apply earth magic*—

She fed in energy and directed her thoughts. —*Senn? Is that you?*—

—*Who is this?*— came the reply.

—*It's me, Lieh. Your mother. I . . . I've been looking for you. Now I've rid myself of Tamesis with this sword Aidan had, and I'm free of that cursed demon. Are you . . . alright?*—

—*Aidan's sword . . . are you here in Islingin? Come to the courtyard of the Keep, we're all here!*—

—*Sure, give me a minute*— Lieh picked herself up, sheathed the sword again, and tested her powers. After a few hours of sleep, her magic had recovered more than enough for a short ride through the air to the courtyard. She levitated from the wall, sailed over the eastern battlements, and came down in the center of the open area. People and animals were everywhere. Senn and six companions sat in a circle, while eight disheveled men and women in fancy clothes slept on the ground nearby. Her son stood up and ran across to meet her, swerving around a big lynx, a falcon, and a fox.

"Mother! You're alive!" Senn threw his arms around her in a strong hug. He pointed to the sleeping men and women, "They were the Spirit Council. But I freed them, and now they're sleeping off the effects of fish poison. Well, actually Talen freed them from inside the Orb. Still, he was mostly drawing on my magic. Oh … one of the Council Magi is Darin's father from the south!"

"Senn, slow down," she said, returning his embrace. "I'm just glad to have you back. I learned a lot during all this, and there's so much to say … I never thought I'd have this chance again. If only I'd paid more attention to you instead of focusing so much on the clan. I want you to know, I'm proud of you—whatever you do."

"Thanks, Mom! Now, you have to come and meet my new friends." He grabbed her arm and pulled her toward the circle.

After the events of the past several moons, Senn was glad finally to have a break. The survivors had moved into several of the homes on the streets nearest the Keep. The structure of the Keep itself needed a lot of work after the damage it had sustained. One tower was missing, the front wall was partially collapsed, and the interior of the north wing was completely burned out. Yet there was hope for the future now, with the spirit killing sword (which Rikk had taken to calling Demonkiller) and the runed Spirit Chamber offering them a chance to free themselves of the demon invaders once and for all. Certainly it would still require a lot of work, so that evening they planned to meet in the overgrown square to roast some game and discuss the future. Senn's mother was manning the kitchen, which meant good eating. There was nothing like a barbecue to make one forget about the summer heat.

"Come eat while it's hot," Lieh called from below.

Senn stood up from his bedroll after a well-deserved afternoon nap, rubbing Keegan's head. The two of them descended the stairs of their newly adopted dwelling, walking to the roasting oven that Lieh had prepared out of stones from the rubble.

His mother was sweating from the heat of the oven as they arrived. "Keegan, that was some fine work hunting. We'll be eating well for days! And Senn, if you have a minute . . ."

"Of course. What is it?"

Lieh set down her cooking tools and sighed. "I haven't always been completely honest with you. You know I love you, but in the past I focused too much on the clan and on my own ambitions of power and knowledge. Perhaps during your childhood I still dreamed of my good times with Marek. However, while traveling with Tamesis and Xipil, I realized those aspirations are not the right ones for our kind to follow. As your father found out, they only lead to darkness."

"Yes. Talen knew it from the beginning of Marek's experiments, so he created the Orb to hide himself. In the end it was Talen's magical knowledge that sealed the gap. Mother, I'm sorry, too . . . sorry that I lied about the Orb. Talen instructed me on how to break the seal that hid him, and that was what attracted all those demons to our clan."

A shadow came across Lieh's face. "That was unfortunate. But at least the loss of our clan was not in vain." She looked down at her feet, "Talen was right not to trust me with his secret, or with the Orb's full power. If I hadn't been imprisoned by Tamesis, I might have ended up following Marek as well. And, Senn, one other thing . . ."

"What's that?"

She touched his arm gently. "I'm sorry about Aidan. Everything that happened led me to believe that he was Marek. By the time I found out otherwise, it was too late."

Senn frowned. "I know. He took a lot of risks to enable us to succeed. Now he's in the spirit world with Marek and all the rest." He looked up. "Still, it was his choice, and I'm sure Aidan would risk himself again and again to provide mankind with this chance. We just have to use the opportunity he's given us—to make his sacrifice worthwhile."

Slowly the others filtered out from their new quarters along the street leading to the Keep. Helder had pieced together a long table from lumber he'd scavenged, and they all sat down along its length. Darin was overjoyed to have found his father, Chelan Lang, who had apparently been the first of Xiuhcoatl's kidnap victims. Darin, Chelan, and Ziya were busy getting reacquainted, and they sat among the recently freed Spirit Council Magi to swap stories. Senn and Lieh sat next to Keegan, who required no chair.

"So, Rikk," Senn asked, "what are your plans now? Will you stay and help us rebuild?"

"Sounds tempting, I just might do that. Maybe I can do a bit of work with the Demonkiller as well, to show these clans around here that there's nothing to fear anymore. We'll probably experience more attacks once we persuade people to move back into the city."

"That's true. But now, every demon we throw in the Spirit Chamber or slash with that sword will be gone forever . . . so fighting demons will be a lot easier than it used to be." Senn turned to Nic and Piet. "What are your plans? Your clan isn't so far from here as Leikton, just a couple of weeks' ride."

Nic shook his head. "Just a couple of weeks? You make it sound as if that were nothing. Yes, we're planning to head back and break the sad news about Aidan to the clan. For certain, his sacrifice will never be forgotten. We'll celebrate and toast his life with a party the likes of which haven't been seen in fifteen years." Around the table, everyone agreed with that. "And I guess," Nic nodded at the lynx, "we'll have to tell Keegan's mother that her daughter might look a little different the next time she sees her." Piet laughed and nearly spit a mouthful of roast across the table.

The lynx licked her lips. —*At least I'm still good looking, which is more than I can say for you two*—

Senn looked to Darin and his crew, who were carving up a deer halfway down the long table. Senn asked, "Darin, how about you? Are you three going to stick around here and help rebuild Islingin?"

Darin laughed. "Well, that would be one idea. But I think Ziya and I are going to head south with my father and take some of this knowledge to Leikton. Maybe we don't have a Demonkiller sword, but we can create some of these demon coffins with the earth magic runes you taught our people. We need to spread this lore, if we're going to rid Kartus of these demons. Helder, what about you? Are you coming with us?"

The gruff archer put down the haunch he was working on and furrowed his brows. "Not sure yet. Me and Rikk, we think alike. I might stay up here with him, slow down some o' them demons with my arrows, give him a chance to stick 'em with ol' Demonkiller."

Lieh asked, "Speaking of demons, that reminds me. Where did Xiuhcoatl and Shyama disappear to?"

Senn just smiled. "Well, you know they made a little deal with Aidan. We would leave them alone if they didn't cause any trouble here in Kartus. I think Demonkiller made them more than a little nervous, because they left a couple of days ago with hardly a word about their destination."

High over the eastern ocean, two giant petrels soared over the waves, playing together as they dodged the salty spray from below. They fed on fish and squid, enjoying the change of pace from the prey they were accustomed to hunting on land. Xiuhcoatl was glad finally to be free of the worldly cares and responsibilities of working for Marek. Even his brief time assisting Aidan and Senn had required a lot of energy, although he had helped them voluntarily after realizing they deserved to live free as well.

—*Shyama,*— he called to his new mate. —*Do you see that swarm of fish below us?*—

—*Yes. Good eyes, Xiuhcoatl. I won't go hungry with you around, now will I*—

They dove down and plucked several fish from the surface of the sea. It was a good life, and it would be even more interesting once they arrived where they were going. If Xiuhcoatl's experience since returning to the physical world had shown him one truth so far, it was that he could choose his own path through life. Not everything was under his control, that was for sure, and someday he would probably end up back in the spirit world for good. Still, as long as he followed his instincts and stayed true to what his reasoning told him was right, he kept coming out on top.

—*Xiuhcoatl. What do you think about our human friends. Will they manage to rid Kartus of the spirits?*—

—*Now that's quite a puzzle. With that sword and those spirit-proof runed boxes, they should be able to send back most of our kind in a few years. In the long run? I suspect there will always be a few of us hiding in the shad-*

ows. Who knows, perhaps there are even a few spirits left as clever as the two of us—

—Now, Xiuhcoatl. There's clever. And then there's you. I don't think the word does you justice—

—Well, thank you, my dear. We shall have to put that to the test once we get across this ocean, shan't we?— He pumped his wings harder, and the petrel gained a bit of altitude. From here he couldn't yet see land. But he expected that any day now, Hyanto would be visible. A new land of opportunity filled with creatures to inhabit and secrets to discover, and most importantly: no one there had ever heard of spirits returned from the dead. It was a land ripe for their enjoyment, promising freedom for as long as he and Shyama could make it last. Fates willing, that would be a long time.

Appendix: Cast of Characters

<u>*Morel Clan*</u>
Lieh Morel—Magus and survivor of Islingin who formed a clan
Senn Morel—Lieh's teenage son
Jarel Linker—strongman in his mid-20's who wields an axe and keeps dogs
Lani Telus—young woman and Minor Adept, Jarel's lover
Wildon Herst—the clan's aged magic tutor, a Sabi with withered magic
Rikk Janus—strongman in his mid-30's who wields a sword
Artie Tenko—strongman who wields a battle hammer
Sephora—small child
Namee—young woman and Minor Adept
Kettin—young man and Minor Adept
Beagan and Elam—archers

<u>*Alkar Clan*</u>
Aidan Alkar—Magus in the Janklo region who formed a clan
Nic—archer in charge of weaponry
Piet—Major Adept in charge of magical equipment
Keegan—young woman and Major Adept
Jann—strongman and helmsman aboard the *Janklo's Pride*
Merle and Uri—sailors aboard the *Janklo's Pride*

Lang Clan
Chelan Lang—Magus who formed a clan near Leikton
Darin Lang—Chelan's son, leads the clan after his father's disappearance
Helder Stowe—strongman archer and Minor Adept

Marek and his Followers
Marek Seltin—husband of Lieh Morel and leader of the spirits
Xipil—demon spellcaster and leader of the trio hunting Senn Morel
Shyama—demon lynx in Xipil's trio
Tamesis—murderous demon in Xipil's trio, bent on destruction
Xiuhcoatl—demon who finds Magus forms for Council members
Umkoome—demon Major Adept who guards the Spirit Chamber
Clayne—gatekeeper of the spirit world
Tynan Maltus—first Spirit Council member
Rook Valtis and Sel Spali—Council members, husband and wife
Zin Wisner—Council member and Hyanto expert
Jarl Meita—Council member and weapon maker
Kelti and Raeta Sul—Council members, the twin seductresses
Strago Seltin—Council member, father of Marek
'Treeface'—member of the Spirit Knights, led by Umkoome

Various Spirits
Talen Morel—Lieh Morel's father
Kert, Darcy, and Dolf—demons who twice attack the Morel clan
Fynn, Alina, Elias—demons near Silville

Others
Rylan—traveling outdoorsman near Silville
Kenzie Merril—Minor Adept in the Islingin region
Ziya Rell—Greater Adept near Silville

About the Author

David Douglas is a Mechanical Engineer, recently employed testing DRAM memory chips. But, due to a price war among the Koreans and the eventual death of the last trench-memory-cell manufacturer, he now finds himself busy with other activities: riding the seas of Kartus, bringing demon spirits from the other side, and concocting stress-induced romances that would make even the most jilted of lovers wince.

In his spare time, David is a carving snowboarder, Ultimate Frisbee player, sometimes skydiver, runner, world traveler, and bass guitarist/singer. He lives in Munich, Germany, home of the Oktoberfest, which strangely enough takes place in the end of September.

See David's latest adventures at http://blog.daviddouglasbooks.com

www.ingramcontent.com/pod-product-compliance
Lightning Source LLC
Chambersburg PA
CBHW031257170626
46807CB00001B/189